Eutopias
Or
Outopias

Choosing To Design
And To
Make Good Places

Alan Wittbecker

Books by Alan Wittbecker

Eutopias: A Poetic Commonwealth of Earth

Ordering Space and Living Places: Aesthetic and Ecological Dimensions of Place

Poetic Archaeology of the Flesh: Creative Language, Physics and the Ecology of Being

One Earth Many Worlds: The Role of Cosmologies on Ecological Impact and Accommodation

REviewing REthinking REturning: Essays of Life, Ecology, Design, and Forestry

Good Theories Good Practices: Essays on Radical Ecology, Ecosystem Medicine, and Ecological Forestry

Eutopian Essays: Towards Making Good Places with Thought Experiments & Ecological Designs

*Eutopias: Making Good Places Ecologically & Culturally Using Thought Experiments & Informed Designs (2006, online at:*www.eutopias.net*)*

Eutopias
Or
Outopias

Choosing To Design
And To
Make Good Places

Alan Wittbecker

Sarasota
Urania Science Press
2006

Published by Urania Science Press & 3 Muses Books
SynGeo ArchiGraph
8051 North Tamiami Trail, No. 32
Sarasota, Florida 34343
www.3MusesBooks.com
editor@3musesbooks.com

For more information on sites and projects in text:
     SynGeo ArchiGraph Co.: www.syngeo.net
     Ecoforestry Institute: www.ecoforestry.net
     G. P. Marsh Institute: www.gpmi.us
     Pan Ecology: www.panecology.net
     Rian Garcia Calusa: www.re-design.us
     Eutopian Ecologists: www.eutopias.net

Library of Congress Cataloging in Publication Data

Alan Wittbecker 1946   Eutopias or Outopias

  Includes Index.
   1. Man—Response to catastrophe. 2. Human Ecology.
I. Title.

GF75.W5851

ISBN 0-911-385-24-X

Book Design by Rian Garcia Calusa
Printed in the United States of America
10 9 8 7 6 5 4 3 2 1

To Arne Naess for letting me work on the Wolf Project and lecture at the Center for Nature at the University of Oslo one spring (1987), between hiking, climbing and swimming expeditions. I know this effort may not be rigorous enough for Arne, but it is philosophical, and I now claim his excuse for writing it this way—I am too old to fill in details and I should not be held accountable for not filling them in.

And, of course, my continued gratitude to Michael Barnes, Alan Drengson, Michael W. Fox, Buckminster Fuller, Garrett Hardin, Twila Jacobsen, Neil Keefe, David Klein, Nadya Kristoforova, Boyd Martin, William Odum, Nela Rachevitz, Paul Shepard, Emerson Wittbecker, Margaret Wittbecker, and Precious Woulfe for their unselfish criticism, suggestions, support, or assistance. Finally, if I had not been trapped in a mountain snowstorm on Mt. Lemon in early 1973, I might not have read books by Theodore Roszak, Ivan Illich, and Leopold Kohr, and become determined to continue exploring these topics.

Sources for Excerpts

Ordering Space and Living Places: Aesthetic and Ecological Dimensions of Place. (Printed Bound Essay). Newark: Shamrock Press, 1970.

Eutopias: A Poetic Commonwealth of Earth. (Printed Bound Essay). Newark: Shamrock Press, 1970.

"The biological definition of good places: Eutopias." *Proc. Marsh Inst.* 2:3-19. 1977.

"Human populations related to ecosystem productivities." Contributed paper, Ecol. Soc. Am. Annual Meeting, Grand Forks, 1983.

"Quantitative determinations of minimum wilderness areas for the planet as a whole." Contributed paper, 3rd World Wilderness Congress, Findhorn, 1983.

"The role of radical ecology in making humane places on earth." Contributed paper, AAAS annual meeting, San Francisco, 1984.

"A Palouse ecoregion reserve proposal." Contributed paper, 4th International Congress of Ecology, Syracuse, 1986.

"Eutopias: An annotated outline." *Pan Ecology* 5(2):1-16, 1990.

"An empowered United Nations: Proposals for cooperation and survival." *Common Voice*: 1(1):1-8). 1991.

"One earth, many worlds: A framework for cultural preservation." *Pan Ecology* 6(4):1-16, 1991.

"The corporation in the community." *Pan Ecology* 7(4):1-11, 1992.

"Setting community limits for long-term stability." Contributed paper, International Forum for Biophilosophy, Budapest, 1992.

"Eutopias: Making good places ecologically," *The Trumpeter* 11(3): 85-92. 1994.

"Saving common places: The Palouse," *Wild Earth* 5(1):54-58, 1995.

"Death and taxes in forest ecosystems," Invited lecture, University of Idaho, Martin Peace Institute Symposium, 1997.

"Varieties of interaction in nature: Exploitation, disturbance, and interference," *The Trumpeter* (.athabascau.ca/ trumpeter) 1999.

"Ecological Thought Experiments" *Sofia Echo* Vol. 5, Issue 31, Aug 3-9, p. 12, 2001 (1st of 12-part series).

Eutopias Or Outopias

Contents

Exploded Contents

1.0. Preface: Making Good Places—The Idea Repeated

This project was started in 1969, inspired by works by Paolo Soleri, Garrett Hardin, Lewis Mumford, John B. Cobb, Jr., Leopold Kohr, Thomas Paine, Eugene Odum, and others. I thought that their ideas could be combined into one synthetic project. The first draft resembled a series of footnotes to their works, with a meek extension of their ideas. The book surrounded the idea of place with statistics and problems. The statistics on suffering and loss were disturbing and depressing—and are even more so now. I was working as a psychologist at a local hospital and taking graduate courses at night; in a geography course, we played a City Land-Use Game (CLUG), which lead me to pay more attention to urban places. So, I tried to concentrate on the psychology of urban places. Driven by a sense of urgency, several of us at this small state university started the Marsh Institute for Research and Education in Ecology; our first paying project was to clean up after Earth Day—there were two that year, 1970. In 1971, a partial draft was published by Shamrock Press (Newark) as a bound monograph, *Ordering Spaces and Living Places*, and circulated to a limited readership; then the notebook was bound as *Eutopias*.

After courses in international communications and philosophy, I expanded the outline as a utopian project. Dizzy with enthusiasm, I came up with many brilliant and original ideas, from an explication of the good side, "eutopias," to the correlation of crowding and ugliness to sickness and crime. Then I found that most all of these ideas had been described already— eutopias addressed by Buckminster Fuller and the correlations charted by Ian McHarg. After reading Ian McHarg's *Design with Nature*, I played with his idea that the relative beauty of a place could be correlated with illness and crime. People seem to be unhappy for an indefinite number of reasons, such as lack of food or prestige, too few symbols, like money, or lack of meaning. I considered that living in good places would increase human happiness; good places could provide food, security, and meaning. So, I tried to locate good places everywhere and the describe them. Then, I started to define what made them good. And then, I tried to figure out how to design good places, to define the kind of changes that would result in good places. At this time I was teaching physics laboratories at a Canadian university.

At first, I wanted to show what good places looked like and then to distill their common features. The more I looked, the more I realized that it was almost impossible for good places to exist without a network of connected, surrounding good places. Even enclaves required a relatively stable environment and exchanges with an outside society. So, good places had to have good environments and good social contexts. As I traveled and began to describe places, I saw that they were already changing, because people like me wanted to live in good places, and if the places existed, then people would move there and enjoy them. Alas, when many people move to a good place, the place changes, and the reasons people move there are overwhelmed and disappear. I moved to a place that I had identified as good and began teaching philosophy there, in Idaho, as a graduate fellow. I did not want to advertise good places only to have them be swamped and diminished by people who wanted to find a good place, rather than to stay in place and build good the qualities they desire (the irony of my own decision was not lost on me). I played with alternate titles: Big Planet Small Worlds, The Big Picture, or perhaps Another Great Design.

So, I rewrote the manuscript as a discussion of the kind of problems that existing communities had to respond to in order to survive. I sent out a section of chapters on the metaphysics, metaphors and metaecologies of place in 1976; it was accepted by Libra Press (New York), but published by Reason Wolfe (Wilmington) as *The Poetic Archaeology of the Flesh*. I was teaching ecology in Oregon, as a teaching fellow, trying to finish a degree. That same year, with my partners, I started a comprehensive design company, Nieman Ryan Community Designs (Portland, OR)—we designed everything from books and posters to wetlands and forests.

No longer comfortable listing examples of good places or emphasizing problems, I rewrote the book as an abstract discussion of the differences between utopian and eutopian thinking about societies and places. Then I immediately rewrote it with an ecological perspective, expanding the discussion of good places with ecological definitions. This continued to the early 1980s, while I was teaching computing and mathematics and attempting to finish my formal education in Los Angeles, at a small institution dedicated to tutorial learning. Having learned from books, from teachers I had never met, I jumped at the chance to work with the brightest and wildest thinkers of the time. International let me select my own tutors: Buckminster Fuller, Paul Shepard, Joe Meeker, Michael W. Fox, John B, Cobb, Jr., Arne Naess, Paolo Soleri, David Klein, Henryk Skolimowski, and Neil Evernden. Fuller decided not to be an official tutor, but suggested new directions and ideas. Shepard did not like anything I had done, but that forced me to examine and criticize his ideas, before I incorporated them into my project. Meeker praised my integrative skills, but suggested I was more interested in collecting big names so I could bask in their reputations—perhaps that was some part of my choices, but the glow never paid the rent or got anything published. Fox took over as my chief advisor and introduced me to the whole dimension of inhumane farming practices and the misuse of science. Fox, Klein, and Naess encouraged me with wolf projects. Soleri and Skolimowski invited me to work at Arcosanti. Skolimowski and Cobb required numerous rewrites on ecological philosophy and process theory.

So, I thought of just describing a cosmological framework. But, the more I understood about human psychology, the more I realized that not all people would want good places. Like many mammals, some people preferred suboptimal environments, that is, they preferred danger and change to a safe comfortable environment. So, I realized that the framework had to be suboptimal and loose. It had to be culturally flexible, yet protective of each region. After a while, the manuscript incorporated many of the design ideas from our work in Oregon, Washington and Idaho; another version was circulated in 1983, and articles from it were published in several journals. Slowly, problems were replaced with cultural descriptions and ecological descriptions of good places, which fed back into our design work. To meet degree requirements, I focused only on a framework for human cosmologies; this excerpt was accepted as a dissertation and published in a limited edition in 1984 as *One Earth Many Worlds*.

Our design group realized that although we could influence local design, there was a whole dimension of untapped regional and global design possibilities, so we started an offshoot, SynGeo ArchiGraph, for that kind of design in Seattle in 1991. We approached global corporations, cities, and nations to offer ecological planning and design services that addressed populations and styles, as well as multiple scales and ecological principles. We finished several *pro bono* projects on regional design, including a design for the North Slope of Alaska, but were unable to interest anyone in using this approach or in hiring us for a design. Financially, the business was a failure. We took part-time jobs designing books, boulevards, forests, and streams in Massachusetts, New Hampshire, Washington, and Oregon. The book was expanded to include the designs of good places. To supplement my income, I taught courses in environmental science in Seattle and Vancouver (BC).

With another set of colleagues, I helped to set up education and training for the Ecoforestry Institute in Portland; we also assembled an Ecoforestry Management Team to manage forests. We cofounded the Forest Stewardship Council in Oaxaca, Mexico to try to set high standards for forest product certification. Many of the examples in this book are from our research, management and restoration experience with northwest coniferous forests. I taught workshops in forestry and courses in forest ecology and planning; finances improved. Modified further with global ecological designs, the manuscript was sent out again in 1992 and 1997.

After brief participation in wolf projects in Alaska and Siberia, both truncated due to lost funding, I worked on a wolf survey in Bulgaria for two years with the Peace Corps. There, I was invited to submit regular essays on ecology as a newspaper columnist (in English) and a series of articles on ecology and forestry to a science magazine (in Bulgarian). I tore apart the book and rewrote it as a series of essays, mostly from previously published articles. My quiet interludes of writing were punctuated by the excitement of being lost in a blizzard, being caught in an avalanche, climbing mountains bare-handed, encountering fantastic wildlife, trying to teach English to children raised with television, walking the country, and getting married to a naval engineer.

In 2002, I sent out a series of essays from the book. One publisher suggested putting all the published reviews and essays together in one book, *REviewing REthinking REturning*, which they published that year, and which won an award for best nonfiction book on the web. The following year, Cambridge Press and Ebooksonthenet published a second collection about forestry design and practices, *Good Theories Good Practices*. And, the next year, a third set of essays taken from this book, all previously published in journals, magazines, or other books, became *Eutopian Essays* (Urania Science Press 2004). Although I worried if these books would have any effect, I also wondered if my predecessors and professors would approve of my use of their works. Of course, I am not a professional. I am an amateur in the real sense of the word: I love playing with ideas and forms. If I am not skilled enough or persuasive enough, that fault lies with me and not with the teachings or ideas.

I reintegrated some of the essays into the matrix manuscript, concentrating more on the politics of place and international order. I kept working, planting trees and creating landscape designs. I started teaching courses in anthropology, ecology, and design at a small college in Florida. I continued teaching distance learning courses on forest ecology and design to students in Canada, Armenia, Chile, Germany, and Romania. These college and independent courses allowed me to try different approaches dealing with culturally specific alternatives.

I kept working to involve people, not only in celebrations, such as earth day, but in lifestyle changes and joyous living. One of my arguments was that we had to treat the dismal effects of modern civilization, from deforestation to global disease patterns, as a catastrophic emergency that required immediate action, but we should not let this slow, global emergency overwhelm all joy and creativity. As I was writing about why it was necessary, I participated in animal surveys and planted thousands of trees to restore overused forests.

1.2. History of the Form

This is an excerpt from a source book, *Eutopias: Making Good Places Ecologically and Culturally,* that was written and rewritten over a period of thirty five years. It parallels the philosophical discussion of an early draft. In some places, I have left it the way it was originally, even though some of the ideas have been presented later by others. In other places, I have quoted their works, especially where they have presented things better or things that I did not consider. Very few arguments are used in this book. Many good arguments for cultural collapse and ecological damage have already been made. This book assumes those problems and offers proposals that might dissolve the problems. Arguments for or against these proposals might come later.

This project, has dominated my thinking for over thirty five years. It will never be finished to my satisfaction, but I want to present these ideas in raw outline form as a series of questions and suggestions. It remains an ambitious outline with many empty spaces. Of course, empty space may stimulate the creativity of others. The book was first written as an expanded outline. It was revised as a series of essays that made specific arguments. It was revised again as a series of answers to specific questions. The binding idea has always been the ecological and cultural creation of good places.

The form of this work reflects an effort to describe the ideas and creation of good places. It is not a linear path leading to a definite conclusion. It is a dialectical spiral, which gathers facts and ideas and reforms them in wider contexts, then tries to use repetition and charm to lead readers to agreement. But, it also requires more effort from you, the reader. The work presents its subjects in a loose form, with a slight similarity to the *lebensforms* of Ludwig Wittgenstein. If the metaphors and ideas stretch too far to hold, perhaps they are, as Wittgenstein wrote of his propositions, all nonsense, to be read and left behind.

2.0. Prologue: Places on Earth

Human consciousness of our effects on the planet and each other has gradually increased, as shown by recycling programs and by celebrations such as earth day, which has been getting larger every year, as a celebration. But, celebrations did not seem to have lasting effects. Environmental deterioration has worsened in some places. Levels of consumption have increased; populations have increased.

This year's earth day celebration (1990) is over. What were we celebrating? That we *are going* to save the earth or maybe just still think about it? Perhaps we were celebrating our intention to go on a material diet or an opportunity to spend money on t-shirts and buttons. Perhaps earth day is a new spring-time variation of a new year's resolution—a temporary awareness, a limited intent, and a reason to party before business as usual. Or, perhaps it is a modern penance that allows us to buy a place in heaven by promising to save the earth with small tokens.

The token changes and vows do help, but are they enough? Will a little conservation avoid a great human disaster? Are these easy remedies reminiscent of medical cures for diseases and problems, such as smoking, overeating and stress, that could be avoided by simple denial. The implication is that a few small things, such as using less water or recycling bottles, will save the earth—that ozone depletion, rainforest destruction, population growth, and the polarities of wealth will somehow be corrected automatically, as governments and industries continue as before, adjusting their labels by using greener colors.

We have been told that saving the earth starts in the home. No wonder corporations give their blessings to this event—most pollution and waste is industrial and agricultural! Which issues have higher priority? Deadly local ones, such as toxic waste dumps or topsoil loss, or deadly global ones, such as greenhouse gases or chemical runoff? Is an alarm justified, or is caution enough? Should we listen to ecological Cassandras or to economic Neros?

Are we too lazy to follow through with the effort that we already celebrated? Are we too cheap to deduct a required percentage from profits to pay the real environmental costs? Are we too crazy to stop our material and biological growth? Where is the will and the vision necessary to really make radical changes? We have, in fact, taken the easy way at every branch. We have assumed that corporations will choose the proper path of production and regulate their pollution. Yet, we know that they put profit first and only prevent pollution when forced to do so by public action or government regulations.

We have wasted thirty years attacking the symptoms and not their technological or social origins. We must acknowledge the failure of our remedial efforts, and our failure even to address the flaws of our designs and ideologies.

I do not want to participate in the wrong games. I do not want to drive fewer miles in a high-powered gas guzzler—I want to travel by train; I want my radio shipped by train and not truck; I do not want my vegetables shipped at all, but grown locally. I do not want farmers to do slightly less aerial spraying of fertilizers and biocides, I want organic produce. I do not want to recycle aluminum and plastic, I want returnable glass containers. I do not want safer coal-burning centralized power plants, I want local solar power. I do not want to give more money to the homeless, I want my tax money to help them build and keep their own homes. If industries cannot help me with what I want, then I want my government to encourage them and channel them, tax them and regulate them. And, if my government cannot do that, I want to encourage a change in government and support better candidates.

Leaders, corporate, religious or political, rarely decide the direction of development. People living in communities decide that. Decisions bubble up through consciousness. People get tired of consuming and seek more meaningful ways of living in nature. And, out of frustration, they participate in selecting leaders or run for office themselves, or, in my case, write a grand outline about it. The history of the book has ranged from statistics to the psychology of place, from the ecology of place to the politics of place.

This work is a collection of thoughts, but as Aristotle said about emotion: Thought by itself moves nothing. Our living together, and our ancient social tendencies, give rise to a shared morality that directs our behavior. I would want nothing more from this book than it direct a discussion and perhaps suggest good behaviors.

We need to propose and execute national policies to steer technology. I want my representatives to ban CFCs, to ban burning, to tax nonrecyclables—and if they do not, then I will run for office myself. We do not have time to look at all the information that we have collected, or to convert it to knowledge. We never have had time. We cannot connect with all the information flows. So, we will have to act as if the information we have is enough for wise decisions.

The earth does not need to be saved or healed, as if we could do either. The ways of life that we remember and prefer, the places that depend on other species and natural processes—these can be saved. Our own divided minds, that let the poor be enslaved by the wealthy, that let 'good' animals be domesticated and 'bad' animals be eradicated, can be healed. The sacrifices will have to be great; the changes will have to be radical. But, the celebrations will be meaningful only then.

The local environment, and that of the region and planet, offer opportunities and challenges to all living organisms. How humans respond to these things results in accomplishments or problems, in creations or deaths.

2.1. Facing Losses & Challenges

Every year numbers are collected in every area of human interest. Those numbers indicate the deterioration of water and air quality, the erosion of soil and land, the destruction of forests, the decline in health and longevity, the deaths of people, the fracture of cultures, and the wobble of planetary cycles. In the past few years, the numbers have worsened dramatically.

The numbers of changes are incredible: For the first time in human history, in the year 2000, as many people lived in large communities (over

20,000) as in small communities (under 20,000). Sixty percent of Earth's inhabitants are expected to live in cities by 2030, according to the United Nations—the same year global carbon dioxide emissions are expected to increase by almost two-thirds of what they are today. By 2025, worldwide energy consumption is expected to grow by 54 percent, while worldwide oil production is predicted to begin declining in 2016.

The numbers of differences are revealing. The inequity between people continues to increase. In 1996 the UNDP estimated that the wealth of the world's 358 billionaires exceeded the combined income of nations that are home to 45 percent of the world's people. And the gap grows. If we added millionaires, what would that be?

The numbers of human deaths are far more disturbing. There have been massive human die-offs in the past 106 years since the start of the Twentieth Century. These numbers tell a story of big death. From democides—the intentional killing of races, nations, tribes or communities—total deaths may range from a minimum of 150 million to a possible 350 million people, who were shot, knifed, burned, suffocated, poisoned, starved, crushed, drowned, hanged, bombed, or buried alive, in a plague of violence. This includes Josef Stalin's 1932-3 forced famine that killed 7 million people, as well as the Nazi holocaust (6 million) of Jews and Gypsies under Hitler by 1945, the current deaths in the Congo (by 2006, 4 million), Pol Pot's Democratic Kampuchea, Khmer Rouge 1975-79 (over 1.5 million), Sudan (1985-2004, 2 million), Ethiopia (1978, 2 million), North Korea (1948-87, perhaps 2 million murdered), and Pakistan (1940-50s, 1.5 million murdered). Rwanda (1994) and Bosnia-Herzegovina (1992-5), add 800,000 and 200,000 to the total. Is it possible to even imagine that number?

Deaths as the result of formal or declared wars are surprising less than democides, which are often internal to a nation, at about 61 million dead. The war between China and Japan, before and during the second world war (1932-1945), resulted in 14 million dead. The rest of the world may have experienced twenty one million dead during the six war years.

Famine, once the greatest producer of deaths in agricultural nations for thousands of years, may have killed 32 million in this century.[1] One of the largest modern famines was the Great Famine in China, centered in the early 1950s; it killed 10.7 million people. There were two famines in India, in 1942 and 1965, that each killed 1.5 million people from drought. Two famines in Korea, in 1948-87 and 1995-8, each killed over 1 million people.

Disease, once the greatest producer of deaths during early phases of globalization, has killed many millions, especially at the end of the Roman empire, when the Justinian plague in 540-590, might have killed 100 million; the Black Death of the 1300s in Europe and Asia, and the beginning of the Spanish Empire, produced 46 million dead. In the Twentieth Century, the influenza pandemic in 1918 killed over 20 million people, and possibly as many as 50 million. The recent AIDS epidemic, from 1978 to 2001, counts for over 23 million.

Disasters, from drought, flooding, earthquakes and other regular planetary events, killed 21 million people. Accidents, from transportation from horses to space shuttles, killed half a million people. Murders and terrorism killed hundreds of thousands (perhaps 0.02 million). Nations, such as the U.S. or the United Kingdom, have killed thousands of innocents; the U.S. is guilty of indiscriminate bombings of Germany and Japan in 1945, then later in parts of Africa and the Middle East, and the U.K. caused thousands of deaths with its 1914-1919 food blockades of Germany and the Middle East. Such a list would also have to include Afghanistan, Angola, Albania, Ethiopia, Burundi, China (1917-1949), Croatia, Czechoslovakia, Indonesia, Iraq, Turkey (1919-1923), and Uganda.

Many of these overlap by category. For instance, ethnic cleansing can start from changes in the distribution of food, that lead to famine and disease. Poverty is never listed as a cause of death, but over 15 million, perhaps as many as 30 million people, die from a lack of clean water, food, medical services, or shelter, every year, including 2006.

The numbers on the living environment are disturbing and critical: The list of animal deaths in the United States[2] in 1984 reads like a doomsday book of atrocities: 22,078 North Pacific fur seals clubbed to death; 17 million mammals trapped for fur in the U. S.—303 million throughout the world; 12 million unwanted pets put to death; 70 million laboratory animals used in experiments; 3.5 billion chickens killed for food; 700,000 cattle dead from transport-related injuries; 598,757 animals shot for sport on wildlife refuges. Although species are still being identified at the rate of 8,500 new insects species and 100 new fish species per year,[3] probably 400 species are driven to a premature extinction and 1,000,000 species are threatened every year.[4] Statistics for habitats are almost incomprehensible. Three billion cubic meters of wood are consumed annually. Twelve million hectares of forest are cleared annually and 10 million hectares are degraded. Marsh lands are filled in; coral reefs are mined; and grasslands are paved over.

Possibly 59 percent of arable land degraded; 50 percent of fresh water co-opted for human use; 50 percent of the planet's wetlands modified, drained or destroyed; 50 percent of the coral reefs damaged and perhaps 20 percent destroyed; extinctions that are uncounted, perhaps uncountable.

We tend to think of problems as unwanted 'side-effects' of the wanted main-effects, but all effects are equal, as Buckminster Fuller noted, and must be addressed as equal. A problem, from the Greek words 'to throw forward,' can be considered as a question proposed for solution. Most things identified as problems are embedded in a network. Nothing is simple; there is not one truth, there is not one way, there is not one goal. Problems could be considered also as challenges that we must respond to continuously, in the process of living, not as puzzles that have to be solved once for all time. A challenge is a calling into question or a demanding task (a challenge is 'a call to take part in'). It is about consciously choosing to see what can be done, rather than dismissing a conflict as terrible and unsolvable. When challenged by some situation, we react by habit, although this may be disconnected from other habits. Habits protect us from many problems. Addressing a problem often has to do with a power struggle, which becomes part of the problem of the problem. If problems are regarded as challenges that require a social response, then much of the conflict can be avoided.

The problems of cultures, of natural ecosystems, and of modern, industrial, corporate, urban civilization, have been documented quite thoroughly. We have identified most of the problems in the problematique, from erosion, pests, and fertility loss, to population migration and diseases, and we have addressed them separately, using technological innovations or political adjustments. But, we have not dealt with them in a whole pattern. We have not understood them as complex large dynamic systems.

Sometimes we forget, however, that the decisions of our ancestors can saddle us with losses, just as our losses will encumber our heirs with deforested landscapes on depleted soils, despoiled by exotic chemicals and hazardous wastes, in a network of impoverished habitats with an unstable climate, and of course, compounded by large intergenerational financial debts. The losses indicated by these numbers can be categorized simply.

2.1.1. *Eight Terrible Losses*
This network of problems can be grouped under eight large categories, each of which contains a multitude of related problems. Each category extends numerous threads to the other categories.

2.1.1.1. Loss of Nature (Habitat Species & Pieces)
The overuse of ecosystems results in deforestation, devegetation, and desertification, then in the depletion of raw materials and the depletion of agricultural productivity. Economic and political pressures, derived ultimately from population pressures, force farmers to intensify their efforts to increase crop production, instigating a dismal cycle of population expansion, environmental deterioration, and human poverty.

This overuse results in the attendant losses of many habitats, species, and individuals. Many species are not hunted to extinction; they are being lost as a result of the simplification of their habitats for human uses, from the expansion of agriculture to the pavement of cities and road systems. The rates of extinction are now far higher than the normal, unassisted rates. The loss of habitat also decreases any new speciation processes. Demands from a growing human population, as well as their violent conflicts, accelerate the losses.

As the human world becomes more abstract and separated from the wild worlds, it becomes more isolated and human specific. As our habitats become more removed from natural processes, we tend to think they are all self-created and controlled, at least until a dramatic hurricane or earthquake overwhelms our abilities at control.

2.1.1.2. Loss of Culture
With the globalization of trade and the domination of national languages, smaller cultures are being absorbed into larger ones. Although people retain some of their traditions, the loss of their language means that the whole perspective of their culture, related to the uniqueness of place and human adaptation to place, is being lost. Knowledge of plants, animals, and processes is being lost at a time when modern science is half-heartedly trying to catalog

knowledge of every place. A lack of knowledge is often related to illiteracy—or the lack of numeracy or ecolacy, to use Garrett Hardin's words, but this kind of loss is personal and cultural—it had been learned once and is lost as a result of a set of circumstances where it is devalued and ignored. Smaller, less-competitive cultures are being abandoned by new generations of people or subverted by global comparisons of luxuries and expenditures.

Population pressures, resource shortages, and manufacturing 'side-effects' cause instability in many societies. Militarism, intolerance, crimes, and health problems are symptoms of the instability of cultures. Confusion and misinformation contribute further to the destruction of cultures. If cultures are lost and new forms cannot fit themselves to the patterns and uncertainty of natural systems, then people may not be able to adapt to the continued development of the earth and its ecosystems.

2.1.1.3. Loss of Health

The instability of cultures, as well as stress, insecurity, and insufficient diets, results in physical and psychological problems for people. Individual powerlessness and disillusion provoke further disintegration. With disruption of agricultural and manufacturing productivity, as a result of conflicts, people have less food and fewer necessities. Hunger affects over half the people in the world, in every culture, including many of the dominant cultures in China, Russia, and the United States. Extended hunger not only alters behavior and intelligence—that is the ability to evade hunger—but it allows diseases to run rampant. Many diseases have made dramatic comebacks where people live in large groups in unsanitary conditions with inadequate food.

Health can be reduced by long-term trends in lifestyles, from sedentary work to family size. The size of families is crucial for mental health, for instance. Basically, extended families allow more outlets for communication and spread the stress among members. Small families have to bear much more stress and members often become unhealthy. Loss of health leads to other losses.

2.1.1.4. Loss of Fitness

Fitness is the ability to function under normal environmental conditions. Fitness can be measured quantitatively by testing aerobic and anaerobic power, the capacity for sustained exercise, respiratory and heart rate markers; pulmonary gas exchange, mechanical power and strength, body composition; range of motion; and stamina. Stress, obesity, illness, erectile dysfunction, weak sperm, social conflict, and other kinds of dysfunctions, can reduce fitness. Some of this reduction, evidence of poor personal or reproductive health, is caused by chemicals, especially persistent chlorinated organic chemicals, such as polychlorinated biphenyts (PCBs), dichlorodiphenyltric hloroethane (DDT), and dichloro-liphenyldichloro-ethylane (DDE, a stable daughter compound of DDT).

Some of these chemicals also reduce our ability to reproduce, raise young, make good decisions about consumption and social conflict, and to persevere in general. The cost of fitness ranges from lower fertility and sperm viability to early death. However, a lifestyle dependent on physical and energy slaves, not to mention a diet riddled with addictions to cheap fats and sugars, decreases our fitness. All of the elements of a true addiction are present: We get a short term high, and we suffer long term health problems. The air pollution, the sedentary life styles, and the global warming are all injurious to health. Exposure to toxic chemicals and stressful city environments makes things worse, even as we acquire more information about the dangers and options.

Perhaps this fitness problem is a result of a long-term trend. As scavengers we had to gather seeds roots and fruits, as well as dead animals. As hunters we moved quite a bit; as farmers, we had to work harder and longer, planting, harvesting and storing food. Then we started using animals and better tools and fossil fuels; we invented labor-saving, and activity-saving, devices. So, now exercise is simply an activity outside the education or work day. As human populations expand and shift to cities to live, they are losing the ability to fit with natural ecosystems.

2.1.1.5. Loss of Equity

Although many resources are distributed unequally over the globe, as a result of different kinds of historical geological processes, trade can allow access to those resources. However, as a result of long-term processes of inequity, from keeping people enslaved to cultural hoarding, many people have far less than others. This has resulted in permanent overclasses and underclasses, which are maintained by physical force, as well as by the force of economic and religious myths. These myths tell all people that they participate in the "best possible economic system" regardless if it justifies the differences of inequity based on history or on perceived racial abilities. Most people are hungry; few people are fulfilled. Even low average levels of food and fulfillment can be maintained only through theft from other species and from future human generations, and through the degradation of billions of humans as well as the ecosystems on which they depend.

Other myths, such as the "market is free" or "growth is beneficial to all," suggest to people not to try other economic forms. But, the market is not free; it is orchestrated to benefit the rich. Continued growth is amoral and pathological, benefiting the elite of authoritarian regimes as much as the oligarchs of democratic ones. It refuses to recognize, much less to pay, all of its costs, such as depletion, loss of security—which may be most important—or extinction. The entire system perpetuates mass poverty and justifies it by blaming individuals, but the system itself fails to reduce inequity or poverty. This loss reduces effort; it is responsible for tiredness and low kinds of health, productivity, and esteem, things that are necessary for personal and systemic renewal.

2.1.1.6. Loss of Renewal

Self-renewing systems renew themselves through a process of renewal—yes, the definition is self-defining and circular. But, renewal is limited when too much of the system is lost through waste. Manufacturing for a large population in "free" economies results in the production of waste, and in the storage of solid wastes in landfills. The waste is unavoidable in the current system, which is unable to renew itself and has to force a linear flow and trust that natural recycling systems will be able to adjust to immensely higher volumes. Much loss in the current economic system is wrongly identified as waste. It is simply not economical to recover this waste in this system, due to the volume of "free" resources and goods from nature. The current political and economic systems are unable to use the unwanted or unexpected products of their systems.

Waste is a strangely inappropriate category; the waste of one system is almost always a potential resource for the next system. Even the waste of the sun, light, is a resource for plants on earth. People themselves are treated as a waste product of capital-producing system, although the system could be viewed as a waste-producing system that also produces capital.

Pollution is not so much waste as a kind of resource out of place, for example, in the acidification of rain, in salinization of waters, and in the eutrophication of water bodies. Many new chemical products, such as carbonated fluorocarbons (CFCs), pollute the atmosphere and water. Pollution interferes with natural cycles of renewal, from atmospheric cooling to purification of water by plants. Many manufacturing processes result in the production of new dangers, such as modified and uncontrolled genetic fragments, nuclear wastes from reactors and weapons, and new substances and products, which are not easily incorporated into natural cycles. The loss extends to human lives, as well.

2.1.1.7. Loss of Accord

As a result of the unequal distribution of natural resources, including unincorporated waste and pollution, and the unequal distribution of materials and wealth between people, economic conflicts arise, often becoming violent political conflicts. Accord, by definition, means agreement or the concurrence of will or action. It can mean harmony of mind, as well as harmony of sounds. As an agreement between the parties in a controversy, by which satisfaction for an injury is stipulated, accord allows people to reconcile their injuries and interests.

Because many national boundaries were drawn as a result of colonial expansion and contraction, many cultures are artificially combined in large territories or stretched across several traditional territories. This has created the conditions for continuing cultural and political conflict. In addition to the normal conflict between different cultures with different ways and values, usually resolved by trade or distance, this new conflict resembles small permanent wars over large numbers of territories. This kind of hot conflict not only destroys habitats and resources, but it causes immense human suffering. As the rules change, and conflict includes noncombatants, as well as plants and animals, there is less accord between conflicting groups. Accord requires the ability to trust, which requires self-reliance and confidence. The lose of accord leads to other related losses.

2.1.1.8. Loss of Design

During the evolutionary development of human responses to environmental challenges, people tested many kinds of designs for their tools, houses, and living habits. These initial designs often worked well in situations of limited resources or limited power. With the application of more power and the acceleration of the interchange of dominant designs, we have been able to force standard designs to work under almost any conditions, often replacing adapted designs.

Many of our current problems are design problems, Victor Papenak judges, that is to say, bad design causes all varieties of suffering and waste; it causes death, from accidents or collapses, and immense waste by relying on power to overcome its flaws. Many of these problems could be solved by better design, not just by more comprehensive industrial design or political design, but by the ecological design of entire processes and places. Of course some problems are caused by gravity, wildfires, or earthquakes, which are a natural part of the planetary system. While they may seem unsolvable, we can adapt to them with better designs, for instance, by reserving flood plains or landslide areas as parks without houses or buildings, and by adjusting the houses that are built to local conditions. Other problems are caused by human demands and the design response to them.

2.1.1.9. One Bad Combination of Losses

All of these problems interact, so that it becomes difficult to isolate separate problems. These longstanding problems result from longstanding challenges to human health and happiness: Food shortages, disruptions in distribution, violence, stupidity, greed, forgetfulness—not just personal forgetfulness but larger forms of cultural amnesia, old diseases and new, lust for power, and the lust to consume. These problems result in the death of many individual plants and animals, as well as entire species and whole habitats and ecosystems.

People die for many reasons: Environmental catastrophes, such as earthquakes, accidents, old age, lack of food, diseases, or personal violence. We know that people also die "indirectly" as a result of the destruction of natural ecosystems, specifically, as an example, the lack of clean, drinkable water. People die for economic reasons, such as not having a job to afford food, or not having a place to live, as a result of war or dislocation. It is almost impossible to calculate how many die in each category How many die directly from hunger, since hunger leads to disease, such as pneumonia, and disease gets the credit; how many die from unclean water, since the contaminant or the accident gets the credit? It is also difficult to calculate deaths from theft, economic dislocation, lack of planning, bad designs, or depression. Cause and effect make a complex dance of candidates in a network of things. Only specific diseases, accidents or bullets seem to be unambiguously fatal, and even these are often causally linked with many other contributing factors. We need to use better tools to understand and solve these problems, as well as to understand how a cosmology or economic system can promote the problems and then fail to solve them.

2.1.2. *Perceptual Challenges & Networks of Problems*

Many challenges to, or problems with, civilization are caused by our classical logic, which, in the western civilization, is deductive and bivalued; that is, we arrive at decisions from an overall image, and develop categories that are mutually exclusive. This binary approach results in an "either/or situation," rather than a "both/and" situation. For instance, the argument is tossed back and forth about whether our approach to resources should be anthropocentric or ecocentric, when in fact it should be neither. This argument occurs due to a misunderstanding of the concept of frame and focus.

2.1.2.1. Focus/Frame

Everything that we focus our attention on can be seen to be of a larger framework. Focus and frame can be understood metaphorically—and, in fact, metaphor itself can be understood as consisting of two parts, according to Max Black: Focus and frame. The focus designates the figurative term signified through the process, and the frame refers to the subject or context.

Using this distinction, it can be seen that most of the fuss in ecosystem-based activities, such as forestry for illustration, has occurred at the focus level. Modern foresters have so long focused on trees that they forget that the forest is a frame that holds many foci, or points of view. Alan Drengson is fond of saying that we do not see the important operations of nature because we are looking through the wrong paradigm—a paradigm acts like a pair of glasses, focusing on what we want to see.

The elements of a forest are related psychologically, by foresters, as focus or frame, as contrast or uniformity, as dominant or recessive, or in a number of other pairs. For instance, forests can be considered by scientists as either matter systems or energy systems, but the focus on either frame permits subtle differences and limitations in interpretation. Some scientists describe organisms as being configured by energy through time, but, organisms are material patterns in space as well. Furthermore, it is not quite right to say that ecological forestry is ecocentric, because it is actually concerned with the frame and not the focus, the periphery and not the center; perhaps it should be called 'drymoperipheral' instead.

The anthropocentric needs of people can be contrasted with the needs of the forest itself. This dilemma can be answered by considering the focus/frame character of the situation. Both of the two basic views are merely aspects of one view of good forestry. Anthropocentric values that focus on commodities can only be considered in the context of the values that are contained in the whole; that is, they are derivative from the frame. Furthermore, it is not necessary to ascribe conscious purpose to the latter view. Massive disruption often results when a community falls out of balance with its local forest environment, and in fact industrial forestry only avoids the penalties for such disruption by trading advantageously with other communities in less powerful areas. Emphasizing balanced use, including natural forest requirements, rather than perpetual growth, as is done now, would permit the frame to stay pluralistic and multidimensional, and still provide resources to human populations.

2.1.2.2. Small & Large Scales

Switching our attention from a focus to the larger frame usually involves a change in scale. Scale has several meanings. Basically, as it is used here, it has to do with the level of measurement in a space/time energy/mass context. For instance, in forestry the measurements of leaf litter by foresters can be made at several scales: Single tree, stand, annual measurements, or stand life measurements. Processes that are unimportant at a small scale might be vital at a large scale. Too much litter in one stand in one year, for instance, might suppress a soil cycle; too little litter over a century might interfere with several regional or global atmospheric cycles.

Some patterns in forests are scale-dependent; for instance, hemlock trees may dominate small clusters, but be scattered all across the entire forested landscape. That is to say, the pattern changes with the scale. This is true of processes in forests as well. Canopies shade the understory annually, but fires in a lodgepole pine forest may increase dramatically the amount of light to forest floors once every 200-300 years.

The scale of the system defined, for example, wooded patch, ecosystem or temperate broadleaf forest, depends on the scale of the phenomenon being addressed. Mangrove forests are in phase with the frequency of hurricanes, although hurricanes may not influence the life histories of short-lived organisms as much as daily or seasonal cycles. Microbes, for instance, are affected more directly by short-term cycles of precipitation and temperature.

Problems in forestry arise where applications that work on a small physical scale are expanded to large scales, without thought for the difference or changes in patterns. For instance, it is well-known that a Douglas-fir tree is shade intolerant and grows best in openings that get light. Rather than simply remove single trees or small groups of trees, and release or plant the fir in the openings, industrial forestry applies the treatment to the entire landscape with large clearcuts, which alter the other conditions that firs require: Some shade, water, protection from browsing, and associated species. This is similar to the formal operation of Greek tragedy—applying a good idea to another situation or scale where it does not fit.

Other systems of cutting, such as high-grading or thinning from below, may also have unintended effects with changes in scale. High-grading is a form of group selection, in which the "best" and largest trees are removed. The practice was not overly destructive on a small scale, with many of the matriarch and patriarch trees remaining, but on a large scale, all old, large, heritage trees were removed. Thinning from below may be a good idea in a stand, but like high-grading, it is a form of biological selection—the gene pool is altered as the small and suppressed trees, some of which may be genetically superior to larger ones, are removed.

An inappropriate time scale, its shortness and urgency, is a cause of many other problems in industrial forestry. Although forests are considered renewable resources, they are slowly renewable, requiring hundreds or thousands of years to renew from catastrophic disturbance; this time is far longer than any economic plans, and really is nonrenewable on a human life scale. This has important implications on sustainability. For instance, we cannot keep cutting on short rotations without destroying the character of the forest; we need to plan for 500-year or 2000-year rotations.

Really large scales, bioregional or global, are not considered often at all. At large scales, other factors have to be considered. Many cosmic tendencies, such as disorder (entropy) and order (ektropy), as well as change, creativity and temporality, are relevant to forestry. But, managers tend to emphasize only those tendencies that seem positive, such as creativity, diversity, and order, and not those with negative connotations, such as entropy, death, and uniformity. The universe comes with the whole package, and we risk serious error by choosing only the tendencies we want.

2.1.2.3. Global & Local Fields

Differences in scale are often called local or global differences. Concepts of scale apply to physical and biological fields. Local fields or events are those separated from other fields or events and exert minimal influence on the others. That is, the internal connections inside a local field are stronger than the connections between local fields. Both quantum theory and relativity consider that local fields are generally noncausally and nonlocally connected—that is, no communication is instantaneous—through higher dimensional realities.

Local ecosystems are unique and original. In an ecosystem, each locality supports a segment of the total species population in a unique context, with a particular set of predators, competition, food, or physical habitat. The environment requires an enormous amount of minuscule local adaptations between the earth and its users. Production of pine cones, for example, is adapted to the local microsites; Loblolly pine planted fifty miles north or south of the seed source are less vigorous. The chemical DNA seems to reflect local conditions. Local ecosystems are separated from one another, not only in space, but by differences. For example, Dutch elm disease is a local problem, even if it seems ubiquitous in all forests with elms, produced by local actions and requiring local solutions.

Local systems, however, can affect global systems. Cutting down local forests may contribute to the discharge of greenhouse gases, such as carbon dioxide, into the local atmosphere. This may have the effect of increasing quantities in the global atmosphere, creating a global change, possibly a runaway increase in atmospheric temperature.

Local systems emerge from a global system, which has characteristics that emerge from the interplay of local systems. Global systems have properties that no local systems have, such as an overall atmospheric temperature or global biogeochemical cycles. James Lovelock suggests that the interaction between hardwood forests and softwood forests may act as a global regulator of oxygen for the planet. Many things, such as human poverty and species extinctions, only seem global because they are happening in many local systems at the same time, and may effect global cycles.

2.1.2.4. Minimum & Maximum Limits

Our western civilization has become enamored with the idea of the maximum; it is the goal for many kinds of planning and operations. Agriculture, for instance, is concerned with maximizing its products and profits, but it also narrows the ecological basis of world food production and decreases human livelihood in the long run. We also strive to maximize good for ourselves, and the diversity or yield for nature, without a good grasp of what a maximum or minimum is.

In some senses, nature does try to maximize or minimize certain conditions. For instance a bubble minimizes surface tension by assuming a spherical shape that contains a maximum volume. Of course, we could also say that the bubble is an optimum form for the least possible surface area for a given interior volume. In principle, mathematicians reduce the question of maxima and minima to a geometric construct, often a three-dimensional surface with peaks and pits. In trying to apply the idea to a tree, however, the calculations become incredibly complex. A tree appears to create a maximum leaf area to collect radiation and a maximum number of seeds for reproduction, but it also tries to minimize evaporation and energy for its metabolism, both of which would set a smaller leaf area. So, leaf area reflects a compromise between gains and losses. The tree puts out an optimum or at least a satisfactory number of leaves. A forest is even more complex. In reality, the processes of trees and forests have many local maxima and minima; these can be represented graphically as surface potentials on a catastrophe field, as Rene Thom has done.

To survive, an ecosystem depends on the interactions and balance of many variables, most of which are not well understood. In agriculture or forestry we try to maximize one of those variables. When that happens, the balance or harmony is altered, and although it may take decades or centuries for the consequences to be known, the system is affected.

Many scientists and ecologists argue that we should maximize diversity. Diversity is an emergent property of ecosystems, arising from the activities of multitudinous beings learning to use the productivity of the system to augment their own flesh. The ecosystem is self-organizing, but diversity is not a goal of the system. Diversity is just a characteristic of mature ecosystems. But it is never an independent thing by itself; to think so is to be guilty of misplaced concreteness, according to A.N. Whitehead. In fact, nothing exists by itself, that is, not in relation to other characteristics, activities, or systems.

While it is meaningful to speak of an optimum diversity, as the result of limits and the interaction of many factors, a maximum diversity may never be reached in any system. As Paul Weiss noted, the patterns of organic nature are a combination of order and diversity; order involves constraint while diversity requires freedom for difference. Maximum order would result in a static universe, where a maximum diversity would create a nonordering chaos.

Few mammals—and humans are mammals—try for a maximum condition. Few mammals even try for an optimum; most strive for a satisficium, that is a satisfactory amount, according to Francisco Varela. Some animals, individual rats, for instance, seek substandard, or more challenging, conditions. Varela analyzes the evolutionary process as satisficing rather than optimizing; that is, a suboptimal solution is adequate to continue living; striving for an optimum or maximum does not pay off in terms of investment of effort.

Individual people are concerned with having maximum freedom or producing maximum values, and in fact, the idea of unlimited value tends to encourage the effort. Values may be indefinite, but they may not be infinite. Like the principle of limited good, there may be a principle of limited value. Even aesthetic appreciation requires limits, to avoid having our over-appreciation overwhelm the values evident in nature.

2.2. **Fashioning Tools**

A tool is a material object, or idea, that extends the human body or human thought. Technological things, such as tools or artifacts, are extensions of our physical being. The spoken language, using sound, engages and extends all the senses. The written language, using visual symbols or glyphs, can also engage and extend all senses, if the body resonates with them and recreates the full environment.

The users of tools had to have the ability to copy tools. Copying behavior may have shifting goals depending on context. Chimpanzees can learn to crack open oil-palm nuts using tools. This may start with young copying the mother's behavior, to be like her or to please her as part of the mother-infant bond. Young chimps may have to practice for three years to be able to coordinate hitting nuts with one stone as an anvil and another as a hammer. This nut-breaking is most often done at the end of the fruit season, when fruits are not available. The animals can get nine times the kilocalories that they put in as effort. Tool technology is a critical skill for eating and maintaining health. Stones are often kept at the nut "factory" although mothers may move the stones to familiarize infants with them. The copying has a lengthy investment by parent and child. The identity-based learning may shift to reward-based learning as chimps mature.

Tools may have first been used to acquire or store food, then to extend the efficiency of those processes. Tools have affects on human beings, from psychological distancing from things, as the tool is intermediary to a thing, to intimacy with the tool. There are physical effects as well: Loss of use of teeth, muscles, memory, loss of hand-eye coordination and perception of wild, but increase of the hand-eye coordination of tools. Each tool has an ideological bias, as skills or behaviors are amplified or ignored. To a man with a hammer, everything looks like a nail. To a woman with a grade sheet, everyone looks like a number, to a man with a computer everything is data, and to a woman with a camera everything is an image.

For tool-using cultures, tools had to do two things: First, they had to solve specific physical problems, and second, they had to serve the symbolic world of art in the construction of things, such as homes or monumental buildings. There are effects of tools on human cultures. The complexity of tools leads to rules for their use, and for who uses them, such as trade unions and clubs like masonry. Numbers become a tool to assess someone's behavior or worth. And, there are effects of tools on ecosystems, from the disturbance of soils to scale effects. Tools play a central role in the thought world of a culture, according to Neil Postman. Tools are not simply integrated into culture, they can reorder the culture. They may undermine the ideas in a culture or dominate them completely. At an extreme, tools may eliminate traditional world views and reduce the meaning of life to machinery. New technologies compete with old ones for dominance in a world view. The medium of technology contains an ideological bias. Tools attacks tools, according to Postman; printing attacks manuscripts, television attacks printing, painting attacks rock art, and photography attacks painting. Tool use has many effects, so care must be taken to use them consciously aware of their impacts and limits.

2.2.0.1. General Tools

Some tools, such as words or logic, we rarely think of as tools. Others, such as habits, stereotyping, myths, and even mathematics, we often use to hide or dismiss troublesome problems. Myths, for instance, are spread and remembered through stories told in every culture. Remembered stories become myths, accepted and not examined. Myths become part of the cultural heritage. The recital of myths is of great importance, though; myths provide a cognitive order for people. Myths are a major way of explaining the universe as it exists and communicating the cultural view of nature. Myths explain that which is otherwise incomprehensible, like death and disorder. To be understandable to members of a culture, the elements of a myth must be taken from the features and values of that culture. Neighborhoods share a common store of general myths of a larger field of culture or a nation, in which their local areas are embedded.

Myth sometimes starts as a cosmological account of the past. Any account of the past that is believed to be true is mythical. All interpretation and recounting of the past is a form of mythmaking. That is why myths reflect the details of a culture. The experiences of many lives, in their daily succession, are coded in myths, along with the natural phenomena, features of the culture, supernatural beliefs, and moral values, in a social order in a physical place.

In the simplest human societies, mythology is the text of rites of passage. In Hindu, Chinese and Greek philosophy, it is the picture language of metaphysics. The first function is extended by the second; both harmoniously bind people to their world in its visible and transcendent aspects. Ludwig von Bertalanffy proposed that myth, magic and language are interconnected near the origin of symbolic activity, for instance, in the new stone age drawings at Altamira. Mythology can be said to be the womb of a person's initiation to life and death.

Levi-Strauss thought that mythology was explanatory, a product of observation and a reflection of reality. Myths often were created, however, out of inherited ideational pieces through fitting together. But thought proceeded through understanding, with the aid of distinctions and oppositions. Levi-Strauss argues that all myths conformed to a small number of structures. Most myths, for instance, have a built-in binary opposition. He cites the Zuni origin myth, where life and death are in opposition. He also contended that the oppositions were attempted to be resolved with an ambivalent mediating term; in the Zuni, this term was hunting, which was life-producing and death-producing. Levi-Strauss reasons that the human mind operated using oppositions, that were reflected in myths, and attempted to resolve them through myth.

Myth and rationality are polar; yet both exercise an ordering function in the world. One dimension may be analyzed by the other, but it is difficult. Mythology is a multidimensional expression, whereas rationality achieves clarity following a single idea in one dimension. One dramatic presentation in mythology could be transposed into rational thought, but it would require a series of analyses. Myth condenses a theme, which serves as a symbol for the interpretation of a situation in the world, thus ordering imagination. Philosophical thought orders reason, by dispersing a theme to trace the logical connection of its structure. The philosophical analysis of myth excavates implicit meanings, and tries to clarify them. It can bring to awareness ideas in the myth, but not replace them.

In Plato, myth and logical thought share authority. In general, myth attempts to explain natural phenomena by going beyond them to imprecisely determined causes, usually gods; reason, on the other hand, limits itself to a sufficient cause. Myth and logic are coextensive in many respects, but some aspects of myth are inaccessible to logic, and likewise some truths of logic are unformed in myth. Beginning with Socrates, and culminating with Aristotle, myth and logic became thoroughly separated; for Aristotle, myths provided material for drama and poetry, while experience promoted the rational sciences. By limiting the area of investigation, and curtailing the range of speech, logic achieved a greater degree of accuracy, but only at the cost of completeness of experience. Mythical thought, with its receptivity of images, has been eclipsed by the untiring activity of logical thought, which attempts to treat everything in its manner.

We have tried to produce a monolithic theory of the nature of myths, by describing them as inadequate attempts to describe nature, or as a protoscience explaining human origins, or as heuristic devices giving the whole vision to be completed by science.

In a scientific view, ethics and cosmology are separate. But in a good mythology, there is a coherence between areas. The individual feeds back into the cosmology in altered form what was received. It is almost like a closed loop between cosmology, culture and the individual. Archaic peoples translate the natural world into the language of myth. Being a narrative, a myth is aesthetic as well as intellectual. Myths develop in terms of their own internal logic, drawing together observations of the world. Claude Levi-Strauss described the process as bricolage, fitting the bits together, identifying impressions of life as sets and forming them into mythical systems; the world picture is a metaphorical puzzle. Bricolage is the mentality of synthesis, a technique for learning, creating, and expressing understanding, using whatever is available from the past and in the present to achieve an integrating form. This is what mythological thinking does, and what scientific thought might do. Mythologies are of major importance in the life of society and civilization.

Although ideology and mythology are systems of thought, they differ in at least one important respect. An ideology is a system of thought that aims to justify and preserve the status quo; its emphasis is on the present. A myth is characterized by traditional consciousness. Its emphasis is on the past and the sacred. Yet, it is a timeless understanding of the cosmos. Archaic myth makes all things into living beings, persons having life and movement. Myths sanctify the existence of a culture by underlining the continuity of human experience with recurring elements. Myths give places, even relatively featureless ones, special significance. Ascribing mythic significance to land strengthens human identification with it.

Joseph Campbell distinguishes three functions of mythology. The first function of a living mythology, the religious function, is to waken and maintain in the individual an experience of awe and respect in recognition of the ultimate mystery that transcends words and names, from which words turn back (the word *mythos* originally meant 'mute'). Myths are ways of teaching unobservable realities by way of observable symbols. This is so the individual has an identity. The second function of mythology is to provide a cosmology, an image of the universe. In fact, the world has to be recognized and assimilated by the mythopoetic imagination. Myth weaves human knowledge, skills and aspirations together in intersubjective realm of image that blends science and art. Mythic symbols can store and convey vast amounts of information concisely. Myth describes the range of behavior that ordinary people are capable of. Myths teach what it is important to know to live in a place. The third mythological function is the validation and maintenance of established order.

Malinowski argued that this function is primary, to justify human activities, in order to have those activities continued. Unless a cultural phenomenon satisfied a basic human need, it would not be repeated. But, myths can also go wrong. They can be constructed for other purposes, to protect interests or to deceive people about what is important.

In the U.S., for instance, the mentality of the frontier bloomed as the physical frontier was being closed. This mentality assumed the nature of a myth, that all people would prosper in the frontier way. Even though the 1890 census recognized that there was no more frontier, and warned people to use what they had, people have sustained the myth of limitlessness. The myth has become stronger than the logic of limits. Corporations and banks have used the myth to offset the dismal flavor of their economics. The victims, from miners to loggers, have been tricked into passionately defending their own exploitation and that of the environment.

The frontier of myth no longer exists. And we cannot understand new frontiers until we are divested of the old one. New myths are made all the time, from poetry and comic books to politics and advertising. Many of these new myths are self-consciously lies, for the purpose of manipulating people, justifying greedy behavior, or enforcing new behavior. We justify our temporarily successful behavior with myths that allow us to continue that behavior without being responsible. The myths of agriculture and forestry, as well as democracy and globalism, and progress and nationalism, are examined for their limits or flaws.

Myths change and evolve. Our old myths, that reality is hierarchical, that the earth is passively female, and that 'man' is lord over the earth, have proven to be dangerous. They should be retired to the scrolls of dead myths. The eighteenth century held that a golden age would appear if the priests and kings were deposed. In the nineteenth century, a central myth, founded at the 1851 exposition, was that industrialization would bring universal peace. A mythology can affect every element of our social, individual, spiritual, ecological and political life, all at once. Myths can be traps, if they are never renewed by every generation. Continued belief in myths about nature in the face of contradictory facts is a trap. Facts are always changing, as are myths, as is nature; and, myths and facts are based on nature and are interpretations.

Contemporary thinkers, such as McKinley, argue that we need a new mythology of humanity in nature. New myths can be developed, such as the myth of participating in organic beauty, where development, not growth, is without limit. The universe is a frontier; the mind is a frontier, but these frontiers are based on a whole and healthy planet and a nature of which humanity is a special part among many special parts. To achieve transformations of human culture, we must go beyond the authoritarian conspiracies and technocratic elitism, to create new myths. We will only learn to treat land as part of our community, and not as an exploited commodity, when we have new myths.

Mythology is a tool that can shape ideas and behaviors, good or bad. Many cultural or ecological problems can be examined using simple tools such as questioning or metaphors. Good words or good metaphors can illuminate a problem better than long explanations and tables of numbers.

2.2.0.2. Words as Tools

The etymological meanings of words sometimes describe the limits of their original uses. We should perhaps heed these limits when we use words in this kind of work. The history of a word sometimes yields clues about how it has been used, as well as nuances of thought.

The word 'nature,' for instance, means, literally, 'that which is born' or 'made again.' Nature is the self-making universe; it is the self-regulating power that moves itself. Nature is the wild environment of humanity, a feeling system that embodies the experience of its inhabitants, with mutual experiences and histories.

'Culture' is a word that refers to a form of human expression that is adaptive to the environment of nature. Culture is the complex whole— invisible, behavioral or material—that includes knowledge, belief, art, morals, law, custom, artifacts, things, and any other capabilities and habits developed or acquired by human beings as members of society in a specific environment. The world 'environment,' meaning surroundings, tends to imply a division between nature and culture. This division has been explored, widened and narrowed by many scholars. Perhaps a new word could be used to describe nature and culture as a whole, 'domiture.'

Domiture, a neologism made from the Greek word fragments for 'home' and 'again,' could do that. The system of culture is embedded in nature; domiture is a larger term to enclose the previous nature/culture dualism. It has to include human reason and human emotion, rather than simply putting them on opposite columns, as with order and chaos, higher and lower, linear and cyclic, as well as agriculture and wilderness. Nature needs a place to play, without controls. Culture needs a place to play, without being forced by nature. Domiture envelopes both concepts.

Beyond being fun, making new words can force us to reconsider certain things. Established words often are bound with connotations and cultural baggage. A new word can call attention to gaps in our knowledge. A new word can suggest new directions for conversation, yet also remind us—if the word is well-made—of its origin. In this sense the construction of words shares the operations of metaphors, by bringing together things from a different context.

2.2.0.2.1. Words like World Nation Place & Home

Other words, such as 'world' and 'nation,' describe whole things. A world is that part of the planet designated by one culture, and the perspective of the inhabitants (from the German word for 'man-image'). It can also mean the entire planet. A nation is a people or tribe or a people living in a territory united by a single government, a stable, historically-developed community of people with a distinct culture occupying a common territory, although it has also come to mean an artificial designation as a result of political violence.

People in a 'domiture' create plans, models and nostrums to improve their situations. 'Plan' means flat; that might imply that our plans are two-dimensional and that being two-dimensional might mean that some properties of three, four or eleven-dimensional reality drop out in two-dimensions. Therefore, we should consider things that might be lost by our planning. 'Blueprint' means a flat in blue ink; perhaps our blueprints need to be four-dimensional (or seven or eleven-dimensional) to be complete. The word 'model' means measure; we need to be sure not to ignore things that are not measurable, such as happiness, health, or completeness. The word *nostrum*, from the Latin word in the plural, means 'our,' and it originally referred to a medicine of secret composition. Often, we offer plans as nostrums to fix a set of problems or illnesses (parenthetically, *nost* in Greek meant to return home, as it is used in words like 'nostalgia').

Human situations unfold in place. The word 'place' comes from the Latin meaning 'open space' and originally from the Greek word for 'broad' as it was applied to a way or street. The use now should reflect the kind of space modified by human interactions, whether cities, homes or pathways. The word 'environment' is from the old French word for 'surroundings.' In normal use, it implies the immediate nonhuman surroundings. We need to make sure that it includes larger scales that incorporate the large cycles in nature, to understand that our local neighborhoods are linked in many ways by atmospheric and hydrological cycles, as well as by elemental cycles. These words are not used in some cryptic way, but just to illustrate what they originally described, in order to understand how people thought, and then to extend those thoughts.

The place is an ecosystem, the subject of ecology, often regarded as a home. The study of life in place is 'ecology' (from the Greek word *oikos*, a dwelling place or house. The word economy derives from *oikonomia*, household management.) Ecology is knowledge of the house, as economy is its management.

Insects and animals displayed a powerful attachment to places, as

Adolf Portmann observed; this attachment was best understood as home. The fundamental ambiguity of existence is that humans have different capacities for feelings and awareness. Some feel strongly about a place or home; others never do. Several metaphors have been used to describe the human place on earth. The earth is a storehouse, property, or a spaceship. But the earth is not a spaceship or storehouse; it is home. Victor Ferkiss proclaimed that: "The world and humanity are one entity, one system in equilibrium. Earth is humanity's only home; humanity is one people in relationship to the earth."

There are a wide variety of meanings of home. It is a place of family residence, the family social unit, habitat, and place of origin. The word 'home' comes from the Middle English word *hom* and Old English *ham*, Old Norwegian *heimr*, Greek *kome*, and Sanskrit *kayati*, meaning village or home. The Old Norwegian word for home meant village or world. The word can be traced through the Greek to the Sanskrit, which meant "he is lying down." Its spectrum of reference is enormous. The word is used to describe house, village, city, bioregion, cultural world, and the earth. Its content is also ambiguous. Home can hold a single person, family, relatives, pets, domestic food animals, neighbors, or others.

Home living is simultaneous on different levels; the importance may shift from city to nation, or nation to state, or house to bioregion, or state to habitat. Each level can be a metaphor for the next. There are parallels between nature and a house, as the basis for home. Solar space is like the landscaping; wilderness is the foundation; conservation areas form the shell and provide services; and each bioregion is a unique room. The analogy cannot be carried too far, but it shows that a house is not, as Le Corbusier said, "a machine to live in." It is a matrix for home. Home is not just a house, either; it is a complex of significant events centered in place. It is the foundation of our individual identity on one level, and our role in the community, on another. What makes home different from house? Participation in its making, or commitment. People invest parts of themselves in a place, to make a home.

The concept of home has a mixed reputation. Paul Shepard finds humanitarians obsessed with the 'homelessness' of stray pets and wild animals. He points out how the fixation on shelter is taken over by the advertising of wood industries, who describe their meager reseeding efforts as 'creating a home for wildlife.' He sees protective organizations swaying to the tunes of propagandist lullabies. Perhaps, he is right. But, there is a misunderstanding of home. A home is not the house, not an undifferentiated place. Animals accustomed to rich woodlands are not at home in a replanted clearcut. The use of the word is a cheap advertising device, yet, it shows the importance of the meaning. A home is living thing, a house is not.

A home is a part of the environment claimed by feeling. Emotion creates an 'in-place.' A place must be found and made. Humans, like plants and animals, identify greatly with local environments. Maybe this is a function of the limbic system of the brain, a function we share with many territorial mammals. So far, no psychologists have studied what happens when a person sees her place, her very context, destroyed. These kind of catastrophes may be the basis for diseases, depression, or cancers, which also may be caused by the invasion of the home place by exotic substances.

The human ordering of the world makes places from wilderness. A place changes qualitatively; it becomes structured. Natural complexity decreases as the human complication increases, although the two are not mutually exclusive. Fitness is achieved after slow, progressive, reciprocal adaptations; it requires a stability of relationships between societies and place. Human places are complex integrations of nature and culture that develop in particular locations. The place precedes knowledge of it. The knowledge of place is one of the first links in a chain of knowledge. This knowing is essential to our existence. Being human is having and knowing a place. Only learning flowing from hospitable presence can promote life and enhance human existence.

Paul Shepard suggests that for each individual the organization of thinking and meaning is intimately related to specific places. Experience focuses on a place, which acts as the background for specific events. The features of the world are experienced meaningfully. The place is a matrix for ordering experience. The specificity of place is important. The earth extrudes itself into particular plants and animals; flexes mountains; and sweats weather. Places animate people (from the Latin word 'anima,' meaning 'inspire').

The inspiration of the sentiment of dependence is called impregnation. Animals and humans are imprinted early in life to particular places.[5] Each difference in the landscape has meaning, that can be perceived, for instance, as when the aborigines of Northwest Australia perceive physical differences and even a symbolic landscape. In fact, they structure space according to myth, where Europeans use buildings and roads for structure. Every place has a unique identity as a result of combinations of factors.

Being apart from home can result in a disease, nostalgia. The word nostalgia was coined by Johannes Hofer a Swiss medical student in 1678 to describe an illness characterized by insomnia, palpitations, stupor, fever, and the persistent thought of home. The disease could result in death. For the Northern Aranda in Australia, as well as for émigré Russians and other groups, it is not possible to stay away from home indefinitely and still live. Nostalgia can be a fatal disease. Thus far, the sense of place cannot be gleaned from an analysis of the human nervous system. Yet a place shapes the nervous system, somehow.

Permanence is important element in idea of home. In English the term for dwelling is 'to stay.' This is the symbolic opposite of moving or changing. It means to 'withstand time.' Dwelling resists and persists. The Royal Commission on Local Government in England and Wales found that people's attachment to 'home area' increased over time. Gaston Bachelard has written much about the significance of home: "For our home is our corner of the world. As has often been said, it is our first universe." The home is a springboard to understanding the universe.

The concept of home is proposed as a metaphor for the development of appropriate attitudes and participation in appropriate ways of living. The Pueblo Indians, for instance, see their American desert as a providential home, because of their attachment and knowledge.

2.2.0.2.2. Words like Ethics & Design

Our attitudes are often expressed in behavior or rules, as an ethics, that we use for making decisions about actions and about making in general. Making is a human activity that involves effort, using tools, in place. To 'make' means 'to bring into being' or produce something physically or mentally (from the English and Germans words, from the Greek meaning to 'knead,' press and stretch dough). It also means to build, fit, or create. The making of a home would be an 'ecopoetic' activity (from the Greek word fragments for 'house-making').

The word ethics is derived from the Greek word meaning 'custom' which itself came from the Sanskrit word for one's 'own doing' (Greek *ethos*, Sanskrit *svadha*). Since it was used in the plural, it meant 'doing together.' The word 'morality' comes from the Latin word for 'will of the people;' the singular meant the 'will' of a person (Latin *mores*, plural of *mos*, from *meare*). It was probably derived from the verb 'to measure,' as to measure one's way or to go one's way. Morals means the 'way of going together.' Ethics means 'doing together,' which of course one does living together. And, in an anthropometric universe, it is entirely appropriate. Ethics is a description of human conduct, or set of rules, determined by custom and culture. Ecologically, ethics is a limit on one's freedom of action in a culture.

Customs and actions combine with history as we redesign ecosystems to provide our needs. The word 'design' means 'marking off a pattern.' Our effort should be to make sure that we are using the whole patterns. Design is a human project in which, as Oliver Lucas says, "visual and physical parts are assembled in order to achieve a specific end result." Ecological design is the creative modification of ecosystems to repair or enhance their ability at self-organization and the maintenance of their complexity and diversity. The word design comes from Latin word meaning 'to mark.' Nature is self-making and self-designing, but we humans now influence every natural system, taking what we need from some ecosystems, enhancing a few, misusing others, and interfering with the rest. We need designs to restore the balance between human needs and natural processes.

Ecological designs focus on whole communities that work in the same self-sustaining and self-limiting ways as nature. By consciously creating meaningful ordered patterns, we can develop ways of producing widespread community wealth while positioning the community for a long, sustainable future in a healthy environment.

2.2.0.2.3. Words like Good

We judge the results of our efforts as good, or not good. Thinkers have puzzled over the term 'good' for centuries, constructing partial theories and contradictory systems. The word 'good' has an interesting and long history. The current version is derived from the old English, *god*, meaning 'suitable' or fitting, similar to the words meaning a 'suitable time' and to be 'suitable' or 'pleasing.' In an organic world, good things are defined by a free interplay of energies. Perhaps, as a working definition, we can just use 'harmony.' In Chinese medical tradition, the highest good is harmony, especially social harmony or good relations. A good person is one who creates and maintains harmony. Harmony is related to wholeness—indeed, the word 'whole' comes from the Indo-European root *kailo*, which is also the root for the words health and holy.

Science is a useful system for realizing new knowledge, but it has trouble dealing with concepts like good or bad. We can learn about ecological processes and try to manage them, but it is problematic to designate good theories or good practices. Normally we do not think of physical or biological events, such as gravity or cell division, as good or bad; they simply exist in a neutral way. But, the effects of these events are valued in the human realm by human intention, which is open to interpretation and ambiguity, and which is described by human symbols and signs.

Signs are arbitrary, as Ferdinand de Saussure noted; that is to say, they have no necessary connection to things. Signs can make many connections to physical and biological events, thus intensifying them; signs can also become dense with human meaning over time. It is the play of signs in human language and human culture that results in judging that something is good or bad; that is, the manipulation of signs, in a field of surprise, due to many levels of meaning or uncertainty, produces degrees of goodness.

Cultural structures provide rules that limit play and action, so that it stops short of death or destruction. All cultures work that way. Ethics and economics, for instance, are rules of behavior; and politics is the practice of changing the rules as society changes. Signal play without cultural structures can result in problems, especially when science or other devices claim to be independent of culture.

Goodness is thus intention and action in the context of the rules of a culture, using ambiguous signs. Goodness is a feature of the path of actions, as is badness, which is sometimes identified in extremes as evil. Of course, many cultural codes divide everything neatly into good or bad, but, everything is not that simple, and goodness cannot be grown and picked like a ripe tomato. By trying to focus on either extreme, of pure goodness or pure badness, we miss the ambiguity and uncertainty of everyday situations, most of which occur in a mixture. Our ethics and ideologies are not comprehensive enough to help us live in this mixture, with the inevitability of uncertainty, and with the possibility of enantiodromia, that is, the creation of the opposite of our intentions. Using new logic and metaphors can help us to adjust to such a reality.

The use of the word 'good' with human places or ecosystems is problematic. Good means different things to different people. Your standards or codes, personally or culturally, might be different from mine. Therefore, the meanings of the words will be different. The search for good is measured by personal criteria, personal judgment, and personal reflection. Furthermore, human beings cannot know, or even think of anything, according to Robert Zajonc, without some involvement of emotion, that is, having at least a vague feeling of good or bad. On the other hand, this sense is complicated by questions of what one 'ought' to do, that is, morality.

When we set goals, as for the goodness of ecological restoration, we base those goals on the meaning of the symbols, which can have many more than one meaning. A shift in context can change the meaning. Because there is no absolute good in our practices, it is difficult to determine the best practice to use, especially when applied to long-lived ecosystems, such as forests and deserts. Goodness is relative, but we must make decisions regardless. Throughout this book, the term goodness is related to overall harmony, but it cannot be considered independent of practice.

Any example of a practice in an ecosystem, such as forestry, can be good, if it follows its methods, regardless if it is totally external, human-centered, rule-bound, or simply pragmatic. Any application of management can be good, if the worker unconsciously follows certain codes or accidentally does the right thing for the ecosystem—the right thing being an absence of interference with the dynamic systems that shape and maintain ecosystem processes. Good management can happen for the most contradictory or trivial reasons: Self-limitation, true love for nature, accident, intention, techniques, or shame—this last may be why management gets altered with public interest and scrutiny.

2.2.0.2.4. Words like Reality & Thing

The word reality comes from the Latin *res*, from which we get the word 'reality,' and it means 'thing.' Being real was being a thing. Reality was thinghood in general. The word thing goes back to Old English words that mean 'object,' action, event, condition, or meeting. It may have originally meant 'something occurring at a certain time.' The word might have been used originally as a metaphor for some event under certain conditions. It might have been used for describing any form of existence, permanent or transitory, limited or determined by conditions. It is now a very general word indicating a form of existence limited by conditions.

According to David Bohm, the Latin word *res* comes from the verb to think, such that things are what are thought about. Perhaps thought is a dance of things in the mind. Occasionally, throughout this book, the verb forms of words is used to indicate an on-going process. In some languages, such as Hebrew of Hopi, the verb is taken as the primary part of a sentence. In other languages and cultures, the group identity, that is the larger subject, is taken as primary, over the separate individual.

Bohm proposes a rheomode, which uses a new grammatical construction, in which verbs are used in a new way; it becomes a new mode of language. Bohm says that words can be brought in to enrich discourse in the ordinary mode of language. The reconstruction of words is not essentially different from the construction of phrases and sentences. This approach is similar to the use of particles in a field in physics. The particles are only abstractions that may be convenient. In ordinary language, for instance, 'truth' is taken as a noun. But, truth is that process which works. We think it is established and stable, but we should recognize that it is constant (from the Latin *constare*, 'to stand together') only within limits of the flow.

2.2.0.3. Logic of Logics

As our words need to reflect a larger sense, so our logic needs to be aware of its scope and limits. Most Western science assumes a predicate logic and is constrained by that logic. This Aristotelian logic is deductive and binary, where categories are mutually exclusive, and substance and identity are permanent. In this logic, contradictions are false by definition. The difficulties with this logic are evident in many instances in physics and ecology, e.g., light cannot be a wave *and* a not-wave, or wolves cannot be a keystone species *and* a species not necessary to an ecosystem. Neither substance and identity seem to be permanent in any human sense of that word.

Truth itself is not an absolute something, or even a relative something. It is that which is lived in connection to the whole web of lives. It is not fixed, static, or a point. It cannot be abstracted by words or measured by numbers. There is no path to it; there are no tools that can isolate it.

Our science and theories are beset by logical problems. Would a more flexible logic solve the problems? A nonpredicative logic? There is another form of this logic that is multivalued, but it is also based on the same epistemology of a hierarchical universe in which values can be rank ordered. Magorah Maruyama calls these logics, and the epistemologies that contain them, homogenistic.

There is another independent-event form, with an inductive, statistical logic, which is used by scientists and existentialists. Independent-event is the reverse of homogenistic logic; both characterize 'Western' logic. The homogenistic logic can be characterized as classificational quantitative, competitive, uniform, nonreciprocally causal, and hierarchical.

Other logic systems exist, although they are not as predominant. Maruyama distinguishes two other epistemologies that have a typical logic based on them: Homeostatic, with a complementary logic, as exemplified by Chinese thought, and Morphogenetic, with a logic incorporating change, harmony, heterogeneity, and unrepeatable and irreversible processes, as demonstrated in Mandenka, Navajo, and Inuit thought.

Morphogenetic logic is quite different from homogenistic logic. The morphogenetic logic can be characterized as relational, qualitative, symbiotic, heterogenistic, reciprocally causal, and interactionist. Reciprocal causal processes can increase structure, differentiation and complexity in natural systems, according to Maruyama.[6] Such a logic is more useful for addressing complex operations in ecosystems. As a many-valued logic, it can address values other than truth and falsehood. It can avoid certain fallacies embedded in two-valued logic.

No superlogic can combine categories, however, since they are based on different epistemologies and cosmologies. Any researcher, using any logic, will filter and distort data to some extent, as a result of epistemological 'selection.' A broader logic, however, such as the morphogenetic, could work at a metalevel and avoid many of the problems of polar thinking.

2.2.1. *Naming with Metaphors*

The concept of metaphor has been defined and used for over twenty centuries. Before that, metaphor seemed to characterize language itself. Metaphor is used in all advanced languages. For Aristotle, metaphor was a trope, the 'turning of phrase.' The word metaphor comes from the Greek word *metaphora*, which means 'carrying beyond.' Aristotle was one of the first to say what it represented in words: The process of transferring a word from one object of reference to another.

There are two principles governing the creation of a metaphor, according to Max Black: First, the just disclosed phenomenon is given the name of a previously identified one that resembles it, and second, this resemblance is discovered in the most 'essential' aspect of the new phenomenon, which calls forth a direct perceptual experience, already named. That is, a metaphor furnishes a label and emphasizes similarities between a known thing and an unknown one. It not only defines and extends new meanings, but also redescribes domains seen already through one metaphoric frame.

The metaphor itself consists of two parts: (1) the focus (or tenor or figure), which designates the figurative term signified through the process, and (2) the frame (or vehicle or ground), which refers to the subject or context. For example, in the sentence, "Light is a particle," the focus is 'light' and the frame is 'particle.' The focus of a metaphor is a primary system that refers to that which is to be understood, a brain or atom, for instance. The frame is a secondary system that provides a pool of names to be used for comparison: computer or solar system. The interactions of systems is mutual; the secondary system imposes a reorganization on the concepts of the primary, but the use of the metaphor alters perception of the secondary as well as the primary. Not only are the two concepts altered, but also the meaning of the concepts is altered. And this 'halo' meaning, in its unique reducibility, permits things to be said that could not be said otherwise. In the secondary and primary systems—for example Karl Popper's phrase "the brain is a computer"—opposites interpenetrate and are unified even though the metaphor is initially and cognitively perceived as absurd.

This interpenetration is a dialectic, where opposites are unified in a metaphorical synthesis that transcends the initial contradictory conjunction of the two systems. Thus, concept formation in art and science is a working out of contradictions, as in Bohr's metaphor, "the atom is a solar system." Logical opposites logically combined assert nothing in traditional logic. Metaphorical logic is not limited to traditional logic. It is more contextual and multivalued. The original meaning of logic in Greek was 'gathering up,' which is what metaphoric logic does. With metaphors, logical consistency is no longer required.

The metaphor is a form of discourse where one of the terms is always denotative. The collocation of terms in a metaphor leads to a sort of intercourse, in the Platonic sense, a transaction or transference between the associated contexts. The focus is responded to as the frame, in addition to its own original, evoked responses.

Some distance between the focus and the frame of a metaphor is necessary; similarity must be accompanied by some disparity. If the two are too close together, then the perspective of double vision might be lost. Samuel Johnson claimed that it was useless to compare a tree with a bush. The power of the analogy is also related to the emotive potential of the matrices. It is equally useless to compare a sneeze to a cloud.

This is a form of reasoning by analogy, not by differences, which a digital computer uses to compare things. Metaphorical expression has an analogical unity in human existence. Its central organizing principle is the single person, with perception and imagination. The expression points the mind toward the broadest meaning. It points, not toward truth, but to an ever-enlarging relational field. It points to the frame, in fact. That which is the frame must be ambiguous. Frames themselves must be used as metaphors. The word 'nature,' for instance, has been used by Western philosophers in over thirty distinct senses. Under ambiguity many meanings may hide. Nature can be regarded as just a 'puzzle' or 'opponent' to be beaten, but both detract from a total experience of nature, in nature.

2.2.1.1. Metaphorical Basis of Science

The entire activity of science can be said to be guided by metaphors. Metaphors can allow scientists to deal with complex situations. For example: "The world is atomic," according to Leukippus and Demokritus; "atoms are billiard balls" for Dalton and Rutherford; "the world is mathematical," according to Pythagoras; "man is an animal" for Karl Pribram; "man is a system" for Ernst Laszlo; and "man is a computer" for Michael Arbib.

Bacon referred to true metaphor as "the footsteps of nature." Metaphor is the vital spirit of a scientific paradigm, according to Thomas Kuhn, and its best organizing relation. The notion of paradigm includes techniques, examples, community values, and a central metaphor. According to Kuhn, there is no methodological evolution of science; rather, normal science progresses by a succession of paradigms, which he described as noncompetitive and open-ended. He stated that paradigms are the traditions described by historical rubrics like: Ptolemaic astronomy or Copernican; Aristotelian dynamics or Newtonian. These examples include law, theory, application, and instrumentation together, and provide models from which the traditions of scientific research spring. In his view, science proceeds by working out problems uncovered by each current paradigm. Should problems occur that cannot be ignored, suppressed or resolved, then a revolution should occur to replace the paradigm. The new paradigm would have to include all the old data as well as the new problematical data. Metaphoric systems are the core of structural coherence of any paradigm.

The word 'individual' is a metaphor. As such it refers to aggregates (sand), functional units (populations), and autonomous, self-regulating beings (a wolf). The word 'whole' is a metaphor. A 'thing' is a metaphor, though it is so old it is considered a real term. A thing (or part) is that which can be separated from other things, thus intimately related to the idea of boundaries. The metaphor has a boundary. The meanings of a metaphor can be ontological (physical things) or structural (quantified or valued). Where we make boundaries usually depends on our past experiences. Interface as a synonym implies that the boundary is Janus-faced.

Metaphors in science are usually termed models and are used to bestow a more precise meaning to expressions. Science makes use of the metaphorical process to construct its models.

2.2.1.2. The Strength of Metaphors

The metaphor of a chain, as in the "great chain of being" described by A. O. Lovejoy, was used to order living beings in a single linear series. This implied that things were level and ordered one after the other. The use of a tree by Buffon to trace the genealogy of dogs in different climates added a dimension to understanding of the effect of the environment on animals. Metaphors are good to think with. The use of the tree metaphor by Ernest Haeckel, as the shape of life, is used in archaic cultures also. After all, the earth is a forest planet; eighty percent of the biomass on the planet is tied up in trees. And, trees are animated water. As a metaphor, a tree conveys strength, growth, and longevity. For the Kwakiutl people, for instance, the chief is the post of the world, the only one standing, the cedar that cannot be spanned, the post of heaven that holds up the sky and bridge it. The chief is the trunk of the cedar, the upper-class people are the branches, and the common people of the trunk. The chief's ancestors are the root of the tribe. If the chief and the heir die, "both tree and root are killed."

Darwin used the 'struggle for existence' as a metaphor: "I use this term in a large and metaphorical sense including dependence of one being on another, and including (which is more important) not only the life of the individual, but success in leaving progeny." The struggle is between individuals of a species, or different species, and with the physical conditions. Darwin's theory of evolution destroyed the tradition of natural economy with its essences ordered by reason, but he still used a rational economics for his metaphors of individualism. The metaphor seemingly arose from the socioeconomic view of the ruling classes of the time, that the suffering of the poor was inevitable. This metaphor formed part of the basis of a new worldview where nature was a theater of violent competition, especially after Tennyson made nature seem more poetic, as "red in tooth and claw." The frame where a metaphor originates often carries the conceptual baggage of that time. It can support the idea of superiority of 'favoured' races in the struggle for existence and emphasize the role of competition in biological and cultural situations, at the expense of other interactions.

'Natural selection' was also metaphoric. Darwin did regret later not calling the process 'natural preservation.' Wallace described evolution as a conservation process, similar to the centrifugal governor of a steam engine. Darwin used the tangled bank as another metaphor. The metaphor of the tangled bank evokes the mutuality and interdependence of the interactions of organisms in webs. Darwin said: "It is interesting to contemplate a tangled bank, clothed with many plants of many kinds, with birds singing on the bushes, with various insects flitting about, and with worms crawling through the damp earth, and to reflect that these elaborately constructed forms, so different from each other, and dependent upon each other in so complex a manner, have all been produced by laws acting around us."

2.2.1.3. Modeling Things

Metaphors emphasize likenesses between things, living things, languages, or human constructs. Metaphor in the broad sense includes similes, analogies, models, patterns, and paradigms. A visual representation of a metaphor can be a model. Modeling can be done with metaphors as well as with shapes and numbers.

2.2.1.3.1. Metaphorical Models

Darwin used 'natural selection' as a metaphor for evolution. Later, the philosopher Maurice Merleau-Ponty used an explosion as a metaphor for evolution. Merleau-Ponty considers that the direction of evolution relies on a pseudo-teleology that is the inverse of mechanism, on a great 'pattern mixed-upness.' Evolution is a radiation of life. Rather than relying on evolution as a basis for metaphysics, he called for a "phenomenal topology" of things as they loom upward bodily around us. Marjorie Grene noted that because the records take one every which way, evolutionary theory was a poor crutch for renewal of ontology.

It is possible to use metaphors for other complex assemblies that are difficult to understand. For instance, it could be said: The city is a sponge. The sponge cannot use the sun to get energy directly, but must use surrounding environment and the productivity of other organisms in the water. Sponges must circulate food brought in, using energy from that food. The city has own metabolism, that is a network of circulatory structures used for exchanges. Of course, the metaphor implies the city is a living organism. Perhaps another metaphor would permit the city to be understood as more self-creating, perhaps if the city were identified as a tree or a box.

Mario Bunge used black boxes as metaphors. The idea of the black box was originally conceptualized by electrical engineers to describe certain unknown systems devoid of structure. Black box theories include kinematics, thermodynamics, information theory, scattering-matrix theory, and circuit theory. The black box approach is useful for all theories whose variables are external and global, that are simple and have a high degree of generality. As theories are supported by observation, black boxes become translucent. Some empirical theories have root metaphors that range from black to almost transparent: 'man is an animal' according to Karl Pribram, or 'the brain is a hologram' for Michael Arbib. When we fill in the box, and make it transparent, we see the interactions of the components. In an ecosystem, if we make the box itself transparent, then we are left with a food web.

The box is a productive metaphor. The box can also be equated to a cage or trap. Karl Marx contended that we live in cages, part natural and part made, although human actions could modify them. The word cage is a metaphor; it implies being trapped. It is, however, a metaphor that can be expanded with a description in space as a four-dimensional box. Perhaps there is a better metaphor, since we depend on nature and society as a foundation for life, that of a trap. The word 'trap' is from the Old English 'to step.' A trap is a device for catching and holding animals or a stratagem for catching people. The idea of a trap can be related to the idea of closeness to limits or to the overconnection of links.

Taken in four dimensions, a trap can be a serial trap: The use of resources by a people, where the replenishment rate is constant ands the rate of use exceeds it. This trap results in ecosystem degradation that is less reversible. The industrial age mistakes the rate of discovery for the rate of recovery. Agriculture is an energy trap, because it allows the concentration of energy, that is, higher yields, but then it requires more energy be put into the system to maintain it. The system has to produce more energy than it uses to be useful. And be sustainable, with a surplus for trade. Instead of being free from economic want to develop their potential as creative human beings, people are trapped in a consumer cycle.

A filter is an interesting metaphor. For organisms, the environment is a filter that allows some characteristics to continue, by providing opportunities and challenges. Organisms put together structures based on historical patterns, and move through a filter of limits like minnows through a fish net. Perhaps, the idea of a filter is too passive. Perhaps a better model might be a kind of sorting filter, a mutual filtering of organisms and environments. Organisms and an environment co-order each other, sorting things out in a mutual process of activities and adjustments. In the next largest system, ecosystems are also filtered or interactively sorted.

Culture is also a filter or mutual sorter. The anthropologist Branislav Malinowski tried to show that almost all of a whole culture is can be seen as a mechanism to modify and satisfy the sexual needs of an individual. What a filter that would be. Of course, you could also argue that the mechanism of culture is to channel energy or distribute material goods. These mechanisms are only parts of a culture. There are some parallels with biological evolution, especially if we use memes as the unit of transmission. Memes are still filtered by the mental environment for fitness to that environment, although in this case the filters are partly due to memes. The scale of replication is related to positive feedback, as when a work of art fetches great sums of money or is written up from controversy. The information that is transmitted is in form. Culture is more than a simple filtering or sorting process. It is more than a formation process. Because it occurs with physical, living, conscious, and social systems, culture is more like a novation process, that is, it recombines things into new orders.

These models of box, trap, filter, and sorter will be used in subsequent discussions.

2.2.1.3.2. Conceptual or Mathematical Models

Models can be constructed with a series of verbal statements or with a combination of statements and mathematical equations, using data. There have been many such models of the world system recently. Each model gathered data, analyzed it, and made a set of predictions based on the data and analysis. Each of the models also recognized having very general problems. For instance, The *Limits to Growth* model had vastly more information than it could use in an orderly way, due to deficiencies in theories of structure. J. W. Forrester emphasized that modeling projects should be global or national, but not regional, and should draw heavily on mental databases. The Forrester model distributes values homogeneously over the globe, disregarding sociocultural and ecological systems. It tolerates an expansionist view of industrial human civilization. But, Dennis Meadows and others recognized the constraints on the planet with limited resources, and concluded that partial solutions could make things worse.

Mesarovic and Pestel established the necessity of using models to represent the objective aspects of world development, and defined a model as "a coherent and systematic set of descriptions of relevant relationships." The entire report used a strict scientific methodology to treat actual data, avoiding any hint of an abstract academic exercise. But, it reduced everything to measurements, perhaps invalid measurements. Although they carefully contrasted their model with the Forrester-Meadows thesis, there does not seem to be any essential difference at all. Their multilevel model is still a reductionistic, as is their attempt at regionalizing cultural areas of the world. They claim a complete set of descriptions, but the subsystems sets are grossly oversimplified, and the results are starkly primitive graphs, reduced to meaninglessness by uniform, noncontextual computer decision-making processes. In summary, their model assumes basic industrial values and loses most human values in the shuffle of facts.

The book, *Reshaping the International Order*, coordinated by Jan Tinbergen, recognizes a need for a new international order. The book identifies problem areas and examines the progress toward their solution. Tinbergen defines a difference between a forecast, as in *Limits to Growth*, and a plan, which is a human effort to control destiny. In fact, the plans described here are based on many forecasts. The second part of the book describes the architecture of the order and discusses strategies for steering change. One aim of development is towards an equitable social order, by reducing the differential between rich and poor. He explores the implications of his own plan, which accommodates the tension between developed and underdeveloped nations. Tinbergen recommends that poor nations negotiate with rich nations through collective bargaining to obtain a greater opportunity and right of equals. This tactic could bring some success.

Where the *Blueprint* group suggested more drastic steps, from disregard for the adaptive dynamics of supraeconomic and ecological factors, Ernst Laszlo's alternative is purposive policies that mobilize adaptive capacities in these dimensions. Focus should be directed toward dynamic equilibrium models achieved without undue trauma, and sustained without repression. The ethical dimension of order relates to attitudes about violence, satisfaction of needs, and sociopolitical conditions compatible with equality and worth of human beings. Laszlo proposes a model which accounts for biospheric and sociocultural inputs from the total environment; recognizes sociocultural systems as converter and subsystematic; relates outputs— material and social technics—to positive and negative feedback. This system is more comprehensive and consciously planned than most.

We have separate kinds of models related to plant productivity, human population, and world games. We can try to generate models dealing, not only with the more constant of natural and human characteristics, but with the limits of certainty and the vagaries of change.

2.2.1.3.3. Theoretical Models
A theory is an explanation or system of everything. It is an exposition of the abstract principles of a science, or it is a speculation. The dictionary

definition states that a theory is a reasoned expectation, as opposed to practice. A scientific theory is a set of general explanatory statements about a natural process; the set is related as a model, which is a human linguistic construction, subject to human perspectives and limitations. Theories may incorporate guesses, critical observations, experimentation, and logical inference, as well as hypotheses and laws. A theory must be a specific enough statement, such that experimental results can be assessed as negative or positive. The results of an experiment can confirm or justify a theory, although other experiments could show that the theory is wrong. Good theories tend to have a limited number of generalizations. Theories can also be nested, so that, for instance, the theory of gravitation might be combined with other theories in a unified field theory.

Science works with theories, that is, specific directions of observation, based on previously identified facts, to lead to evidence, or proofs of hypotheses, about how things work, which can be used to predict other actions in the future. Theory is used to guide experimentation. But much experimentation these days occurs without theoretical guidance, or rather the theories used are not capable of addressing the context itself, so that the experiments tend to go out of control. Many experiments are simply conducted improperly, with no control group, no good theory, or no control of scale.

People who know a lot, but do not have theories that bind them to wise actions, tend to ignore ignorance, or to act in an arrogant manner; such behavior can be dangerous. Theory can reduce this kind of danger. Theory can describe the limits of itself, of knowledge and understanding, so that we do not try to do that which cannot be done, for instance, create perpetual motion machines. That is, theory deals with ignorance, the kinds of ignorance, and especially the kinds that cannot be removed. Theory also deals with ambiguity and uncertainty.

Theory has to account for those things that cannot be reduced or explained or understood. Some mysteries cannot be reduced, cannot be understood with human understanding. Some things are ineffable; even if they are understood, they cannot be reduced to words. Our theories and practices are human theories and practices; they are limited by real human limits, by the dimensions and terms of times that we humans experience.

Theories can help science to avoid claiming what things, either knowledge or certainty, that it cannot claim. Theory can distinguish between knowledge and theory, between theory and the unknowable. Theory needs to address the incompleteness and limits of science. There will always be limits and errors; these cannot be avoided. Theory needs to accommodate this truth. Fallibility is unavoidable; it is a part of certainty from a limited perspective with a limited knowledge; it is part of being incomplete and using incomplete knowledge. But, this is the limit of all being; this is the limit of finiteness.

What we know will always be incomplete, but we have to act under those circumstances, and therefore we have to act on partial knowledge in the face of partial ignorance. Theory is a guide to acting, under different kinds of unavoidable and irremovable ignorance, based on thinking about previous actions and projecting future actions. Theory is not necessary to get more information. But it is necessary to understand what can be predicted or understood. Theory can help distinguish between local and global problems. Theory can describe the fitness of our conduct within an ecological and cultural system.

Most theories in this century have been dominated by the impoverished philosophies of modern industrial cultures. These theories have no way of dealing with the profound changes of global warming and habitat destruction, extinctions, social decay, new diseases, or unrestrained technology. These changes are modifying the planet and may destroy us, as well as those things that we require for adventure or inspiration.

To be really effective, theories need to be rooted in conceptually rich philosophies, such as process philosophy, phenomenology, general systems theory, ecophilosophy, deep ecology, ecofeminism, or radical ecology, philosophies that are more fruitful and considerate of nonhuman beings and systems—and in fact consider such problems as what is good or what are human limits. These philosophies contribute to a new attitude that is more appropriate to the unity and interrelatedness of the earth. These philosophies provide a number of fundamental philosophical, historical, scientific, and cosmological principles that have been presented in other contexts by thinkers such as Cobb, Einstein, Fox, Naess, and Whitehead. Very few of these principles are absolute. Nevertheless, they are essential to the understanding of ecosystems and cultures. Principles, combined with common sense and good judgment, are necessary as guides in the absence of definite knowledge. They give us a deep foundation and a broad predictive ability that we need for good practices.

Good theories are just those that incorporate cultural values with ambiguity and uncertainty. Good theories are grounded in place and in communities. They must be used to place our science and technological capabilities in a culture that has goals and limits for our actions. In this sense, theories are tools for adaptation to place, within place, within specific places that we work towards making good.

2.2.2. *Questioning Things*

Questioning has a long history in human experience. The Greek philosopher Socrates was one of the more renowned questioners. He approached teaching through a disciplined, rigorous dialogue with people he met on the street, often by accident or by design. Socrates tried to get others to recognize the contradictions in their ideas; he assumed that incomplete or inaccurate ideas would be corrected during the process of questioning, and hence would lead to progressively greater truth. He never seemed to reach an end to questioning, however, perhaps because there was no end, that is, the process of questioning could refine any kind of knowledge or ignorance, indefinitely, or perhaps because by itself questioning could only do so much with definitions and concepts. His method was a common search, through conversation, for the goal of truth.

2.2.2.1. The Socratic Method

Socrates asked questions as part of a conversation with others. He seemed concerned with discovering what the opinions of others were based on, an invisible truth. The questioning forced the other participants in the conversation to try to agree on the truths beneath the opinions. Socrates professed ignorance of the truth himself, in fact or in pretense, ignorance being the first step in the pursuit of knowledge. He expressed skepticism that the other conversants actually had real knowledge. The process of questioning subjected opinions to real examples from real experiences—an empirical method—leading to a more general concept—this is the process of induction used in a scientific, homogenistic logic—and then the consequences of the definition were drawn out, through deduction. These definitions were refined by further questioning until all members of the conversation had a better grasp of the concepts. Through thorough questioning Socrates demonstrated that knowledge was quite often uncertain. There was no absolutely certain knowledge. Questions were also meant to examine life as well as belief and truth, and to show that often people were ignorant of their ignorance. Socrates held that disciplined questioning enabled the other to examine ideas logically and to be able to determine the validity of those ideas.

2.2.2.2. The Hardin Extension

For Socrates the goal of knowledge was the acquisition of concepts, such as justice, courage or wisdom. He thought that the truth could be contained in a correct definition. And, he was groping for more abstract definitions. This became a problem, as abstraction became removed from the specifics of living. Socrates was most concerned with examining concepts, but concepts are a small part of reality. Of course, constant questioning of concepts can expose the psychological basis of concepts, and perhaps that is what Socrates meant to do. But, questioning concepts often reaches limits fairly quickly. Socrates never had any answers, although he assumed that an absolute certain knowledge was possible to become established eventually.

The ecologist Garrett Hardin used questioning to illuminate partial knowledge and to track connections between things. Questions establish the limits of assumptions and perspectives. They can clarify the focus of a problem and test evidence related to any problem. Questioning can be used as a device to focus on a specific problem, not only the extent of the problem, but its aspects. Questioning can also be used to explore specific aspects of the dimensions of thought. Of course, questions can refine the process of critical thinking and can allow refocusing in a wider or narrower context. This type of questioning arrives at answers as workable hypotheses or guidelines for making decisions about operating in the world. Without certain knowledge, however, we can make adaptive decisions, based on partial knowledge. His questioning took on the form of asking what happened then, after an answer was arrived at. "And then what?" Hardin asks. Questioning works in a conversational way by weaving ideas. Conrad Lorenz decided that humanity would indeed have destroyed itself by its first inventions, were it not for the very wonderful fact that inventions and responsibility are both the achievements of the same specifically human faculty of asking questions.

More than an annoying part of a conversation, questions are legitimate ways to approach a known or unknown situation. More than just a way to turn around a conversation, questions are tools that allow you to surround a topic and define it more completely. More than simply an admission of ignorance, questions can form a phenomenological spiral that allows you to return to a subject from different perspectives with different levels of understanding.

2.2.2.3. Maslow's Questions about the Norms of a Society

Before even designing a good society, certain normative questions must be answered. These tentative answers are based on those questions first suggested by the psychologist Abraham Maslow. The questions have been slightly modified before being answered briefly.

Is the norm to be universal, national, subcultural, familial, or individual? The norm could have universal elements, not only for humans but for all species impacted by humans. Maslow assumes that different norms must be on different levels, depending on the context. For example, there would be some universal human behavioral standards, but special local expectations, to conform with various cultures.

Should society be selective or unselective? The society should be unselected. It must account for all human variability; and accept it when possible and treat it when necessary. It would have to account for prisoners and misfits. The society should be pluralistic, and accept and use individual differences in constitution and character. Humans are not interchangeable; the insane and aged must be considered. It must integrate all people into a society or work in that direction.

Should society be pro-something or anti-something else? Society could be pro-industrial and pro-intellectual (or scientific), within the set limits of the society and the planet. But, industry must be properly scaled; and science must be cautious. The size of community cultures could be limited by function.

Should it be centralized or decentralized? The global unit could be centralized, electronically, at least, and socially planned; but individual cultures could be autarchistic, based on self-reliance and interdependence. Both should be flexible. Regions could be centralized for some functions.

Should society be tolerant? Society must tolerate all cultures in the nations. Each culture would determine styles and complexity for its individuals. It should aim for taoistic noninterference, but be available for help.

What should be done about injustices? Biological injustices exist and can be ameliorated; social injustices can be rectified.

Should society determine family attitudes? Family or sexual attitudes can be institutionalized by the culture. All group adaptations would be determined by culture.

Should society be open to more than one religion? Society can tolerate any institutionalized religion, so long as it does not impinge on other groups. The spiritual life is a necessary part of a society.

How should leaders be chosen? Leaders within a culture could be chosen by traditional means, within the limits of human laws. Leaders of the international framework could be chosen by global referendum from the ranks of cultural leaders. The leaders would determine the relation of truth to people—who shall know how much about what and when.

For what is an individual responsible? The individual is responsible for the style and simplicity of their life and for its effects on nature and society. The individual is responsible for being tolerant of others, and is free to make many kinds of choices.

How these questions, and many others, are answered partly determines the shape of this project.

2.2.3. *Following Change with Gigatrends*

Things change, sometimes rapidly, sometimes slowly. We often refer to rapid change as a revolution or as a catastrophe; we refer to slower changes as trends or fate. A number of long-term ecological or cultural trends are evident now. A few of them can be fit into the megatrends identified by John Naisbitt over a decade ago.

Naisbitt identified ten larger patterns in society, including the move from an industrial society to an information society, the economic interdependence of the human world, and the restructuring of society from short-term considerations to long-term time frames, that is, he says, from two-year horizons to a "very long-term" time frame of "six to ten years." Some other counter-megatrends (negatrends?), such as the denigration of reason and science in the popular press and media, or the incredible explosion in information—without a corresponding increase or spread of wisdom—he ignored. Negative trends in general are left out of the popular picture. The things that are most popular to society, such as money, real estate, insurance, and politics, are the things that are treated as the most important. The things that will ultimately be most important, such as directing civilization or limiting human activities, are neglected.

The real long trends in ecosystems and cultures occupy the entire human calendar. We might call them gigatrends, since they are larger and more involving than megatrends (*giga* is from the Greek for very large or giant, whereas *mega* means large). Gigatrends are long or very-long-term trends, usually ignored by science and economics, such as atmospheric temperature increases or global deforestation. These gigatrends, on a global scale, include: Human populations increase exponentially; the impacts of a small percentage of people, the wealthy, increase exponentially; humanity takes over the habitats and functions of other animals, eliminating them and trying to take over their functions with chemicals, which is unsustainable for long-term; and ecosystems are simplified and degraded; deforestation, desertification, and exotic take-overs occur on a scale similar to the ice-age or a comet impact, but more immediately meaningful to humanity, since we depend on the ecosystems we are changing. There are, of course, positive gigatrends, although most of them seem to be negative.

Some of the negative gigatrends have been noticeable for thousands of years, but nothing has been done to halt them. Some of these negative gigatrends are hard to see, much less stop or reverse, because they are based on misunderstandings, fallacies, useless myths, and psychological blinders. For example, planners often treat exponential growth rates, such as human population or forest demand, the same as linear rates, such as rice production.

Environmental factors, such as climate or resource location, have shaped the course of human history to a greater extent than has been realized. The decline of Rome demonstrates that ignorance of forest ecology can have important consequences. There have been environmental catastrophes in the Tigris and Euphrates valley, Greece, Khmer, Maya, Midwest United States, and the Australian outback. These civilizations were very successful before they failed. Failure from success is tragic. For the Greeks, the operation of tragedy resulted from success taken to great lengths, that is, where successful behavior in one context is applied to all contexts, with the result that the opposite action occurs from the one desired. For example, humans in moderate numbers were able to take what they needed, such as wood, from natural ecosystems without interfering with the processes. Our dominance, once so successful because of our big brains and tool-using hands, has now become self-destructive. When human cultures adapted to ecosystems over long periods of time, the ecosystems also adapted to human cultures; when the human impact has been rapid and intense, as it has been in North America recently, the ecosystems collapsed or stabilized at a simpler state.

Although many gigatrends are interrelated, they can be discussed is several categories: human populations, human economics and technology, and ecosystems. Positive trends, often smaller and more recent, are discussed throughout.

2.2.3.1. Human Populations & Needs.

With human success has come human influence on ecosystems. Humans have modified animal and plant associations in different ways, simplifying patterns of energy and chemical exchange, and solidifying themselves at the end of many food chains as a dominant species. Our domination is related to our large biomass, our large annual population increase, our high energy use, and our high structural organization of information and matter. None of these effects are exclusive to us as a species, but they are excessive, rapid, compounded, and very large-scale. Basic gigatrends include:

- Human populations increase exponentially; the impacts of a small percentage of people also increase exponentially.
- Humanity takes over the habitats and functions of other animals, but this is not sustainable in the long-term.
- There is a drawdown of nonrenewable resources to support our numbers and lifestyles; this can only be a temporary fix.
- Human interactions become more violent as a result of competition, inequity, and limits in the distribution of resources.
- Local planning ignores limits to carrying capacity, long-term deficits, other species, and ecosystems; regional and global planning are essentially nonexistent.
- The material goods and luxuries of human societies have been increasing. Few people can carry everything they own on their backs, a bicycle, or a bus.

- The social avoidance of hard decisions. No one wants to take responsibility for recognizing limits; no one can say no to their constituents, representatives, or business partners.
- Increase in mind-altering substances, from fermented berries to coffee, tea, sugar, opium, and medical drugs.
- Shifts in our perception of humanity and the earth, from the center of the universe to central inhabitants of the earth to participants in a centerless arena. No culture is the center, or the evolutionary survivor of other cultures. All cultures are part of the web of living cultures of living beings.

Eric Eckholm concludes that the United Nations must identify, analyze and marshal world resources against negative trends. A scientific method would take a long time, however, and poor countries cannot wait. They must attempt a rural regeneration of some kind, to stop urban drift and ecosystem destruction. Eckholm interprets negative trends as indicating the sinking of marginal peoples on marginal lands into a quiet helpless poverty, later leading to urban deterioration, which may be considerably less quiet.

2.2.3.2. Ecosystem Gigatrends

Ecosystems build up information. There are at least three different channels of information in an ecosystem: The genetic, in replicable individuals; an ecological based on interaction between cohabiting species, expressed in changes in their numbers; and the cultural, transmitted through individual learning based on experience. Feedback within the interaction of species is expensive memory with little storage capacity. Whenever succession starts again, after a volcanic eruption, for instance, old information in the form of interactions has not been saved. Genetic memory has a much larger capacity and is long-term. Cultural memory is further enlarged in complex vertebrates. The unconsidered use of information results in still more long-term trends:

- Ecological limits are ignored
- Ecosystems are simplified and degraded; deforestation, desertification, and exotic take-overs occur on a large scale
- Deforestation of the forest planet
- Stress on ecological systems
- Humans simplify ecosystems and keep them at early seral stages to harvest the increased productivity
- Much vegetation becomes a social artifact. In Scotland, for instance, forest cover was reduced from 55% of the total area to 5% by primitive stock-keeping and agriculture; the moors decreased by half, but meads increased eight-fold
- Biogeochemical cycles are disrupted, for instance, atmospheric carbon dioxide has increased since the 1700s. The atmosphere is heating up. Higher temperatures will reduce crop yield. Heat increase will lead to water shortage then food shortages and security problems
- Biological diversity decreases over the same time period. Human diversity increases by leaps or punctuations
- Extinction rates increasing
- Humans take over the productivity of nature. Mathis Wackernagel

estimates all human demands on the environment surpassed the planet's regenerative capacity in 1980. By 1999, it surpassed it by twenty percent. What happens if we extrapolate this to 100 percent? These trends contribute to a shifting planetary system that has less flexibility. Some of these negative gigatrends are hard to see, much less stop or reverse, because they are based on misunderstandings, fallacies, discredited myths, and psychological blinders. For example, planners often treat exponential growth rates the same as linear rates. Thus, if our forests were to last for 400 years at our current rate of use, before extinction, they would only last for 75 years with a demand growing at 3 percent per year, or 50 years at 6 percent—demand is growing now at over 3 percent per year. Dennis Meadows points out the speed with which surpluses disappear with increasing population and increasing per capita demand.

Many predictions about resources are based on fallacies. There is the fallacy of substitution, that states that a substitute can be found for any resource in short supply. This is not always true, especially with cultural preferences. Furthermore, there is a gross underestimation of the length of time for a substitute resource to attain traditional markets. For instance, the transition from wood to coal as an energy source took about 50 years, despite the fact that coal technology was established and attractive. Meadows identifies another fallacy: The expectation that people and institutions perceive problems and react to them rationally, e.g., that with the threat of wood shortages, prices would rise and consumers would value the resource more. Yet, the price of wood is still nowhere the real costs of production and wood is used for cheap, impermanent goods. Meadows suggests that the model of addiction might be more appropriate than adaptation for dealing with consumer demand.

Many of these gigatrends are based on myths, such as the economic myth of forestry, which as it is related by Chris Maser, is based on the rationale of "soil rent" theory, a classic economic theory that assumes, fallaciously, that all ecological variables are constant so that capital investment is easily calculated from the rate of growth of the crop species.

2.2.3.3. Economics & Technology Gigatrends
Eric Eckholm describes how economic and political pressures, which are derived ultimately from population pressures, force farmers to intensify their efforts to increase crop production. This instigates an "utterly dismal cycle" of population expansion, environmental deterioration, and poverty: As the population expands, forests are cleared for land, arable lands are used to capacity—and sometimes beyond; as the soil deteriorates, it requires more fertilizers that cause more hazardous conditions that decrease agricultural capacity; people starve, but the population increases, and marginal lands are used to meet increased demands—or food is imported from other lands, which are also experiencing stress.

Eckholm describes how the usage of such marginal lands could result in dust-bowls, when climactic conditions change. After the U.S. dust-bowl in the 1930s, national conservation programs were able to restore some of the mythical fecundity, through pasteurizing, strip cropping, terracing, and contour plowing. However, current production efforts are causing greater losses of topsoil, and farmers are abandoning some of the conservation methods for economic reasons. Eckholm concludes that free market conditions encourage dangerous trends. The lesson of the latest dust bowl may be forgotten until the next one. As forestry copies the agricultural model, so it contributes to soil losses and destabilizes ecosystems.

There are large long trends related to economics. Economics has been defined as the "way people make their living," although as a discipline it attempts to balance human wants with scarce resources. Over many cultural lifetimes, this balancing has resulted in definite long-term trends:

- Accumulation of goods in human houses.
- Shortages of timber. Most Old-World civilizations faced shortages of high-quality wood, from the Mesopotamians, Egyptians, Greeks, and Romans to the modern countries of Europe. Pressures on British woodlands in the 1300's forced people to turn to coal as a fuel source, a source then regarded as inferior to wood. The timber famine reached Europe in the 1700s. It had existed in China and India over a thousand years before. Countries that exhausted their wood supplies had to invade other countries or to find substitute such as coal or water power. Each substitute required more energy to produce. Eckholm warns that the serious firewood shortage over most of the earth due to population pressures on the remaining woodlands.
- The earth has been divided up; every part is claimed and owned—one would think that this gigatrend of ownership has ended with the finite territory of earth, but it shows signs of continuing through the solar system. With ownership comes management and control.
- Increase of technologies and information to the fewer wealthier countries. The flow of information accelerates into those countries already technologized better. The acceleration of change, as a result of intensity and scale of human exploitation.
- National and international goals (and trading regulations) have become more important than local goals and considerations. According to industrial economic logic it is better to stockpile local forests and import cheaper wood from poorer nations. This puts stress on forests in poorer, or less greedy, nations. Management is becoming more intense. Its goal is always to raise productivity per hectare instead of questioning the demand or other options for getting wood.
- The polarization of countries by wealth, as a result of colonialization and advantageous trading. A small minority of nations controls both resources and productivity.
- Identifying a human minimum. Society seems to be working toward a minimum: a box for everyone, with sufficient heat and light, air and plumbing. Mere existence has become an acceptable option. We have gone from the green forest to the gray box. There is no place to hide, no place on earth that the air cannot stink and the rain not burn, that ugliness cannot reach and misery not touch.

Control has been the goal of science and technology. Scientists are obsessed with the treatment of weeds and vermin. The industrial cosmology has put humanity at war with the planet, which always misbehaves; weeds and vermin threaten us. Stability has been raised to sacred scientific state. Our culture has been distorted by the modern emphasis on the scientific method, with its devaluation of philosophical concepts. Rational values are exaggerated and spiritual events are ignored or suppressed. Most philosophies and technologies are not adequate to deal with nature and ecological relationships.

Even when beauty is considered, it is only cosmetic. Many landscapes and ecosystems are considered too impersonal or "ugly" to be valued. Joseph Meeker judged that a burned forest is ugly because it is truncated; but, a burned forest is as beautiful as a baby, and for the same reasons: it has potential, development, and being in the process of renewal. Our sense of beauty, of what is intrinsically meaningful, dominates our grasp of what is real. Until we understand that all phases of nature have beauty, we will not appreciate the meaning of the entire process.

Understanding beauty could even allow a deeper understanding of the utilitarian. For example, what is the use—or the beauty—of a burned forest, as related to the function of lightning or the planetary carbon cycle? Lightning is essential to life by breaking down amino acids into ammonia, methane, hydrogen, and water. Burned forests are necessary to maintain diversity and keep single species from taking over whole ecosystems. We have been persuaded that humans are able to transform any habitat on earth and benefit from the transformation, but we do not extend that power to nature.

2.2.3.4. Political Gigatrends

These trends are partly the result of our unconsciousness of large-scale, long-term events, partly the result of our cultural amnesia about things that make us unhappy, and partly the result of our cultivated indifference—doubtless from our remoteness from wild nature, remoteness as a result of our tools and the general abstraction of civilization. Many of these trends have to do with war and conflicts.

- Trends in war from amateurs to specialists, from special days to every day, even holy days, from soldiers to noncombatants, from fields of killing to any fields and any places, from destruction of soldiers to destruction of fields and ecosystems.
- Disarmament of civilian populations. In England recently (1995), murder rates were only a tenth what they were 800 years ago and half what they were 300 years ago. The disarmament took place in many small steps from seizures to licensing, production controls, and fewer public exhibitions.
- Stress between countries polarized by wealth.
- Overmilitarization by wealthy countries. Overmilitarization by poor countries.
- The transition of states, from surplus distributors, to tribute-driven, to commercial exchanges.
- The political transitions from leaders, to chiefs, to tribute systems, to economic and political trade systems.

- The reach of the state into individual lives. From tribute to lack of arms, ownership, and licensing, to information-gathering.
- Trust and social cohesion decline.
- Crime rate, disorder, inequity, poverty and development of an underclass, and consumption.

Some of these trends have been reversed for short periods of time, in various places by different cultures, but the overall trend has been negative.

2.2.3.5. Positive trends

None of these negative gigatrends can be really reversed until human neutrality and remoteness is reeducated into participation and attentiveness. There are already a few trends flowing against the tide. Some positive gigatrends include:

- Adaptation of human cultures and ecosystems over time in Asia, Europe, and parts of Africa, resulting in stable domesticated landscapes.
- Setting aside of areas, such as preservation of ecosystem processes, reservation of archaic cultures, and conservation lands, from industrial interference.
- An increase in the scope of ethics, from family, tribe, nation, humanity, to include reverence for all living beings, first identified recently by Albert Schweitzer.
- An increase in the scope of ethics to include land and forests, identified by Aldo Leopold, and later by Ernst Laszlo to include all systems.
- An increase in the scope of law to include legal rights for ecosystems, such as forests, identified by Christopher Stone.
- Restoration of forests from abandoned fields, anthropogenic deserts, and ruined ecosystems.
- Practice of comprehensive approaches, such as ecological forestry and permaculture.
- The number of people investing in small businesses in forest products, businesses that are labor-intensive and practice rather than profit-oriented.

Combined with other new trends in housing—such as arcologies (Paolo Soleri) and ocean arks and bioshelters (John and Nancy Todd), and agriculture—agroforestry, permaculture (Bill Mollison), and tree crops (Russell Smith), these trends may work to counter many of the negative ones.

The intent of describing large-scale trends or patterns is to have human patterns fit with observed patterns in nature; patterns have a form, sometimes repetition, and sometimes regularity, but each of these is caused by some limiting factor. Fitting the pattern can lead to both continuity and predictability, and both of these are needed to adapt human activities to natural limits.

Thinking we have conquered nature and are omnipotent, we have quit thinking. Satisfied with our comforts, we do not ask enough of ourselves. With these gigatrends possibly ending in tragedy for humanity, we must continue to ask questions. What kind of planet do we want? Wild or domestic? Managed or unmanaged? How shall we use the resources of nature? For products? To protect watersheds and maintain global biogeochemical processes? As a home for other beings? For recreation? As some kind of balance? How many different places, different ecosystems, or other cultures, do we need? What kinds, in what forms? How many should be wild? These questions lead to new strategies for living with the forests and wild ecosystems, strategies that we can test with thought experiments.

2.2.4. *Examining Possibilities with Thought Experiments*
Humanity is already engaged in a great experiment with the planet. We are replacing large, old, complex ecosystems with young, simple fragments, in which fires are suppressed, large predators are removed, large herbivore populations are encouraged, exotic species are introduced, soil is compacted, and excessive biomass is removed—all for the purposes of increasing the amount that can be harvested for human use. Our actions are experiments, whether we want them to be or not. Unfortunately the experiment is not only bad science—there is no control planet—it is ill-considered. This experimental course, which may be global and irreversible, cannot be unmade, not by planning or science, much less by our standard methods of ignorance, cupidity, or denial.

There must be a way to refine the experiments, to minimize our impacts, to be less reckless, and to anticipate the outcome of our experiments before we finish performing them. Not all experiments must be physically implemented. Albert Einstein and Leopold Infield suggest that knowledge of laws can be gained through the contemplation of idealized experiments created by thought, Gedanke-Experiment. For example, to address the equality of inertial and gravitational masses, that is, how the problem of general relativity is connected with gravitation, Einstein imagined an elevator at the top of an incredibly high building, and then imagined what research could be done in this local environment. Such experiments might seem "fantastic" in his words, but they might help us understand what we are trying to understand.

Although ecosystems and political orders are orders of magnitude more complex than physical systems, perhaps we could imagine and use such experiments to help us understand what is happening with our complex planet that is composed of many interlocking ecological systems. One of the more comprehensive thought experiments conducted is "Daisy World" by James Lovelock, to show how the evolution of species would lead to the self-regulation of climate on an earth-like world. Freeman Dyson offers another example of a thought experiment from Isaac Asimov: Saturn's satellite Enceladus could be used to provide water and warmth to Mars; a rocket could be sent to the satellite, carrying self-reproducing automatons, which could make miniature solar sailboats to carry small blocks of ice from it—there would be enough ice to keep the Martian climate warm and wet for about 10,000 years.

Thought experiments can give us clues about what can happen and what is the likelihood of that happening. "And then what?" asks Garrett Hardin again. Unlike medical doctors or scientists, we cannot either wait or directly experiment within a realistic time frame or scale. We cannot experiment at all in a traditional sense, where we hold most variables fixed, while changing one or two variables in experimental runs. Ecosystems operate over very long time spans; furthermore, their historical nature means that they cannot be restarted for tests.

Large-scale, long-term experiments are expensive and relatively few. Most experiments are short-range, small-scale, isolated, and detail dense. Most experiments do not present the hypotheses required for the management of ecosystems. Ecosystem management, because of uncertainties, lack of controls, age, and uniqueness, is an uncontrolled, large-scale experiment. Thought experiments can refine the design of our larger experiments by suggesting better hypotheses and considerate behaviors.

Thought experiments can help us avoid being overwhelmed by details. Thought experiments can help formulate goals and interpret information appropriate to scale. The idea of science is to manage our experiences with generalities. Once the thought experiments are started they can be refined with conceptual or mathematical models, which can simulate the changes and historical development of changes. Computer-based models can permit complex explorations, as well as suggest new patterns and further hypotheses. Through thought experiments and models, many of the dangers and expenses of our activities can be avoided.

Thought experiments are vital to understanding the complexity of ecosystems. In practice, erring on the side of preservation—the prudent and conservative course—means minimizing the influence of human activities on the land. It means experimenting cautiously with new approaches to ecosystem management and being properly skeptical about any claims for sustainability. It means drastically reducing our demand for natural products, through conservation, reuse, recycling, and human population control, so that the greatest possible number of ecosystems can be left wild and degraded lands have time to be restored to health.

Thought experiments can also be used to examine possible scenarios of the future based on our actions. For example, if we continue the current trend of disequity, how might things play out? For example if the rich keep getting richer, how will they have to protect their wealth from the poor? Will laws be enough? Will they need ever larger armies of security personnel? With already four times the number of civic police, will they need even more? Will corporate police protect the wealth of their stockholders after the civic police give up? Will the poor collapse leaving rich enclaves that have to grow their own food? At what point will the gap be wide enough that the poor have to harvest the wealth of the rich by force? At what number of poor? Will the poor prey on each other first? At what point will the environment be used entirely for a few more years of life for rich or poor humans? At what point might the environment collapse?

Will regional groups, such as the northern hemisphere, form alliances to keep going, after writing off other regions or the southern hemisphere? Will this block be able to defend its resources? Will that extend the time of any collapse? Or accelerate it?

Will the United Nations be able to coordinate some kind of peaceful reorganization? Can a revitalized UN guarantee a rational economic and political strategy for all nations? Should this UN be dominated by a China or a United States, so that it may operate without as much discussion? Is it utopian to think of such reorganization or redistribution for equity? Is this less naïve than allowing the market to sort out entire cultures and regions and consign them to poverty and violence?

The thought experiment presented below is incomplete, but suggestive of the kinds that we could be creating and manipulating to guide our plans and models.

2.2.4.1. A Sample Thought Experiment with Arcologies

At present over three billion people live in cities, about half of the total world population of 6.3014 billion (revised and estimated for 1 September 2003). What if essentially all people lived in arcologies, except for some small traditional communities living in wild ecosystems?

Historically, human hunting altered ecosystems, then converted forest, grassland, and wetland ecosystems to agroecosystems that had to be managed. Now, the expansion of urban areas with roads, power grids, and other infrastructure, is interfering with the basic functioning of many ecosystems. Modification, conversion and destruction of ecosystems disrupts the complex interactions within and between ecosystems, the hydrology, soil structure, topography, and the predominant vegetation; it changes the complement of species, and it causes a loss of diversity. The new replacement systems are simpler, less mature, and less diverse.

We have achieved great horizontal growth, much like a fungus. However, if we want to be like a smarter fungus, slime molds for instance, we need to learn to cooperate to grow up and be more dense. The larger metropolitan regions are covering wild ecosystems and agricultural fields with single-family houses, malls, building, recreational areas, and roads—all of which are car-centric or auto-morphic. This means that energy and goods are also spread thin. Such systems of things are hard to control, hard to keep safe, and hard to remain interesting. In fact, it might be worthwhile to compare human systems to mature ecosystems; we are creating pioneer individuals that do not live well in concentrations. We are creating edge individuals and not those who can live in interiors and share resources, or can develop new resources with cleverness and intelligence. City designs do exist, however, which incorporate the properties of mature systems, as well as the characteristics of ecological thinking.[7]

An arcology, as defined by Paolo Soleri, is a city which embodies the fusion of architecture with ecology. The arcology concept proposes a highly integrated and compact three-dimensional urban form that enables radical conservation of land, energy and resources. Arcology eliminates the automobile from within the city, and with it, the fifty percent of land devoted to automotive needs. The multi-use nature of arcology design would put living, working and public spaces within easy reach of each other and walking, supplemented by elevators and airport things, would become the main form of transportation within the city. An arcology would use passive solar architectural techniques such as the apse effect, greenhouse architecture and garment architecture to reduce the energy usage of the city, especially in terms of heating, lighting and cooling.

The small footprint of an arcology, combined with many built-in gardens, would allow rural space and agricultural fields to be closer to the city, and a part of the immediate urban environment. Wilderness, also, would be much closer to population centers in arcologies. Psychologically, the intelligent design would be more conducive to inspired living, the kind found in traditional culturally-significant cities at certain times. The proximity of agriculture and wilderness would allow people to participate more in them, with the full range of benefits that comes from growing and cultivating plants, as well as being able to immerse in the otherness of wild ecosystems.

The sizes of arcologies range from 250,000 to almost a million people, although smaller or larger ones are possible. For the sake of argument, assume that the average arcology is the size of Soleri's proposed Novanoah, at 400,000 people. At that size, it would take 15,734 arcologies to house the planetary population; this number is less than the number of cities in the United States in 2004, at 19,354. Assuming that the area under the arcology is about 5 square kilometers (almost two square miles), the surface area taken up by arcologies would only be 78,768 square kilometers, which is only 0.00054 percent of the land area of the planet—that is half of one thousandth of one percent—(149.45 billion square kilometers, or roughly 0.0167 percent of the land area currently under concrete and asphalt now, which is 4.71 million square kilometers or 3.15 percent of the land area of the planet).

The number of roads would be significantly reduced, from 676,750 square kilometers (roughly half of one percent of the total land surface in every country, according to the International Road Transport Union) to 230,000 km² (a generous number to be sure, but it could be as little as 50,000 km²). Over 2 percent of the land is under road surfaces in the United States, with a smaller percentage in Europe, by comparison. Land under agricultural production would also be reduced, from 33 billion square kilometers (22 percent of the land area of the planet), partly due to improved practices, partly due to the integration of many kinds of agriculture into the city, and partly due to the carefully limited use of wild populations, without domestication or containment.

The shapes of arcologies would be as diverse as any. Many of Soleri's shapes are geometric. They could be large pyramids, filled with living and working spaces, connected by transits and illuminated by light wells. The traditional ziggurat modernized would offer a good ratio of sunlight and truck gardens to size. Arcologies could be empty tubular pyramids with modular dymaxion attachments, that could be moved between arcologies or new sites. They could fit the shape of the landscape, as does the Palouse Arcology (Wittbecker 1992). Arcologies could be built around small mountains, in bridges crossing canyons, or threading through coastal seas.

What would such a change mean to most people? Probably, few people would have the need for private cars. A typical day, for most workers, whether administrating, grading papers, policing, or making steel, would start with a walk to work, past local stores and businesses, playgrounds, and microfactories. Work would involve fewer layers of hierarchy; the pay range would only be from 1 to 7 times the minimum salary.

Since Soleri's heroic designs, arcologies have been confined to computer games and have become elements in science fiction and cyberpunk films. With more prototypes being designed, one may be built in the next twenty to thirty years. A proposed project for Tokyo Bay, the Shimizu TRY 2004 Mega-City Pyramid, if constructed, would become the largest artificial structure on the planet; it would be 2004 meters tall and house 750,000 people. The external structure of the pyramid will be an open network of megatrusses, supporting struts made from carbon nanotubes to allow the pyramid to stand against high winds, earthquakes, and tsunamis. The trusses will be coated with photovoltaic film to convert sunlight into electricity and help power the city. The building will be zoned into residential, commercial and leisure areas. Separate buildings for housing and offices would be suspended from the supporting structure with nanotube cables. Transportation would be provided by accelerating walkways, inclined elevators, and a Personal Rapid Transit system inside the trusses with individual driverless pods.

It seems that arcologies would be part of a whole package of changes, brought about by ecological planning on a global scale. The experiment would not require that arcologies replace archaic populations living in human-modified ecosystems, or even all low-density habitations or traditional cities. But, they could be new cities situated in infertile areas.

Many cultures could live in optimum configurations in their territories, as part of wild and domestic landscapes. But, we also need heroic architecture. Heroic design and extravagance in life is needed in general. It is not contradictory or antithetical to frugal lifestyles or to restoring a healthy environment. Life is exuberant; energy is used, lives are lived and used, not wasted or saved. Life is the accumulation of individual experiences that cannot be saved, stored, or owned. The heroic things in life are often those most admired or remembered by subsequent generations.

Thought experiments will be suggested throughout this work. The best response to a question about what would happen as a result of some actions under some circumstances may be a thought experiment. Through that, you can create explanations and discover answers in a dialogue with others.

2.2.4.2. Duality & Conversation

A thought experiment can be considered as a communication: Mind reaching to mind, intention to intention, or as a simple correspondence. Communication is a presentation of one's self to another, through a conversation, in a back and forth process. The word conversation is derived from the French word meaning 'to live with,' from the Latin, meaning 'to turn with.' Since all things are in some sense subjective and unique, the term conversation is appropriate.

For Gordon Pask, a theory of conversation is a theory of participants in conversation; all events are subjective. Conversation creates a domain, which is the appropriate frame of reference. The domain is the environment of a conversation. The conversation is a minimal situation for observing the psychological events of which the participants are conscious. Understanding between participants is pivotal. The conversation is relativistic and reflexive.

The biologist Francisco Varela uses conversation as a paradigm for interactions among autonomous systems. Conversation is direct. Each side has a perspective and this is the heart of the process. When conversation is considered as a totality, there is no distinction about what is contributed by whom. The process is a coherent event shared by the participants, not a simple information exchange. Both Pask and Varela apply their ideas to human systems. But, there is no reason why it could not apply to any interaction between beings.

When different modes of description appear as opposites, it is more satisfactory to consider them complementary instead. This Varela says is necessary with tree/net duality and recursion/behavior duality. Complementarity solves the problem of opposites, such as focus/frame considered under an either/or logic.

2.2.4.2.1. Duality

Duality leads to the philosophical idea of trinity, with some similarity to the ideas of Charles S. Peirce, since the poles are related yet remain distinct; they are not one or two, but are really three. Varela offers the heuristic star, where the star is equivalent to the whole process. Thus:

* = it/process leading to it

Varela proposes that dualisms or dialectical contradictions such as mind/body or whole/part or being/becoming should be conceived of as stars, that consist of an it/becoming-it process. Both sides of the slash must be considered, and the process leading to it. Varela borrows Bateson's concept of minds jointly defined as conversational pattern (left of slash) and bodies as participants in pattern (right). Consider both sides of the slash. The slash is a compact indication of a transition between states. For instance:

* = whole/parts constituting whole
* = stability/approximation in time

The predator/prey pair are not excluding opposites, but both generating a whole unity, an autonomous domain where there is complementarity, stabilization and survival values for both.

* = ecosystem/species interaction

In general, any autonomous situation is on the left of slash, and corresponding process is on the other side: being/becoming or right brain/ left. But that is incomplete; the network is the process that constitutes the trees. The duality is connected with processes in both directions. Varela sees the totality as emerging from part-by-part approximation of the trees (process leading to net). But sometimes the whole determines the parts. Mostly, the process mutually arises. Complementary elements mutually specify each other, so, in a sense there is no more duality.

Even Varela states that in natural systems, there is no real opposition, except where we put our values. Yet, the human brain, encultured, perceives primal dualities. For every apparent set of opposites there is a star that is the left hand of another equation.

Varela suggests using the idea of intersecting triangles, a star, as a solution. The star is an ancient alchemical symbol. Man reflects the macrocosm in a microscosm. The two sliding triangles (remember

Pythagoras) represent Hermes Trismegistus aphorism: As above, so below.

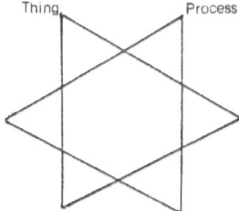

Figure 2-2421-1. The Star

Varela rotates them, however. By using two intersecting triangles in the shape of star, as two levels of logical type, they are noncontradictory and mutually-specifying, manifesting restrained complementarity. The star of Varela differs from dualism and Hegel's dialectics. There is no Hegelian synthesis because there is nothing new, only a more direct appraisal of how things are put together. This view of complementarity is a departure from the classical way of dialectics. Dualities are represented by imbrication of levels, where one term emerges from the other. Their basic form is asymmetry; both terms extend across levels. This dialectic is self-referential: it/becoming-it. The tree is rebalanced by constraints of the network.

The net is prior in relation, however. This explains problem of the space/time energy/mass field much better, where there is network from which space-time and energy-mass can be extracted. The network/tree duality can represent recursion/behavior duality by retaining interest in the connectivity of a system only. The nodes in tree or net represent elements in a system. Their links suggest interactions or interconnections. The reciprocal connectivity of a net suggests coordination; a tree structure suggests the sequential subordination of a system's parts.

But the image of the star is not quite comprehensive enough. The sides of a star are not inversely related. The sides are directly related; as one side increases, the other side increases. The relationship of sides cannot be described as conflict only. For example,

* = whole/part

is not complete. There are parts in wholes, in motion, in context. Similarly, for good/evil, good and evil reside in the knowledge of human actions in cultures in place.

2.2.4.2.2. Conversational Field

Since there are always any number of relations in a situation, the use of dyads and triads can become complex. The metaphor becomes unwieldy. Conversation can replace the idea of duality and triadicity. Four, five or more person relations are not reducible to triadic relations, as argued by Peirce. The upper limit for measurable relations is probably about seven, plus or minus two, as George Miller found. Seven is a magic number in human psychology; it represents the maximum number of items that a subject could reliably remember, as well as other variables. Possibly it applies to the number of subjects having an intelligent conversation as well. Given the indeterminacy of relations between subjects, the use of conversation is justified.

As the science of physics has realized, in its three body problem, the calculations necessary to solve a problem increase logarithmically when the number of bodies is multiplied. In biology, the phenotype and organism generate unpredictability. Neither the organism or the environment knows what the other will do. Species interaction achieving a stable ecosystem can be thought of as a biological paradigm for a conversational domain, the direction of which is unpredictable. Evolution is then the changing theme of the conversation between species and environment. Evolution may be interpreted as the development of new channels for communication.

One paradigm that would suit the needs of ecology is that of personal communication: Mind reaching to mind, intention to intention. Communication is presentation of one's self, of one's life, that may evoke correspondence in others (similar to entrainment). The activities of two communicators combine to make the universe of the observer more ordered and redundant. The nature of meaning depends on the frame of the observer. Ecologists must envisage the notion that nature speaks to us, perhaps using information theory. Anthropomorphic ecology can recapture the experience of personality in nature; this is just the reverse of the pathetic fallacy, which derides the use of human terms to describe natural phenomena.

2.2.4.3. Wild Thinking

What is the proper language for humans? What is the proper diet for all humans? The proper mode of expression? These questions may seem to be too presumptuous to be asked. But, are there other large-scale questions that can be asked? Are there large-scale forms of thought? Is Philosophy one such form? Religion? Ecology? Are such large-scale forms domestic or wild? What is wild? Is it the same as being not domesticated? Uncontrolled or unmanaged? Not cultivated? Untamed? Savage? Wasteful? In a state of nature? Lawless? Wild as a word has ambiguity and reflexion (from the German word *wild*, or perhaps *Wald*, meaning forest).

What is thinking (from the German *denken*)? To revolve ideas in the mind? To design, to imagine, to judge? Perhaps thinking is a dance of the mind, as it flows and merges into a harmonious process in life. Is ecological thinking intrinsically wild? Is ecological knowledge wild? Will Wright suggests that knowledge becomes wild when it is critically reflexive and committed to critical access rather than to a version of absolute reality. If so, such wild knowledge cannot be "domesticated" by one particular social institution. It is accessible by individuals.

Ecological thinking is wild because it has a nonhuman component. By contrast, scientific or religious thinking can be regarded as domesticated or tamed because it is limited by a true version of reality, or a set of rules for observing a true reality. Science is defined in opposition to religion, with a commitment to neutral observation rather than a moral commitment to tradition. Wild ecological thinking combines technique with moral and ecological concerns. The fundamental emotion of wild thinking is astonishment, which literally means 'being struck by lightning.'

Of course, there are other forms of thinking. Religious or scientific thinking are relatively tame. Tame ideas in religion and science are remarkably persistent—for instance, "more is better." George Orwell referred to these obsolete ideas as "wrong-think."

Another kind of thinking, "double-think," is used traditionally to keep some ideas tame. Orwell declared novelistically that "newspeak" was a method for controlling thought through language. Doublethink was a way of controlling thought directly. Newspeak incorporates doublethink, as it contains many words with contradictory meanings, such as 'good/evil', 'truth/falsehood', and 'justice/injustice.'

Doublethink entails holding two contradictory beliefs simultaneously and accepting both of them, deaf and blind to any contradictions. The purpose of doublethink, as presented by Orwell, is to use conscious deception while retaining the firmness of purpose that goes with complete honesty. The deception has to be conscious to be implemented precisely, but also it must be unconscious to avoid guilt and falsehood. It is important to believe the lies and to deny the existence of objective reality, while taking account of the reality denied in order to be satisfied that reality is not violated. It is necessary to exercise doublethink when using the word doublethink, since it is an admission of tampering with reality.

Gordon R. Taylor suggests that "non-think," the failure of good ideas to be recognized or used, is equally obstructive—thus, the idea "to protect the ecological basis of life" is never considered.

Wild thinking is appropriate for "system breaks," that is, the social discontinuities identified by Kenneth Boulding. We have started to identify the forces setting up the next big system break, but we have not defined the forming patterns very well. We need to be rethinking—a form of wild thinking—the basic assumptions of the spheres of civilization, from our economic and political to industrial, religious and scientific.

Talking about wild thinking, perhaps there is another side to it, a necessary social side. Too much anarchy is dreaming; too much feral thinking is noncultural and perhaps dangerous. Too much unanchored thought is unrelated to the important mode of learning by doing.

Is wildness just the nonhuman part of the spectrum? Does it overlap in humans? Is it just difference or craziness? We love and celebrate the wild; also, we fear and suppress the wild. The wild is a quality of being just beyond our rules or outside of our walls. Paul Shepard reminds us that wildness occurs in many places, in any species whose sexual assortment and genealogy are not controlled by human beings. Charles Darwin reminds us that humanity is wild, also. Does the human mind have to be wild? Not necessarily—we can domesticate our ideas.

It seems easy to talk of wild thinking. Is it meaningful to talk of a wild culture, one that intermeshes with the wild of nature? Are archaic cultures wild? Is a model of a civilization without walls, without resources, maxima, or weeds, wild?

All we need is new economic, educational, political, cultural, social, psychological, and ecological frameworks, in which we can try to rebalance our individual lives; try to rebalance the social spins of the patriarchal and matriarchal directions, between the human and ambihuman; try for individual self-reliance and health, try for community self-reliance and health; try for ecological community health, strengthen our community and cultural identity so that the positive aspects of globalization can be internalized without the destructive force of globalization ruining cultures; try to limit the centralization of power and authority, in style as well as trade, reform corporations to act responsibly as public service organizations (not as imaginary irresponsible individuals); try to direct technology in appropriate ways, and set up a global commonwealth for global relations; and, try to live with wildness. How wild humans can live on a wild earth is the subject of this eutopian framework.

2.2.5. *Using Analysis and Other Tools*

Basic analysis means taking something apart to understand how it works. The word is based on the Greek words meaning 'loosen up.' It was first used in the modern sense, as opposed to just logic, by French philosophers and scientists. Once a subject is identified to analyze, the subject is deconstructed, literally. To analyze a rock, it is necessary to break it apart and identify specific elements. To physically analyze a human being, you must cut into the flesh, weigh the blood and organs, and determine the different kinds of organs, fluids, and moving parts.

However, that is rarely enough to tell you how a human operates. For that, you must undertake a functional analysis. You would have to observe a working specimen first: Make a list of characteristics, hair, eye, and skin color and shape, weight, shape, completeness; list inputs, such as air, water, and food; list outputs, such as carbon dioxide or manure; make another list of needs, from shelter to place, security, and social demands; describe the kind of places humans are found, from gardens to factories, and their relationships with other beings.

A lot of time would have to be spent analyzing human communities, at a family and neighborhood level, as well as working relationships and the larger relationships with the environment. Working relationships could easily be expanded into economic analysis. Conversations could be analyzed with linguistic analysis, that would have to delve into the history of language and cultural shifts. A historical analysis of a person could trace the movements of ancestors and their interactions with others and their environments.

A philosophical analysis might be useful to try to understand an individual expression of existence and place. Some philosophies, perhaps all, start with the notion of what it is to be human, even those that start with existence and being start with human existence and human being. But, why not start with what it means to be or to live? "I live here and therefore I am in place and know it."

To understand the workings of complex systems, one could use systems thinking, with its concepts of feedback and emergence. Complex adaptive systems display emergent behavior. As an example of emergence, slime molds can form a community without a pacemaker cell that determines when the cells need to combine. It seems that self organization is bottoms-up. Emergent systems are rule-governed, though; slime molds explore by adhering to low level rules. Individuals coordinate work, even if they cannot assess the global situation. Emergent systems are local; individual molds "think" locally and act locally. Random action serves to explore local space. Individuals pay attention to their neighbors, and patterns emerge from local activity. Simple behavior seems to work, with local feedback, and more sophisticated behavior "trickles up" to approximate a global perception. Mathematical analysis measures those behaviors with standards and converts them to numbers in an abstract space.

Ecological analysis has to be one of the largest form of analysis. It includes limits-analysis as well as footprint analysis. The ecological footprint method[8] offers a way of calculating the ecological capacity, or stock of natural assets, in terms of area, similar to Eugene Odum's method in hectares per person or to ghost acreage calculations by William Catton. The ecological footprint is a measure of the energy and resource throughput of the human economy. It compares human demand for energy and resources with the regenerative capacity of the earth's biosphere for providing these ecological goods and services.

Ecological Footprint analysis adds up the area of different land types, such as forests, fishing grounds, crop land, pasture, that are required to support humans' activities. This is done by normalizing the biological productivity of the different land types in a common unit, such as the global hectare or global acre in the United States. One global hectare (gha) is equal to one hectare of land with world average productivity for all land types. The supply of ecosystem service is called 'biocapacity;' the human demand for these services is the 'ecological footprint.' By comparing supply (biocapacity) with demand (footprint), Ecological Footprint analysis provides a metric for indicating unsustainability. Globally, as of 2002, there exist 1.8 gha per capita of biocapacity available to support human activities, and not setting aside any biocapacity for nonhuman species. In 2002, the most recent year for which data are available, the global human economy used 2.2 gha per capita, resulting in an ecological overshoot of about 20 percent. This means that it takes the Earth about 15 months to regenerate what humans use in 12 months. This condition of global ecological overshoot cannot continue indefinitely. A catastrophic ecological failure may occur if the demands for "natural capital" are not reduced to a level that the biosphere can provide on an annual basis.

Footprint analysis can be subdivided itself, into local analysis or ghost acreage analysis and trade analysis. The geographer Georg Borgstrom in 1961 named "ghost acreage" as the acreage that the average citizen occupies that its out of sight.

Although the footprint is a good metaphor, there seem to be many things left out. Footprints have not only an area, but also a depth, not just a simple size, but a shape. Footprints can be immediately gone or persist for a long time. The footprint adds up all the real and ghost acreage that a country uses, as part of the footprint. That is, the imports are added and the exports are subtracted, although, exports cannot be subtracted from the footprint exactly since they are originally part of it. Wastes are far more critical than resources, as regards ecological cycles. Many uses are not included, so the efficiency calculation may not be accurate. As Rees and Wackernagel admit, the "bio-productive areas that are really needed to maintain today's usage of nature's benefits are most probably larger" than the ones in the calculation. Ecological analysis would force us to look at the obvious—generating nonmarketable use values occupies the center of every culture because it provides a satisfactory life to its members.

The fundamental characteristic of analysis is taking apart. Taking apart living beings or working cycles can result in their death. However, more general kinds of analysis rely on good observations to allow deductions about internal workings. Goethe rejected destructive analysis; his approach was passive attentiveness. Certainly many forms of analysis can approach this level of sensitivity.

2.2.5.1. Linguistic & Historical Analysis

In order to make sense of the sheer multiplicity and complexity of their environments, human beings create abstractions. An abstraction is an idea created to refer to all objects that have certain characteristics in common, e.g., all birds. Abstractions can be generalized, e.g., all things that fly, but at each outer level the objects have less in common; thus flying things include insects, mammals, reptiles, seeds, and spores.

Human beings also classify and label their abstractions. The systems of classification are reflexive and pragmatic; that is, they refer to the classifier as well as to the object, and they are guidelines for how to think about, treat, and relate to an object, according to S. I. Hayakawa. As soon as a classification is no longer useful, people stop using it and become receptive to a better classification. This gives a historical and linguistic caste to analysis, which can be used to differentiate between abstractions and classes.

2.2.5.2. Scientific Analysis

Science uses abstraction and classification to transcend common sense to describe the fundamental structure of nature. Scientists use classes to limit things to their own mesocosmic scale, from geological epochs to species, although the classes are independent from the things. By comparison, archaic (sometimes called pre-scientific) peoples believe that there is a necessary and intimate connection between the symbol and the object, that the name is attached to the object in an intimate way. This "epistemic naiveté" is dismissed by modern science, which uses its own unique method. The general format of the scientific method is the same as that for traditional ecological knowledge. However, science adds measurement to analysis, experimentation to observation and formal hypotheses to guesses:
- Observe phenomena and record facts.
- Analyze the phenomena into components.
- Measure the phenomena (before and after manipulation) allowing the results to be quantified.
- Make guesses and generalizations, using the logic of deduction. A

hypothesis is a statement about relationships that can be shown to be untrue.

- Formulate laws from the generalizations about the phenomena. Such laws may describe the behavior of a natural system.
- Describe the laws mathematically, using numbers.
- Develop a theory to predict new phenomena. Theories can lead to new conclusions and sometimes altered perspectives about phenomena. A scientific theory is a statement that postulates ordered relationships among natural phenomena and explains some aspect of the world. It allows one to ask certain kinds of questions, some as specific hypotheses.
- Test hypotheses and theories in a controlled environment. A theory cannot be tested by hypotheses.

The key ideas here are analysis, measurement, guesses, control, and rule-based predictions, and control. The use of these ideas have brought about keen understandings of parts of nature, from the quantum level to the extent of the universe. And, it has lead to amazing changes, from electricity and hydraulics to medical analysis and computers.

Science works with theories, that is the direction of observation, based on previously identified facts, used to lead to evidence or proofs of hypotheses about how things work, which can be used to predict other actions in the future. Theory is used to guide experimentation. But much experimentation these days occurs without theoretical guidance, or rather the theories used are not capable of the context itself, so that the experiments tend to go out of control, or rather, are improperly conducted as experiments—no control group, no good theory, no idea or control of scale.

Theories can help science to avoid claiming what things, either knowledge or certainty, that it cannot claim. Theory can distinguish between knowledge and theory, between theory and the unknowable. There will always be limits and errors; these cannot be avoided. Theory needs to accommodate this fact. Fallibility is unavoidable; it is a part of certainty from a limited perspective with a limited knowledge; it is part of being incomplete and using incomplete knowledge. But, this is the limit of all being; this is the limit of finiteness.

Good theories are grounded in place and in communities. They must be used to place our science and technological capabilities in a culture that has goals and limits for our actions. In this sense the theories are tools for adaptation to place, within place, within specific places that we work towards making good. Theory describes the fitness of our conduct within an ecological and cultural system. Global theories have trouble passing the test of one locality. But, a good theory has to have a real framework and a real ecological context.

Some mysteries cannot be reduced, cannot be understood with human understanding. Some things are ineffable, even if they are understood, they cannot be reduced to words. Theory has to account for those things that cannot be reduced or explained or understood. Our theories and practices are human theories and practices; they are limited by real human limits, by the dimensions and terms of times that we humans experience. Strangeness, which Edward Wilson expects to be connected and made sensible through a consilience of knowledge, will continue to be strangeness, because of its intrinsic nonhuman properties and our human limits.

In this sense, theory is a guide to action, based on thinking about previous actions and projecting future actions, that is, making thought experiments. What we will know will always be incomplete, but we have to act, and therefore we have to act on partial knowledge in the face of partial ignorance, many kinds. Theory is a guide to acting under different kinds of unavoidable and irremovable ignorance. People who know a lot, but do not have theories that bind them to wise actions, tend to ignore ignorance, to act in an arrogant manner; such behavior become dangerous.

The proper role, ultimately for theory, is to guide us in our choice of tools and strategies for dwelling on the planet. Wisdom is that kind of action, with theory, with understanding of ignorance, that is as if we were wise, according to Jonas Salk.

But, science, like archaic thought or traditional ecological knowledge, makes assumptions in the context of specific cultural situations. Some cultural-scientific assumptions have been incorporated into the works of science by scientists. At the time of Bacon, it was assumed that there was: An absolute, immutable, omnipotent God, everything was sorted into a great chain of being, economic subsistence was preferable, and social inequality was unavoidable. Later, Darwin incorporated a different set of assumptions into his theories: Absolute space-time; atoms as discrete units; economic discrimination, and continued social inequality. These assumptions contributed to the misuse of his theories to justify social and economic conditions at the time. New versions of science have used broader assumptions, but the assumptions still must be recognized for the science to be effective in a larger sense.

2.2.5.3. Systems Analysis

A system is a way to explain part of the universe and to deal with complex behavior. Mario Bunge defines a system as a complex object, every part of which is connected with other parts of the object in such a way that the whole possesses emergent properties that the parts lack. A concrete system is composed of concrete things linked together by real physical, chemical, biological ties. Cells, wolf packs, and nongovernmental organizations (NGOs) are concrete systems. Conceptual systems can be linked by logical relations.

Many concrete systems are open and self-regulated. Many are closed and artificial. Bunge makes a strict dichotomy between formal and concrete systems (conceptual-material). He denies the possibility of mixed systems, but allows real ones to transmit information. He says sets and relations are abstract objects, not identical to concrete objects like molecules. Yet, if the relations are real, are they not concrete in a way? Intrasystem bonds are stronger that intersystem bonds, If not, the system would fall apart.

Social systems have all sizes and degrees of complexity. Governments are more complex than families. Systems can also be constituents of systems, like United Nations (UN). Every concrete thing has properties. Some properties can be known easily; others can be revealed by research. A list of known properties describes the state of the system with finite quantities.

A qualitative description of properties describes qualities of the system. Quantitative descriptions measure quantitative variables. The state of a system, definite and objective, can be conceptualized with theories and models. All concrete systems change as reality unfolds. That is, the properties of systems change through time. Some change, such as growth or decay, is quantitative. Other change is qualitative, resulting in breakdown or formation of the entire system.

Systems theory analyzes events, processes, and patterns in the world. An event is a change of state. An event is described by two points, an initial and final state. A process is a sequence of states, also called a history. A process creates a path, described by a trajectory of states. A process is described as evolutionary if it involves emergence and the creation of new things, as in general speciation; to be a species, however, the novelty has to reproduce, multiply or diffuse.

The concept of state precedes the concept of process, although a process can define a state. In complex systems the past contributes to or constrains the state, from the magnetic hysteresis of ferromagnets to organisms, which have memory.

Changes in systems can be recorded, but only partially and not continuously. The discontinuous recording is digital. The process is continuous, but the measurement is discontinuous.

Regularities in systems are patterns. Patterns can be seen in things or even cultures. For instance, laws of genetics are natural patterns; human customs are artificial patterns. Where the natural ratios of females to males are altered by female infanticide or other action, the pattern is semi-natural. awre

Bunge distinguishes four kinds of real patterns: Laws, trends, correlations, and rules. A law is a stable pattern inherent in things; it is discovered; laws like gravity are boundless; biological laws are bounded, he says. After the "Big Bang," gravity was bounded. There are examples of social or cultural laws: "The inertia of a social system is directly proportional to the number of components and inversely proportional to its cohesiveness." or: "Higher culture does not emerge in society until the basic needs of some of its members have been satisfied."

A trend is a temporary pattern, such as the globalization of capital or fertility. Trends can be reversed. A correlation, usually statistical, is a covariation of two properties, e.g., a correlation of sickness and education— but this correlation is problematic, due to fact that educated are wealthier and report their sickness more than the poor; the real correlation could be reversed. A better correlation is: Single-species forest stands can be correlated with standing armies in the northern hemisphere; standing armies were thought to be characteristic of people in tougher climates, which encourage large stands of trees. A rule (or norm) is a social convention set up by people, in force in a social system. The analysis of patterns is the strength of systems analysis.

2.2.5.4. Ecological Analysis & Synthesis

Analytic science has reached its limits. Data and information developed by hard studies have undercut the paradigms that guided their investigation. The compartmentalization of scientific fields has exposed the complex connections of the subjects. Science does not need to be based on logical positivism and reductionism, though these have allowed great, although insensitive, changes. A. N. Whitehead thought that what had been missing during the formation of science was a sense of relatedness. Early science saw the world as mechanism; modern biology is seeing it as resembling an organism. Organismic trends can be seen in sciences, from relativity and gestalt psychology to ecology.

Ecology deals with the relationships of organisms to environments. It is not a reductive discipline, and not readily amenable to quantification. Even scientific ecology is an integrative discipline that extends beyond the bounds of science. In a way, ecology is an amphibious discipline, with the authority of science and the force of moral knowledge. Ecology, studied through its components and relations, is a perspective, a way of "seeing," according to Paul Shepard. It is a perspective of the human situation in its interconnection. For Paul Sears, ecology is a "subversive subject." Ecology is nonreductive, integrative, and amphibious, having the authority of science and the force of morals. It is normative and sensible. Ecology also offers a "sacramental vision" of nature. Ecology is radical—from the Latin word meaning "rooted"—and forms part of a new metaphor that is more appropriate to the unity and interrelatedness of the earth. Ecology is part of a movement of consciousness, concerned with equality, diversity, health, with humane methods, and with a holopoetic cosmology, and ecology affects them simultaneously. Radical ecology offers a new perspective of humanity in the total field of nature and defines balanced relationships with ultrahuman beings and species. Radical ecology addresses the determination of separate wilderness areas necessary for a healthy ecosphere, and an optimum human population, based on net ecosystem productivities and modified by appropriate technologies within ecological and cultural restraints. It urges local, self-reliant cultures with adaptive cosmologies and natural values in wild ecosystems.

An ecosystem is a complex system that interacts with four large global fields—atmosphere, lithosphere, hydrosphere, and biosphere—and their cycles. The properties and behavior of a complex system are determined by its internal organization as well as its relations with environment. There are two fundamental modes of behavior: (1) Maintenance, based on negative feedback loops and characterized by stability, and (2) Change, based on positive feedback loops and characterized by growth or decline. The two modes can create a typical series of behavioral patterns, from stagnation to rhythmic regulation.

Any large system, such as ecosystem or city, is a high-order, multiple-loop, nonlinear feedback system. In the system feedback loops are the basic structural elements. Each loop is a circular path of interaction between several elements. Ecological analysis forces us to look at the obvious—generating nonmarketable use values occupies the center of every culture because it provides a satisfactory life to its members. These values are represented in a unique image of the world for a culture.

2.4. **Connecting Images—Outopias or Eutopias**
Earlier and foreign images of the world are dismissed as being outmoded, useless, or unrealistic. Utopias have been offered as ideal schemes for social and political development. Sometimes, utopias offer memorable images. But, most utopias are rejected as irrelevant dreams and self-indulgent imaginings. Yet, as Pierre Dansereau has said, the failures of pollution, poverty, and urban decay are failures of the imagination. Rejecting the solutions of imagination, therefore, can only make the suite of human crises worse.

While utopian ideas might be stimulating, other traditional or accidental ideas might be applied more rapidly. Political realism dismisses utopian ideas as naïve and impractical. People are afraid that such ideas would destroy their investments in power and in collections of wealth. Political realism, however, is deficient in imagination and results, as well as deficient in courage and imagination. Despite great revolutions in technology and intensification, most people are still poor and threatened with displacement. Despite great revolutions in technology and living conditions over the past several thousand years, people are still very much shaped by unique cultures and small groups. These traditional institutions work very well on a local scale in a specific place. The information is available, but there is no framework to make it work, yet.

The word utopian was meant to be ambiguous, either no-place (*outopia*) or good-place (*eutopia*). Perhaps the ideas of no-places have less relevance. The images of good places, however, might be worth considering.

Buckminster Fuller was one of the first to consider this second meaning. In the 1920s, Buckminster Fuller began work on an Air-Ocean World Map, as an alternative eutopia that sought to define civic and ecological order through maps of known areas. In 1927, Fuller sketched the World Town Plan, a map that preceded and directly influenced subsequent maps. A 1943 issue of Life published one of Fuller's maps that could be cut up into fourteen pieces and reassembled in the form of a Dymaxion globe. Fuller saw his map as a populist construct to be used as an operational tool by the members of the global citizenry.

In 1954, Buckminster Fuller published the Raleigh edition of his project on the Dymaxion Air-Ocean World Map. In the dymaxion series of maps, Fuller superimposed a spherical icosahedron grid onto the earth's surface to limit the distortion of the relative size and shape of its components. The projection of Fuller's map represents all areas with equal weight. In Fuller's map, the North Pole is the neutral center around which land mass and ocean unfold. Fuller's town plan map, in its projection method and form, highlights the connectivity of his "one world island."

One of Fuller's objectives was to establish a map that does not prioritize cardinal direction, political entities, or hemispheric organization. Instead, the Dymaxion map provides a base for presenting global themes such as human migration, natural resources, and population distribution. Temperature replaces politics as the organizing map feature. In this map, world climate is shown in a range of coloration from warm reds to cool greens and blues. Even though highlighting a specific theme, Fuller's map emphasizes wholeness across the global surface.

A complete eutopian structure would start from such an image of wholeness. A eutopian structure, one that is unambiguously good, could be designed and described. It would outline a science and politics adequate to deal with the creation of good places on earth, where all beings are equal within a framework of high human culture within nature. It would propose an adaptive cosmology to place human values within a global ecology and to balance human development and the preservation of wild places. The framework could protect the integrity of culturally-based nations and to address global issues. Global and local issues would be differentiated; the myths of global communities and one-world people would be explained and discarded. Pretending to be world people is a mistake based on a misunderstanding of human limits. People are the products of places and cultures, of land and nations.

Unlike either the political realism of nations or the ideal designs of utopias, a eutopian plan would be based on traditional human and cultural realities and would propose only modest and reasonable changes at local and international levels. For example, there are 500 million indigenous peoples in fifteen thousand distinct groups, such as the Uighur in China or the Kuna in Panama; and, there are over two billion people in hidden nations within massive political structures, such as the Azerbaijanis in the Soviet Union, the Kurds in Turkey and Iraq, or the Tibetans in China. Furthermore, there are regions in some countries, such as the Pacific Northwest in the United States or Wales in Britain, that may prefer independence to forced membership in a confederation. A Eutopian plan could allow any indigenous people with a traditional culture to become an independent nation without fear of conquest or compromise by existing political states. The benefits would outnumber those of a global monoculture and the negative aspects would be more manageable.

Such a eutopian process would solve many problems, from problems of scale to political inappropriateness. Not only would more nations exist in the framework, but alliances and networks would form and reform, as they do now. How would it work? A political framework, based on traditional cultures, coordinated by a global 'regulating' body, based on a modified United Nations, would be possible and desirable. The holistic framework would protect the creation of thousands of good places, or eutopias, based on human cultural realities and on the ecological limitations of places, that is, on homelands. These models already exist—they just need to be better defined and then protected from misguided ideas of growth and progress, as well as from the dominant, consuming industrial culture. This framework would also reconcile the well-being of society with the health and continuity of living ecosystems. The international framework would provide paths for policing, international education, and other national needs. This plan would provide a path to independence and formal interdependence.

Before trying to build this framework, however, we first need to understand ideal fictions and images.

3.0. **Utopia: No Place**

Felicity's Children
Wherefore not Utopie, but rather fitly
My name is Eutopie, a place of felicity

The City, Amanote, speaks these lines in Thomas More's 1516 fantasy, *Utopia*, about a perfect commonwealth, a society without the problems and poverty of a young English capitalism. While relating his story in Latin, More made puns on the Greek names he used: The name of the city, Amanote, means "dream town;" the name of the traveler himself, Hythlodae, means "dispenser of nonsense." The title is also a word play; to the Greek word meaning place (*topia*), could be added a prefix meaning no (*ou*), or good (*eu*). He used 'u' as an ambiguous prefix; no place sounded like good place.

Utopias are fictions by definition. More had said that it was a fiction whereby the truth might "slide into men's minds." More invented and named the modern utopia. Unlike the earlier *Republic*, which Plato presented as an aristocratic ideal to be contemplated, More's utopia is meant to be a description of an achieved egalitarian society.

The citizens in More's utopia were uniform and regimented: Everyone had the same clothing, housing, and work schedule. Strong peer pressure existed for people to use their leisure time constructively for the public good or to improve their personal virtues. The electoral unit, the family, was autocratically ruled by the patriarch and a hierarchy of princes. Decisions were made by councils elected from public officials, who met regularly with these princes. The utopians solved the problem of population growth by setting up external colonies, where it was considered unjust for natives to hold onto land that they were not 'using'—much in the way the Spanish and English approached colonization in the Americas during the same century.

In *Utopia*, Thomas More comments on why there is less need for work or long working days: "for where money is the only standard of value, there are bound to be dozens of unnecessary trades carried on, which merely supply luxury goods or entertainment. Why, even if the existing labor force were distributed among the few trades really needed to make life reasonably comfortable, there'd be so much overproduction that prices would fall too low for workers to earn a living."

The basic argument, that a few hours of labor a day for everyone would be sufficient to supply all the necessities and comforts of life, is a good one. The residents of Utopia reject beautiful clothing. More used a monastic metaphor, associated with strictness and deprivation. But, More neglects the importance of aesthetic needs. Having everyone have one simple garment would not be acceptable. People like to improve their things. Clothing, for instance, can reflect differences in taste or status, and people will devote much time and money to clothing.

In Utopia, money is eliminated, and therefore many crimes no longer exist. But, More does not adequately consider the human need for prestige and honor. People kill and cheat for prestige and honor as often as for any gold or symbols.

For More, Nature deserves respect, if for no other reason than she is capable of turning against us, and must be treated with care. But, nature is regard as endless and can be converted to cities and fields with each new utopian colony.

More expected that part of the meaning of Utopia would be carried in the dialogues inspired by the book. Chronologically, More created a good place first, and a society constructed from the moral and rational ideals of More himself second. As More wrote, he realized that humans can make any good place less good, that they can seek less than the optimum, or reinvent original sin. Human nature creates conditions that reverse its good. Absurdities are invented, toyed with, and embraced. It is human nature, to attempt to escape all control, or to express the desire to be wicked. More's vision had an immediate effect on literature and ideas, but less of an effect on the growth and development of his country.

Utopias as visions of ideal societies can be found in almost every culture: In prophecies, visions, dreams, myths, and ideologies. George Orwell suggests that the utopian vision has been consistent since Plato, with its dream of justice through reason, through the elevation of public life, and through the regulation of private life, community property, and good breeding. Utopias are not just visions of nowhere, but of otherness.

The ideas of a golden age and an ideal city were combined in modern western utopias. The discovery of new continents opened new possibilities for utopias. Utopias have always been placed in distant lands, populated by people with strange customs. Plato envisioned a perfect model for the Athenian form of social organization; his *Republic* was located on an island in his present (2500 years before our present). In response to Plato, Aristotle[9] suggested that it is impossible to say which model for a society is best. No organization can be ideal under all conditions and at all times. The organization depends on many factors, from social organization and size to the state of relations between neighboring states.

Christian utopias, such as Augustine's City of God, began with inward change, but lead to heaven. These first utopias were idyllic; they described the good life, either material or spiritual, as tranquil and unchanging, but located in other places. In these utopias, liberty was less important than happiness or goodness.

Many utopias try to control society through the state—as in Plato, More, Fourier—to ensure safety and peace. Other utopian writers, such as Morris, Kropotkin, and Bookchin, suggest abolishing the state entirely. Another distinction in subsequent utopias is between private or collective ownership, with the degree of openness, or with the level of technological solutions.

In many utopias, nature, rather than be protected or preserved, is deliberately transformed, according to geometric and scientific models. Francis Bacon, in *The New Atlantis*, writes: "the fathers of Salomon's House summon natural phenomena and create new species to dominate and transform nature, even to the point of eliminating it and making it superfluous." The goal of Bacon's utopia is the inflation of human power over the universe, to create human ease and human happiness. The simplicity of earlier visions was due to the assumed scarcity of goods.

With the exploration of all the continents and oceans, utopias began to be located in other times, the past or the future. For Saint-Simon, Fourier, Comte, and Marx, the good times were in process, and the goals for the future were fixed and codified. The predicted Utopia would be achieved eventually, given institutional and technological propensities. Morris and Howard rely on the garden metaphor. This requires complete design and control in some instances. The garden is dominated by external design without internal human changes.

Later utopian thought put less emphasis on individual and social content. Theilhard de Chardin regarded man as the spirit of the earth, part of a process leading to the "hominization" of the earth and the spiritualization of humanity. The present is also rife with unanticipated developments, such as population growth, blossoming energy use, and waste that follows use everywhere. Other thinkers, including Skinner and Maslow, emphasized the psychological dimension of utopias, recommending personal changes.

In the past century, the concept of place began to be combined with different prefixes to indicate wrongness (*dys*) or badness (*kako*), as in dystopias or kakotopias. Among others, Huxley and Orwell traced paths of visions gone awry. Huxley relies on a wilderness metaphor, with a simple natural lifestyle, characterized by a hands-off approach. But, is there recognition of the human contribution to the goodness of place? Is there enough respect for the power of nature? We recognize that nature may treat us well; we should recognize that nature will provide opportunities for us, but also that it may remove them through the occasional violence of its chaotic systems.

As the visions became less positive, utopias became less adequate and less desirable. Few utopias, although Ernest Callenbach's *Ecotopia* is an important exception, have been created since the 1940s. Callenbach and Bookchin suggest alignment with natural cycles, preventing disruption by eliminating pesticides and using only renewable energy. Marius de Greus suggests that this model is the most neutral and has the fewest weaknesses. Even ecological utopias can be static, however. Callenbach, for instance, offers a static model in the Northwest. Most utopias still tend to be isolated, since they could not compete with the expanding industrial system. Modern utopias present a very limited set of lifestyles, usually revolving around the simple good of a frugal lifestyle.

Utopian thought has a reputation for being unrealistic. This thought is considered to be the dangerous dreams of unreal fantasies. Many commentators, such as Frank and Fritzie Manuel, conclude that utopia is dead. Perhaps this conclusion is just the recognition that reason is not enough, and that human technological power over nature has a higher price than we thought we would have to pay. Perhaps it is the conclusion of people without a strong system of spiritual beliefs.

Utopian thinkers, in questioning the whole of society, often urge its total reconstruction. Utopias have had a great influence on modern industrial society, with their ideal visions of society and their promotion of the benefits of scientific technology. Ironically, these tendencies, especially detachment and nuclear weapons, have the possibility of making real kinds of utopias, literally 'no-places,' on earth.

Traditional utopias look towards a past of ideal peace or a future of ideal post-industrial technological harmony. They do not look enough into the present, into other cultures. In present cultures, however, lie suggestions of the size of society, limits to growth, and appropriate technology.

The value of utopian thought is in questioning all the presuppositions of today. The question: To what extent are problems inherent in the existing social economic or political order? Or rather, in the scale of that order? People want to break from the problems of the past and yet keep the positive aspects of it. They want to have dreams and create their societies in the images of those dreams.

3.0.1. Images Cast Shadows

Our dream of civilization and nature in modern industrial culture is the dream of order and beauty, but as Aldous Huxley notes, the dream of order begets growth and tyranny, and the dream of beauty ends in monsters and violence. Striving for the good life for many has left us with crowded roads and regimented jobs; trying to build beautiful cities has given us gigantic boxes and neighborhood violence. Trying to fulfill our dreams of comfort and security has provoked global threats and local nightmares. The dream is a nightmare that reflects an unbalanced and immature image of the earth.

The collective image that people make of their place on earth is a world, derived from the German word meaning 'man-image.' The image is constructed metaphorically, but considered 'as if' it were true. Each world is based on a root metaphor, according to Stephen Pepper, which is a good device to discuss them. Root metaphors are comprehensive and dominate our attitudes towards things. If the image is incomplete or does not fit environmental conditions, it may fail. People who constructed their worlds from preconceived notions sometimes did not survive. The Aztecs, for example, based their cosmology on the belief that the sun needed human blood to survive, and so they sacrificed great numbers of lives to ensure the sun's life. Their political policy was based on raids for victims, and this policy contributed to their overthrow and decline with the arrival of the Spanish.

The use of flawed images can destroy the environments of cultures as well as the cultures themselves. When Easter Island was settled by Polynesians around 1500 BP, it was fertile and uninhabited. Despite their technological and food-producing skills, ideas on how to deal with surface stones to increase productivity seems to have precipitated genocidal warfare between two groups of believers, those who wanted to keep the stones and those who wanted to throw them into the sea, although stresses from deforestation, erosion, and limited kinds of crops may have contributed to the violence. By the time of the island's rediscovery by Europeans in 1722, mortality from social chaos had reduced the population to about 1100, significantly less than the approximate high of 8,000 (estimates have ranged as high as 20,000 or 30,000). The population dropped to 155 by 1886, although at an increase of 3% per year since then, the population is now over 2000 and supported by tourist trade.

Root Metaphor	Function	View
Animism (Mythology)	Identity	Identity
Formism (Rationalism)	Substitution	Similarity
Mechanism	Decoration	Similarity
Contextualism	Utility	Congruity
Organicism	Wholeness	Interaction
Holocosmology	Frame	Star

Table 3-01-1. Root Metaphors. By contrasting the views of metaphor enumerated by Max Black with Pepper's four root hypotheses, a rough correlation emerges. Two other hypotheses can be added to the schema: animism and holocosmology, which considers all views valid to some extent.

Modern industrial cultures also have defective images. Our root metaphor of the machine extends down through all levels of society to the economic and the personal. An image of a culture can be stated as a series of principles, such as: "the universe is mechanical; humanity is master of the universe; and all persons are equal." These metaphors have allowed inhabitants of some nations to treat people, plants, animals, and nature as robots that can be modified or replaced. The cost of that image has been the diminishment and destruction of lives and environments.

Metaphors can limit cultural possibilities. For example, the metaphor "labor is a resource" implies that, like any common resource defined by industrial society, labor is cheap and can be used up. Modern economies, embracing another metaphor "nature is capital," draw on the accumulated "capital" of ecosystems for production. By ignoring the real cost of the capital, as well as the costs of natural services, such as nutrient recycling, soil building, and atmospheric renewal, these economics create a temporary wealth that will disappear when the capital is exhausted or the society collapses. Decisions regarding resources are made on short-term economic grounds and lead to material shortages and environmental degradation.

Powerful images can influence cultures over centuries. The principle of plenitude, restated in Christian terms, presents that an intelligible creator gave an earth of unlimited bounty to humanity for its use. This principle seemed to be confirmed in the Renaissance with the discovery of the richness of heaven, microscopic life, and unexplored continents. Many modern political ideologies and economic systems have been shaped by the principle of endless wealth. Adam Smith calculated that the real price of anything was just the toil acquiring it.

These ideas are parallel to the idea of unlimited good, where anything, even virtue, can be multiplied indefinitely. The invalidity of this principle comes with the recognition of limits. Without limits any good becomes devalued and is wasted. Limits contribute to value. The universe is limited; the earth is limited; individuals have limits. These modern metaphors are defective because they do not fit our surroundings. The crises of cultural images have tremendous physical consequences.

For most of human history, the habitable earth has been a mosaic of separate territories and peoples. Different groups developed distinctive ways of dealing with their nonhuman surroundings. Each way of dealing can be referred to as a culture, a pattern of behavior based on shared beliefs adapted to the local environment. Culture can be expressed as a symbolic language. The particular symbols concerned with cultural institutions as manipulative objects are political symbols. Politics deals with words, which are arbitrary symbols for events or things. The wrong relationship of things and symbols can result in misguided politics and violence. Political decisions are made on narrow political and economic grounds. The gradual narrowing of the focus has resulted in a citizenship in industrial cultures that is the abandonment of responsibility on the assumption that others know how to manage things; government itself is the assumption of responsibility, without sufficient knowledge that result in a suite of problems.

Wrong decisions and wrong relationships have resulted in creating places that are nowhere. To create our nowheres, we have accepted the gifts of bigness, speed, uniformity and allowed the thefts of life, intelligence identity, and choice to negate any gain from them. Combined with our own failures of charity, imagination, will, and courage, using piecemeal knowledge and unrelated ideals without regard to traditional knowledge and practical experience, we have created common faceless cultures to sit on our flat, placeless utopias.

3.0.2. One World Through Reason (The Place of the United Nations)
After the war in 1918, there was a popular vision of one world, without walls or barriers. The most desirable way of creating the "one world," as Wendell Willkie called it, was through reason, although reason has not been used historically to consolidate or shape nations—France, Germany, the U.S., and Italy, among others, were united by force. The notion of a world government seems to satisfy a basic human craving for unity and order, but, at the current stage of international relations, there seemed to be no agreeable path toward a single benevolent world order.

The partial adaptation of international institutions is insufficient for a world order, especially if these bodies are only advisory. The United Nations (UN) is the only body with the machinery for constructing a world system; the beginnings of ecological politics can be found in the special services of the UN—UNESCO, FAO, WHO, and the various technical aid services. As long as ecological and political problems are addressed in a framework of nationalism and military power, however, these organizations are treated as peripheral and relatively impotent.

Despite its good-hearted programs on disease and education, the UN cannot deal with wide-spread starvation, or acid rain or the whole complex of global problems. The UN does not seem to have a good grasp on global problems either. The 6th and 7th special sessions recommended financial aid, annual transfers of resources to poor nations, and a charter of economic rights. It is unlikely that this will happen. There are too many vested interests.

It has been said the UN has no use beyond recommending the avoidance of violent conflict. As it is, the UN has found many uses in setting standards for human health and education, as well as with human rights.

It has not been as effective recently at stopping genocidal behavior in some countries.

As it is structured, the UN is not capable of handling the responsibility for international order. Despite its emphasis on peace and international security, the UN has been able to mount only a relatively few peace operations—perhaps only one every two years for its sixty year history. Although many of these have been successful, they have had to be approved by the Security Council and to be run understaffed and underfunded. The peacekeeping efforts in Bosnia were not effective. Not in Somalia either. The attempt to guarantee democracy in Cambodia was not effective.

Milton Eisenhower had said at the UNESCO conference in 1949 that for the UN to be effective, it would have to have a police force stronger than any nation's armed forces. While that could work, few nations would permit an international superpower. Most nations would also consider it to be an intolerable burden and worry that it would control the world in a unity that would have no liberty for any nation.

Is the UN due to be a monster world-state? Perhaps healthy small states could be united into healthier larger organisms. But, the UN cannot survive on good will. As it is now the UN is a union of some large powers and many small ones. The UN functions only with the consent of the reluctant four or five biggest states. Their veto power is a reflection of their power and might.

It has been said that there are no fundamental disagreements in the UN, now. But, then, this is a limited UN, not much trusted or invested in. It has also been said that there are no universal agreed-on truths of social organization. This is not a problem, because cultures organize, then societies. All an enhanced UN would do is keep standards and coordinate cultural organizations.

It has been said that the UN is a forum for the same power politics in disguise. That has been a problem with the original establishment of the UN and its reflection in the Security Council. The universal values of the UN Charter come from the victors of the world war in 1945. The UN was never meant to be for free nations. The Security Council was the preserve of great powers, with the undemocratic veto power. Restricting membership in the Security Council to great powers, and its use of the veto principle, indicate that the UN is imprisoned by the status quo. The values and memberships simply need to be modified and enlarged. Should the UN get rid of all veto power in Councils and return to persuasion?

It has been said that the UN bureaucracy worships consensus, otherwise called the "handmaiden of evil" by autocratic states. But, consensus is what allowed human societies for millennia to reach decisions.

It has been said that there is a danger in having a strong Secretary General powerful enough to prevent war. No Secretary General has had the power to prevent wars. Is preventing war less dangerous than allowing uncontrolled conflicts?

It has been said that public discourse would be suffocated in a peaceful world. That is always possible, but we know that it is suffocated in a warring world, even if it is a multitude of small, undeclared wars. Discourse is considered unpatriotic for criticizing bad decisions made in wars or in 'undeclared conflicts,' the current political euphemism for wars, but discourse should not be suffocated by unevenly applied ideas of patriotism.

It has been said that a vision of world peace is unrealistic; leaders would have no tragic memory of the latest conflict and little earned wisdom in dealing with conflict. It is argued that these "shallow, callow, child-like leaders and their advisors" would commit some grievous miscalculation leading to a holocaust or war. My answer? Three words: George Double-U Bush. For the most part, the current leaders have power expressly due to their skills of manipulation, not due to experiences of tragedy. Furthermore, peace would not be the end to struggle or conflict. Natural limits, human conflicts, and the long adjustments to peace and equity would provide many large challenges.

It has been said that the UN dominates the world, that it is inflexible and unaccountable. But, it is no less accountable than any elected body. Officials and programs can be changed or removed.

It has been said that international goals are best realized through national self-interest. This must be the old wisdom. It might have been true, if nations were perfectly rational and knowledgeable; they do not seem to be. Nations now seem to be the handmaidens of corporations, whose interest is only in profits for shareholders. The views of shareholders are notoriously short-sighted.

The UN is limited by images and ideals of progress. The UN's solution to economic problems is "sustainable development"—that is, "growth that respects environmental constraints," as if growth respects any constraints. The Bruntland Report indicates a five to ten-fold increase in world industrial output within the next hundred years before population stabilization occurs. While the appeal of growth is unarguable, it is really not likely to be sustainable in any meaning of that word, since sustainable growth does not recognize known ecological limits. Furthermore, the UN has no power to coerce its members when it does make good recommendations.

Our attempts at social improvements have proceeded without order, without sufficient insight and perspective, without sufficient confidence, without a comprehensive plan, and without a great dream. Our politics has been corrupted by special interests. The structure of our civilization comes from anonymous builders and mediocre designers, minimal engineers and rapacious financiers. We work within the rules as they have been for decades, rejecting any alternatives as too utopian. The rules themselves have been shaped by centuries of social metaphors and utopian ideals. The rules within which we have been operating for the last sixty years, or even since the Treaty of Versailles, are inadequate. It is not a matter of what is the best thing to do within the rules as they are at the moment, it is a matter of changing the rules.

3.1. **The Lure of Nowhere**

The idea of 'nowhere' is attractive. It has a spare simplicity. We believe that we can shape it. It represents the search for perfect predictability, for sameness, for comfort from sameness, and the known. There are few uncertainties, fewer threats, and less to fear.

3.1.1. *Getting Nowhere*

Our fascination with nowhere has allowed us to create nowheres, big, impersonal flatscapes with nothing unique to recommend them. We are comforted by uniformity, but not necessarily when every single place is or looks the same.

3.1.1.1. The Gift of Bigness (The Curse of Corporate Bigness)

Early in our history, when the very success of the species was in question, we humans learned to reproduce more rapidly than our rates of mortality. To extend our families, we have increased our numbers and our rate of increase exponentially. To ensure the success of our species, we have appropriated the places of other species. Our overpopulation has led to aggression against other cultures and species, then to indifference at their suffering. Even low levels of food and fulfillment at our current size can be maintained only through theft from other species and from future human generations, and through the degradation of billions of humans as well as the ecosystems on which they depend.

To provide for the needs of many and for the extravagant luxuries of some, we have produced waste and pollution on a geological scale, from islands of garbage to skies of acid rain. Manufacturing processes result in the production of new dangers, such as recombined genes, and new substances, which are not easily incorporated into natural cycles. The overuse of ecosystems results in deforestation, devegetation, and desertification, then in depletion of raw materials and depletion of agricultural land. Economic and political pressures, derived ultimately from population pressures, force farmers to intensify their efforts to increase crop production, instigating a dismal cycle of population expansion, environmental deterioration, and poverty.

To provide for our needs efficiently, we have increased the scale of our activities. But we have decreased the diversity of habitats by filling in wetlands, felling forests, plowing grasslands, and irrigating deserts. Agribusiness has caused widespread landlessness; people who try to grow their own food are forced onto marginal lands or off the land. Acquiring fossil fuels also creates landlessness; coal mining in the Black Mesa mountains of the United States, for instance, may force the resettlement of twenty thousand Hopi and Navajo people. Without land, and the economic independence it allows, cultures are more likely to disintegrate.

Our local communities are proud to attract more people and larger industries, but do so thoughtlessly, without regard for the limits of population size or the rate of energy use, without sufficient consideration of the effects on the quality of our lives or on the quality of the environment. Although we make plans for people and their activities, the plans are usually reactions to growth and change. The formal development from planning results in a complex of problems, from pollution to ugliness.

Our societies are big. Our corporations are big. Our impacts are big. This creates discontent because people feel powerless. They feel powerless because they feel that democracy is not working. The country is run by the rich, rich corporations, rich people, rich politicians, and they secure their needs for more money first. In fact the decline in earnings, relative to costs of goods, forces people to struggle with jobs and increased conflict everywhere. Now, at the perceived "end of history" and the "victory of democracy," it is difficult to imagine a better future, at least without questioning the rich, the ideals of democracy, and the corporate good will to society.

We have economic growth; we can see the numbers. But, the growth is premised on saving costs by forcing down wages, or by reducing the number of workers in the name of efficiency, and forcing overqualified workers into service jobs. The growth promotes inequality, improvement for a few and impoverishment for most. It is the growth of a tumor, issuing a healthy glow from a fever and the false image of health. Profits go up, but public services decline for lack of funds. There is no money for schools, none for libraries or parks, little for private institutions, and little for national, state or local governments. Where did it go? Profits? Profits for individual corporations, profits for individuals? Could we find them, can we track the money? We should be able to, since the management revolution has made paper trails everywhere. Perhaps the trails are too complex.

Bigness overwhelms the ideals of cultures, which is why large nations such as China or the United states cut their forests, regardless of respectful religions or special cultural values regarding nature, regardless of the desires of local communities. The nations are willing to sell the wealth of the provinces, even though the provinces want to conserve them.

Something is wrong. But whom is to blame? Where is the target? People rail against liberals or conservatives, against corporations or protesters, against big government, or big corporations, big permissiveness, big violence, the lack of faith or lack of prayer, the failure of responsibility or the failure of nerve, against guns, leniency, illegitimacy, bad rock, bad lyrics, bad welfare, bad politicians, bad people, and bad police. But, the real enemy is unseen. Who can argue against democracy or corporate wealth or the general vague feeling that things have improved? Against a reasonable system? Against the bigness of the system?

The course is downward now. How can it be turned? How can we diagnose the problems? How can we suggest a path to health? Charles Reich says that we need a science of social change. Ecology is science-based. Conservation is science-based. Even management is science-based. Now economics and politics needs to be science-based, instead of dominated by an old ideology and weak mythology. Reich suggests that between citizens and government is a third entity, economic government, to which has been ceded power to determine the direction and type of economy. The only knowledge we get is knowledge from the economic government, and the numbers look good. We have no other knowledge, except for a weak self-knowledge, and vague social knowledge, that tells us something is wrong.

Leopold Kohr identifies the basic conflict between man and mass, citizen and state, large and small communities, as a result of bigness. Kohr's theory of size states that the cause of most forms of social misery is bigness. We have always tried to exceed the physical and biological limits of places rather than recognize them and be guided by them. Every advanced country is now over-technologized. Past a certain point the quality of life diminishes, not improves, with each advance. Big science serves big technology, which supports and is supported by big government. And there is no science like big science, and no administration like big administration. But this enthusiasm is misdirected. Scientific advances and technological changes result in unforeseen consequences, good or bad. They cannot be controlled or legislated against before the fact. But the investment seems too big to abandon.

The planet, including human society, is threatened by the bigness of things. Although nature is big, it has evolved slowly; human size is new and sudden. A snail's pace is good enough for nature most of the time, but with our brief life span, we argue that we need quick changes. The technological advances have not been paid for yet, although the cost in pain and death is incalculable. We will be paying for hundreds of years for those past advances. The economic style is too great, and reckless for ecological systems to absorb its impacts. The scale of things is an independent problem, that can ruin the best intentions of policy. A bigger system to control systems that are now too big might be a mistake.

But some solutions are even bigger. Buckminster Fuller, Alvin Toffler, and the Club of Rome favor a supertechnocracy. Science fiction visions predominate: Gerard O'Neill's orbiting cylinders or Simon Calder's floating domes. R.A. Smith, in "Unibutz," claims that we could achieve a pantheistic-humanistic-cosmic awareness, in achieving technology without materialism, plenty without selfishness, and community without tribalism. His Unibutz is a global goal for leaving the earth and reaching the stars. The voyage would help shape new world structures and give a purpose to humanity. But to what end? Bigness and wealth elsewhere?

Perhaps big science and big technology have too much momentum. Theodore Roszak acknowledges its schizoid attraction and repulsion, with the twin promises of glorious accomplishment and hideous death. Who could escape being torn between yes and no, if even our end would shine with radioactive, Promethean grandeur? Our image of big science—the scientist as tragic hero, isolated in chaotic nature, but strong in his proud individuality, perhaps driven to research by hubris and madness—is a barrier to any new vision, especially a small vision.

3.1.1.2. The Lure of Speed

To achieve even greater efficiency, we have increased the speed of our activities, converting materials and cultures into new designs without consideration of the meaning of, or need for, efficiency. The speed of our economy is too great for many cultures to adjust to; and the thoughtless transformation of cultures may result in great, irreversible mistakes. The speed of our conversion of wild habitats to domesticated lands is too great for many species to adapt to.

Alvin Toffler foretells a dramatic redistribution of power, from slow countries to fast. Speed is the critical factor for Toffler, who states that, historically, power has shifted "from the slow to the fast," whether speaking of "species or nations." Certainly, being faster to the industrial market has advantages for many international corporations. But, this kind of speed is not applicable to species. Slow species have survived as well as fast, either adaptively or neurally; many fast dinosaurs perished before their slower mammalian contemporaries.

Toffler notes that the industrial revolution stepped up the metabolism of economies, but does not seem to make any distinction between good or bad metabolism—fever as well as excitement speeds up a metabolism. Truly, we are speeding up our use of resources without knowing where they are coming from or going to. Modern economies, embracing the idea that "nature is capital," draw on the accumulated "capital" of ecosystems for production. By ignoring the real cost of the capital, as well as the costs of natural services, such as nutrient recycling, soil building, and atmospheric renewal, these economics create a temporary wealth—similar to the healthy flush of a fever, perhaps—and a long-term imbalance. When an economy falls out of balance with its local environment, massive disruption often results; industrial economies have only avoided disruption by trading advantageously with other economies, by using fossil fuels, and by promoting general institutional inequality.

Continuing his paean to speed for its own sake, Toffler states that fast economies generate wealth and power faster than slow ones. But, what kind of wealth? Financial or cultural, agricultural or symbolic? And, what kind of power? Mechanical or organic, political or personal? Industrial economic wealth is merely a small part of the wealth of the earth and humanity, most of which has little value to that economy.

Toffler describes an acceleration effect that makes each unit of time saved more valuable than the last, creating a positive feedback loop— inadvertently identifying the archetypal problem of modern economics: Runaway positive feedback loops leading to catastrophe. The fast economy he describes seems to depend on fleets of hypersonic jets racing around the world with the elite and their tonnage of possessions. Telecommunications, transportation, and tourism will accelerate, blithely unaware of their impacts on family structures, biogeochemical cycles, including the ozone layer, and wilderness. Have we learned anything?

Toffler sees revolutionary consequences in new management methods, but not the negative effects. Managerial decisions regarding resources are made often on short-term economic grounds and lead to material shortages and human and environmental degradation. Newer methods seem only to offer a higher degree of impersonality.

The new wealth creation system, Toffler claims, holds the possibility of a better future for the vast populations of poor, if their leaders anticipate changes. The new system for making wealth consists of an expanding global network of markets, monetary, and production centers in instant communication with increasing flows of data and information, but not necessarily wisdom or understanding. He argues that the availability of this information flow gives more power to consumers, voters, workers, and small businessmen, taking it away from a centralized few. The potential is there, but Toffler does not go far enough to envision alternate economies and communities. The power still operates under the old assumptions and divisions in his speedy synthesis.

Of course, Toffler is right to recognize the problems of nonindustrial countries, many of whom depend on cheap labor or strategic military location for foreign investment. But, where does that "investment" go? To the local poor or to remote, rich politicians? Wealth could be distributed fairly, depending on many factors, such as synergy, generosity, reciprocity, and cooperation, but it is not. The gaps are growing. Toffler acknowledges that they will keep growing. But, we can redistribute wealth without industrializing. We should try to achieve economic justice before accelerating to new glories.

Toffler concludes that a great technological and cultural wall will separate the slow from the fast, making problems for joint ventures. But, what are the products of these ventures? The debris of advertising fads, such as mink toilet seats, or the tools of real needs, such as evaporative water purifiers? Toffler foresees the emergence of an electronic neural system for a global economy, without which any nation will be doomed to backwardness. What kind of backwardness? Lack of fast things? Lack of professional enslavement? Lack of art, play, or culture? Lack of food, tradition, freedom, or happiness? Perhaps these have already been stolen.

3.1.1.3. Grand Thefts

Despite our bigness and speed, most of the world's human population goes hungry; even fewer are fulfilled as actualized human beings. The utilitarian aim of greatest good for greatest number has been vulgarized to mean the greatest number of goods for those who can afford them. In our attempts to manufacture the good life for everybody, we have deprived everybody of clean air and water, quiet nights, darkness, open spaces, and other indefinable qualities. Soils are destroyed, wildlife is killed. We devour nature to assuage our disease; we try to fill our emptiness with goods. We can only gain past a certain point before our gain causes the loss of something else that we need to be healthy.

Modern technological society ravishes nature and mutilates humanity with the products of its materialism. Industrialization has distorted people's lives and cheated them of bread and justice—during the time it takes to read this manuscript, over 10,000 people will die as a result of nutritional deficiency. The cost of the paper and processing for this manuscript could feed twenty people for one day in many poor countries. Reluctantly, I rationalize that an idea is a better and more effective solution to global problems of production and self-reliance than a one-time aid or just ignorance, but the rationality does not sit well in the dreaming mind. Oppression darkens the mind and narrows the spirit. In a mass consumption society, people impoverish themselves spiritually while impoverishing others materially. This is theft. As with the Christian ten commandments, most loss can be reduced to theft, whether of a life, mate or name. Most of our modern problems can be considered the consequences of forms of theft.

3.1.1.3.1. Theft Of Life

The relationships of humans and animals have changed drastically. The increase of humans and the destruction of animals have unbalanced the relationships. The destruction of habitats is accelerating. Up to a point, niches can be enlarged or increased, but with so many humans, it becomes a case of supplanting other species entirely.

The loss of cropland and soils, and the disappearance of genetic stocks essential for crop breeding, may eventually cause the collapse of the biological basis of our food supply. Huge quantities of fertile soil are washed away each year as a result of deforestation and poor land management. It has been estimated that Colombia losses 400 million tons of soil per year and Ethiopia 1 billion tons per year. In The U.S., in spite of its soil conservation service, almost 5 billion tons are lost annually; these losses over the past decade may have cut the potential to grow food by ten to twenty-five percent. This increases our dependence on oil imports, since $1.2 billion of fertilizer was needed to replace the nutrients lost through soil erosion in the U.S. in 1978, for instance. Increasing amounts of fuel equivalents are used every year to offset erosion.

In developing countries, hundreds of millions of rural people strip the trees and shrubs around their homes for fuel. In Gambia, it takes 360 woman-days per year per household to gather wood. Even when firewood is available for sale, it may be beyond the budgets of the poor. In South Korea, it can cost up to fifteen percent of a household budget; in the Sahel, it can consume twenty five percent of a budget. When wood is scarce, the poor are forced to use millions of tons of crop waste and dung, which should be used to regenerate soils. The poor are destroying their means of survival, in order to survive now. Then, the soils on which they live become even more vulnerable to erosion. Deforestation causes siltation, which cuts the useful lifetimes of reservoirs in half, decreasing hydroelectric and water potential. Deforestation causes floods, which devastate settlements and crops, incurring even greater replacement costs. Lack of soil and forest conservation contributes to rising energy costs and the financial costs of providing essential goods and services.

Tropical rain forests, genetically the richest land environments on earth, are being felled and burned at the rate of 27 million acres a year—50 acres a minute (in 1972). At that rate there will be no more tropical forests left by the year 2050. The lowland forests of Malaysia, Indonesia and the Philippines are being ravaged the fastest. The rape of the tropics is endangering hundreds of thousands of species. Over 25,000 known plant species and over 1,000 species of mammals, birds, reptiles, amphibians, and fish are threatened with extinction, as their habitats are eliminated. Many of these species may be economically and culturally important; others are different and unique. Unknown species, perhaps half of all species on the planet, are not valued at all because of our ignorance.

Irrigating marginal lands causes some loss from salinization. Salinization is responsible for the degradation of over thirty percent of the arable land in Iran. New energy uses further degrade a portion of land in more industrialized nations. At the present rate of cropland impoverishment, one-third of the world's cropland may disappear by the year 2000. Deserts are expanding at the rate of 23,000 square miles per year (for contrast, the nation of Belgium is 12,000 square miles in area). Eight million square miles more are seriously affected. Desert conditions jeopardize the survival of almost eighty million people now; 550 million more could be threatened. Desertification by overuse of land afflicts almost seven percent of the earth's surface.

Drought is blamed for arid land problems in Australia, but drought is inevitable. Aridity is determined by air currents and topography. Rainless episodes are normal in regions of erratic rainfall. Sensitive pastures may be overgrazed in good years, but the damage is not apparent until a drought. Sheep during the Australian Gascoyne droughts starve; there is enough water for thirst, but not enough for plant growth for food. Survey teams in the Gascoyne region recommended the most ecological strategy was to temporarily abandon the affected sections. The recommendation also was made to graze only half as many sheep. These recommendations were ignored by grazers, who needed the income immediately.

Even the sea is not invulnerable to human impacts. The most productive areas, which are close to shore, are being polluted, overfished and destroyed. Estuaries and coastal wetlands are being destroyed. Overfishing has deprived people of millions of tons of seafood. Overfishing is destroying the fisheries' support systems. In the U.S., losses to fisheries from shore "improvement" and degradation cost $86 million a year.

The relationship of humans to humans has also changed in the past thousands of years. Human lives are stolen, not only through war, but large-scale murder, as well as through diminution of human value and denial of resources.

3.1.1.3.2. Theft Of Common Sense (& Humility)
The industrial machine is out of balance and defective, but we have been making it run faster to process more material. Western civilization still selects cultural changes in terms of wealth and power. This is destructive to most individuals, as well as maladaptive for a society under ecological restraints. Over the past two centuries, industrialized countries used great quantities of raw materials to create luxuries. Then they disseminated the ideas of wealth, equality, opportunity, and indulgence to many countries without industrial opportunities. There can be no peaceful future for civilization when such disparities, and popular knowledge of them, exist. The cult of competitive consumption seems to be the universal solvent of the modern world. Everyone wants what some have. The industrialization of Asian nations is seen as a solution to shortages of manufactured consumer goods, although imbalance and pollution are down-played. Even worse is the unavoidable waste. Probably over fifty percent of the productive effort in United States goes into making things which contribute nothing to the material standard of living.

Consumer desires must be satisfied promptly or despondence results. Although life, art and science depend on organization, the civilized consumer feels that organization implies stasis and death. Believing the line of succession ends with his claiming of the inheritance, the industrial consumer feels no obligation to provide for the next generation. The consumer justifies narcissism as a preliminary condition in the search for consciousness, truth and morality. Consumers become embroiled in their own causes, locked in the idealism of adolescence, and repudiating the lessons of history. Hegel noted that the greatest lesson of history is that nobody ever learns the lessons of history. And, Cicero wrote that those who do not know the past are like children. Americans and the people of some other nations seem intent on validating these insights.

This repudiation of history creates a historical amnesia. Consumers retain little more than a dim notion of the past. Universities report a lack of interest in events that occurred before the current year's athletic season. The sense of time falls in upon itself, collapsing like an accordion into the present. Knowing nothing of history and expecting nothing of the future, people cannot escape the fearful isolation of the present. They join together in a melancholy herd, clutching at everything, but holding nothing fast.

Even good eating habits can be forgotten in quickly. The eating habits of many people in industrialized countries are unrelated to nutrition. There is no instinct for good nutrition; it is a kind of empirical learning from trial and error, although young children are often good choosers. As South Africa became colonized, for instance, the natural diet of Zulus changed from millet to corn. Malnutrition also resulted from this overdependence. Yet after a generation, tribesmen thought they had always eaten corn, even though their ancestors were stronger and healthier than they are now.

Without the depth of history, experience is shallow and short, and intelligence is thin. Technology has reduced the globe to a single, closed system, which humans can share according to their financial powers. Our direct experience of the world has become shallow, in spite of faster travel. Travel used to broaden the mind, but now it narrows it. We travel in sealed corridors like boxed goods, comforted by homogenized foods and the English language. Our cultural adaptations to the pressure of homogenization throttles individuals and groups.

Our overweening bumptiousness, which the Greeks called hubris, lets us behave as though we were too privileged to be members of the earth's ecological community. We name things and dismiss them. We draw lines around them to separate ourselves. We build our own environment, mathematical and sanitary.

John Fowles observes that most of us remain firmly medieval and distanced from what we cannot own or fully control. We assess most of nature as what is not clearly *for* us must be *against* us. We cannot accept indifference, the nonhumanity of nature. We seem incapable of realizing that the destruction of the Amazon, much as we deplore it in its remoteness, is our responsibility; we consume the materials from tropical forests. Our growing emotional and intellectual detachment is the greatest threat to nature. Heroic narcissism has replaced nature with humanity; nature no longer provides the mirror to reflect human aspirations, a televisions screen does. Narcissism is a threat to nature and humanity.

Unbridled consumption in a laissez-faire economy for fifty more years will probably carry humanity beyond a point of no return, leaving industrial society with insufficient resources to maintain itself and insufficient flexibility to retract. If lack of planning permits rapid increase in population and consumption, then our options may be diminished to two: A nasty, overplanned existence, or a squalid collapse. But the future seems as unreal as the past. The historical origin of the ecological crisis is in the failure of people to use their intelligence to anticipate the long-range consequences of their activities; this is a perennial human problem.

3.1.1.3.3. Theft Of Choice

We follow false models. Our civilization is dominated by all of the ideas of the industrial revolution, which form the outlines of a tragic world view: The primacy of humanity, anthropocentrism, the supercesion of the individual, the achievement of happiness through the accumulation of things, the perception of the incompetence of nature, the requirement of humans to control the environment, the expansion of the frontiers of technology and opportunity, and the identification of solutions for every problem. But, these ideas are false; programs that assume them for conditions are doomed to fail eventually, and perhaps destroy the kinds of environment that humanity needs. Cities and factories reproduce themselves exponentially through a industrial genetic code. They are the addicts' dream of affluence using science to create a dream pill from the dust of a bare earth. But, simply removing the causes of unhappiness may not produce happiness.

Industrial culture has been distorted by the modern emphasis on the scientific method, with its devaluation of philosophical concepts and emotional values. Rational values are exaggerated and spiritual events are ignored or suppressed. Most scientific studies seem specialized or irrelevant. Some parts of problems are identified and analyzed, but the conclusions are trivial and weak. The ethical impulse to solve the problems is even weaker. We choose to let them slide, or to label them as nonproblems.

The unified direction and responsibility of science is nonexistent; there is not even a concept of what is good. Control has been the goal of science and technology. Scientists are obsessed with the treatment of weeds and vermin. The industrial cosmology has put humanity at war with the planet, which always misbehaves; weeds and vermin threaten us. Our path has been worn so deep, it would be difficult to leave it. Stability has been raised to sacred scientific state. The interlocking of technologies and institutions makes it impossible to reform policy in any one part, separate from the other parts. This interlocking also makes people powerless to choose any alternative. The systems managers are preparing to operate the planet, according to systems principles applied in routine methods.

The safety of the environment is too important to be left to scientists, even to ecologists. The crude history of science shows that scientists fall willingly under the dominion of money and power, like Christianity, communism, and most movements. The movements of science and industrial culture reduce the possibilities of choices.

3.1.2. *Being Nowhere*

Most humans are dominated by the idea of competition: It is us against the environment, us against others, and us against ourselves. Everywhere antagonism pervades our society—college presidents lead their groups into battle for bestness; political parties blame each other for one hundred years of bad planning; we compete for jobs, status, dollars, and mates. Conventional violence—war, murder—captures news headlines, but structural violence—mining, schooling, hospitals—pervades society unacknowledged. Most relationships seem violent in a competitive society.

Many human societies advanced by fighting and expanding. Fighting is a common form of human behavior, occurring in children, as a ritual limited by pain, and in adults, as failure of communication or understanding. The growth of the brain and its capacity for abstract thought seems to have bypassed the ritualization of social conflicts common to other mammals. Human fighting is not as formalized; and, this is what permits humans to slaughter one another. Most tribes followed two standards of morality: One for insiders and one for outsiders. Most aggression was directed outwards and the losers were often exterminated.

Many tribal groups federated into national units. A nation, by definition, has a single, central government representing people who occupy contingent lands and are consciousness of a common identity. The professional ruling class is divorced from kinship bonds; structure is stratified and internally diversified. Almost the whole land surface of the globe is divided into centrally governed states. Human affairs are managed within the framework of these autonomous units. Decisions are made on narrow political and economic grounds, rather than on environmentally sound principles.

3.1.2.1. Trapped in Images: Myths & Peace

The two great myths, progress and nationalism, arose with the industrial cosmology. The author Aldous Huxley[10] described progress as the theory that one can get something for nothing, that the gain in one field is not even paid for in another. Progress assumed that all consequences could be foreseen, and that the ideal ends in the future justified the most abominable means: Robbery, murder, or cheating. Progress was considered good, and primitive groups only obstructed the civilized nations' march toward paradise.

According to Huxley, nationalism was the theory that the state was the only true god; all others, especially other states, were false. Conflicts over prestige or power were crusades for progress and nationalism, for the Good and the True. Lord Acton observed that nationalism aims solely at making a nation, the abstract idea of the political state, and not at liberty or prosperity for people. He also predicted that the result would be moral and material ruin. Nations are basically exploitative of other nations and smaller cultural groups, which may not be considered nations because they lack a permanent military: The United States concentrates on Latin America; Europe on Africa; Japan over Southeast Asia; Russia over Eastern Europe; and China over Tibet. The reasons for this continued behavior include: The rapaciousness of society; the acceptance of war; and the economic advantages of large-scale operations.

The cultures of industrial nations are based on unethical accumulations of materials. Inequality is maintained by power, not persuasion, and also by the assumption that solutions are extrinsic and external and have to be found by spreading out rather than intensifying efforts to find solutions at home.

National powers work, through progress, to maintain the good life for their leaders and followers. Major powers deal formally and informally with each other on survival problems, such as nuclear crisis or ecological crisis, but compete on other issues. Politicians should think about the hunger and squalor of billions of human beings and the destruction of habitats with billions of ambihuman lives, before dedicating themselves to their personal fortunes and the missiles needed to protect them. The system of management, like all paradigms, slowly becomes a means of excluding experience foreign to the notation. It becomes a form of authoritarian control. Programs become responsible for dimensions of misery beyond any considered.

Our politics will improve when we realize that we are the biggest ecological problem. Ecology studies the details of the binding of all beings in the earth into a whole. Ecology, like god, is not to be mocked, as Gregory Bateson said. There are no such things as little sins. Even human plans are now part of the ecology. Bateson warns that all ad hoc measures leave the deeper causes of problems uncorrected, or worse, permit the causes to be compounded.

3.1.2.1.1. War

Those who believe in the theology of nationalism are committed to fight. War is a way of conquering or creating new nations. It is a nonprogressive way of promoting progress, especially innovations in certain kinds of technology. What have been the causes of war? We know some causes from hunting societies or chiefdoms: Insults or broken agreements, or competition for resources, from food to land. Nations created new causes: To unify other cultures and resources, or to deunify the enemy and to unify the aggressor.

The war ethos has been expanded and reduced to absurdity. War has become so big that there can be no victories or victors, and possibly no survivors. The only remaining purpose can be the total destruction of the combatants, as nations, as well as natural habitats. Sadly, the only people who do *not* know this, or admit it, are those in decision-making positions, who are compelled to prepare for what they subconsciously know would be a terrible disaster. Their power has trapped them in the momentum of their nation, afraid to be caught in any criticism. Yet, they direct the money, skill, and knowledge of their citizens into projects that lead to misery, servitude and hideous death, and not to life, liberty, and happiness.

The intellectual rationalization for the continual preparation for war is the old Roman adage: "If you want peace, prepare for war." This adage has been so completely taken into the modern heart that most of the larger nations have spent over half of every century in war, according to Pitirim Sorokin. Preparation for war has always lead to war. There seems to be no reason that the present arms race will lead anywhere else, even in times of relative peace.

Power politics makes problems that cannot be solved except by war. Questions about defining the best nation or the best religion lead to organized slaughter as the answer. "War is not merely a political act," said Clausewitz, "but also a political instrument, a continuation of political relationships ..." As long as human institutions were large and brittle, war was an effective way of disassembling them. This form of social renewal, however, was very expensive. Marx may have been partly right when he said war was necessary under certain conditions, as a last resort. But, those conditions no longer exist. His observation may have been true from the 1830s to the 1940s, but it has been rendered false by modern weaponry. Nuclear war can destroy the parts as well as the connections, cultures and ecosystems, as well as senile political structures. It may not be able to discriminate.

War has become an integral part of the modern economy. The war industry, as measured by expenditures, is on the order of $200 billion a year. Defense problems in the U.S. are perceived as problems of hard technology; psychological and social research is considered irrelevant. Security is analyzed in terms of Newtonian physics: Blocks, actions and vacuums.

There are other dangers and benefits to war. There are, of course, benefits to war. It equalizes opportunities for some. It foments change, any kind of change. It gives a sense of the past, if the past needs to be measured by conflicts and victories. It leads to more advanced technologies and to faster social responses.

The economic rationalization is even more crucial for nations. Armament piling has become a vital part of the U.S., Russian, Iranian, and North Korean economies, among others. The recovery from the U.S. depressions in the 1930s was not complete until the rearmament surge to combat the Axis powers. The Korean and Vietnamese wars also spurred the U.S. economy. U.S. prosperity has its basis in the preparation for death. The fear of Russian competition (in 1970) ensured government expenditures of billions of dollars for 'deterrence.' The vested interests in this system are almost insurmountable. The concrete companies and bomb makers put up their own puppet politicians to guarantee their part of the spoils.

The dangers include the fact that war has been regarded as meaningful struggles against people who would kill or enslave others. The 'side-effects' are rarely considered or counted. War also leads to an overweening respect for large government. The cost of war excludes the social distribution of wealth. Consider the plight of the Russian or the U.S. poor. The situation is much worse in disadvantaged countries. The war industry, as measured by expenditures, is on the order of $200 billion a year. Kenneth Boulding says that it is an unrecognized paradox that the cost of maintaining the war industry is greater than any possible damage that could be inflicted by an enemy. Furthermore, war intensifies the depletion of resources; therefore, it is counterproductive to fight to steal another nation's resources. For centuries, warfare has resulted in incredible wastes of resources. The latest multinational conflict, which began in 1914, and has been hot and cold during this time, has been the most wasteful

The winners of a large war will need to be pitiless, according to Kurt Vonnegut, for pity will be suicidal when resources become exhausted. War is considered to breed strength and nobility. The values of strength, nobility and bravery were suitable for certain hunting societies. But, even the weak and lazy can get food and shelter in this world without plundering. Humanity is clever at taking more than what it needs from nature. Evolution is thought of as the survival of the fitter. Nobility and cleverness may not best fit a species for survival, if they require competition and war. Perhaps mankind will perish for its nobility—but is it noble to be extinct?

Perhaps it is the fate of humanity to die a radiant death, taking most other living beings with them. Who could resist the glory of complete annihilation? Perhaps that is the fate of humanity. But what is fate? The hand of God, or the idea of Tolstoy—that historical events are determined by the summation of innumerable decisions by the anonymous masses of humans that add up to a tendency. In particular terms, the small decisions to buy automobiles, poison coyotes, plant trees, or live simply, add up to fate. Fate certainly concentrates power in corporate, military and political hands, which still belong to human beings, who cannot find consolation in mega-deaths.

Nuclear war is unthinkable. Limited disarmament is unworkable. Human and environmental degradation are unconscionable. Is anything thinkable or workable without being hopelessly utopian? The problems of aggression, nationalism, war, and peace are problems of human nature, symbol, culture, politics, ecology, and size. They are not simple problems and not easily solved. They are interrelated as human groups are technologically, economically, ecologically, and politically interdependent. Human interactions have been dominated by symbols. The most powerful set, embodied as nationalism, has a direct relationship to war. Large-scale war can create utopias, places that are nowhere, on earth.

The United Nations made war illegal; one nation cannot attack another. But, that has not made a lot of difference. Cultures try to destroy other cultures. Big nations try to absorb or punish small nations. The aggression by the United States against Iraq is a crime against humanity according to the Nuremberg principles established by the victors of the conflict in the 1940s. Those principles were enforced by hangings at that time. The war was sold to the U.S. Congress with lies and propaganda, but even exposure was not enough to reverse the decision to stay the 'course.' Perhaps U.S. citizens are naïve about their role in making peace or securing its need for oil. Perhaps that naiveté has to do with the luck of never having been invaded, flattened or destroyed by another nation.

3.1.2.1.2. Peace
What is peace? The absence of war? The absence of large-scale organized conflict? Peace means, in the original Latin, 'confirming to an agreement.' An agreement is part of a conversation between two or more people, which usually results from an effort to avoid some kind of conflict. Peace requires conversation, the exchange of opinions, wants, and problems within the context of meeting.

Robert Kaplan states that tragedy "requires a sense of history," implying that war is tragedy and peace is timeless. He suggests that peace leads to a 'preoccupation with presentness, the loss of the past and a consequent disregard of the future.' He continues arguing that because peace is pleasurable and pleasure is a momentary satisfaction, therefore pleasure, as well as peace, is inseparable from convenience, a temporary, timeless, uniform satisfaction. Should we not outlaw lovemaking and eating as well? Or all momentary pleasures? These are strange arguments: People in war time damning peace, as if it were the worst threat to the planet. Have we ever had such a dull time of peace? And, did the people who experienced the satisfaction of peace complain and lust for the tragedy of war?

Why is universal peace something to be feared? Would it lead to great dullness or great evil? Tragedy does require history, for it cannot operate without it. Peace requires history and tragedy as well.

Is peace without a sense of history? Peace seems unchanging and historyless, with fewer dramatic changes, but people seem to want to sacrifice anything for it. The common, written history of reference is the usually the history of the victor, with great leaders and great changes, but that itself is a small limited mythical history. Real history includes all kinds of changes, from geological ones to the development of cities. Perhaps people mistake peace for a static vacuum.

How did we get this way? Bad genes? Bad images? People have images of nature as violent or of humans as naturally violent, which contrast with other images of nature as cooperative and humans as peaceful. Some of the logics of our cultures promote a dualism where either one is true, but not both. The logic of opposites creates a false dilemma, a fallacy, where there has to be a winner and a loser, where opponents have to fight over one thing or one way. This logic has the advantage of simplifying complex situations into one adversarial relationship, which can only be decided by conflict. But switching logics, or expanding the logic that dominates global conversations, can allow seemingly contradictory ideas to exist together, such as simplicity and wealth, or peace and artistic creation.

Overwhelming desires? In Buddhism in general, desire is an obstacle to peace. Suffering can be reduced only by following certain practices. There is conflict between desires and suffering, between needs and wants, between ideals and actions, between expectations and real events. Neither desire nor suffering can be totally eliminated by behavior patterns, which will always cause more desire or suffering by the very nature of human wants. Peace for Baruch de Spinoza is a virtue that springs from force of character. It exists with other virtues, such as self-control or self-regulation. Some desire and suffering can be reduced through education. Art educates and liberates the individuals of society in a gradual and peaceful process. In spite of the cultural forces dominant at any moment, an individual has the potential to determine a different course. Art can reduce or rechannel desire, and thus reduce the suffering that comes from maximized desires.

Runaway scale? As long as there is no limit on violence, wars can continue to engage plants, animals, even entire habitats and civilian populations, as often as soldiers and weapons. Conflict has to be descaled. It could be limited to a small number of representatives from each culture or group, so that the scale of peace would always be larger than the scale of conflict.

So, if we made an agreement to limit conflict to certain arenas and to certain sizes, that could be a form of peace. Peace could be a process of resolving conflicts between cultures. Some conflict is unavoidable, due to human nature and ideas of honor and possession, due to different images and beliefs about how the universe operates, and due to misunderstandings and accidents. Much conflict is related to fear, fear of loss, loss of security, loss of effort and opportunity. However, as long as violence is an accepted response to conflict, events will continue to be violent. The proper response has to be self-restraint and mutual constraint. Conflict has to be delinked with violence. All conflict is not bad. It is a challenge and stimulant to an individual and a culture. But, it has to be responded to in such as way that people think and develop, and create a considered response. Limited peace would to match the limits of conflict.

Peace is also a freedom from public disorder. Disorder is also unavoidable. But, it has to be kept below a cultural ceiling where it could destabilize the culture. That requires the agreement of a culture and inhabitants. Like conflict, disorder is a challenge that requires a creative response, rather than attempt to destroy disorder.

Is peace just nonviolence? Nonviolence is a psychological choice by an individual; it may be a cultural rule if enough people practice it. It is a way to resolve conflict through nonresistant awareness, which includes witnessing and understanding, conversation and mutual constraint. Conversation, remember, involves listening as well as speaking, in responding to another person. It exposes common themes and builds trust. So, nonviolence, or peace, is not a passive, head-hanging response to dominance. Bearing witness to injustice, that is to the results of dominance and violence, of inequity and prejudice, is a form of action that requires courage and persistence, and results in knowledge and the spread of awareness. The Quaker tradition of bearing witness is a turning towards events, and participation in those events. There are degrees of witnessing from observing to communicating, such as writing letters or making telephone calls, to acting nonviolently and negotiating for changes in events. Nonviolent action can neutralize aggression by refusing to offer positive feedback, that is, more violence in response.

Is peace just cooperation? Conflict is the result of differences in perception or needs. But differences can be resolved without conflict, without automatically assuming an adversarial stance. The subject of the conflict can be recognized as a common challenge—more than a problem that requires a solution, or a final, one-time fix, challenges are opportunities for change and development.

When conflict was thought to be the primary mode of operation in nature, it justified human conflict and violence, not just to fellow humans, but to animals and all of nature. With the scientific understanding that cooperation is much more prevalent in building guilds among animals and stable habitats, the operation of nature becomes more understandable. Cooperation builds partnerships and mutually beneficial relationships between individuals, species, and communities. Cooperation is more than the avoidance of conflict. It is the recognition of emergent benefits. It is finding security in sharing, or in new ways of being, rather than by eliminating competitors.

Cooperation is one aspect of peace. Ways of cooperating include communicating needs and negotiating for redistribution of resources. As it goes along it may be necessary to mediate two desires, or to arbitrate a decision. But, this is done though sharing in a conversation, by building consensus through common themes and conversation, by identifying shared goals and needs, in an atmosphere of trust, where feelings and ideas are shared, taking as much time as necessary, with as little outside agenda as possible, to be committed to the benefit of both groups in the process.

Is peace just harmony? Peace can also mean harmony or concord. But, harmony can contain discordant notes and themes and weave them into a rhythm. Harmonious action can change patterns of domination of cultures and individuals. Harmony has to include conversation with other species, and trust in nature as a generally beneficent system, our mother system and home. Although humans cooperate with each other, cooperation with other species is best characterized by allowing them opportunities for living, despite a measured exploitation.

Peace is unknown territory, *terra incognita*. We have not been there often, except by accident. The path to conflict is easier to define—it results from fear, from the desire to defend and to be violent. The new path requires as much bravery as violence does; it requires patience, it requires effort to find out why and what is needed.

There are, of course, numerous ways to achieve peace, such as requiring everyone to belong to the same religion or social class. This tactic has been tried; it did not work. Perhaps we could limit conflict in new ways, such as personal conflict between leaders or their champions. Or, assign all power to an Association of Nations. Or change the focus of war to nonhuman astronomical events, such as meteors.

3.1.2.2. Achieving Placelessness

By accident, we have created the opposite of peace, and the opposite of place. De Tocqueville had previously identified a trend of human uniformity in the 1830s, when he wrote that variety was disappearing, and the same ways of acting, feeling and thinking were copied around the world. A number of scholars, including Christian Norberg-Schulz and Edward Relph, have noticed that we are creating flatscapes, devoid of depth and providing only one mediocre possibility, a chrome-plated chaos.

Placelessness begins with adoption of an attitude, an abstract, geometric view. With an inauthentic technique, places can be treated as interchangeable and unremarkable. Nothing is significant there. Cutting historical roots and eroding symbols contribute to an awful placelessness, an alienation to place, an inability, finally, to have a home and to live there. This becomes the fate of millions, and it increases.

After shaping ourselves to technology and necessity, we have lost the knowledge of how and for whom to care. We have learned not to care, to be dispassionate (uncaring), unattached (placeless), and objective (uninvolved). Other animals have used languages and tools, so it is not those things alone that account for the lost knowledge. We 'not-care' because we are confused. Our confusion results from being out of place and not having an identity.

3.1.2.2.1. The Loss of Identity (The Ninth Loss)

People use to identify with place. In fact, many names are merely place names given to people. Other names come from what kind of work people did, or who their parents were. Thankfully, we have stopped naming people for place and jobs. What kind of names would we expect to use now? Frank Paperpusher? Berty Mallpack? Joe Truckaimer? Mary Asphaltlot?

The gain of a global monoplace has led to a loss of identity. The mass production of homes, as well as of music and art, has led to fewer creations. The commonness of culture, at a low common denominator, has led to fewer identities to choose from.

3.1.2.2.2. The Scope of Failures

Acceptance of limits is not a kind of failure. One speaks as best one can. Awareness of inadequacy, as of ignorance, is a positive accomplishment. True failure is indifference to inadequacy. The failures in our character or group or national character, can be seen to be responsible for the problems identified by Konrad Lorenz as the seven deadly sins of civilized humanity, from destruction of nature to the loss of civility. These failures can be described as a series.

3.1.2.2.2.1. Failure Of Perception

Perception is defined generally as the mental ability to grasp objects or qualities through the senses, resulting in understanding or knowledge. The number of things that we grasp, however, is limited by our senses. We see very little of the spectrum. We are limited by our size, our positions, and by our life span. These limits make it difficult for us to perceive very slow or large changes or to anticipate them.

In a market economic system, we have the perception of progress without the recognition of the costs of bigger cities and bigger farms. We have a perception that efficiency is related to maximum productivity, without regard to human health and happiness. Wealth and power are treated as primary needs, more than health or self-actualization. Failure of perception results in the inability to see the long-term results of economic actions that maximize profits through direct competitiveness. The same inability shows itself in the political frame where political cycles are limited to two, four, or six years.

Much of the environmental crisis is caused by the failure to understand patterns of cycling. This is especially true with industrial agriculture, which tends to break up cycles. Like most human endeavors, agriculture ignores cycles, as well as physiology, metabolism, and diversity. It fails to accommodate the reciprocity of the living environment—life does not adapt to a passive prior environment, it produces and modifies its surroundings.

We seem unconscious of the failure of cities and walls to lock out wild nature. This failure had mythic origins. After the Sumerian king Gilgamesh killed the great spirit of the forest, Humbaba, he became possessed with the fear of death and tried to lock out nature with the great wall of Uruk. It did not work, but it contributed to our historical domination of nature and others. Our fear of the wild, undomesticated, uncontrolled profusion of nature has lead to our war on forests, rivers and winds.

We fail to see the incredible interdependence of humanity and nature, of diversity and success. We do not seem to be able to see others as feeling human beings, or animals and plants as feeling beings, or rocks as experiencing beings. Domination and conflict reflect our inability to perceive other human beings as equals. This failure reflects our inability to perceive the complex operation of nature, from the links of fungi to large-scale developments. The failure of perception also leads to the disappearance of strong passions and emotions, as we avoid unpleasant realities and pamper ourselves with visions of separateness and superiority.

3.1.2.2.2.2. Failure Of Intelligence

Intelligence is the ability to learn from experience, retain that knowledge, and use it effectively in new situations, with common sense. Although we learn limited lessons from the short-term experiences of some people, we sometimes apply them unthinkingly to other situations. For example, British and U.S. farmers tended to take their success with monocropping to every other ecosystem, from tropical forests to deserts, with disturbingly bad effects. Explorers and scientists failed to learn from earlier archaic cultures that had adapted to places over thousands of years, again with disastrous results. Intelligence by itself is obviously not enough to guarantee our success. We even have special behavioral sinks for intelligence when it is too active but unattached—habits, computer games, and television, for instance.

Beliefs, also, such as the belief in progress and technical improvement, can lead to the failure of intelligence. Therefore, intelligence has to analyze beliefs and myths, to make sure that they reflect ecological realities.

Perhaps the problem lies in a broader kind of intelligence, social intelligence. Ants have a swarm intelligence, where the swarm is smarter than the dumb individual, that is, greater intelligence emerges. Small insects are not smart. But, in hives, their social intelligence allows for smarter behavior and better designs. Humans on the other hand, are smart as individuals, but seem to demonstrate the opposite trend. Humans have mob intelligence, where the mob is dumber than the smart individual, that is, intelligence submerges. Rather than becoming smarter in mobs, people act less smart. Nations may be cross-cultural mobs. What is the solution? Being led by a few smart individuals? Democracy? Is there a way to replace cultures with other alliances, such as those for bioregions, totems, or economic systems? Could common sense save us from the failure of intelligence?

Common sense is the combination of intelligence with feeling and everyday experience. Common sense flows from the way people live in place and expresses what they want. Intelligence also grows out of living, but it is abstracted. Common sense is part of a conversation that results in cooperative behavior in the face of environmental and social challenges. Of course it is not perfectly transparent; people sometimes do not communicate exactly what they mean, which is why the context and body language of conversations are so important.

It is common sense that allows us to realize that our bodies and minds are real, that the world is a strange, wonderful, and dangerous place, that the earth has existed for a long time, with many radical changes—the shift from a methane atmosphere to an oxygen atmosphere was certainly radical—and, that people in other cultures have different, equally real and important experiences. It is common sense to realize that gardening is more productive than war. It is common sense to realize that enlarging a place is better than destroying a place where other live. It is a failure not to.

3.1.2.2.2.2.1. Laziness in a Maze

Economic decisions have provided short-term benefits for many and great wealth for some, but we have been unable to figure out a way to improve the lives of everyone. We have failed to consider the impact that an increasing population with increasing per capita expectations will make with competing demands on natural resources. Surpluses will disappear overnight, as they did when the U.S. switched from oil exporter to oil importer in the 1970s. The U.S. exports raw logs to Japan and China, without considering unemployed wood workers in the U.S., and without considering who will supply the U.S. with wood, or where that country will get its wood.

Our leaders make decisions based on polls and the likelihood of re-election, without considering that they were elected for some purpose beyond re-election. One frightening aspect of government is the total failure of our leaders, both national and international, in political and economic spheres, to learn or understand the simplest facts of science or technology, much less ecology and long-term development. Our leaders separate these other spheres from politics, impressing us with their facility with words and their images on television bites., but that is not enough to hide the failure. Isolated problems stir only a mild reform, but no problems are truly isolated. Modern citizenship is the abandonment of responsibility on the assumption that others know how to manage things. Modern government is the assumption of responsibility, without knowledge or group intelligence.

The failure of intelligence leads to our adopting useless traditions and buying habits, and to genetic deterioration from weak selection pressure and from lack of preservation of norms of social behavior. Neither liberals or conservatives recognize the fundamental conflict between political government and economic government. Therefore, there is no attempt to resolve it, with changes to structure, tradition, or new invention. Perhaps this is laziness. Laziness results in cultural amnesia or political amnesia, where people cannot remember the good decisions they made or good habits they had a generation earlier.

3.1.2.2.2.2.2. Dance of the Fallacies

This failure of intelligence results in the use of many fallacies in reasoning. Economics has not been unsuccessful with its models, for instance of buying behavior, but it has become a highly abstract academic discipline. All its abstractions are applied to the real world without acknowledgment of the high degree of abstraction involved. The philosopher A. N. Whitehead warned that the economic method would triumph if the abstractions were judicious, but even judicious abstractions have limits, and the neglect of those limits leads to disastrous oversights. Considering a fictitious human nature under imaginary circumstances and thinking it is real is the fallacy of "misplaced concreteness" according to Whitehead. Hermann Daly and John B. Cobb Jr. suggest that the classic instance of the fallacy in economics is "money fetishism," where the characteristics of an abstract symbol, such as limitless growth, are applied to real commodities and values. Misplaced concreteness also occurs in forestry, where wood is given a status that trees and forests are not. Genetic reductionism is another good example of the fallacy. Genes are not independent creative beings; they only function within the organism, in this case, a tree, which is the creative being.

Many predictions about resources are based on fallacies. There is the fallacy of substitution, that states that a substitute can be found for any resource in short supply. This is not always true, especially when cultural preferences are considered. Furthermore, there is a gross underestimation of the length of time that it takes for a substitute resource to attain traditional markets. For instance, the transition from wood to coal as an energy source took about fifty years, despite the fact that coal technology was established and attractive.

Dennis Meadows identifies another fallacy: The expectation that people and institutions perceive problems and react to them rationally, for example, with the threat of wood shortages, prices should rise and consumers would value the resource more. Yet, the price of wood is still nowhere near the real costs of production, and wood is used for cheap, impermanent goods. Meadows suggests the model of addiction might be more appropriate than adaptation for dealing with consumer demand.

These fallacies, as well as others, such as the fallacy of complexity, the fallacy of the false dilemma, the fallacy of begging the question (*petitio principii*), and finally the appeal to authority (*argumentum ad vericundiam*), are used to deny intelligence. The fallacy of the false dilemma restricts decisions where only two alternatives are claimed and one is considered unacceptable, as in: Either A or B; not A; therefore B. Either war or peace. Either tax cuts for billionaires or economic chaos. Obviously, there are more than two possibilities. Preservation is not the only alternative to clearcutting. War is not the only alternative to peace. Engaging in this fallacy allows us to stop using our intelligence.

3.1.2.2.2.3. Failure Of Imagination
Imagination is the act of forming mental images of what is not present or has not been experienced to deal with new experiences. The world of many people is simple because their image is simple, so they think there are simple solutions to simple problems. Many people believe that energy and food increase automatically as people multiply, and that simplifying ecosystems can increase their productivity. This exemplifies the failure of imagination. We should not confuse the limits of our mind with the limits of the world, as the philosopher Schopenhauer warned. We seem not to have the ability to see what we have lost, in our rush to be civilized and big.

This failure of imagination limits our understanding and visions of a future. We have the ability to explore planets and modify genes, but cannot seem to offer functional education or meaningful jobs, dignity in retirement, or goals for living. Oddly, we seem to have adequate imagination to describe space colonies and interstellar migration. Will we develop them just to take the same inequities and problems with us? Humans can even create virtual worlds by limiting what could be received; for instance, if a being could see in the x-ray part of the spectrum. Yet, human imagination is as limited as human knowledge.

The failure of imagination leads to the inability to recognize or use the good ideas of others. This is obstructive to our adapting to a changing ecological contexts—thus the idea "protect the ecological basis of life" is never considered. We think that we have to address things one at a time, that we cannot see ourselves or our actions in the whole ecological system, partly because we are interested in continuing our immediate pleasure, even if over a short-term human lifetime, without regard to the indirect and shared costs to the system and to others within it, and partly due to a failure of imagination.

Every proposal to build a dam, to widen a highway, to cut down another forest, to turn wetlands into salable real estate, or to bury unwanted waste products is sure to have unintended consequences. But, we never elaborate the possibility of these consequences or what actions we would take if they occur. Instead, we label them as 'side-effects' and try to ignore them.

We do not try to imagine the connections between things that we do not know about. Not knowing how trees provide wood or how people cut the trees and process them, we feel no responsibility, we feel no connection. When we do not feel the connection to land, or understand what it does, in terms of cleaning water or providing food, we do not create groups to protect the land, or a constituency or a leadership.

Many organisms exist of which we know nothing. Their worlds have little meaning in a human world. We know what it is to be human, but spend little time imagining other forms of existence.

The failure of imagination has lead to the human overpopulation of many ecosystems and perhaps the planet. Although small bands have some problems keeping their numbers within limits, we fail to understand the differences in scale, and use common resources, like the ocean, without common rules. Extreme change, as regards climate switches or cultural collapse, lies outside our experience and our ability to imagine that change.

We never imagine long stretches of time, thus we fail to anticipate the changes that occur in long time periods. Can reason comprehend deep history fully? Tending to think things too complex, or too expensive to change, we are not able to make good decisions to adjust to large or slow changes.

Perhaps this is a failure of ability in general. This inability to imagine the differences in situations and the consequences of our actions leads eventually to tragedy, which is the failure of a guiding image of the world, often referred to as a cosmology. In a theatrical play, the tragic hero triumphs at first, and incorporates the successful behavior that lead to the triumph. This behavior, employed in new circumstances, however, leads to disaster. The hero refuses to give up a particular role or strategy or to imagine how to change in new circumstances. Hence, the failure to give up a chosen role or pattern of behavior leads to great loss later. The play reflects our actions in the environmental play. The real-world tragedies result from the failure of our working images, the products of our imagination: Humans are responsible for the consequences of actions based on certain images, not on chance or fate. We can choose between the tragedy of the commons or the tragedy of total control, or we can expand our cosmologies. We are tragic because we have to accept responsibility for our actions.

Ultimately, many failures, as Dansereau has said, the failures of pollution, poverty, and urban decay, are failures of imagination. Rejecting the solutions of imagination, therefore, can only make the suite of crises worse. Will the failure of imagination condemn people to partial solutions or ignorance? We seem condemned to the weak trials of the past. Utopias are dismissed automatically as imaginary places. We can only imagine a society without any history or without a real place as being desirable.

3.1.2.2.2.4. Failure Of Integrity

Integrity is the state of being complete or whole. The term is applied to art, music, ecosystems, wilderness, computer databases, or people; it implies that these things have not been corrupted by natural process or human actions, a form of natural process, of course.

Integrity can be related to the general character of a human being, having to do with the integration of the self, into an identity that represents things beyond it, but also referring to a way of acting morally. Acting with integrity on a particularly important occasion could best be explained by the general presentation of that character and life.

The failure of integrity leads to both the breakdown of tradition, as we pretend that ubiquitous behavior forms a global culture, and to the destruction of natural habitats, as we take key elements from the ecosystems. We must acknowledge the failure of our remedial efforts, our failure even to address the flaws of our ideologies.

The failure to value those things necessary for life, of a person or a habitat, is a failure of integrity. Value, as an expression of worth or exchange, cannot be limited or ignored. This keeps values and morality as local effects. We do not extend respect or love to distant others. Our personal values and beliefs do not let us.

3.1.2.2.2.5. Failure Of Will (& Courage)

Will is the power to make a reasoned decision, with a strength of purpose, with a firm attitude to control one's actions, with courage or nerve. Courage means an attitude of dealing with anything recognized as dangerous, difficult or painful. Nerve means strength, emotional control, or endurance.

Will fails daily. We refuse to share or to help others even when it is easy. If we cannot imagine extremes, it is hard for us to have the will to sacrifice things to avert it or ameliorate it. For all our cleverness, we still emulate flies and grasshoppers, when it comes to acting always in short-term self-interest. During the good weather and the good crops, we expand to or past the limits of water and food.

We lack the political will for sacrifice or planning. The failure of will leads to susceptibility to indoctrination by governments and even by advertising schemes. Policies are not implemented, due to social differences, corruption or war. What does this failure mean? Living in fear? Fear is not necessarily bad. Fear serves a purpose in human affairs. It is a warning system against unknown or overwhelming facts. But, fear can get out of control. Fear builds barriers. It also can lead to the hatred of ideas and languages.

Too much fear can lead to the failure of will. Afraid of failure or of being unpopular, many politicians, perhaps all politicians, exercise too much caution. They refuse to stray from their opinion polls and say what they believe. They refuse to initiate actions that they know are correct.

Disarmament, for instance, is a simple rational idea. Our failure to disarm, especially nuclear weapons, is a failure of will. Perhaps will is undermined by comfort and security. Perhaps the lack of security has allowed fear to dominate our decisions. Courage requires understanding of humanity and the planet, what to affirm and what to negate, as Paul Tillich says. We can have the courage to be, to become, to transcend our limits, Tillich believes. The roots of courage are moral, as Henryk Skolimowski notes, the result of moral conviction, where reason alone is not enough, and belief is required. Lack of morals, which come from community life, can lead to failure of will, decision or resolution.

The chaos of climate, with an increase in extreme conditions and warming of the global atmosphere, has been observed and linked to human industrial activities. Yet, we do not have the will to make changes that might keep the climate more stable.

No one wants a blasted world for their children, or for others' children or for other humans, animals and plants. The problem seems to be why do we act as though we want such a barren wasteland. Failure of imagination? We seem incapable of imagining large scale and long term consequences of our wants and desires. So, we buy that gigantic sport-utility vehicle, so we can see over traffic and be safer from traffic. We cut down a grove of trees for more houses; we pave a few more streets. After all, what difference can a few more things mean?

Few people are without some goodness in their hearts, so that may not be the problem. But, few people have long-term, large-scale ecological intelligences in their brains. Almost nobody wants to try to plan for some kind of mutual constraint to allow the rest of the planet to breathe. After all, it's just one more pair a shoes and a filet for dinner. What harm? And the answer is very little harm at all—it's just that on a massive scale, little sins can kill numerous species and destroy large habitats. And, few of us see the results. Just fewer bees and songbirds. The Gulf of Mexico west of here is dead for hundreds of square miles. Why? Garbage, phosphate dumping? Who knows what combination exactly, but it killed the fish, crabs, and almost everything except red tide bacteria.

Until people hearts respond to what's in their heads, we can kiss our asses goodbye, and many other nonhuman asses as well of course. Until our larger selves, that is the self of our places and environments, get to speak and express their hearts, the small hearts cannot do much. Until then, we will need laws, prescribed limits, taxes, injunctions and maybe new social rules, which can come from the heart, of course.

Perhaps people's hearts are barren and fruitless and they would prefer the challenge of a desert world. After all, many of our religions came from the world views of desert peoples; perhaps they believe that god wants a desert domain to rule. Perhaps it is just our desire to simplify the earth to an extreme. After all, a desert would be easier to manage and it would be quite stirring visually. Many cultures that live in deserts love that unique environment.

We know what we have to do, really. But, it seems that only in times of war or great catastrophe do we have the nerve to do something, although we do not seem to have the nerve to avoid those catastrophes or wars that could be avoided by planning and conversation. Perhaps it is fear of pain or change. Perhaps it is a character flaw in the species, the failure of nerve at critical junctures. Perhaps it is just the lazy habit of mob thinking. But, we must overcome it and plan dramatic changes.

The failure to change, to choose real equality and real peace seems to be another unique kind of human failure, the failure of will. We may not have the courage for some to give up their lavish lifestyles and extreme comforts, their extreme profits or gargantuan excesses. Somehow, we need to commit ourselves to a revolution in distribution, equality, and kindness.

3.1.2.2.2.6. Failure Of Charity

Charity is love of others or the act of goodwill towards others; it refers also to the feeling of benevolence or kindness in judging others. In traditional hunting societies, charity was expressed through reciprocity, or mutual sharing. In urban societies, sharing was more than just an exchange; it was characterized by generosity. In early industrial societies, the views and practices of others who shared resources or places were met with tolerance.

In archaic societies, charity may just be sharing food. In more stratified societies, charity tends to be part of an institution, that may be modified by greed, laziness, or the arrogance of charitable workers. The failure of charity leads to the rat race of competition between human groups, at the expense of many human and ultrahuman groups.

As money and power lead to detachment from agricultural and natural cycles, from reciprocity and concern, charity disintegrates. Humans have the power to alter vast processes in nature, but do not care enough to refrain from trying. Power without charity is a satanic theme. Sigmund Freud wrote that Satan desired to be father for himself, an agency without community. Many governments have the same desire. Governments also have knowledge without charity, which was a demonic theme for the Christian church (the word 'demon' is from Greek word for knowledge). Power without knowledge, and knowledge without charity, are frightening possibilities.

Of course these failures occur in endless combinations. Maybe the failure of our modern civilization is a failure of imagination compounded with a failure of nerve. We cannot imagine an alternative to war, and we cannot act beyond emotion. We cannot imagine beauty in the old and messy nature, and we are afraid to try to do without luxuries or to try to sacrifice anything to try to change the momentum of industrial civilization.

3.1.3. *Leaving Nowhere*

Are we doomed by our failures to live in nowheres and nonplaces, to have the same jobs and the same common rewards? Is being placeless hopeless? Is hope what we should depend on?

3.1.3.1. Habit & Hope

In his writings, H. G. Wells prophesied the collapse of civilization and the reversion to barbarism, with the eventual rescue by a race of supermen. Human nature desires a grand explanation to place its daily doldrums into a grand frame. We must abandon the Nineteenth-century grand design approach, however, with its attractive simplicity, and substitute an awareness of humanity as participants in nature, within natural laws. The complexity and fluidity of problems exclude simple, rational argument. Until recently, attempts to resolve contradictions created by urbanization, centralization and bureaucratic growth were viewed as a counterdrift to progress. Any critic was a treated as a discounted outcast.

There is a conflict between economic growth and the preservation of the environment. Economic growth usually triumphs, but it upsets natural rhythms. The devastation of the biosphere is the greatest threat to the survival of humanity. It may not be perceived as such by most people or their governments because of more immediate concerns, such as war, poverty, epidemics, energy, inflation, and unemployment. Nevertheless, the failure of conservation is a direct cause of the worsening of these problems. Society may hinder human understanding with a burden of distractions, injustice, and inferior loyalties.

Most of us will occupy ourselves with externalities, and hope, in the traditional sense, that our children will be wiser—but how can they ever be with no one wise to teach them? Children are cultivated as the leaders of the future— they expected to solve the problems that adults failed to solve. This future is the keystone of the salvation-through-schooling mystique—if it was true once, there is now too great a lag time between taking a civics course in junior high school and using it as adult forty years later. These things need to be taught to adults or especially to the old, who are traditionally leaders. The dying and the old hardly matter to the young and ambitious; their feelings lie as lightly on the scale as their own future. The old themselves default in their responsibility and the young in theirs. Responsibilities are passed down through generations without ever being taken.

Any mind, even most ingenious and fertile, may fall back on habits of its cultural inheritance; humans are social animals with cultural heritages. The outlook of merely a secure and satisfying life, without great ease and rich comfort, may be threatening to many consumers. The contest is not between us and them, but between the reasoning mind and biological limitations. Can there be a leveling up, now, or is there only the possibility of leveling down? The crisis emerges from our state of consciousness. It may be infinitely more difficult to transform human sensibility than to pass laws. We are isolated from the past and future by a disease.

3.1.3.2. Hope & Science

Technology offers human beings a vision of a world with a stable population, freed from poverty to live in peace, sharing the world's resources. Industrialism, more than that, promises humanity a paradise on earth, after displacing the promise of paradise in heaven. Now, psychology promises its own myth of paradise through self-knowledge and medical improvement.

Science holds great promise for improving the human condition, through understanding the climate and ecology, improvement of agriculture, and the development of soft energy sources, but the lead time for research is long and unpredictable. Interest in ecology has inspired a number of plans and models of the world. The worst are disoriented, useless and uninspiring. The best are notable by their criticisms of the former.

Most popular plans are based on thoroughly terrifying assumptions: Continued, accelerated economic growth, as well as population growth; further industrialization; less distribution of wealth; continued inflation; continued centralization; and complicated technological solutions. Many of these plans rely heavily on scientific studies (MIT SCEP), computer models (Forrester and Meadows), or even science fiction (Kahn). We hope that we can avoid the worst of those assumptions. However, as Ben Franklin noted, those who live exclusively on hope may die fasting.

The present causes of the ecological crisis lie in the combined action of technological advance, population increase, and conventional, erroneous ideas of the nature of humanity and the environment. Garrett Hardin asserts that the problems of the ecological crisis are direct results of the tragedy of the commons reproduced on a global scale. Therefore, overpopulation, pollution and resource depletion can have no technical solutions; they can only be ameliorated through political reform, which can only result from changes in perception.

3.2. Designing Nowhere — The Ideal Place

The result of hope is the quest for an ideal place, without problems, without stress, and without hope. In short, a place that can only exist nowhere. This quest is achieved by subtracting place, by removing diversity, and by ignoring inconvenient truths.

3.2.1. *Designing Nowhere*

The title for Sir Thomas More's Utopia is a pun. To the Greek root word *topia*, meaning place, could be added *eu*, meaning good, or *ou*, meaning no. Good place sounded like no place. Utopianism can be found in almost every culture, in prophecies, visions, dreams, myths, and ideologies. In general, utopias have been preoccupied with static societies that were egalitarian and open. They tended to emphasize a purposive world characterized by moral order. They usually tended to refer to the past or future, and to theocratic salvation or rational achievement.

Utopias started out as models for interpreting and remolding society (Plato). Christian utopias began with inward change but were located in heaven. By the 16th century, they were located in other lands; but, by the 19th they had to be located in other times. As Plato's city was tied to the cosmos,

Augustine's was to God, Hegel's to the spirit, and Machiavelli's to Florence.

Plato's *Republic* envisioned a perfect model for the Athenian form of social organization. A fully communalized, small population was supported by agriculture and crafts. By contrast, Augustine's *City of God* neglected social and political life and emphasized the ideal human relation with God. Other medieval utopias shared this emphasis. At the beginning of the Renaissance, economic requirements for the good life were given more attention, although ethical civilization was the ultimate goal. Religion still played a major role, however.

Thomas More's essay, *Utopia*, was completed in 1516. It depicted a perfect society, without the problems and poverty of the nascent capitalism in England at the time. The electoral unit was the family, which was autocratically ruled by the patriarch. The government consisted of several levels; the lowest was elected from constituencies of thirty families and the highest was a hierarchy of princes. Decisions were made by councils elected from public officials, who met regularly with the princes. Utopia was uniform and regimented; everyone had the same clothing, housing and work schedule. There was strong peer pressure to use leisure time constructively for the public good or to improve personal virtues.

Popular welfare, to be achieved by experimental science, rivaled virtue as a goal in Francis Bacon's *New Atlantis*. Traditional values of Christianity, monarchy, and agriculture were maintained. Bacon suggested a domination of nature instead of a stable balance within nature. Surprisingly, however, scientists were expected to be ethical and withhold discoveries that would not be beneficial to society.

Denis Diderot used his *Supplement to Bougainville's Voyage* to call attention to the natural qualities lost to civilization by glorifying the peoples of Tahiti. But Edward Bellamy based his vision of the future on increased industrialization. *Looking Backward* was placed in the year 2000 to view the compulsory conscription of labor for a state enterprise which had eliminated poverty and created a satisfying life where the burdens and benefits are equally shared.

Francois Fourier's model eliminated the drudgery of work, but segregated workers by emotional tendencies in specially designed structures called phalanxes. His scheme emphasized decentralization and autonomy. Each individual was simultaneously capitalist, worker and consumer.

William Morris moved utopia from factory and barracks to a romanticized version of the English village. In a democratic anarchism, people worked only at agreeable activities; either there was a perfect fit of people to activities or some things did not get done. Decision making was completed locally with majority rule. People wore pleasing clothing and lived in comfortable buildings. The undesirable products of industry were neglected.

Utopias often emphasize a perfect social structure, without the dynamic aspects of a historical process. In the 1800s, however, utopias were considered as possible future societies, with a history. Karl Marx and Frederick Engels rejected utopias as being out of step with economic development; utopianism was considered as a naive, prescientific mode of thought. Marx dismissed utopian planning since the socialist utopia was on the way, regardless of intentions or plans. More modern writers have created other alternatives.

Although concerned for individual liberty, H.G. Wells advocated government centralization in his book *A Modern Utopia*. He concluded that utopia could only take place on a global scale. The global government was ruled by people reminiscent of Plato's philosopher-kings. Criminals and misfits were exiled to prison islands. Unfortunately, nature was regarded as unmanageable.

In Aldous Huxley's *Island*, the inhabitants have mastered the technological impulse and managed to live naturally. Their utopia, however, proved no match for the industrial expansion of the outside world. *Ecotopia*, by Ernst Callenbach, was a secessionist state in North America. A decentralized society tried to develop modes of social organization in balance with the natural environment, surrounded by industrial areas.

The number of bad places, dystopias, described since the sixteenth century has increased with the decline of the quality of life. Nicolas Berdiaev warned that utopias were more capable of realization now and that our problem was how to prevent them. The dreams of communist Russia, industrial United States and fascist Germany became nightmares. And, as Eugen Weber noted, those who have had nightmares are reluctant to dream further.

3.2.1.1. Utopian Inadequacies—General Characteristics
Utopias sometimes search outward or inward; some believe that utopia exists somewhere on new frontiers, for instance, with O'Neill's space colonies. An inward utopia is sought in the self, in the human quest for perfection. Most utopias deal with the same questions: What is society, how is it organized, what are its forces? How does it continue, or change? Plato questioned the best kind of social system in *The Republic*. Since then, many thinkers have dealt with the problem of political order, social stability, universal justice, and individual happiness. So little is known about any society that it seems futile to design whole societies. Most utopias would be unworkable and unsatisfactory.

Classical utopias were literally no place. They were anthropocentric and ignorant of ecological restraints, technological consequences and historical trends. Most of them dealt exclusively with technological change and material wealth. In fact, society and nature were interpreted by physical metaphors. Utopian city plans from Plato to O'Neill have been perfectly mathematical. Perhaps they could exist only in a desert. Plato's vision, echoed in Wells and others, had its roots in the first cities of the Near East. Mumford claimed that in fact cities were machines powered by conscripted labor, whose power to transform mud and rock into edifices captivated the imagination. The archetypal image of the city, and utopia, is characterized by hierarchy, rigidity and coercion. Mumford feared that all ideal models had the same life-arresting or life-denying property: Static order.

Utopian laws were usually traditional or arbitrary and not concerned with the laws of nature. Early philosophical utopias ignored ecological factors and considered only ethical and social relationships. Even at this, no utopias were multiracial and multicultural. The best was unfit for human habitation compared to the simplest life in tribal society. Idealistic designs for peace lacked a theory of change, and were based on an ethos antithetical to balanced conflict.

Utopian design concepts have been harmed by other basic defects: No concept of transition linking the present to the future; and, a solution by replication of local power-authority concentrations on a global level. An adequate conception of social justice is crucial to utopian planning; attention needs to be given to rights of all members. Refuse disposal has been a major limitation on human progress, and one of the problems confronting utopian thinkers.

Utopias provide images of ideal societies in abstract settings—literally nowhere. Utopias promise newness, order, happiness, and re-inheritance for the disinherited. They banish the irrational, the irreparable, and all conflict. Common ideas can be discerned in a reading of utopias:

- The quest for human perfectibility—the dismissal of social causes of disharmony—through constant attempts at self-improvement;
- The emphasis on order—the elimination of chaotic, uncoordinated, accidental events that cause waste and conflict—in a predictable society with planning and control;
- Universal fellowship, which is brought into being by removing barriers to harmony, such as private property;
- The expansion of consciousness with new, cohesive rituals; creation of new social forms—often a radical departure from old conditions, with plastic variance in all aspects of life from diets to dyads;
- Location outward in a distant place, an island or space colony, or time or inward frame of mind.

The common characteristics of many utopias, however, make them unworkable and unsatisfactory. Utopias tend to be ungrounded, static, teleological, ingenuous, simplistic, homogenous, and incomplete.

3.2.1.1.1. Utopia is Ungrounded

Utopias are literally no-place. They do not exist in place, either a human place or an ultrahuman place. They are designed to be no-place, without weeds, storms, or hard ground. Because they are nowhere, utopias lack any reference point. Because utopias are not grounded, their ideal qualifies do not have to fit together; any combination of details is possible, regardless of whether it ever could work together.

3.2.1.1.2. Utopia is Static

Utopias present a static order. Many utopian plans emphasize the physical order of a model city, a perfect design centered in a mathematical space. The perfection of the social structure of the inhabitants reflects this ideal physical order. The utopia arises fully formed, not as the result of a historical process or of a dynamic movement, and so it shows no concept of transition. If the utopia operates at all, it does so without problems; everything is managed according to one plan. The interpretation of society and nature is limited by physical metaphors, especially those based on physical mechanics. The shape of the city and the development of the people are set and unchanging.

3.2.1.1.3. Utopia is Teleological
Utopias assume the possibility of human perfectibility. They present a final state of society, where perfection has been achieved. The characters, who are symbols and not inhabitants of a place, lack a psychological dimension because the irrational, the internal conflict, and the irreparable have been banished from the ideal and from the brains of the characters. Human happiness is determined by reason and intention in a single, inflexible, final order. A utopia tends to impose a monstrous discipline on the activities and interests of the society.

3.2.1.1.4. Utopia is Ingenuous
In order to eliminate uncertainty, many utopias construct one ideal community of immense size as the model for all communities. Utopias tend to be centralized. H. G. Wells, in seeking to protect individual liberty through government centralization, concluded that utopia could only take place on a global scale, ruled by an international government of Platonic philosopher-kings. The subjects naively would derive their identity from the global structure. Some utopias tend to universalize the best of a society, so that all societies may fit the mold. To ensure continuation of the best, they rely on segregation to resolve social difficulties. For example, Fourier segregated workers according to emotional tendencies, while Wells exiled criminals and misfits to prison islands. Furthermore, nature in utopias has been regarded usually as unmanageable, by Wells for instance, or totally manageable, by Saint-Simon in another instance. Waste is not considered. Good, however, is considered unlimited—the metaphor of unlimited good, however, leads to devaluation and waste.

3.2.1.1.5. Utopia is Simplistic
Utopian laws are often simple and arbitrary and not concerned with the laws of nature; they try to comprehend, predict, and control human behavior on the basis of a materialistic philosophy. Utopias deny the depth and complexity of social, biological, and even physical problems in emphasizing a simple model. The excesses of geography are removed; utopias are rarely cold or too hot or too wet or too dry—the very places that are still wilderness on the planet. They remove the "useless" and unfriendly animals and plants. Utopias neglect the element of chance, in the form of earthquakes, fires, comets, and most natural disturbances. Most utopias ignore the problem of scale. What can be done on a small or imaginary scale may not be possible on a large scale; there are simply too many factors and connections. Ubiquitous problems, like hunger or illiteracy, are considered wrongly as global problems; and, they are usually coupled together.

3.2.1.1.6. Utopia is Homogenous
The creators of utopias conceive of their inhabitants as one people, with a common color or temperament, regardless of real social, cultural, or biological

differences. Clothing and housing are often uniform. With undifferentiated growth, the monocultural mass produces beauty and satisfaction for everyone. Nothing like this seems to have happened in mass societies, although monumental and heroic structures have been produced. A utopia uses its central technological, political, or moral theme to solve all problems; thus, all problems in a typical utopia are solved if every member of society has a radio, commits to be a communist, or acts like a Buddhist.

3.2.1.1.7. Utopia is Incomplete
Other societies have been ignored in utopias, except as examples of errors of thought or false images. Utopias have been blatantly anthropocentric in their concerns. Hence, utopian topics include industrialization, modernization, food capacity, housing, population explosion, and material possessions, but not the presence of foreigners, the necessity of wilderness or the rights of animals. Nature is regarded most often as an object of conquest or a storehouse of resources than as a mutually-created matrix.

3.2.1.2. Goals & Failed Designs
Regardless of how ineffectual utopias seem, they express human truths, for instance, 'with voluntary cooperation, state compulsion is unnecessary' stated William Morris. They present new possibilities, such as 'welfare through science,' thought Francis Bacon, or the recovery of lost 'natural qualities,' believed Denis Diderot. And, they have the power to transform society, as could be done by the rational state, according to John Locke, or the classless society, predicted Karl Marx.

Utopias are not just irrelevant fantasies; they have guided many of our modern qualities. For instance, contemporary industrial culture has mimicked utopian models in allowing for the interchangeability of people and places. Like utopias, modern industrial landscapes are flatscapes where variety disappears and significance is ignored for the comfortable standards of meaningless continuity. The characteristics of industrial cultures bear a strange resemblance to the characteristics of utopias, from simplification to ingenuousness, homogeneity, and incompleteness.

3.2.2. *Implications of Good & Evil*
The public gets used to messages of doom, but there are evils that survive identification in the light, and yet go on, like the reification or deification of money or war. Simple codes divide the world into good and evil too neatly, whether in the Christian bible or Reagonomic policy. The world is not simple, alas, and goodness does not grow like tomatoes. By trying to focus on either extreme, of pure goodness or pure evil, we miss the ambiguity and uncertainty of situations, most of which occur in a mixture. Our ethics and ideologies are not composed to help us live in a mixture, with the inevitability of uncertainty, or with the possibility of enantiodromia (a thing turning into its opposite).

Humans usually distinguish unambiguously between good and bad; most ethics intend to further the good and suppress evil. We search for essential difference between good and evil in vain, because the constituents are the same. The distinction lies in the way the pieces are assembled, the structure. The universe is comprised of good and evil, that is, it is agathokakological. Everything seems to work by complementary opposites. Not all good things go together in the same category, exclusive of all evil things. The attempt to isolate the good accelerates enantiodromia and can actually create evil.

Good can be defined as intention and action in the context of the rules of a culture, using ambiguous signs creatively. A sign is anything that signifies something other than itself. Signs are arbitrary, according to Ferdinand de Saussure, that is to say, they have no necessary connection to things. When we set goals, as for the goodness of our forestry practices or charitable institutions, we base those on the meaning of the symbols, which can have many more than one meaning.

Signs make many connections to physical events, thus intensifying them as well as miniaturizing the events in the signs. Signs become dense with meaning. Patterns are available to the mind, and the reality of patterns emerges from events and becomes as real. But, also a reality that can be extended. The play of signs results in good or evil; that is to say, the manipulation of signs, in a field of surprise, due to other levels of meaning, can be interpreted as good or evil.

Culture provides rules that limit play, so that it stops short of death or destruction. Games have rules. All cultures work that way. Ethics and economics are rules of behavior; politics is the practice of changing the rules as society changes. Politics, however, is changed by scale from good to evil; there are too many of us in each system to share discourse. This is much more so on an international level.

The rules of a culture can be expressed in signs or words in the context of the culture. A shift in context can change the meaning of a word. We do not think of physical events, such as gravity or fusion, as good or bad; they simply are. A physical movement is turned into action in the human realm by human intention, which is open to interpretation and ambiguity. Signal play without cultural structures can result in evil.

Words have meaning because of their shared history and context, by their place in a whole language, which adds to meaning of the word. The combination of words in a conversation, with body language and intent, are more important than individual words. The dialogue process helps get past dualities such as good or evil. Metaphor and humor lend new clarity.

In having good as a goal, we cannot calculate the result. Good is a feature of the path of actions, as is evil. We cannot aim at it and shoot, or even stare at it. We must approach sideways, through a field of good and evil. This is one thing a conversation can do, or a poetic series of statements: Let us approach sideways.

3.2.2.1. The Possibility of Good
Good is an interesting word, with a long history. The current version is derived from the old English word, *god*, meaning suitable or fitting, similar to the words meaning a 'suitable time' and to be 'pleasing.'

Humans cannot know, or even think of anything, according to Robert

Zajonc, without some involvement of emotion, that is, at least a vague feeling of good or bad. Good is problematic. The search for good is measured by personal criteria, personal judgment, and personal reflection. On the other hand, there are questions of what one *ought* to do, that is, morality. Good and bad mean different things to different people. Your standards or codes might be different from mine. Therefore the meanings of the words will be different. Furthermore, doing bad to one person sometimes results in good for others, or vice versa. Sometimes, just to feel good, people destroy the works of others, or living beings, or an entire ecosystem.

I still have trouble deciding between good and bad (or evil) personally. I have no doubt that when I do more good, more bad is also created. For instance, when I started trying to restore my forest, that is, the forest that owns me, the best knowledge at the time insisted that I should clean the fallen trees out of the stream and remove flammable brush and woody debris from the forest floor. I started to do this in a beautiful cedar grove, but I spent too much time sitting on the ground looking at the trees—I could blame Artemis, goddess of forests, solitude, young girls, and the hunt, for possessing me, I suppose. Then, scientific knowledge advanced, and I was advised to drop trees into the stream and leave all the woody debris and brush. Had a been less contemplative, or lazy, I would now have much more work to do, to undo the previous good. Was what I did good? Then or now? Do I need more training to determine what is good or bad? Is the failure to do the good of now, then, bad? Did I fail from ignorance or conflicting intentions? That is one problem with ecosystem management today: Which action is good? Which is bad? Which should we do? In an organic world, good things are defined by a free interplay of energies.

In the long run, as John Fowles suggests, maybe all our judgments of good and bad are meaningless. All actions, good or bad, interweave so extensively as time passes that their individual goodness or badness disappears. Each becomes lost in the other. One should do good for one's health, for instance, or the health of the forest community, not because the action is an action or for the sake of doing something good. In doing, we choose between good and bad actions; the judgment makes us human and susceptible to error. We just have to be aware that choosing good can result sometimes in its opposite, through enantiodromia.

3.2.2.2. The Necessity of Evil

Evil is a disintegration, a juxtaposition of opposites, with some parts striving to suppress others. Good is the synthesis and reconciliation of the same parts. In ancient Hebrew, good and evil is a single word meaning 'everything.' Everything is disintegrating and synthesizing all the time. Disintegration is necessary to the process. We are aware of values as conflicts tear us; we can reconcile values in just proportions to resurrect whole body.

3.2.2.2.1. Size and Evil

Humans became more and more prone to alter the earth, because of an increase in the human population and in the means of destruction, not necessarily because of a change in attitude. Both American Plains Indians and Africans exhibited this change in their situations. Indians, for example, used the newly acquired horse and gun to become more efficient, and careless, hunters. Although our behavior may not be qualitatively different from our remote ancestors and the worst pathologies of wild animals, which usually result from miscommunications under certain circumstances, it is quantitatively different. More and more activities affect larger and larger parts of the planet; many problems have global effects now.

In tropical areas in the past, people practiced land use that permitted the vegetation to maintain itself despite human exploitation and the constraints of soil and climate. With population and production pressures, tropical areas everywhere are rapidly being exploited. The consequences may be disastrous.

Size is almost always the greatest threat. In spite of the fact that many Buddhists planted trees regularly, the Buddhist traditions of wooden temples and funeral fires contributed to the denuding of large areas of forest. It is our misfortune to live at a time when the accumulated effects of the conversion of nature for human ends are becoming obvious and cutting into the survival potentials of many other species.

3.2.2.2.2. Perfect Separation and Evil

From medieval times, scientists found that glass could separate materials and distill liquids. Astronomers and microscopes found that glass could be shaped to focus light waves to reveal the very small and the very distant. Portions of the universe were placed behind glass in a laboratory world. Glass was very useful. Scientists came to rely on its advantages, but they were unconsciously imprisoned by its limits.

As science cut the connection to direct observation, it became as blind as mathematics to the 'outer' world. The formality of science made statements about the outer world tautological. This proved to be a problem with quanta, species fitness, and psychological needs. Scientific hypotheses form filters like glasses. They cannot be shed entirely, but their effects can be understood.

Glass has advanced our civilizations by permitting the easy separation of fluids and reactions. But, it leads to an objective attitude towards living beings and nature. Being "behind glass" has become the metaphor, first for a scientific approach to knowledge, then for a utilitarian ethics and a teleological ethics. Only recently, in theoretical physics and in ecology, has it been realized that there can be no perfect detachment and objectivity. There can be no perfect insulation from the object of study.

Scientists have experimented with biological processes behind glass (*in vitro*) in the laboratory. The primary commandment of Jacque Monod's ethic of objectivity is observers should not participate in the workings of the world. But, detachment from nature is detachment from the basis of knowledge. We distance ourselves behind glass. This detachment is the greatest threat to the welfare of nature. It permits the vivisection of the "voices of existence," as Neil Evernden warns.

We have created a hard glass between the mind projecting and the object receding. Sometimes we doubt if there is anything on the other side that can be seen. Glass also forms a window for consciousness, which swamps the mind with the 'error of the eye,' in Marshall McCluhan's phrase. Vision, whose mode is successive and not simultaneous, is emphasized and split away from the total sensorium. After human consciousness places the glass, human needs shape and tint the glass. Utilitarianism casts a thick, convex glass, to focus on the individual. Romantics use a tinted, concave glass, the better to see the whole.

The evolution of human mentality has put us all behind glass. We use glass to protect ourselves from the ambiguity and messiness of nature. We have made an experiment of ourselves; our mentality has evolved behind glass. We have isolated ourselves by technology. We have seen more on television, but are moved to do less. C.P. Snow has commented that watching deaths by starvation in Africa on television screens could mark the end of any moral community of humanity.

We are behind glass and fear it will break. Augustine remarked to the Romans: "What glory is there in the largeness of empire, bright and brittle like glass, and forever in fear of breaking." Reason alone cannot cure what it caused. Glass cannot divide humanity and nature; nor can we humanize the planet without dehumanizing ourselves. We can put things and beings behind glass, but we lose them. Relationships are so strange and complex that they cannot be understood behind glass. The glass creates an illusion of objectivity. Being behind glass allows us to pretend that we are separate; this pretense allows evil. We need to break the glass. We need a sanctified vision of life from a deep participation.

3.2.2.2.3. Freedom and Evil

Freedom is a description of possibilities. Freedom allows many values and behaviors, but not necessarily all. Freedom is considered the opposite of determination. Most theorists are worried that freedom would be denied in any modern utopia or dystopia. Both Fritz Schumacher and Eugene Odum refute this in numerous arguments. Some freedom is needed to realize human potential. A right amount is needed; and this amount can be determined ecologically and ethically.

But, in addition, one must understand that existence is already half determined; freedom and necessity must be balanced at about fifty percent (compare with the fifty percent redundancy requirement in information theory). Too much freedom, the refusal to acknowledge what is determined, would inflict the self-determination of each on the self determination of the many, resulting in social chaos, and reducing other freedoms. Too little freedom, the refusal to acknowledge what can be done, results in stagnation. Recognition of the laws of nature is what allows the only real freedom within them. We do not eat poisonous plants, or breath water, for instance, although both can be done with adequate preparations.

3.2.2.2.4. Knowledge and Evil

Knowledge increases our opportunities, that is, our freedom; we pay for freedom with the risks of mistakes. Knowledge is power and power can possess its owner. Humans have the power to alter vast processes in nature, and not enough care to refrain from trying. Even if we know better, we must care to act with concern for others.

Once we become aware that the unintended byproducts of industry are harmful to a species population, then the destruction of that species becomes an intention if we do not alter our behavior. Destruction is then a matter of choice and responsibility rather than ignorance.

3.2.2.2.5. Intention and Evil

The first act of a utopia must be to come to terms with the evil seeds of good intentions. Evil can arise because of the contradictory nature of reality, the nature in which all institutions subvert the values for which they are founded; all values seem to be achieved in conflict with opposites. Does evil come out of our efforts to do good? Developed nations are in a double bind in dealing with famines: If we do not feed starving people, they will die; but, if we do feed them, more will die later, unless they have renewed their crops or reduced their populations.

The process by which a movement turns into its exact opposite has been identified as a swing of reversal; romanticism rejected industrialization, but became mechanized. The German attempt to unite Europe left it divided. The line curves upon itself. The rise of ecological consciousness is an offshoot of the space program's view of the planet. Values too strenuously proclaimed often go to their opposite.

Aid is an illustrative example of this kind of swing. Basing foreign aid on a belief in spurring industrial development is a tragedy. The second outcome of a massive distribution of food to poorer countries is often a depression of local agriculture. Common-sense solutions to some problems just worsen the problem. Michael Gordon illustrates the pitfall of half-hearted help.[11] Aid can be the prime cause of suffering that it is intended to relieve, increasing the sum of human misery. Medicine and infant care can be cruel, if the infants are neglected later. Aid humiliates the receiving country, Gordon says, and corrupts or angers the donor country. But the innocent suffer with the guilty. The alternative can be greater starvation a few years later. Aid as a program for action is incomplete and too simplistic. Schumacher stipulates that the best aid that could be offered is intellectual.

The editors of *The Ecologist* are even more radical in their recommendation: In view of the psychological and material debacles thus far, no aid at all is best. Even intellectual aid is questionable; our ideas and inventions may not even be applicable. Now, with our proliferation of information, especially concerning products like cars, vacuums, clothes, and grooming devices, we raise people's aspirations without satisfying any of them.

The author H.G. Wells invented the idea of futurism, predicting and planning a culture for future global development. "The future cannot be predicted, but can be invented," according to Dennis Gabor. The first step in inventing is to learn everything possible about the past and the present and then try to identify those possibilities that may be realized and then to choose from among those possibilities to invent a desirable future.

Karl Marx realized that ideas become a material force when they take hold of minds of people. But, first the ideas must be formed. We may remake our part of the earth, which is part of a solar system, which is part of a galaxy of over 100 billion stars in an archipelago of galaxies. If we are unable to create a place here, the fault will probably be, to paraphrase Shakespeare through Cassius, in ourselves, and not in the stars.

3.2.2.3. The Tragic Species
Or why humans will not change—even to save themselves. Human beings have been very successful at monopolizing nature for themselves and their own purposes. This very success, however, may lead eventually to failure, as the tactics that worked so well in an uncrowded world rich in resources are applied to a humanized world with immediate limits. As the Greeks recognized, success can lead to failure and to tragedy.

3.2.2.3.1. Theatrical Tragedy
In defining tragedy in terms of its formal characteristics and emotional effect, Aristotle characterized it as "the imitation of an action that is serious and also, as having magnitude, complete in itself; in language with pleasurable accessories, i.e., rhythm and harmony, each kind brought in separately in the parts of the work, i.e., some in verse, others in song, in a dramatic, not a narrative form; with incidents arousing pity and fear, wherewith to accomplish its catharsis of such emotions." For Aristotle, tragedy was the mimesis of a good or noble action.

In a theatrical play, the tragic hero triumphs at first, and incorporates the successful behavior that led to the triumph. This behavior, employed in new circumstances, then leads to disaster. Hence, the failure to give up a chosen role or pattern of behavior leads to great loss.

Disaster results from breaking of the principle of temperance (*sophrosyne*), or "nothing in excess." Reversal (*peripeteia* in Greek), the change of a situation to its opposite, is an important plot mechanism. When the principle of temperance fails, the actor sees "the transformation of his action into its opposite." This antinomy illustrates the Heraklitean notion of the return swing of the pendulum (*enantiodromia*); human ideals seem to swing back and forth in dynamic opposition. In Greek tragedy, a single element of value grows cancerously and destroys the whole. The Greek tragedy showed the process by which absolute values swing through reversal to their opposites. But the anomalies in tragedy called for a creative response—a higher level of moral awareness born from the dialectical union of opposites, especially for the wise observer.

Virtue is steering between the intellect and impulse. Folly is a misjudgment in combining values, missing the just proportions. The tragic error in Greek theater is a mistake of being in an evil predicament. Oedipus did not sin—he was caught in contradictory circumstances.

The fundamental notions of tragedy are hubris and nemesis: Hubris is an arrogance that arises from a form of blindness, and nemesis is the eventual consequence. The hero builds up an interpretation of events that conforms to her ideal. Hubris leads to a decision made on the basis of the hero's mistaken interpretation of circumstances; the decision leads to ruin. The quality of irony brings with recognition of the situation a decree of necessity. The hero recognizes her ideas in terms of laws. This is purgation. The Greek tragic hero was a typical man or woman isolated and projected onto a larger background of fate. Theatrical tragedy stresses the price of consciousness.

Joseph Meeker judges that the tragic view of life, as embodied in Greek tragedy, is based on a deep conviction that humanity has no part in nature, that human behavior must conform to moral laws that are extranatural. This view also assumes human superiority over nature. Obviously, an assumption of human superiority would cause conflict.

Humanity can still be a part of nature, however, and still be tragic. Even if moral laws are natural. Tragedy is more than an ethical conflict. Tragedy can imply conflicts larger than the individual or even society. Ernest Becker claims that the tragedy of evolution is that evolution produced a limited animal with unlimited horizons. For him, tragedy is wanting an earth that is perfect, a heaven abstracted from imperfection, a utopia, perhaps. Of course, the swing of the pendulum ensures that humans cannot create a perfect place. In the sense of employing a successful strategy in all circumstances, perhaps natural selection in evolution is tragic, the tragedy of reality—Michael W. Fox and Garrett Hardin hold this view. Modern science is one-sided or single-visioned, in denying poetic and other kinds of knowledge. The attempt to avoid the pendulum, enantiodromia, without understanding the operation of nature, ends in tragedy.

The definitions of tragedy can be linked to the cosmology of a culture, the image of the place of humanity in the universe. Tragedy challenges the external order of things, the cosmos, even if the cosmos is only the size of a city (*polis*). The fatal flaw if the individual is the fatal flaw of the world-view of the individual. This is the root of Hardin's Tragedy of the Commons—people are locked into a system of self-interest through economic gain without being bound by traditional rules for sharing or cooperating. Hardin's own definition of tragedy is "the working of fate." But, this kind of tragedy results from a failure of cosmology; humans are responsible ultimately, not fate or chance. Humans are tragic because they are responsible for their actions. They can choose a tragedy of the commons or of dictatorial control—or they can expand or alter their cosmology.

3.2.2.3.2. The Human Comedy

In *The Birth of Tragedy*, Frederich Nietzsche suggests that tragedy is dead. Meeker suggests that the moment after tragedy is a comic moment, where the actor steps out of tragic action, observes herself and her former universe, and laughs. The actor is then free of evil, restraint, body, and death. Laughter involves detachment, which is a fundamental form of freedom; freedom, according to Meeker, is the central value of comedy.

The comic actor tries to create a new and better universe, Meeker argues. The attempt is a celebration of human freedom. Farce, in opposing aging and death, affirms life through a comic recognition of the impossible. Comedy strives for freedom. The farcical hero demands the universe to be changed; the comic hero demands that society accommodate itself to his will; and the absurd hero sees the universe as a hoax and makes no demands. Comic heroes lack self-awareness—if they had that, the collision of will and act would be tragic. Comedy, however does not trivialize what is important, although it deflates what is overinflated.

The comic mode of behavior, as defined by Meeker, is a genuine affirmation of the instinctive patterns necessary for biological survival. Comedy is concerned with muddling through, not progress or perfection. Meeker argues that evolution shows all the flexibility of comic drama. Evolution is a 'shameful, opportunist comedy' whose object is the proliferation of life without regard to morals. The participants must adapt, diversify, and accommodate. He contends that events in tragic literature could not occur if comic principles are observed. Comedy encourages necessity and acceptance; tragedy avoids necessity to try to accomplish the impossible, Meeker claims. Comedy assumes that all choice is likely to be in error. To comedy, as in evolution, nothing is sacred but life itself.

Western images are tragic because death does not imply rebirth or living continuity. By comparison, Indian images of life are comic because death does imply rebirth, as rebirth implies further death. The comedy here depends on surprise—death is really an illusion. Immortality, however, is the shift of identity from an ego to the universe, the one universal rhythm that exists in all beings of all sizes. This is the Indian rhythm of the juggler, balancing worlds; and if one seems to fall and shatter, hundreds of new jugglers are born.

Cultural heroes, by contrast, represent cultural ideals. Cultural heroes are often mythical beings, of human birth, who restore the balance to the people. Unlike theatrical heroes, who precipitate a tragedy by not changing, cultural heroes change to avoid tragedy. For example, many Japanese heroes change their roles as the play develops. The hero becomes multifaceted— ferocious, then poetic, after success followed by loss. Many Japanese legendary heroes, like Yamako Takeru, have a time of success followed by failure from the application of the strategy that made them successful in the first place, quite similar to Greek tragic characters. This behavior is called the Nobility of Failure, *mono no arvare*, or the pathos of things.

3.2.2.3.3. The Nobility of Failure
Despite the arguments of Hardin and Meeker, evolution and ecology cannot be compared to comedy or tragedy, which are descriptions of the fitting of human images and behaviors to a changing environment. In the end, both comedy and tragedy encourage the acceptance of human limitation. Meeker emphasizes that comedy is immoral, like evolution, but he is wrong. Comedies of manners and types do have a lesson to teach: Moderation and control are affirmed, rascality and immorality are denied. High comedies show that the world is basically good and that evil is introduced by humans who lack control or moderation.

Tragedy proceeds by analogy and homogenous substitution in the rationalization of the hero. Events are controlled to be consistent with an idea; the direction of expansion is integration; and, it ends in cumulative catastrophe and purgation. Comedy proceeds by wide variation and heterogeneous substitution. Every action discovers inconsistency. Expansion is a phase of discrimination. Ideas have continual purgation. Comedy plays with the ideas that tragedy discovers. But, the play of ideas is hedged with the mystery of tragic issues.

Reason moves between tragic pain and comic disillusion. Comedy offers a rebirth as a solution. Tragedy also offers a way out, but it is through death. Tragedy confronts evil; comedy avoids it. In comedy, frames of reference collide and shatter harmlessly; in tragedy, the frames conflict.

Furthermore, the comic mode is an incomplete strategy for living. If the comic attitude is necessary for survival, then it must be moral, at least in the etymological sense of having rules for living together. The comic mode, as described by Meeker, cannot be reconciled with natural patterns of reproduction and death. But, life is no more sacred than rock or air. What Meeker has described is not comedy, which is an analog of complete freedom, which cannot ever occur, but compliance, that is, the acceptance of partial freedom and partial conflict. The reduction of behavior to a comic mode would be tragic, in the Socratic sense, because it would refuse just proportion; it would be single-sided.

A complete strategy must include ecosystems and other species, those systems and beings on which our lives depend. We have already made a start in considering them, as when we suggest that each species has a characteristic face. And, each face is capable of a variety of expressions: Fear, anger, humor, indifference. Thus, a bear may appear curious, a wolf noble, or a chimpanzee sad. These stereotypic expressions become as masks, although we risk fooling ourselves by limiting a species to one mask.

Human faces seem more dramatic to us, as evidenced in the Greek standards for tragedy and comedy—the two masks often displayed outside theaters. The mask is seen by an audience as tragic or comic. The mask offers a surprise. The surprise catches the hero or the audience, and the audience cries or laughs. The play is tragic or comic only from perspective—the difference between comedy and tragedy is in the point of view, not the subject matter. The mask of tragedy and comedy reflects this duality: The refusal or acceptance of the inevitable, detached indifference, comedy, or compassionate concern, tragedy. Both faces are combined in one mask.

From a cosmological perspective, there is no tragedy or comedy: Everything simply is. Thus, the human situation is tragic or comic to humans only; other species, ecosystems, and geological cycles will continue or not. Responsible human behavior may avoid human tragedy. As de Montaigne wrote: "Our great and glorious masterpiece is to live appropriately."

3.3. **The Potential of Somewhere: Eutopias as Real Places**

Most Utopian discussions have to do with places as literature or as literary alternatives to real world ecological and political situations. Marx and Engels criticize utopian thinkers for lacking a thorough analysis of power relations within a society, as well as of economic developments that bring about changes. Karl Popper criticizes utopian engineering for expecting to make massive changes that would affect the entire human society. He says, correctly, that our knowledge and experience are too limited to expect that such changes would benefit society and people. It is too limited; there are far too many uncertainties and risks.

Nevertheless, utopias serve a vital human need. One important and valuable aspect of utopias is their play with new ideas or combinations of ideas. The other sense of utopia, that of good places, should not remain silent. We need utopias to define visions for the future, but we need a different kind now, not the visions of no-places or of the wrong-places, but of good places—Eutopias.

In that sense, eutopias fits in the tradition of thought. The approach is both descriptive and prescriptive in novels, which allows readers to interiorize the system and appreciate the details of the life within. Eutopias is a thought experiment to apply real alternatives, derived from the baseline of cultural experiences, to the problem-ridden monolithic applications of industrial civilizations.

Utopias may be impossible, but good places are possible. Good places already exist everywhere. There is a place in Africa, by the northern Abderes in Kenya, where a stream winds its way through gardens and orchards, by low houses, and crowned cranes stalk between rows of vegetables; flocks and herds graze on fenced pastures, and wild animals fed nearby. Such places can be found in every place of the world. Perhaps by logically working out the limits and adaptability of humanity, good places can be created for almost everyone.

In totalitarian utopias, people must be controlled, the threat being that, without discipline there would be immediate disorder and the utopia would collapse. As we know, it is impossible to avoid disorder, which is a necessary part of any physical and social system. A system with flexibility, such as a eutopian system, could incorporate disorder without being destroyed.

Taking it cue from utopian writings, eutopias asks the broadest questions about society and the environment. Where would you like to live Urban or rural or mixed? How close to nearest large store? How often should your neighbors visit unannounced? Once a week, a month, always, never? What should your neighbors do? Be artists, scientists, laborers, game players, or be multi-faceted?

Rather than a single nonnegotiable truth, as would be imposed in Plato's *Republic*, the inhabitants of eutopias would "play" with truth. In fact, their education, taking cues from Schiller, would encourage play at all levels.

Culturally-based nations can provide a greater spectrum of intricate descriptions and possible relations than any one single thought experiment. That is why they need to be the basis of good-places-in-the-making. The framework is enriched by the ideals and visions of nations. This is consistent with the intuitive knowledge that many styles of life are sustainable.

This is where eutopias would work effectively: Accepting the unpredictable nature of natural and social processes, yet managing adaptively on a micro-planning level. Eutopias would incorporate tradition and working past elements, rather than breaking with them. As Edmund Burke, reflecting on the French Revolution, notes that society has gone through a natural process of development, forming traditions and institutions that provide rules of behavior known to the people. We tend to forget how much discipline already exists in every society. People abide by most rules, from driving on one side of the road to preserving their children from molestation.

In eutopias, it is important to work with what exists, with what has already worked in place, with history and culture. Eutopias can start in California, Sri Lanka or any place that can support a nationhood aligned with a cultural history, without having a standard army or special currency.

The eutopian vision would start with immediate needs for everyone, but then allow people to be as extravagant as they want within the general social limits. Most people like the place they live, and they like their culture, so it is not necessary to force them to stay in place or be what they are. That does not mean that they do not want to live better, just that they do not all want to be Swiss or U.S. citizens.

Despite the eloquent pleas of Wendell Berry and Gary Snyder, that people ought to stay put and put down roots in a home place, we may not want to base the frame of eutopias on that idea. People have been nomads for a longer time than farmers or city dwellers. It might be better to accept that movement and dislocation is part of the harmony of life and try to minimize the negative effects, especially combined with consumerism and energy waste. The civilization of cultures is not a steady state, but it can be accommodated in a flexible framework. Flexibility is an important eutopian characteristics, along with resilience, adaptivity, and surprise—that is danger; Callenbach recognized that in his *Ecotopia*—places need to offer excitement and danger.

A new model may solve some problems but will definitely create new problems; Niccolo Machiavelli reasoned that this would always happen. This is a good argument for eutopias, since changes would occur mostly on a small scale, easily correctable. That is why eutopias can be a framework, by limiting human evil and good to small places, with minimal control or competition.

There is no single model of government that will fit all cultures, all traditions, all needs or all nations. But, governments can be held to common standards through an international body. Eutopias tries to structure the global commonwealth of nations by proposing specific common goals, regarding weapons disbursement and population limits. It offers a consideration of distributive justice among nations and between the generations of every nation. It offers visions of culturally-based nations in equilibrium with nature, using ideas from ecological design and conservation biology.

The eutopian framework is more than is a simple perspective; it is a design for a self-renewing process using proven cultural methods to improve human situations and environments. The frame is not a final goal but a way to allow the many small useful, culturally determined (or limited) changes that we need for our survival on the planet as we like it.

Eutopias is a cheap solution because it uses the parts already in place. It is within reach of any people in any culture, regardless of how fast or technological. And, because it limits the ways of big, expensive solutions.

Eutopias is not a big law; but, it is a big story, large enough to allow all other stories. It is changing and open-ended. It is conservative, but that becomes an instrument to create peace and justice everywhere. It keeps human rights connected with species rights and land rights.

Eutopias is a framework that holds all the other pieces of solutions and makes them part of a whole thing. It helps us to understand the whole thing, the whole set of relations with people, land, and other beings, with other cultures and the ranges of technology. Eutopias is a framework that holds many centers, beginning with the centers of different human cultures and including the centers of nonhuman communities and guilds.

Eutopias has to address the whole, because the health of the whole depends on the health of the wholes that make it up—the health of wildernesses, the health of civilizations, and the health of ecosystems, that is, inhabited places that are made through living.

4.3.2.4.3. Wooing the Earth

From Tagore, Rene Dubos takes the heroic love-adventure of humankind to be the wooing of the Earth. The wooing of the earth is both sweet and sour; sweet because humans can create enchantment within nature, and sour because they can spoil desirable places—possibly to the point of ruining nature's recovery mechanisms. The wooing of earth implies more than converting wilderness into humanized environments. It also means preserving natural environments in which to experience mysteries transcending daily life and from which to recapture an awareness of the natural forces that have shaped humanity.

Dubos celebrates the human ability to woo the earth by creating new environments that are "ecologically sound, aesthetically satisfying, economically rewarding, and favorable to the continued growth of civilization." While that is noble and just, and realistic, there are two erroneous assumptions contained therein. First, civilization does not have to grow to develop, and it is development that is important, not growth, which is plainly unfeasible. Second, "to woo" means to solicit love or to make love; Dubos assumes we will remake nature in our image. And love, as everyone should know, entails respect or reverence. It does not remake the loved one in one's image, it respects and allows freedom. That is the larger meaning. We should "improve" on nature where we live, but we do not need to improve on all of nature. We do not need to domesticate all beings for human use. Joseph Krutch recognized that ecology without reverence or love is only shrewder exploitation.

We can create places only by living there; by slowly adjusting all to all. Human modifications of earth can be lastingly successful only if their effects are adapted to the invariants of human and physical nature. Ecological management can be effective only if it takes into consideration the visceral and spiritual values that link us to the earth. Although some of nature can be regarded as a garden to be cultivated, large areas should be preserved as untouched reserves or necessary systems for global balance. Other areas could be studied or urbanized as population centers. Our tendency to redesign nature, rather than tolerate and cherish, is dangerous; it leads to "curing" abnormal people and "solving" weed problems. We do not respect the wild, complex side of human nature.

4.3.3. *Making Good Society in Place: Characteristics of Good Societies*

Because the characteristics of good societies depend on the characteristics of good ecosystems and good places, good ecosystems and places have to be preserved.

Stable, good societies must pass the social institutions to a new generation, but without sacrificing everything for posterity. The traditional object of economics is the administration of scarce resources; this needs to be extended to a line of generations. There is the question of the quality of life from one generation to the next; possibly the distribution of a dowry to all succeeding generations

4.3.3.1. Method as a Characteristic of a Good Society

Because human beings exist as part of the natural order, the characteristics and principles that underlie good societies also underlie ecosystems. Method is such a characteristic and it allows the development of society through differentiation and recombination. It allows the development of society through the use of energy and self-maintenance. Growth, for instance, allows society to avoid stagnation or collapse, although only for a time, then it has to split or adjust its size through emergency measures. Feedback, positive or negative, is method for society to adjust to various natural or social limits. Feedback can allow a society to deconstruct or reconstruct itself as it progresses. Society has to weave a course between its successful competition to support and renew itself and its tendency to overdevelop and destroy its habitat and place.

Human societies in place use methods to create their societies and these methods have characteristics based on the characteristics of files, ecosystems, and good places, such as process, change, course, conduct, and action. Methods are the motors of change that drive the development of societies. Methods may conflict or fit together but their action causes human bonds to be more flexible. Method addresses the efficacy of society; it is method that can fragment the image of or world or place and reduce fitness. It is method that can work up appropriate beliefs and behaviors. Methods of observation, for instance, can determine what is seen or important. Methods of behavior can lead into the character of the society. The world and society are accessible through methods of describing, analyzing or synthesizing. A poor method can lead to the fragmentizing of society or nature.

A method is a way of doing something or the regularity and orderliness of the actions of doing (from the Greek words for 'pursuing a way'). Goethe said that 'the methodology of forms is the methodology of transformations.' Goethe attempted to use his method to produce an organic and morphological world-history. This methodology is part of nature. It reflects nature. Rilke wonders whether or not all the dynamics of nature, including those of human society, are hieroglyphics of the methodology of thinking. Early science saw the world as mechanism; modern biology is seeing it as resembling an organism; perhaps it will be seen as spirit or as a composite of all. Science accepts the sentience of plant life, but does not adjust its methods. Human knowledge grants emotions to animals, but uses them badly anyway. We turn inward from the earth, for human purposes. The scientific method multiplied human dividends with the industrial revolution, but it destroyed the fabric it was examining. New ways of thinking are being developed in terms of instructions and normative modes, and that these are beginning to provide methodologies capable of achieving the necessary, challenging tasks.

4.3.3.2. Self-extension as a Characteristic of a Good Society

The characteristic of self-extension, and its corollary ideas, uniqueness, design and centering, emerges from the characteristics of good human places, ecosystems, and the field: Individuality, Self-extention, Ordering, Identity, Boundedness, Autopoesis, Wholeness, Form, and Uniqueness. It is those characteristics modified by adaptation and ethics.

The individual extends far beyond the skin. Extent can be more than just in space. People extend themselves in time by planning for their heirs. The extensions are connections, not only physical connections but intention as well. Extending the place into other ecosystems allows nature do the work. Whitehead seems to find it necessary to divide the cosmic process into two characteristics, extensiveness and aim. Extensiveness means that the process is spread through space and goes on in time. In fact, he considers extensiveness more basic than the arbitrary factors of four dimensions or "electromagnetic laws". Extensiveness is the binding of the physical world by relatedness.

4.3.3.3. Variety as a Characteristic of a Good Society

The characteristic of variety, and its corollary ideas, valuation, consciousness, and self-analysis, emerges from the characteristics of good human places, ecosystems, and the field: Richness, Challenge, Diversity, Openness, Flexibility, Difference, Discretion, and Limit. It is modified by adaptation and ethics.

Flexibility is potential for changer within a system. Variety provides flexibility in systems. Flexibility is needed to correct our mistaken allegiance to the machine image of life. If we survive then we need to always preserve more flexibility for future mistakes. As we know, it is impossible to avoid disorder, which is a necessary part of any physical and social system. A system with flexibility can incorporate disorder without being destroyed. What barriers are there to renewing institutional flexibility? or restoring ecosystem flexibility.

The realization of hard realities does not mean a return to a dark age. We will have more flexibility if we choose our way, and salvage much of the industrial revolution. Natural systems are characterized by resiliency and flexibility, and high productivity, too. We need efficiency, but a higher efficiency—an efficiency in life, not one department of life. There must be a positive flexibility; potentials not used must be preserved for future use to accommodate dead ends, mistakes, or change.

Civilization will have to follow a circuitous route, practicing rigorous self-discipline and economy, more than if we had started earlier. There must be far fewer people than now; the mess and heat generated by vast multitudes will always be ruled out by the natural laws within which all things function.

Zonal diversity can be used to develop different resource production systems in a local area. This increases the likelihood that production will fluctuate nonsynchronously so that support for human populations is constant. Of course, keeping flexibility and reserves could have the same effect. By forming a complex society, the scale of production is raised from a local group in limited territory to a regional population in diverse territories. Even hunter/gatherers engage in similar "energy averaging" systems. A smaller size could mean more flexibility and faster response to local conditions.

Plans can be made within the limits of variables, although it is not safe to be limited by lethal variables, as Gregory Bateson recognized; closeness to limits reduces flexibility, that is, uncommitted potential for change.

4.3.3.4. Cooperation as a Characteristic of a Good Society

The characteristic of cooperation, and its corollary ideas, awareness, complexity, intensity, and patterning, emerges from the characteristics of good human places, ecosystems, and the field: Conviviality, Adaptation, Awareness, Intensity, Development, Complexity, Participation, Integration, Connection, and Infolding. It is modified by adaptation and ethics.

Cooperation implies convivial or appropriate technology. The word convivial means social, from the Latin word "convivium," meaning living together. Ivan Illich, in *Tools for Conviviality*, sketches a meaningful community where workers have control of their tools and their lives.

There would be a selective reduction of industrialism. Large industry might still be needed for certain things, such as televisions or computers, but the technology of the future must be valid for all peoples for all time. There should be a proper mix of handicraft labor, intermediate technology and heavy industry. Economics would become characterized by friendship and cooperation. The root problem is how to live with technology in a mature manner. We need an ecological awareness at all levels; a human, existential ecology, where humanity is part of system, with an awareness of awareness.

There is no reason not to develop complex instruments to monitor and analyze the environment. Machines do not need to be dismantled. Technological developments are more easily assessed by a small, self-supportive community, where they are not necessary. Necessity was not the mother of invention; curiosity was. And curiosity needs time, not pressure. Small communities could use sophisticated but unobtrusive technology. Evolution occurs in small populations, demes, in which a mutation has taken place. Thompson claims the metaindustrial village is such a deme. With desk-top computers and microfiche libraries, satellite and cable television, advanced science would be possible in the most rural setting. Kohr states that small firms have been shown to be more productive as separate entities.

Human power is found to be incredibly wasted by nonproductive ways. By giving technology a human face, Schumacher proposed that directly productive time in our society should be tripled, at least. Engaging in real work, as opposed to busy work, would be of tremendous therapeutic and educational values to workers. In tandem with the Intermediate Technology Group, of which he is a part, he advocates production by the masses to replace mass production. This group, ITG, complements another headed by Victor Papanek, as described in *Design for the Real World*, that has invented technologies appropriate for underdeveloped areas, capable of making everything from televisions to automobiles. Schumacher believes that 3rd world development can only be possible with appropriate technology. In order to be applicable, such technology must maximize opportunities for the unemployed, without trying for a maximum output per worker, as is the case in highly industrial countries. Increase value on labor by one-to-one with product. Productivity will go down, but quality will go up.

A biotechnology would function most effectively at the lowest levels of society, by being comprehensible by the poor. It would be based on ecological and economic realities, and it would permit local economies in local communities with a minimum of financial support.

The main concern of intervention into nature is productivity and efficiency, measures of economic perfection and reward, but the end products produce profound changes on the quality of human life and environment. But these changes can be diminished with new methods of production, new patterns of consumption and new life styles.

Technical progress in certain directions should be dictated by an awareness of need for appropriate technology. Miniaturization of technology reduces the scale of impact of industrial civilization on the biosphere and correct the maladjustment to nature. Scales of economies are reduced. Cybernetic technology allows citizens to participate in electronic democracy.

Schumacher dispels the illusion of the myth of production. A new economics must correct the failing of the old, the inability to distinguish between capital and income. But the solution is really a personal one. In "Peace and Permanence," Schumacher contrasts the Keynes plan with the Gandhian ideal: peace depends on wisdom and wisdom is found only in ones self—not being greedy, using good sense.

We need open our hearts and let empathy catch up to creativity. We look back to where we have been in history, gather up the old economies, and turn on the spiral in a new direction (spiral history, turning of universe, in and out).

With modern electronics and miniaturized technology, we do not have to return to the idiocy of rural life. History is a spiral, not a circle. We can spiral back to the country—old labor turned to form of art and sacred ritual. Ritual of communal labor might bring community together for a few hours a day in global village; rest of day devoted to individual creations. According to Thompson, in such a village, nature could be great, machines tiny and man in proportion. In contemplative cultures being is the source of identity, as it is in nature.

4.3.3.5. Loyalty as a Characteristic of a Good Society

The characteristic of loyalty, and its corollary ideas, equity, attachment, investment, and love, emerges from the characteristics of good human places, ecosystems, and the field: Consistency, Abiding Restraint, Tension, Stability, Accommodation, Constancy, Investment, Love, and Regularity. It is modified by adaptation and ethics. Loyalty is the constancy of a place modified by attachment to and investment in a place, by the members of a good society.

Loyalty is defined as the faithful adherence to an ideal, cause, duty, nation, or place. It implies an obligation to support or defend those things. People give their loyalties to family, culture and place. Loyalty can form the context for agreement or dissent.

Loyalty can be corrupted or bought, however. Capitalists, for instance, can generate consumer loyalty through a massive scale of gift-giving, which allows the capitalist system to survive for a while longer.

4.3.3.5.1. Loyalty & Stability

Loyalty increases social stability, whether loyalty to the family, place or political system. As loyalty is transferred, the criterion of rights is transferred from the nature of 'man' to the community of persons; both law and justice, as well as obligations and rights, are reduced to equity issues. Thus, new nations demand to participate in a common justice, as opposed to the extension of natural rights.

4.3.3.5.2. Plenitude & the Equity of Wealth

A powerful arbitrary idea, such as the Christian principle of plenitude, can influence many cultures over centuries. The principle states that an intelligent creator gave an earth of unlimited bounty to humanity for their use; this seemed to be confirmed in the Renaissance with the discovery of the richness of stars, microscopic life, and unexplored continents. Many modern political ideologies and economic systems have been shaped by the principle of endless wealth. Adam Smith calculated that the real price of anything was just the toil acquiring it. These ideas are parallel to the idea of unlimited good, where anything, even virtue, can be multiplied indefinitely. The invalidity of this principle comes with the recognition of limits. Without limits any good becomes devalued and is wasted. The universe is limited; the earth is limited; individuals have limits. These metaphors are defective because they do not fit our surroundings.

Our modern cosmology, with its basis on machine metaphors and the principles of plenitude gets in trouble because it does not understand how basic the concept of limits is to the physical universe, to life, to ecosystems, and to human constructs, such as cities and economics.

4.3.3.6. Harmony as a Characteristic of a Good Society

The characteristic of harmony, and its corollary ideas, balance, education, care, and acceleration, emerges from the characteristics of good human places, ecosystems, and the field: Health, Meaning, Vitality, Productivity, Renewal, Cycling, Process, Movement, and Flow. It is modified by adaptation and ethics.

Harmony comes from the Greek word *harmos*, meaning 'fitting.' Extended definitions of harmony include: The combination of parts into a pleasing or orderly whole; or, an agreement in feeling and action. To harmonize means to associate different things in a proportionate arrangement. Proportionate is the due proportion of two things having a reciprocal relationship or an equality in measure. If nations were defined as having an equality of measure, not necessarily size or force, then the harmony of nations could be promoted.

In Chinese medical tradition, the highest good is harmony, especially social harmony, or good relations. A good person is one who creates and maintains harmony. And, harmony involves the body and emotions. Perhaps this is the best working definition of health. It is harmony that comes from adaptive history. It is not the musical kind exactly, but more like the mutual restraint of groups of organisms.

Harmony is the agreement of method, extension, variety, cooperation, and loyalty in a social and ecological context of good societies in good places. Harmony in a society is the agreement of actions, feelings, ideas, and interests that results in peaceable relations. Harmony is society can be reduced or destroyed by cheaters, 'free-riders,' or anti-social individuals. But, society itself may select for traits of reciprocal altruism or altruistic punishment in other individuals.

Harmony is mutual constraint plus a shared adaptive history. It is constraint that limits the scale of a society. Harmony requires understanding and then planning for adjustments. Harmony requires adequate ecological information and the infusion of its significance in human affairs. And, it requires the time to do this, with the practices of caution and reverence.

4.3.3.6.1. Opportunity for Meaning

People need to have the opportunity to find meaning in work, community, and their cosmology. Livelihood is vital because it is the source of meaning. It represents the place in the order of things. Losing it means a loss of meaning. Disconnect and dehumanize. Then blame for being disconnected and dehumanized.

The definition of wealth must be enlarged to include meaningful work that would bring fulfillment in addition to a living wage. It must include the whole wild environment that provides services.

What determines the quality of life? Energy, luxury, affluence or abundance? Gratification, strong community with meaningful relationships? Sacrifice? The greatest human dignity follows from respectfulness of everything as meaningful as ourselves, the entire earth.

4.3.3.6.2. Balance for Health

Health is a balance of the material and spiritual, between challenge and well-being. Furthermore, the organism must adapt to the environment, which implies having a memory and being capable of learning, and must reproduce, that is, duplicate its pattern in a separate being. Organisms are goal-seeking, and often stability is sought above change or complexity. The individual is a subject centered in a milieu. Because of this implied point of reference, Rodman concludes that ecology is teleological. Often organisms strive for well-being beyond just survival. Their goal is to come into the fullness of being. A. N. Whitehead considered that all organisms have three urges: to live, to live well, and to live better. Living better is being more attuned, stimulated, flexible, receptive, spontaneous, and integrated.

The well-being and flourishing of human and nonhuman life; all beings have value in themselves (synonyms: intrinsic value, inherent value). These values are independent of the usefulness of the nonhuman world for human purposes. Life includes individuals, species, populations, habitats, and all human and nonhuman cultures. Deep concern and respect for cultures. Ecological processes should remain intact.

Psychologists have recognized the need for diversity for people's quality of life and emotional well-being.[12] Ecological diversity in the forest has been reduced by human activities, such as planting or grazing. The overall landscape diversity of many forests has not fared as badly, due to the addition of human artifacts, which increase it. An increase in ecological diversity would lead to an increase in diversity of the landscape, however.

Ecological forest design is the design of communities. We should design places as organic wholes to promote the well-being of individuals and the common good. The immediate goals of design are to reverse degradation and reclaim places for communities

Now, a place is a society of plants, animals, fungi, and humans, with biological, economic, and spiritual significance. This last definition represents a turning back to more traditional beliefs that place was a home and economics was how you lived at home. The entire community is considered. Human communities are embedded in forest communities; our cultural and spiritual achievements occur in the larger community, which supports human endeavors.

The relationships of cultures (nonindustrial) to forests is intimate, complex, and spiritual. Forests provide cultural metaphors; forests provide places for rituals; and forest wilderness provides places for human independence (or anarchy).

Places have provided the resources for civilization and human expansion. Forests influenced the first spiritual and religious expressions of people living in or near them. Forests provided interactions with animals that humans used as companions, labor, or food. Forested places provided sanitary conditions for people: clean water, clean air and reduced pathogenic microbes, and moderate weather.

Theodore Roszak realized that human beings, and especially economists, focus their consciousness on the visible parts of the world, and forget the invisible that makes everything possible. The necessary invisible background must be described. He characterized economists as urban intellectuals automatically endorsing growth with ecological stupidity. He called for a nobler economics, one that is not afraid to discuss spirit, conscience, moral purpose, and the meaning of life. Roszak, Schumacher, Boulding, Daly, and others have grasped that economics is a subdiscipline of ecology.

Skolimowski states that spirituality is a state of being where the world is experienced in a state of grace. Reverence, compassion and love are forms of spirituality. The quest for meaning is a spiritual quest, which is also a public quest for many great civilizations.

Our education can not be just verbal and scientific. It has to be emotional, spiritual, and nonverbal. Aldous Huxley thought that we should *hope* that a nonverbal education could counter the effects of technology. Earlier, in *Poor Richard's Almanac* (1736), Ben Franklin wrote "He that lives upon Hope, dies Fasting." But then Franklin had confidence that the system was in balance, that not everything needed to be controlled all the time.

4.3.3.6.3. Education & Care for Continuity
Our curiosity is subverted to hunger for news of the human world, and a total lack of interest in the nonhuman. Sociality is frenzied restlessness. Society bombards its citizens with knowledge, with facts already observed and processed. Ignorance results from too little or too much of this knowledge. As Whitehead stressed, education should aim at the effective utilization of knowledge. Merely having the facts does not guarantee the formation of new patterns. One must rearrange the facts into ideas.

The current form of our education is a spectator sport. The format of our communications, also, leads to a spectator view, by not providing any participation (feedback). Maybe people are too illiterate to participate in anything. People want to learn. We now are educated to become something, to achieve a capability, sufficiency, respectability and power. Education is a perversion of learning. Students are taught to prey on society and nature. Everything becomes a struggle for victory. Changing technology seeks young graduates who may have learned the newest techniques; older, experienced employees are retired. Education has become almost exclusively associated with youth and believed to be completed after an age limit. Most people are left with the information and attitudes vaguely associated with social awkwardness and dietary problems. The social system in advanced countries encourages the self through education, but denies it the opportunities of adult fulfillment. We cannot solve environmental problems until we learn or teach to enjoy life as it comes, satisfied with wonder and mystery and not dwell on future prestige.

The wholeness of humanity needs to be affirmed, but from a firm cultural base. The complete surrender of cultural identity is as dangerous as too little openness. Every culture needs its own local, sacred center, which cannot be broken if the group is not to perish.

The state of one's knowledge is an important characteristic of the state of one's being. The young are lost because there is no relevant knowledge to guide them; they are furnished with bits of information, which are relevant to the concept of world as factory.

Education can encourage cross-fertilization and technological advance. A creative person pioneers, and fails often, but is productive in the long-run. Curiosity-oriented research has provided many new technologies. As knowledge diffuses organically, an innovation will be modified a thousand ways as it spreads, and no one will worry about credit for the idea. Equal access to information is necessary as well as to resources. Interaction is one stage above toleration. Cultures could borrow and learn from one another without being homogenized; they could converge in interaction.

Knowledge enlarges the range of options. It generates innovations, but it constantly surprises because new discoveries and applications are so unpredictable. Thus knowledge makes people receptive to new attitudes and willing to change their ways. A contextual education might have immediate consequences. The move from growth to need might entail economic well-being, and with that, the desire for silly extravagances like golf carts and electric swizzle sticks and for fashions in clothing, housing and transportation might disappear. On the positive side, manufacturers could concentrate on durability and reparability.

Norbert Weiner has characterized the world as consisting of "to whom it may concern" messages. Unfortunately, these messages are incomprehensible as spectacles. They are clothed in form, which requires understanding to decipher. Thus the ecological crisis is a result of a perceptual crisis. Human beings destroy whole threads of the web of life because it is not seen as a web, a complex network of totally interactive beings. What kind of animal we are is determined by our perception of the world. Spectators, aided by computers, may solve technical problems, but not the environmental problems that require participation. An ecological education would provide participation. Leopold has said that the only true application of recreation engineering is to promote perception in people. But weeds in a city lot convey the same lesson as unique canyons.

Education is such a delicate necessity; it could enlarge or alter the perceptions of all human beings on earth with the selection and presentation of relevant information. Ecological consciousness could be fostered almost immediately. The basis of an effective participant education must include the application of perception research to ecological concerns and the promotion of ecological wisdom in a healthy world view.

Specialization and ignorance (of science) are working against that. Schumacher presents the leading ideas of the century—evolution, survival of the fitter, Marxism, Freudianism, relativism, and positivism—and distills them from one common denominator: that the higher is merely a manifestation of the lower. This is a metaphysical assumption, in modern education, that causes us to suffer a metaphysical disease; the cure is also metaphysical, however, and can be affected through an ecologically wise reeducation. Education is defined, through A.N. Whitehead, as the transmission of ideas that enable man to live above meaningless tragedy or inward disgrace. G. Hardin has written that the essence of tragedy is the remorseless working of things. Education properly could allow people to escape the tyranny of physical and biological laws by understanding them. The most important part of ecology is the education of its laws, which are not part of the science. Ecological education is necessary mechanism to produce individual and social changes to steer society away from disaster (from the Latin, educare, to lead forth).

Fuller states that the educational revolution is the highest priority of all; it should be based on synergy, here the total effect is greater than the combined actions. Synergy is the behavior of whole systems unpredicted by the behavior of any part separately. It would require interdisciplinary approaches. Interdisciplinary cooperation is a revolt against separation of arts and sciences. A general education is in contact with world order in the universe of knowledge and the community of cultures. The way to effect a cultural transformation is by surrounding society with a new field of consciousness, not by attacking institutions or society.

On a sailing ship (after Fuller), everyone cooperates spontaneously because they all know how to sail and what their functions are, in fair and foul weather. Humanity will only cooperate spontaneously when all humanity understands their role as part of the earth. That is the foremost purpose of education: To make individuals aware of how their lives and the earth work.

4.7. Expressing the Place: Ecopoetics (or Art & Design)

People express a place, taking on the characteristics, and reforming hem to human ideals. The extension of human identity with places expresses the places. Of course, the characteristics sometimes get expressed through human cultures. More often, places become expressions of human ideas and human patterns. Art is the process of expressing things in materials, or art is the expression of patterns.

The spirit of each place is unique.[13] Place is not just location; it is the total sum of objects in the landscape combined into a unique whole. The identity of place often leads to human identity, thus people call themselves after places. The more unique a place the stronger the emotional attachment of the inhabitants. Every place has certain characteristics that enforce the spirit of place, for instance, a strong definition of place or indicators of great age, or where a place distills the essence of larger landscapes. A sense of wildness and water also contribute greatly to the spirit of place.

Every organism creates an image of its place from what is meaningful to it. This image is what fits the organism to its place. Suckers and caddisworms have simple images; coyotes and humans have more complex ones. Boulding (1956) notes that the image as a cognitive construct of the world has several aspects: Spatial, temporal, personal, relational, value, and affectional (emotional) for each individual. The total sum of individual images is a world. Some of the images we impose on nature result from idealized notions of pastoralism or technological futures. Thus, landscapes abound in nostalgic or consumptive trends on many levels of explication—some are iconic, some invisible. We originally perceive the landscape symbolically, but the landscape has other functional dimensions that increase according to use.

4.7.2. *Design of Places as Ecosystems*
Nature is self-making and self-designing, but we humans now influence every natural system, taking what we need from some ecosystems, enhancing a few, misusing others, and interfering with the rest. We need designs to restore the balance between human needs and natural processes.

Ecological designs focus on whole communities that work in the same self-sustaining and self-limiting ways as nature. By consciously creating meaningful order, we can develop ways of producing widespread community wealth while positioning the community for a long, sustainable future in a healthy environment.

There is no guarantee that nature can provide humans with everything they want. Recognizing the lack of guarantee simply recognizes that nature is wild and we must come to terms with nonhuman beings and processes. It is not enough to arrange trees in rows to maximize future harvests; it is not enough to preserve small areas of old-growth without natural disturbances. We must pay attention to the processes that make up the entire habitat, for example, the role of herbivores on trimming vegetation and diversifying it by predation. The design of the ecosystem and its management must ensure that the processes operate to maintain a dynamic state. Furthermore, the context must be conserved. The ecosystem, however, cannot be considered outside of the context of the entire landscape, including human images and institutions.

A number of ecosystems, everywhere, are still wild. Many others have been impoverished, but have the capacity for regeneration. As afforestation proceeds to reclaim wasted lands, as it has in England and Europe, more attention will be paid to the shape of the forest ecosystem. Design principles can guide our decisions. Although design in Europe has primarily been concerned with artificial forests, many of the ideas can be applied to wild forests. Human design, until now, has been primarily visual. It has emphasized aesthetic reaction to a place, but also the uniqueness of a place. It is not enough to create ragged edged forests to satisfy human eyes; it is not enough to leave beauty strips of real forest to fool travelers. Design is needed to create natural spatial patterns and temporal phases across watersheds and entire landscapes. Ecological design considers the whole context.

4.7.2.1. Definitions of Ecological Design

Landscape is a heterogeneous area composed of a mosaic of interacting ecosystems of various sizes; an ecosystem is a community of organisms living in place. Design is a human project in which, as Oliver Lucas says "visual and physical parts are assembled in order to achieve a specific end result." Ecological design is the creative modification of ecosystems to repair or enhance their ability at self-organization and maintenance of their complexity and diversity. Diversity, as in biological diversity, means species richness, different age and size classes in a population, and genetic differences in a species, as well as kinds of habitats present in an ecosystem and the kinds of communities occupying the habitats; and the kinds of ecological processes that maintain habitats; and the variety and richness of the planet's genetic heritage. Ecosystems that do so are healthy. A definition of health is the condition of being sound in body or well-being.

Signs of ecosystem health include the homeorhesis of the system (after Waddington), the stability of the system (that is, its resilience after stress, such as floods), the diversity of its components, the continuous recycling of elements, and flourishing. The ecosystem stocks and flows are determined by stochastic variability due to random factors. Ecosystem health seems to mean the links between human health and ecosystems. Robert Costanza stated that: "an ecosystem is healthy ... if it is stable and sustainable—that is, if it is active and maintains it organization and autonomy over time and is resilient to stress." Health as related to ability of ecosystem to continue to provide services.

Health is related to stress, both good stress and bad stress. Stress may be related to the rate of change for the system, in addition to loss or gain of components or changes in structure. Health is the overall ability of a system to maintain itself under a normal range of environmental conditions. Obviously, a pioneer community may change the conditions to favor a new level of the system with new components.

A ecosystem can be characterized by a number of words: productivity, openness, efficiency, maturity, stability, durability, self-making, flexibility, diversity, richness, wholeness (matrix), and dynamic. This list is not meant to be exhaustive.

Living communities are self-organizing systems with emergent properties; they maintain themselves in a state of flux; species are always coming and going, and changing proportions. In a living system, nothing keeps growing forever; things die and are reborn in cycles. The continuation of the system depends on these cycles. The cycles are bound by limits. Both individuals and communities are usually bound by one or two specific limits. Ecosystem health occurs within those limits.

4.7.2.2. Characteristics of Ecological Design
The characteristics of ecological design have to address the characteristics of ecosystems and places. The courses of the design have to imitate the processes of systems and places. The wholeness of the design has to address the ideas of spirit of place, and sensory force. After the processes are identified, they have to be related to the patterns. Design may have to try shortcuts, unless it can afford to take the ecosystem time, which is often many human lifetimes.

4.7.2.2.1. Imitating Courses
Design has to identify patterns of movement and construction, then it has to imitate the processes and patterns, modifying them to include more things of human interest and need. This is more difficult than copying a shape or a structure. Fortunately, imitation is a human strength, even if the recognition of complex, long-term, moving patterns is not. Courses can be thought about using topological and mathematical models representing a four-dimensional landscape.

4.7.2.2.2. Extending Identity & Wholeness
Ecological design has to capture the integrity of a place, or restore it. Unity is a fundamental objective of landscape design. Unity is the way the elements, including shape and scale, of a landscape are combined.

For instance, visually, a forest ecosystem usually dominates the landscape. From a distance, even-aged forests have much the same impact, in terms of color, shape, and scale, as uneven-aged forests. Diversity becomes more important visually at a smaller scale. Natural forms of the forest are unified with the landscape because the margins are very uneven, and open space in the forest is part of the mosaic caused by birth and death of individual or groups of trees.

4.7.2.2.2.1. Spirit of Place
The spirit of each place is unique. Place is not just location; it is the total sum of objects in the landscape combined into a unique whole. The identity of place often leads to human identity, thus people call themselves by their place names. The more unique a place the stronger the emotional attachment of the inhabitants. Every place has certain characteristics that enforce the spirit of place, for instance, a strong definition of place or indicators of great age, such as trees or rocks, or where a place distills the essence of larger landscapes. A sense of wildness and water also contribute greatly to the spirit of place. The spirit of the place is the best guide to design.

Each place expresses a unique combination of elements, including contrasts, dramatic features, and the presence of water. Design can work to be consistent with the recognized spirit of place. If the design recognizes this aspect of the landscape, it may be stimulated by spirit and it may further enhance it—what it should not do is degrade it. Forest design can emphasize some features above others.

Goals of good designs include: To relink people with genius of their places, to revivify image and identity with places, and to develop and maintain the identity of places.

4.7.2.2.2.2. Sensory Force.
All the elements of design can be combined in an image. Every organism creates an image of its place from what is meaningful to it. This image is what fits the organism to its place. Suckers and caddisworms have simple images; coyotes and humans have more complex ones. Kenneth Boulding (1956) notes that the image as a cognitive construct of the world has several aspects: spatial, temporal, personal, relational, value, and affectional (emotional) for each individual. Cognition is an active relationship that is creatively shaped by the participants. Participation is not an option by the way—every scientist or inhabitant becomes part of the system of observation. The total sum of individual images is a world. Some of the images we impose on nature result from idealized notions of pastoralism or technological futures. Thus landscapes abound in nostalgic or consumptive trends on many levels of explication—some are iconic, some invisible. We originally perceive the landscape symbolically, but the landscape has other functional dimensions that increase according to use.

Visual force is a psychological interpretation of perceived power in a landscape. As a principle, it is embodied in psychology, art, graphic design, and architecture. The human mind responds to visual force in predictable and dynamic ways, for instance, visual forces in landscapes draw the eye down convex slopes and up concave ones—the strength depending on the scale and irregularity of the landform.

The effect of a forest landscape is not completely visual, however. Smell, sound, touch, and even taste play a large part of our appreciation of forests. Crawling, which is highly recommended by Gary Snyder, climbing, listening, and tasting things, such as soil, bark, or lichen, can expand our perception of other aspects of the forest. De Tocqueville commented on the ceaseless noises in the forests he encountered in Pennsylvania and Ohio—they kept him awake.

4.7.2.2.3. Enhancing Openness & Flexibility
Because the operation of the universe tends to change systems, the design of a place should be open to the types of processes that could destroy the design. Furthermore, flexibility, defined as the unused capacity for change, can be designed into the system. The parts of a system have to maintain the potential for all possible behaviors that could flow from any other part of the system. Openness and flexibility are characteristics of healthy ecosystems, and they can be considered and enhanced by design.

4.7.2.2.3.1. Anticipation

To anticipate means to look forward, to think about possibilities or to expect surprises—n a way it is to create thought experiments about possible future events. Responses to things can be worked out.

4.7.2.2.3.2. Playfulness

Playfulness is a fondness for play, for engaging in activity because it feels good. Play is an activity that can lead to relaxation, or practice for more serious things relating to food and mating. In another sense it means to move freely within limits.

4.7.2.2.4. Participating in Co-constrained Construction

Designs are limited by the real biological constraints of ecosystem processes and biogeochemical cycles. We must know the constraints in order to create a healthy design. The design has to work within the constraints of the ecosystem. Rather than emphasize static equilibrium, the design should emphasize heterogeneity and learn to adjust to disturbance

People have needs, animals and plants have needs, the site does have constraints, and these things can be married into a good pattern. Harmony is a constraint of the whole system. Design is the participation in the process of the ecosystem as a harmonious system, with mutually restrained conflicts and constrained influences. An ecological design is a form of co-constrained construction, where the organisms, environment and designs are co-implicative, co-defining, and co-constructing. They all engage in a process of self-assembly, where the whole is the whole system.

4.7.2.2.4.1. Participation

To participate means to take part with others in some activity. Designers should participate in a complete design process, guiding involvement and commitment to the art of living together as a community.

4.7.2.2.4.2. Adaptation

Adaptation is a process of making fit by adjusting to circumstances, environmental or cultural. Here it means fitting into an ecosystem, within established cycles and functions. It is adaptation that improves the chances of survival for a living being.

4.7.2.2.5. Investing in Stability & Constancy

People often judge the health or wholeness of ecosystems, or the goodness of designs, by how they look. Traditional design has emphasized visual results above all else. Ecological design, however, achieves the same results by paying attention to the structure and function of the ecosystem first. Design has been concerned for centuries with making domesticated landscapes out of wild ones. Now, design is addressing the opposite problem: How to preserve or provide the conditions for wild ecosystems so that they are stable or constant within the processes shaping and affecting them.

Signs of ecosystem health include the homeorhesis of the system, that is, the stable, directional flow of the system capable of resistance, resilience, and accommodation. The design for an ecosystem describes the system in a comprehensive interdisciplinary approach, using dynamic concepts such as constancy and stability.

4.7.2.2.5.1. Plurality
Plurality is the condition of being numerous, the existence within an ecosystem of distinctive living patterns. This conditional applies to cultural and political patterns as well; it allows many values.

4.7.2.2.5.2. Frugality
Frugality means being economical, avoiding excess and waste. It is the style of use of things. According to Henryk Skolimowski and others, it is a necessary lifestyle in a crowded world.

4.7.2.2.6. Stimulating Productivity & Health
Most products of an ecosystem are produced and consumed and recycled within the ecosystem. Humans need to minimize the external inputs in the form of energy and exotic substances. The community must be restored to health. This means balancing human needs with bird or fish needs in a sustainable pattern.

Ecological design is the creative modification of ecosystems to repair or enhance their ability at self-organization and maintenance of their complexity and diversity.

Health is the overall ability of a system to maintain itself under a normal range of environmental conditions. Ecosystem health is one of the goals of design. The goal, of course, is not an end point that can be reached once, but is rather a continual striving.

4.7.2.2.6.1. Respect
Respect means to show regard for, or to avoid interfering with, others. It means recognizing the "beingness," value and rights of the ecosystem itself.

4.7.2.2.6.2. Responsibility
Responsibility is the condition of being accountable for one's actions or obligations. Here it means undertaking all aspects of a design, regardless of the expected level of success.

4.7.2.7. Applying Ecological Designs to Places
All design elements are related psychologically by designers, as focus or frame, as contrast or uniformity, as dominant or recessive, or in a number of other pairs. Good ecological design means not violating any of the aforementioned principles and ideas.

Design can improve the results of bad practices. Bad forest harvesting practices often result in geometric wastelands. Good design can correct reliance on straight lines, parallel lines, right angles, and perfect symmetry. In cutting or planting to improve natural appearance a number of things have to be considered, including the age of the forest, windthrow, the width of corridors, and the minimum size of the habitat.

4.7.2.7.1. Ecological Design of Place

There are basic geometric elements of any design, from three dimensions (volume) to 2 (plane), 1 (line), and 0 (point) dimensions. These elements can vary in numerous ways, by number, position, direction, size, shape, interval, texture, color, and temporal. Furthermore, the elements can be organized into groups by nearness, similarity, and difference (diversity), into structures by rhythm, tension, balance, and scale, and finally into a whole with sensory force and a spirit of place (genius loci). All of the elements interact in complex and unpredictable ways. The spirit of the place is the most important principle to be conserved or enhanced.

Geology, climate, disturbance, and stability all produce diversity. Landscape diversity is linked to ecological diversity, which depends on diversity of the substrate. Different ecosystems introduce diversity into a landscape, but different ecosystems often can look similar. Excessive diversity can lead to confusion in a landscape design. Increased diversity also has the effect of reducing scale, so adding diversity can be used to do reduce the scale. A high level of diversity is acceptable if one element is clearly dominant or if the differences cannot be recognized from a distance.

Psychologists have recognized the need for diversity for people's quality of life and emotional well-being.[14] Ecological diversity in the forest has been reduced by human activities, such as planting or grazing. The overall landscape diversity of many forests has not fared as badly, due to the addition of human artifacts, which increase it. An increase in ecological diversity would lead to an increase in diversity of the landscape, however. It would also tend to reduce the scale, but this would not be a problem in large forests.

Process applied to components yields pattern. Nature is composed of patterns. Organisms have characteristic patterns, such as the branching of trees or the cloud forms of tree crowns. Lichens have lobes, wood grain under stress has spirals. The cracks in tree barks form nets. Patterns are not still. A circular pattern through time can be recognized as a spiral (the earth's orbit for example). The pattern should allow for surprises and discontinuities; it can do this if it is flexible. The design of forests is vulnerable to surprises because nature is chaotic (unpredictable) and science itself is uncertain (by definition) about patterns of change in forests.

4.7.2.9. Ecological Design Limits

People often judge the health or wholeness of ecosystems by how they look, as a function of richness, despite the fact that ecosystems have to fit into extreme climates and places. Traditional design has emphasized visual results above all else. Ecological design, however, achieves the same results by paying attention to the structure and function of the system first. Design has been concerned for centuries with making domesticated landscapes out of wild ones. Now, design must address the opposite problem: how to preserve or provide the conditions for wild ecosystems.

Design must address the common good, that is, the good of the entire ambihuman community; it can do so by: Promoting the well-being of all individuals in larger community, deciding what is preferable, attempting to regulate and anticipate all effects, encouraging convivial activity, recognizing links and dependencies, mediating the relation between technology and community, and alleviating some of the problems of modern industrial society.

Designs provide a framework for natural and artificial processes to work in. The patterns in design are echoes of patterns in nature. Good designs learn to embrace error and failure, so necessary in open systems. Most ecosystem designs will not be restorations, because of the uncertainty about the kinds and associations of native vegetation. Furthermore, humans are now an large part, although not yet an integral part, of the system; therefore it could not be restored to a premodern or prehuman state, even if we knew the proper or historical state. This design is not the biotechnological design of a new ecosystem, either; we cannot accurately control and predict ecological events in most ecosystems. However, we can steer some of the events in a known direction—known because we have historical records of the system, although not complete. We can also reduce those human activities that we know alter the conditions of the forest, such as overcutting and pesticide use.

Although ecological design attempts to restore some kind of balance, the balance does not exclude human activity. Rather, it integrates it into the larger community. A moderate number of human impacts can be absorbed by the system—too many destroy the systems capacity for self-maintenance. The design should be open to evolution and to human technological and social development. The design should be based on a model of ecosystem functions, considering diversity, complexity, and the maintenance of natural process— natural here meaning a self-sustaining system composed of elements now lost through human disturbance.

How do large-scale processes influence design? That is, how can design be flexible and open enough to cope with change? How does design accommodate those processes? The processes provide constraints on the designs, which when implemented force some constraints on the processes themselves. The question is how to limit the latter constraints so that the processes are not fundamental shifted into a new regime. For example, a dam is located depending on waterflow, canyon walls permeability, location, rainfall, and other factors. After being built the dam changes rainfall, erosion, waterflow, species groups, and other factors.

The role of designers is to optimize or satisfy the fitness of people with their environments. To fit cultural goals to ecological characteristics and limits. It is adaptive creativity, not just for the current technology, but because it needs to adapt to the technological and natural environments. An ecological design involves designers and people in reshaping and recreating a self-sustaining community. Individual resources are limited. The relationships to strive for here are community relationships. Furthermore, there are limits for human manipulation of other communities. Total control has limits, also. We should not aim to try to control the forest and its habitats. We have to trust that natural processes are self-correcting and organizing.

An ecological design is the creation of a clear vision of the ecosystem that is aesthetic, useful, and self-sustaining. Ecological design fuses art and ecology from the work on forests and rivers to agriculture and buildings. Some of the relationships can be captured by maps and drawings, but not the dynamic four-dimensional qualities of the system itself, which can only be understood by dwelling there for years. Nevertheless, a simulation of the view from foot or airplane is more compelling than a recital of the statistics or species lists.

The goal of ecological design is not to restore, but to revitalize and reinhabit the forest. We do not want to live in the dead bones of a mechanistic failure. We want to live in a healthy environment with aesthetic appeal—aesthetic appeal is a requirement for human health. Every system has physical, biological, economic, and political characteristics. The design, planning, and management for a forest, for example, describes the system in a comprehensive interdisciplinary approach, using dynamic concepts such as feedback and stability, recognizing limits to change and sustainability with different levels and scales of structure and function in an anticipatory, flexible planning approach, recognizing human and nonhuman goals, and incorporating personal and institutional interests.

Ecological design is the design of communities. We design places as organic wholes to promote the well-being of individuals and the common good. The immediate goals of design are to reverse degradation and reclaim places for communities, but also to work to increase public awareness of the interdependence of communities, to create environmental quality, and to transform public values by generating new metaphors for living. Unlike what many say, regional design cannot ignore culture, politics, and economics. Design has to commit to limits, constraints, and optima (physical, biological, and social). Ecological design can restore the interconnectedness of the systems, especially ecological and human social systems.

5.0. Eutopias: Good Places

When the word 'Eutopias' has been used in literature, on occasion, as a counterpoint to 'utopias,' to describe a dream world of contradictions between rusticity and civilization, as in Bernard Mandeville's verse:

T'enjoy the world's conveniences,
Be famed in War, yet live in Ease
Without (great) Vices, is a vain
Eutopia seated in the brain.

This second meaning of utopia, eutopia, is not used often. It means simply 'good place.' Good places do exist. They can be described, and even expanded. Some of the traits that make them good can be understood and repeated. A formal compilation of general characteristics of good places, a eutopias, a general description of good places, extends the application of utopian thought. Perhaps the number of good places can be increased with understanding of traditional ways and with more effective metaphors. Good places, and good societies, can be partly understood through certain paths of ecology, economics and politics. These paths are now be explored.

5.0.1. The Lure of Good Places

What does lure mean? Something we desperately want? We have often moved to places that we have only heard about. If we do not live in healthy places, we want to move to healthy places. Sometimes, we remake our places until they have the characteristics of good places.

5.0.2. The Existence of Good Places

What does existence mean? Good places do exist. People in optimum size groups, with strong ethics and common beliefs and understandings, either by respecting limits or keeping well below them, can make good places through their actions.

5.1. Describing Good Places Somewhere

Good places are a confluence of good human societies in healthy ecosystems. We have described some of the qualities of healthy ecosystems. And, we have described some of the qualities of good human societies. To have good societies in good places will require good images and good actions.

5.1.1. *Characteristics of Good Places in a Eutopian Framework*

From political character studies to technological promises, utopias have kept close to the contemporary forms of society. The possibilities described for the future seem to be circumscribed by the limits of human imagination. The entire literature of utopia, imaginative as it is, cannot match the actual diversity of cultures for richness or the depth of nature for wonder.

Many archaic societies employ a set of principles, different from industrial cultures, that may be more adaptive to place. Instead of regarding the "universe as mechanical, humanity as master, and all persons as equal," the Yaruru consider the "universe static and internal, humans sensible to other's wants, and all beings equal;" by contrast, the Navajo consider the "universe personal and orderly, events primary, and the family first." The ways that people live in place reflect their principles. For instance, the Yaruru are much less likely to overwhelm their home place than any industrial culture.

Other modern metaphors can promise more adaptive behavior for industrial culture. A machine metaphor used by Kenneth Boulding, "the earth is a spaceship" suggests the limits of the earth and the value of its life-support system, but it masks other realities. The metaphor of the spaceship is a closed system model, which leads to inadequate understanding of open, natural systems. The earth is an open system that sustains life. The earth has no single captain with authority. In fact, the image of a spaceship does not fit a large, organic, nonmechanical system. Alas, the earth is not a spaceship. It is far more dangerous and uncontrollable. It is clear that many human behaviors and many human institutions in the past, which may have been appropriate to a large planet, are entirely inappropriate to a small closed spaceship. "We cannot have cowboys and Indians, for instance, in a spaceship, or even a cowboy ethic," Boulding says, "We cannot afford unrestrained conflict, and we almost certainly cannot afford national sovereignty in an unrestricted sense."

Another metaphor in popular use, such as "the earth is a garden," is a better model for reintegrating humanity into a balance with nature, because the garden is a small balanced system directed by humanity, and part of the larger environment, and dependent on it. The rule of the garden is empirical and based on observation: If you do something, then something else happens. Even so, the metaphor of the garden has important limits. Humanity does not have adequate knowledge to direct all of the processes of nature.

In naming a new science of ecology, Ernst Haeckel combined two Greek words (eco-logos) meaning "the study of the house." Ecology relates to dwelling, to the frame that contains us. The desire to refine a focus on our problems has allowed the frame of reference to be neglected. This metaphor has turned attention to the whole. But, it too is limited. The house herein is not a construct any more than a spaceship. And, there is not just one house; there are many unique ones with individual characteristics and connections.

Eutopias, as a general description, uses a root metaphor of many places, in different bioregions. This eutopias is a framework for human cultures, to preserve the unique image that a society needs to guide it and to make it different from others. To be effective, in contrast with the ideal characteristics of ideal cities, a eutopian framework embodies attributes that are compatible to the values and norms of living cultures.

By being attentive to the characteristics of place, and those of a good society, a eutopian framework can be described by its own characteristics from groundedness to comprehensiveness. These characteristics are quire different from the characteristics that can be observed with utopias or industrial designs.

5.1.1.1. Eutopias are Grounded
Eutopias are grounded in places, and grounding may resemble a knotting in the physical process of existence. Eutopias are realizations of human ideas

and designs. The making of places is an ordering of a distinct structure and with an important center. Humans and their communities are embedded in places. The Taureg of the Sahara have created an image, a world, that cannot be relocated to the rain forest of the Campa in Peru. When the symbols of a world lose their meaning, through wrongful application or abstraction, sickness and disintegration result.

Being grounded in place allows us to rediscover a participating consciousness and a symbiotic connection to the living earth. The organization of perception, meaning, and thought is intimately related to specific places. The commitment to a place implies acceptance of its limits. Place is a focus of meaningful events and a platform for ordering a world. The individual image of a place is modified by memory, experience, emotion, imagination, and intention. The social image of a place is influenced by individuals, myths, history, and consensus. The images reinforce each other over time. Each place and culture is unique.

5.1.1.2. Eutopias are Dynamic

Eutopias are dynamic expressions of the productivity of places. Nature and human nature are not static orders; they are flexible, historical, and irreversible. Worlds have been built by peoples over so many thousands of years that it is not necessary to start from raw sensations for a new image. Societies build images that reflect knowledge of themselves and their environment. The problems of many human societies can be rooted in their anthropocentric images of the universe. But, the solution cannot be a uniform cosmology of the earth. The strengths of cultures lay in the diversity of values and in their fitness to particular places. A holistic eutopian cosmology can preserve the differences in a whole image of the earth. The image cannot be a rigid shell to contain everything, but rather a flexible, organic network holding all human and natural groups. The eutopian cosmology recognizes the value of a whole dynamic biosphere. The eutopian order permits traditional cultures and natural processes to be self-ordering and self-renewing without the imposition of a rigid order from above. They allow cultures to be healthy and harmonious.

5.1.1.3. Eutopias are Adventitious

Societies are part of an unending, imperfect process, without a final state. Furthermore, the attempt at perfectibility through self-improvement causes disharmony, which is part of the same imperfect process. Each eutopia is a practical application to place. It is open to the differentiation and diversity that exists. It accepts confusion and conflict—but constructive, scaled conflict, not insoluble, that can lead to education, understanding, and the abandonment of stupidity. Many utopias imply that society can be remade according to reason. But reason is not large enough. Experience is necessary; the unconscious is necessary, and ecological design is necessary. Utopias pretend that all factors governing a system are known and that their effects can be calculated. Unknown factors determine a large part of the operation of any system. Furthermore, there is chaos in every system; there are plagues and random frenzies. Eutopias recognize and absorb unknown factors. They enhance the richness of place.

5.1.1.4. Eutopias are Sophisticated

All the contents of the human species cannot be captured by a single policy. The eutopian framework protects difference and diversity from a uniform global policy. Within the framework, cultures are decentralized and autonomous; people identify with their local culture. Because the earth is finite, there are physical and biological limits to growth and progress. Eutopias voluntarily limits human influence within ecosystems. This does not mean that humanity cannot modify some ecosystems or become space-faring—just that it should not dominate every ecosystem or transform the entire matrix to human products, in order to luxuriate or to explore space. The process of producing goods results in waste, even at low rates of use. The principle of limited good is respected; desired things exist in nonexpansive quantifies. Eutopias is an approach that respects limits, maturity and subtlety, as well as beauty and elegance.

5.1.1.5. Eutopias are Complex

The eutopian framework is multidimensional and pluralistic. Balanced development, rather than growth, is emphasized. When a culture falls out of balance with its local environment, massive disruption often results; industrial cultures have only avoided disruption by trading advantageously with other locales, using fossil fuels, and promoting institutional inequality. Small cultures have built-in checks; furthermore, their cultural definition of good helps to maintain balance between other species and the use of ecosystem productivities. This allows them more stability.

Gross imbalances of wealth and health are the unforeseen consequences of exploration, colonization, science, and management. These imbalances will become more unmanageable with time and television, or with any communication. The primary obstacles to equity and justice are political and managerial, not to mention inertia and poor priorities.

Regional areas are limited in size, to avoid problems of scale. Historical smallness, even lacking natural resources, has not been an obstacle to wealth for many countries, for instance, the sovereign German states of Hamburg or Bavaria. The merits of urbanization do not require a large population. Local concentrations of artists, philosophers, and scientists are capable of creating a distinct civilization. Cities fifty times as large as classical Athens or Florence have not been fifty times as creative. Eutopias would generate loyalty and complexity within limits of size and impact.

5.1.1.6. Eutopias are Heterogenous

The eutopian frame is unselective. It accounts for all human diversity and variability, for prisoners and misfits, artists and technophiles, and for the insane and the aged. It is pluralistic. It rewards and uses individual differences in constitution and character. Humans are not perfect or interchangeable. It accepts inequities, although biological injustices exist and can be ameliorated, and social injustices can be rectified. The eutopian frame is flexible enough to incorporate the positive features of traditional civilizations. Through its respect for the validity of all cultures and understanding of the responsibilities of cultures, it works to define an authentic concept of humanity. It tolerates fluctuation, irregularities, uncertainty, and diversity, which are characteristics of open systems.

5.1.1.7. Eutopias are Comprehensive
The levels of application of human norms are both universal and local, depending on the context. For example, there are some universal human behavioral standards, such as a prohibition against incest or against eating human flesh, but local expectations conform with cultural values—and indeed, cannibalism and incest have been important parts of some societies at times. The eutopian frame tolerates and integrates all cultures. Each culture determines the style and complexity of its individuals. Eutopias strives for concerned noninterference, but offers advice and assistance to all cultures to integrate new attributes or common concerns, such as the equality of women, into the culture.

Eutopias considers the total community as a self-making whole. Human cultures make a place within nature. Culture is an immeasurable complex of material and spiritual achievements inside nature, by modifying and using nature. Nature changes with culture. Nature is the locus of the centers and images of all living beings. Nature is thus an important basis for all cultures. The self-ordering processes of nature must be protected through formal preserves of areas or through limited human impact on other areas. The eutopian framework allows people to identify with their domiture, that is, nature and culture.

5.1.2. *Describing Dynamic Structure and Framework of Good Places*
The characteristics must be preserved by action. Characteristics are part of a structure of a good place. Characteristics can be described, but some of the pieces could be missing. The structure is necessary to contain and fit the characteristics, regardless of what is missing.

5.2 **Thinking about Making Good Places in Context**

People are in place. One secret is to have the places be good places, so that people might develop their potentials. There are many potential levels of action, many ways of being, starting with the individual and continuing through the international. However, individuals are part of families, which are part of groups that often include extended families. Larger groups may include clubs or corporations, communities or counties, states or regions. For the sake of simplicity, communities are considered under the heading of individuals. States and regions are considered under the heading of nations.

5.2.1. *Being Individuals in Good Places*
From a cosmological or ecological perspective, living organisms interpenetrate deeply into nonliving forms and the earth. Individual organisms are woven into a complex fabric. Their activities reshape the fabric. Human beings, to make good places, have to consider their individual and social actions, their participation, as responsibilities.

5.2.1.1. Individual Participation in Place
To make a good place, individual participation is required. In order for places to continue, participation is necessary. Participation enters the constitution of place; it is not a fusion where things lose their identity, but a mutual folding together where each becomes part of the identity of the other. Without it things would have no existence. To exist is to participate in place. Participations are felt, not thought. Participation leads to knowledge, science, and mystical experience.

There is no way to validate the wholly subjective experience. Each human being inhabits her autonomous world. The autonomy of consciousness lets us believe the lies and the truth. As William James and Paul Tillich have argued, beliefs about reality affect real human actions. This can introduce the new into the world and permit respect for difference.

Ervin von Weizsacker is convinced that our actual task is the realization of the human self, that the possibility of world peace stands or falls on that success, although he is skeptical that it will happen. The world transforming idealist can be as neurotic as the rest and works against himself. The Buddha says the cause of suffering is attachment. Perhaps, but attachments grant status to the other. Perhaps suffering is unavoidable. A worse threat to human being and the safety of place is detachment.

The absolute individual reflected the absolute state. The absolute individual becomes more self-important through detachment from the environment and personal nets. The state gave the individual a vote, which many people use to reduce participation. The decay of mutual participation and constraint has led to alienated individuals.

The locus of political sovereignty is individual, who is limited in giving away proxy rights. Politics has to be a participatory process, where the individual has some power over decisions effecting them. Participation is necessary, not only politically, but to establish the existence of perspectives throughout the population as a whole.

Many other aspects of human social existence can vitiate our responsibility to participate. Aldous Huxley noted that there are three things we center our existence around: Technological gadgets, political power and morality. Each center can be used as a means to solve problems; sometimes people believe that their problems would all be solved if everyone had a radio or computer, were a communist, or were a Mormon. As the collection of gadgets for some grows, the cost to others creates more problems. With the emphasis of political power, only the mechanism changes—from a dishwasher to the corporation or from the toaster to a political party—but, the problems increase. Moral systems allow automatic decisions also, but to no better effect. The idolatries of gadgetry, celebrity and morality occupy our attention. People struggle and suffer in the resulting turmoil. While these concerns are necessary, it would be better to focus consciousness on the unity of the situation, not on single filters of experience.

A rotation of civic, vocational and professional responsibilities would awaken different senses in an individual and round out self-development. Complete society might create complete humans. A eutopian framework could deepen the sense of personal worth, allow spiritual growth, and augment people's need to participate in governing institutions. People are capable of being the most delicate gauge of the health of a place and ecologically intelligent scale.

5.2.1.2. Responsibilities of Individuals
Each individual has responsibilities that cannot be evaded or given away. Some of these responsibilities are: To cultivate the self, that is, to be healthy and fulfilled; to engage in meaningful work; and to practice simplicity.

5.2.1.2.1. To Cultivate the Self. To be Healthy and Fulfilled
Each individual is responsible for her body, for her health, and for the direction of her education. Education is a life-long project, involving the investigation of and respect for other points of view. The idea of a right to health and education is less important than the moral obligation to preserve one's health and educate one's self. The possibility of transformation and peace stands or falls on the success of the realization of the human self. The individual is responsible for the style and simplicity of her life and for its effects on nature and society. The individual is responsible for being tolerant of others, and is free to choose work, mates, or places. An individual can achieve self-realization through participation in place, that is, home.

5.2.1.2.2. To Find Good Meaningful Work
One should choose work that is interesting and positive, that uses proper technology and fits in the system. Work should be respectful of resources, foster a cooperative approach to economic problems, and promote self-help and self-sufficiency. For the individual work should be a form of right livelihood, which was a step on the Buddha's eight-fold path to purification and liberation. Work would be expressed as the needs of the place dictate, regardless of economic incentives to convert a place into a set of commodities. Work would be expressed with an efficiency that comes from experience.

Work is done with other people; in that sense it is moral, also. In her study of the moral underpinnings of work, Jane Jacobs, through a Platonic dialogue of her characters, collected and sorted them to find that they fit two patterns of moral behavior that were mutually exclusive. She calls these two patterns "Moral Syndrome A," which is a commercial moral syndrome, and "Moral Syndrome B," which is a guardian moral syndrome. She claims that the commercial moral syndrome is applicable to business owners, scientists, farmers, and traders. And, she claims that the guardian moral syndrome is applicable to government, charities, foraging societies, and religious institutions. She also claims that these moral syndromes are fixed, and do not fluctuate over time. It seems likely that MSA developed from MSB as a way to cope with the changes as a civilization of strangers developed around agriculture and cities. Jacobs suggests that the mixing of these two moral syndromes can result in the work underpinnings of the Mafia, communism, and New York Subway Police.[15] MSA can produce goods that are harmful to people and destructive to the environment.

5.2.1.2.3. To Practice Simplicity
Responsibility for the ecological production of goods is important. Choosing for yourself involves knowing an ecology and knowing a politics, that is, being astute, and protecting what is valued. The people of industrial nations could cultivate voluntary simplicity, living in a way that is outwardly simple and inwardly rich, by consuming less. Simplicity can be carefree and joyous, without being a form of self-punishment and asceticism. To live on earth with a minimum of influence is a noble goal. Each person has the responsibility to change the self and to abandon behavior that is inconsistent with acceptable practice. We have an obligation to make the world livable, not only for ourselves, but for other native species.

One should share with others, practice stewardship of domestic landscapes, and be frugal. Simplicity also involves not interfering with self-governing nature and not imposing one's personal morality on others. Physical enjoyment and cultivation of the inner life are valuable. The desires for superfluous material goods, for praise and power, for moral superiority and fixed opinions, are not as valuable. The manifest goal of all activity is the attainment of felicity, a subjective state. Meaningful satisfaction comes from enjoyment rather than the consumption of commodities, for instance, from walking through a forest, listening to birds, enjoying flowers, and watching a sunset, without destroying any of them. One goal, shared by all living beings, is the richness of experience. People can enhance richness and minimize the destructive results of their participation in the process.

5.2.1.2.3.1. To Limit and Value Possessions
Among Australian aborigines, a sense of responsibility was continually renewed by visions of Dreamtime, through which people were restored to unity with heaven and earth. There is an alternate reality where an individual can be healthy and complete, and be concerned with a healthy and complete system for all life. The Greek ideal can be inferred from qualities of ancient sculpture: Simplicity, proportion, and harmony. Plato's *Republic* was designed

to avoid certain evils, most among them, the overcrowding of the economy, the proliferation of needless goods and services, and the infiltration of those who supply them.

People in industrial nations could cultivate voluntary simplicity, living in a way that is outwardly simple and inwardly rich, by consuming less. The main aim would be spiritual, but a lesser aim would be to acquire a minimum wealth to maintain life. This attitude would also require new values: Stewardship, not progress; austerity, not affluence; permanence, not profit; responsibilities, not rights; people, not professions; betterment, not biggerment; and enoughness, not moreness.

Lao Tse recommends cutting out the desire for superfluous goods, then the desire for praise or fear of blame, then desire for power, morality, and opinion. For him, physical enjoyment and cultivation of the inner life are best things of all. The desire for superfluous material goods, for praise and power, for moral superiority and fixed opinions, are expressions of greed and strife. H. D. Thoreau emphasized the necessity of natural simplicity as a way to avoid the desperate life of those weighed down by strife and greed. A Harris survey in the U.S. in May 1977, showed that people are expressing choices that are reflecting changing values towards simplicity, although the survey did not indicate how they would face the consequences.

People can exercise personal choice: Choosing to keep an older bicycle or car, buying fewer clothes, and traveling less. The planet is being transformed for human comforts. Freedom has come to mean being 'without limits.' Two reasons for not acquiring material possessions are the ecological responsibility for their production and a goal of personal development. Each person has the responsibility to change the self, to abandon behavior if it is inconsistent with acceptable practice. People have an obligation to make the world livable, not only for ourselves, but for native species; to try to stop destructiveness exactly in proportion to the destructive results of participation in the process. People must realize that the more we are removed from a ruinous process, the less is destroyed, disturbed, or achieved. People need to learn deny things that work against thinking and living as simply as possible. Then, they will have time and the ability to find a responsible ecology, to find meaning in appropriate environments and to discover our potentials.

5.2.1.2.3.2. To Have an Appropriate Diet & Food Production
Although human dietary habits were stable for long periods, they have been changing, for economic, personal, and social reasons. Many people limit their intake of animal products to milk, butter, and eggs. Some are vegetarians or vegans; others concentrate on fruits. Humans have been represented as omnivores, carnivores, or fructivores by different factions. In view of human control over animal and plant populations, a reexamination of the use of animals and plants is critical. There are both advantages and disadvantages to strictly carnivorous or vegetarian approaches.

Humanity has a long history of eating animals, and traditions of eating are important to the integrity of archaic cultures. Besides flesh, animals provide many high-quality materials that cannot be duplicated by an appropriate technology: Wool, leather, lard, tallow, and manure. Most animals eat food that humans cannot; they concentrate protein and convert low-quality protein to high-quality. Where animals are allowed free range, they graze in nonproductive places, such as steep, rocky slopes. There are good reasons for livestock production—ruminants can harvest vegetation on marginal lands not suitable for cultivation; they also consume roughages not suitable for human consumption. Many native grasses yield one and a half times as much energy per acre as potatoes and 2-3 times as much protein. Nonruminants, such as chickens, are useful as refiners of plants and wastes into processed foods. In periods of abundance, animals could be fed surplus grain, then eaten in lean years. Food animals would serve as shock absorbers. Foods of animal origin provide essential amino acids in which plants are deficient, and which the human body cannot make. For example, plants lack the vitamin B12; plants also may be inadequate for reproducing females. The energy efficiency of eating animals may be low, but there are other factors, including quality of protein or taste.

There are many arguments against eating animals, especially as practiced in industrial cultures. Often, animals compete with humans for the same food, corn and soybeans, for instance. This is especially noticeable in western societies, where food animals are fed corn and soybeans for fattening. In 1980, livestock ate enough food for 14 billion humans. Intensive meat production causes tremendous organic waste and water and air pollution. The intensive production of large numbers of animals for consumption causes great organic waste and pollutes water and air with animals wastes and process byproducts. Much land is not suitable for factory farming or industrial agriculture. These methods often ruin habitats.

Moreover, factory farming methods are inhumane—calves, pigs, and poultry are squeezed into the smallest possible spaces. Currier Holman said that his business at Iowa Beef Processors "is very much like waging war." And, as in war, the innocent suffer. The inhumane treatment of food animals results in lower-quality protein, while drugs and chemical additives, beyond the toxins and saturated fats already in meat, increase the danger to consumers. Circulatory and heart diseases are linked to a diet based on animal foods.

Wild animals are still taken by some cultures. It might be possible for industrial cultures to also take wild animals in limited numbers. Wild animals are already adapted to their range, which is often unsuitable for domestic animals. They are usually more efficient converters than domestic animals. For example, the oryx (antelope) needs only one-third the water of cattle and is immune to many of the diseases that affect domestic cattle. It is twice as efficient at making flesh, and it is immune to most diseases that afflict cattle. And wild animals are adapted to an ecosystem. However, wild animals are unsuitable for domestication, so the take would be limited by health, habitat and reproduction.

Aquaculture has many advantages. Fish are better converters than mammals; fish would have a better distribution and be more acceptable to many cultures. Fish protein is readily assimilated by humans.

Insectaculture would have more advantages. Insects comprise over 80% of all animal species, and they are edible. Their advantages for diets include: fast breeding: many insects breed extraordinarily fast and occur in great numbers. One aphid, if all offspring lived, could produce 1,560 sextillion aphids, equal in weight to all of humanity. Most insects are high in protein and calories. Insects are cleaner than that cleanest of domestic farm animals, the pig. Insects are an abundant, but neglected, source of food.

Limiting the diet to plants avoids the suffering associated with food animals. The practice is more efficient overall; more people can be fed per acre. Vegetarianism could allow vastly more people to be supported on the same acreage. It would encourage humans to explore and use wild plants. Much animal suffering would be avoided. As early as 1961, the Journal of the AMA stated that a vegetarian diet could prevent 90% of thrombo-embolic disease and 97% of coronary occlusions. Plant protein produces lower levels of cholesterol in the body than animal protein. Cholesterol levels in the blood have been linked to heart disease.

By eliminating the cereals fed to animals, the acreage in production could be reduced by 51 percent. Grain is an efficient food, having a high calorie to waste ratio. Furthermore, technology could reduce the area needed to produce edible plants by 95 percent, with greenhouses, hydroponics, and alternate sources, such as algae. Vegetables offer other, untapped, sources of protein, for which appropriate technology currently exists: leaf protein, which is abundant, efficient, inexpensive, and suitable to tropical and subtropical growing areas; algae, which is efficient and protein rich; single-cell protein, from yeast and fungi, which is fast, efficient, waste-free and pest-free, and can be grown on petroleum waste. These new microbial foods could lessen the burden of land use. Furthermore, the use of wild vegetables could encourage the exploration for and use of neglected and unknown plants.

But, there are disadvantages to vegetarianism. Plants are living organisms, also, and many plants are living when they are eaten, although sentience is a more important criterion. Many of the alternative sources, such as single-cell protein and algae, are deficient in amino acids or are of poor nutritive quality. Cereal crops, by themselves, do not provide a good balance of proteins, so many kinds of plants would have to be used. In some areas, this would mean importing protein, at the risk of economic imbalances and threats to local self-sufficiency. Plants also have poisons, to discourage their predators, human or invertebrate; many plants must be cooked before being consumed. Much of the land pressed into production by industrial agriculture is not suitable for domestic plants; habitats are ruined by the development of land for special crops, such as chocolate, tea, coffee, and tobacco.

It is obvious that humans are not pure carnivores, but it is less obvious that they are not pure herbivores or fructivores. Physiological evidence, such as the shape of teeth or length of the intestine, points to an omnivorous existence for many thousands of years. Although some human cultures concentrate on large animals or on roots, most cultures depend on a combination of sources of food.

Consumers cannot afford to be uninterested in nutrition, agriculture, health and ethics. Health is rooted in wholeness. Vegetarianism is not a compartment, separate from agriculture, social living patterns, or wilderness. It is an ethical response to factory farming. If humans eat animals, let them eat the whole animal, and use it completely. We must know the animal we eat, whether it is wild or domestic.

Vegetarianism is an ethical response to the suffering promoted by factory farming. But vegetarianism is not a compartment separate from industrial agriculture, social mores, cultural traditions, the rights of wild beings, and the necessity of sufficient wilderness. Diets are part of the cultural traditions that provide individual identities for all people. Cultures maintain regional differences and emphasize the unique social aspects of consumption; meals often provide important social and psychological benefits.

Many of the problems associated with human patterns of consumption are problems of scale, efficiency of exploitation, and a universal, commercial diet. Our lust for food has resulted in a war against other species, less reported than human conflicts, but waged more constantly, viciously, and mostly out of sight. We cannot eat without killing animals or plants. Human cultures are based on killing. Often, our wants and charities result in deaths. If we have zoos, to save a few species after destroying their habitats, then we must kill for those animals that are carnivores, as we do for our pets.

Killing has been disconnected from necessity. Humans must eat to live. For food, it is necessary to kill. But food should not be wasted. The fruits of nature are not to be destroyed for temporary gains. The consequences of all acts should be examined as thoroughly as possible. When we recognize that animals suffer, we act humanely toward them. When we recognize that their interests might collide with ours we must learn to act justly, also. Are animals interests completely identified with needs?

Knowledge of our carnivorous history should not paralyze us with guilt. Rather, as Raymond Durgnat says,[16] it is "a reminder that what is inevitable may also be spiritually unendurable, that what is justifiable may be atrocious, that the best we can do will always be an organized butchery—and the possible best is itself light-years from fulfillment." Durgnat concludes that when we realize that society is "an organization of deaths as well as of lives, can we become more aware, gentle, alive, sad, free for a Schweitzerian reverence for life ... for all lives, and not just the next one."

Knowledge makes us aware of the costs of eating and, perhaps, inspires us to eat simply, as part of a simpler and more frugal pattern of life. To make choices, we need a way of calculating. Michael Fox presents a scale of suffering of animals.[17] For example, dairy cattle are the least intensively raised while veal calves suffer the most inhumane conditions; turkeys have better conditions than battery hens. A conscientious person minimizes animal suffering by limiting diet.

For understanding the ecology of beings, Aldo Leopold offers the image of a biotic pyramid; individuals at the top, fewer and usually larger, are more complex and capable of feeling. We argue about the extent that each species can suffer, think, or anticipate, but there is evidence of feeling on all the levels of being. As John Cobb implies,[18] the entire pyramid must be healthy and whole. Human health is rooted in the integrity of ecological systems. Physical, mental, and spiritual well-being are dependent on a good diet. Being a vegetarian may be the best option for the urban residents of industrial cultures. For archaic or post-industrial cultures, where human needs are kept simple, limits are respected, and all beings are revered for themselves first, being a conscientious omnivore (the term is from Michael Fox, who is a vegetarian himself) is a middle way that preserves the meaningful rituals of eating, yet uses animals and plants in an humane and optimal way.

5.2.1.2.4. To be Peaceful: Gandhian Nonviolence
Some groups of people, concerned with defending vacant lots, wilderness areas, ecosystems, and the earth as an organic body, have advocated using any means necessary. Earth First!, for instance, showed many of us arm-chair sympathizers that saving the earth requires more active participation than just letter-writing and circulating academic articles. They were among the first to put their bodies where their ideals were, and their stance has made some profiteers and environmental rapists more cautious. But, Earth First! made its wild reputation by monkeywrenching. Although the group has been effective so far, there is a possibility that its tactics may cause long-range difficulties in the form of violent retribution or the overreactive destruction of wilderness, as well as polarization inside other environmental groups. This discussion contrasts the tactics of Earth First! with a Gandhian nonviolence.

Dave Foreman of Earth First! has said, "Monkeywrenching is nonviolent resistance to the destruction of natural diversity and wilderness. It is not directed towards harming human beings or other forms of life." Many Earth First! tactics, however, make this statement questionable. Is Earth First! really nonviolent, at least according to Mohandas K. Gandhi's definition and practice of nonviolence?

To be peaceful, one has to practice nonviolence towards people and towards the ecosphere. One should be vigilant against military intervention, practice conciliation, and resolve differences face to face. Individuals could try to deinstitutionalize legal confrontations.

Gandhi characterized his ethics of group struggle by the Sanskrit word *ahimsa*, meaning "nonhurting" and "nonviolence." Ahimsa is a closely related set of prescriptions and descriptions. Gandhi said: "Ahimsa means avoiding injury to anything on earth in thought, word, or deed." He adopted a wide interpretation of 'injury.' The subject 'anything' included all living beings and perhaps nonliving things. Ahimsa is the absence of *himsa*, meaning hurting from the root *hins*, meaning hurt, a form of the root *han*, with a larger number of meanings, such as strike, kill, destroy, or dispel. Gandhi mostly had living beings in mind, but injury to nature, to natural processes, could come under the general principle of ahimsa.

Indeed, the concept of ahimsa is so wide that it could be interpreted to be an act of violence to abstain from efforts to prevent injurious acts, such as the exploitation of wilderness for profit. But, Gandhi referred specifically to destruction, as part of sabotage, as himsa, even if the things destroyed were not the property of anyone.

Gandhi also said: "Ahimsa really means that you may not offend anybody, you may not harbour an uncharitable thought even in connection with one who may consider himself to be your enemy." Mental forms of injury include hurting people's feelings, their dignity, or their relationships— but the feelings and relationships must be positively valued, that is, it would not be himsa to hurt feelings of hatred, nor to save a victim from wrongdoing. Furthermore, some actions may be in accord with ahimsa if they are performed 'wholly unselfishly', although Gandhi does not accept the postulate of unselfishness as sufficient for the qualification of nonviolence. Most selfless terrorism, however, is still *not* nonviolent.

5.2.1.2.4.1. Injury & Hostages

Mental forms of injury seem to occur in Earth First! campaigns, from name calling and humiliation to suggestive publications. By its verbal and physical stance, Earth First! seems to be violent towards many groups, including loggers and RVers. Foreman tacitly admits this when he makes the distinction between blockades, which are forms of nonviolent civil disobedience, and monkeywrenching, which involves conscious destruction of equipment, while recommending that they not be combined in the same campaign.

By its attitudes Earth First! polarizes most people. The Earth First! slogan is, after all, "No compromise in Defense of Mother Earth!" This really polarizes the opposition. One problem with opposition is its either/ or character: "if you're not with us, you're against us." This of course is a logical fallacy. Positive action does not have to be bilateral or dualistic; it can transcend simple opposition and be positive without being adversarial. Gandhi was always willing to compromise on nonessentials. He characterized himself as a man of compromise because he was never sure that he was right. Compromise is an essential part of the nonviolent person, *satyagraha; ahimsa,* as unselfish love, demands compromise. There are principles that admit no compromise, and furthermore, if the compromise fails, the *satyagraha* is ready for "battle" (in Gandhi's term).

Could Earth First! be truly nonviolent and still be effective? Could Earth First! be more visible and less destructive? Perhaps it could, with the adoption of a Gandhian campaign to defend wilderness. Before this campaign is presented, however, consider how violence may be a dangerous tactic for groups interested in preserving and protecting wilderness against an industry-dominated consumer public.

1. The hostage, wilderness, is very large and vulnerable to counter-attacks, as well as to swings in fad (which often determines how people vote to dispose of the object of the fad).
2. The destruction of materials, such as bulldozers, is usually illegal. Property is considered sacred in The U.S. and Norway, as well as in many industrial and consumer countries.
3. Violence tends to polarize opponents and some of the undecided against the long-range goals of a group, regardless of how well supported and argued.
4. Wilderness is symbolic of people's right to earn a living—even if the people in this case are loggers, drillers, or roadbuilders, who may destroy it in the process of using it.
5. Violence leads to escalation by opponents to protect their equipment and property. Violence leads to violent conflict as a *style* of opposition.

Most of the thousands of direct actions on behalf of the environment have been nonviolent in the Gandhian sense and some have been effective. The "hug the trees" movement in India, for instance, physically blocked excessive logging in the Himalayas. The Chipko (meaning "hug" or "cling to") movement started out to preserve trees by embracing them before axes could be used and has resulted in a ten-year ban on tree-felling in over 550 square miles of the Uttarakhand in India, a major source of timber and water power. The main goal is the "judicious use of trees," according to Chandi Prasad Bhatt, the founder, and not complete preservation. The movement is pressing for a complete remaking of forest policy; they are also responsible for planting trees (over a million so far). One tenet of the movement is that the erosion of human values follows erosion of the land.

Both ecology and human ecology offer the best support for saving wilderness and humanity, which depends on wilderness. The principles from these sciences can inspire a series of norms that are the foundation of a Gandhian nonviolent campaign.

5.2.1.2.4.2. Hypotheses & Campaigns
Certain hypotheses can be suggested and segregated by common themes so that the derivations are more obvious and can be linked more easily. In this instance, hypotheses are presented through the process of induction. This procedure is genetic rather than logical.

The first set of hypothesis notes that humans have the same genetic stock and the same basic interests: Food, welfare, self-actualization, love of place. Human make their worlds of facts from observations and theories colored by needs and wants, within perceptual and imaginative limits. Humans live together in human communities within biological communities in geographic places. Humans can communicate and do so to build cities and make art. Humans are capable of great trust and exhibit this in their use of automobiles, weapons, and money. Humans are capable of violence, for many reasons, from self-preservation to misunderstood symbols. Living in separate locations with differences in languages and cultures can lead to misunderstandings. Humans are autonomous beings and can choose their behavior. Humans can change their behavior. Nature is self-making and self-maintaining. Where nature is left alone, by definition wilderness, animals and plants reach their own balance. Animals and plants live in communities in geographic place. Animals and plants are autonomous beings.

The second set suggests that all beings (human and ultra) have long-range interests, especially in the continuation of their ecosystems. The presentation of facts, as uncolored by needs and wants as possible and within the limits of perception and imagination, increases the probability of understanding. Living together in the same community fosters cooperation and understanding on immediate, common goals. Working together on common projects increases cooperation. Constructive work is more binding; a constructive program is more meaningful and generates trust and communication. Work abstracted from the community can cause its opposite (enantiodromia), that is, destruction instead of good. Misunderstandings can be corrected in peaceful confrontation. Constructive confrontation concentrates on faulty understanding in a situation and not on the opponent's action or personality. The focus on misunderstanding reduces violence.

Humans are responsible for their own actions. Humans enjoy being with animals and plants in general and being in wilderness and using it for living and recreation. Human economies are based on wilderness, ultimately. Wilderness should be saved for many reasons.

The campaign to save wilderness should be constructive and positive and be addressed to issues and relationships, using unbiased facts. It should be well-advertised and simple, sticking to goals. The campaign should be nonviolent and given to the possibility of agreement, including compromise on some aspects. Violence against transgressors of wilderness may result in further violence against wilderness or perhaps further violence on the part of defenders to guarantee wilderness. The campaign should apply to a local area and address those who are knowledgeable in the local community. Responsible persons, acting in a group with an appropriate lead time, concerned with their own community, present an undeniable case.

From these hypotheses can be derived norms that regulate personal and group behavior in a nonviolent campaign. Here are some examples of norms. Live in the community with your opponents. Formulate the essential, shared interests and try to cooperate on the basis of these interests. Refrain from provoking or humiliating your opponent. Seek personal contact with your opponent and his group and be available for meetings. Trust your opponent. Learn about wilderness.

Act as an autonomous, responsible person. Choose attitudes and actions that reduce conditions that lead to violence. Find common interests to build on. Present unbiased facts. Be flexible and ready to compromise. Be constructive. Suggest alternatives. Trust people, at least until that trust is betrayed, then respond in kind.

Act nonviolently, peacefully, and responsibly. Defend wilderness. Do not stop, even if it seems to be saved.

5.2.1.2.4. Tactics & Norms

The Marsh Institute, for instance, uses an educational tactic by offering to performing a consulting service for free on a small scale; the farmer and logger then can compare directly the results and the methods, such as pesticides versus integrated pest management to reduce aphids on a barley crop, or sanitation cuts versus single-tree trimming to eliminate dwarf mistletoe infestations. Then, there is defensive monkeywrenching, such as tree spiking—with signs notifying cedar thieves, and passive resistance, such as not informing hunters or biologists of the whereabouts bears or other wildlife. In general, logging and farming prices are unrealistically subsidized by free goods from nature, as well as by government subsidies. Prices should be geared to costs, and tariffs and taxes used to balance trade discrepancies. The answer is not to fight over trees in wilderness areas or to give up wilderness as a one-time boost to timber interests. It is to attack the old, unreal ways of cutting, and to attack unrealistic economic policies. The long-term strategy is to save wilderness as completely as possible and to include the cost-benefit analyses of alternate plans. Sawmill workers have been complaining that wilderness removes real jobs from their grasps; this misperception needs to be exposed as the short-coming of a problem economy.

Anti-ecological decisions usually come after years of planning by government or industry bureaucracies, at extravagant costs. Therefore, it is best to seek out and address plans at the earliest stages, before momentum can carry the plan. This is hard to do when the bureaucracies resort to secrecy. One of the goals of Earth First! is exposure of destruction and the increase in public awareness. It might be more effective to team with reporters and send news flashes on destruction and illegal use than to destroy equipment.

These norms provide a consistent guide to reacting to dishonest or violent opponents in the struggle. For instance, if your opponent uses biased reporting, merely provide a factual presentation, with evidence, without resorting to provocation or name-calling. Although the stupidity or badness of opponents is not an issue, some people are stupid and bad, so it is a factor to be considered. The stupid and bad must be neutralized some way, by simple diversion through relatively harmless assignments.

Nonviolence is easily misunderstood. If your opponent respects violence in defense of property, and you misjudge your opponent and offer nonviolence, which is perceived as weakness, prompting him to violence, what should you do? Perhaps, you should stay in the center of the issue and be active, but do not respond violently yourself. Most such opponents eventually recognize perseverance as an indicator of strength.

It is important to formulate one very clear, concrete, easily understandable goal for an action and alert the opponent to that goal as soon as possible. This is very hard to do when it is difficult to know who the opponent is and how to reach them. Any action can be part of a larger campaign, however, and this may be important for psychological reasons, since many actions are unsuccessful in reaching their goals, although that does not reduce their importance. The success of the campaign does not depend on the success of each single action. One effect of actions is to attract the attention of the public, who might act rightly with knowledge.

A campaign may be part of a larger movement, such as one to eventually put 40 to 50 percent of the landscape (of North America or the planet) into special preserves. Such a movement may take many campaigns and a hundred years. But, the goal is important.

Wilderness campaigns are not really constructive in the sense of architectural or educational campaigns, because they are defensive. Furthermore, what is defended is, first, in the process of change, so it can not be saved as it is; second, it will always be vulnerable; third, wilderness is an ambiguous concept misperceived by opponents; and fourth, it is ultrahuman. What is to be saved is the potential for the evolution of uninhibited development of species and ecosystems.

Violence polarizes opposition. A stance of "no compromise" polarizes opposition. To turn your opponent into a supporter, compromise is far more effective than violence or coercion. We have to compromise. We don't know enough not to—we are not sure enough of the consequences of our actions, which often have the opposite effect of the one intended. Furthermore, compromise can be such that it satisfies the opponent's ego without giving up much, because it creates a state of cognitive dissonance, where a little token is enough to convince people that something is owed in return, a much bigger concession in this case, regardless of whether they know about or care about how cognitive dissonance works.

The code of nonviolence, as presented by Gandhi, is not a rigid system. Exceptions are possible and, under some situations, even desirable. Arne Naess suggests that a small piece of a technical installation, a dam, for instance, could be destroyed in order to avoid the greater destruction of an area. Nevertheless, this violence is an exception and not a norm. Earth First!, by compromising on nonessential issues and using violence only as a warning, might increase its effectiveness. Either way, Earth First! already exemplifies an important, and neglected, aspect of Gandhi's philosophy: *you should follow your inner voice whatever the consequences.*

5.2.1.2.5. To Share in Governing Process.
One should get involved in government and change, focus on political effort, and work to decentralize and debureaucratize institutions. We need to work to make laws to equalize representation, encouraging the poor as well as the highly privileged, who are less likely to accept far-reaching changes, to participate. We have to work to create new goals and purposes for society, especially those related to survival and happiness. We need to offer service to others, to volunteer for civic groups, and to challenge discrimination and prejudice. Involvement means to recognize and participate on at least three levels, from the local and regional to the global.

5.2.1.3. Individuals in Communities
There may be a genetic tendency for individuals to live in groups and to behave altruistically towards their kin. Individuals rarely exist outside of families and larger groups. Living in groups can be related to Maslow's list of human needs, especially to the satisfaction of needs such as self-actualization. The groups inculcate values, behaviors and language into individuals, so it is difficult to consider an individual without the presence of their group culture. Culture is everything created as a group, tribe or nation, physical or ideal, in the past or present. This embraces cookware, arrows, steam engines; artworks, books, legal codes; symbols, values, social structures. A cultural system surrounds the network of human interactions with raw materials, forms of life and other humans. Culture includes all of the expectations, understandings, beliefs, and commitments that influence the behavior of human groups. Many social ceremonies reinforced the cohesion of a group. Gatherings were regular, to celebrate the first fish or last crop of berries, as well as social ties. People of different groups visited, traded, played sports, and gambled. The band was the economic group. Food-sharing, division of labor, diet with variety. Most sets of ethics make the rules easy to follow. They emphasize the differences (relativism) or similarities (absolutism) of human beings only; or of the individual or the group; or of good feeling, reason, or desire. But ethics has to confront the individual, embedded in a community, located in a bioregion, on earth.

The fundamental organizing principle of human communities was kinship. The first social networks in human history were symbolized by reciprocity; relations were more important than the gifts. Reciprocity becomes established in a group with the internalization of norms. Internalization of norms may be a gene-cultural co-evolution. So, altruistic behavior can be internalized, like any other trait, as long as the costs are not excessive.

Cooperation could become stable under Darwinian conditions in large social groups, provided that defaulters were punished. Reciprocity, it seems, can be positive or negative. It seems that people are willing to punish "free-riders" at a cost to themselves and no benefit; this is sometimes called altruistic punishment. People may be motivated to punish by strong feelings of resentment; even if they personally have not been directly cheated, they may want the punishment out of fairness. Traditional theories of reciprocal altruism cannot account for this kind of punishment. Maybe groups select for the traits, since free-riders could destroy the trust and harmony of a group. It shows that individuals will cooperate in a reciprocal fashion without regard for future rewards. Strong reciprocators that punish others may help the group survive, especially under crisis conditions such as famines or earthquakes. Is this a cultural form of punishment, as opposed to an individual one? Perhaps it can be understood in terms of group dynamics rather than selective advantage or cost/benefit.

Humans have a habit of structuring the world with their own group at the center. This ethnocentrism is evident in small tribes as well as in large empires, such as the Roman or Chinese empires. The center of a cosmos is usually the place of living, the locality of the group creating the cosmology. It is the center for individuals and groups.

5.2.1.3.1. Kinds & Importance of Groups

There are several basic types of kinship groups: The nuclear family, the expanded family, and various types of descent groups, that is, a group of people who claim common ancestry, such as lineages or clans. Each type can be characterized by its size, formal political system, marriage forms, and leaders. Nuclear families last only as long as parents and children live together; descent groups are corporate groups in that they are permanent units that continue to exist even though their membership changes. Membership is usually determined at birth and last for one's lifetime.

Other groups, such as tribes and states, are not based on kinship, although component groups may be. A tribe is a group of nominally independent communities occupying a specific region, sharing a common language and culture, which are integrated by some unifying factor. A chiefdom is a regional polity in which two or more local groups are organized under a single chief, who is at the head of a ranked hierarchy of people. An individual's status is determined by closeness of one's relationship to the chief. The state is the most formal of political organizations with political power centralized in a government which may legitimately use force to regulate the affairs of its citizens, as well as its relations with other states. States maintain civil order and socioeconomic contrasts through a central government and specialized subsystems. The populations are divided into socioeconomic classes, or strata, and states draw a line between elites and masses with the former clearly separated from the latter in activities, privileges, rights, and obligations. The major concerns of government officials are to defend hierarchy, property, and the power of the law.

One function of a community is to free people to follow occupations of their own choice in which they may cultivate their gifts, and grow in strength, skill, understanding and achievement. Another function is to give them the opportunity to make their contributions worthwhile to the group.

5.2.1.3.2. Responsibilities of Communities

The responsibilities of a community are: To educate people, in schools, corporations, libraries, and museums; to protect people, with public health programs, sanitation, hospitals and fire departments; to keep the community heritage, through cultural events, shared customs, festivals, art displays and museums; and, to create community wealth, in the form of parks, wilderness areas, monuments, and public buildings

5.2.1.3.2.1. To Educate Individuals

The community teaches an individual its language, behaviors and values. Sometimes we forget that people want to live their traditional ways of life. They are willing to make sacrifices to preserve it or to reestablish it. The Inuit of Chesterfield Inlet in Northern Canada, for example, have established a community like that of their ancestors, rather than embrace mainstream Canadian industrial values. Language, for instance, is an emergent property of a group of human beings.

5.2.1.3.2.2. To Ensure Health & Safety

Groups must ensure the health and safety of the group, of individuals and of the local environment. People live in a mixed community of beings. In archaic cultures, other beings were considered equals, with their own homes and territories.

5.2.1.3.2.3. To Ensure Resources & Food

Communities used enforce rules about common resources, from hunting grounds to sheep pasture. Although an individual hunter can choose to hunt and live outside the territory of the group, the group has to be sure that the territory it claims can support all the people in the group. Communities are the matrix of inspiration for the use of resources for tools an d the use of tools for resources.

5.2.1.3.2.4. To Provide Ways of Transport

Paths are structures that enable people move easily, knowledgably and efficiently from and to special areas. A walking community is highly permeable. As paths become wider more permanent structures that can accommodate wheeled vehicles, their edges interact with human places. Streets are public places. Other public ways are developed for towns and cities, from escalators and conveyer belts to buses and mag-lev trains.

5.2.2. *Being National in Good Places*

A nation is an independent and self-guiding conglomeration of people—sometimes with more than one culture. Nations often have special properties, such as a national currency, flag, and armies. Formerly, nations were as self-reliant as communities.

There is an operation of metalysis with nations as well. Through isolation and identity, people divided into cultures and nations. Nations have unified and disunified. The reason for nations is the desire for autonomy, to practice unique cultural beliefs and traditions. For nations, sovereignty is limited to culture (or subculture?). Isolation and commerce have to balance. Free movement would cause an imbalance.

Nations usually form during violent conflicts, sometimes as a result of settlement patterns, language and geography, sometimes from ethnic cleansing, war or partitioning. National formation has never been entirely rational and planned. The nation states are closely related to large scale violence, usually having to do with trying to consolidate their power (global war). They then have a monopoly on power. Often, a nation will specialize on political and economic issues, for instance, when the Spanish ransacked the planet for gold. They enlarge and consolidate their territoriality, which gives them increased capacity for marshaling resources, that is trying to maximize global functions with minimum territorial burden. But they have not been stable; there are violent fluctuations. They are part of long cycles.

People are parts of community, but they learn to become part of a nation. They have to learn how to interact as members of a nation.

5.2.2.1. The Import of Recognizing Nations

A nation can claim a measure of truth and reality, but, it does not need to contradict the truth and reality of other nations. A nation often sees the source of its identity in people, and more, people in place, unique peoples in unique places, with unique histories, stories, traditions, and values.

Preservation of a nation appeals to qualities inherent in established ways and to people's moral right to maintain their distinctive customs against change. There are also esthetic reasons for preservation: to preserve styles, merit and achievement. Ethnic identity and consciousness of gender make finer grids of groups.

Groups progress when inspired by a common vision and supported by common values. Cultures need to be reminded of the values already woven in fabric of existence. Reinterpret old beliefs, base a vision of the worlds in places on earth, to be.

Devotion to nation, community, groups, clubs, corporations, teams, and co-ops, can provide a better personal identity. But, humans require more than what is local. They require broader horizons or larger identities. The larger culture or the nation provides this. Forced cultural integration, however, breeds tensions, as it has in Zanzibar or Rwanda.

Humans also require less than a global identity; they require a measure of provincialism. The provinces would be defined by culture, by region and language. Individuality requires distinctive features. When these are stripped away by global coca-colonization, people fight to preserve local culture; the Irish fight to use Gaelic, the Welsh for self-rule. The real feelings of innumerable groups of people center on much smaller regions of the world than nations. For example, Britain is composed of Scotland, North and South Wales, Northern Ireland, Anglia, and Saxony. It may mean more to be Quebecois than Canadian, Kurd than Iraqi, Mongolian than Chinese.

5.2.2.1.1. Regional Differences between Nations
After the differences in environment, and different historical directions, people have different ways of imaging their places, of distributing their wealth. Variations of custom, languages, religion, organization, philosophy, and perception between communities are what enrich the totality of national experience, as the talents and skills of individuals enrich communities. People need to realize potentials as member of the human community and nature.

Herbert Read presents differentiation as a measure of social progress. "Progress is measured by the degree of differentiation within a society. If the individual is a unit in a corporate mass, his life will be limited, dull, and mechanical." But if a unit on his own group, with space and potentiality for action, then he can develop. People need to work on their own solutions in their own places; this would allow maximum diversity and satisfaction.

Heterogenization is beautiful. It is beneficial to all nations; it enriches the cultural resources, provides niches for individuals, and supplies many patterns that may be adapted. It also increases the speed of cultural evolution or the richness of exchange. The process of heterogenization may proceed by localization or interweaving; this is interlocality differentiation. Yet, some homogenization is equally important. This is intralocality differentiation, where each locality heterogeneity increases while differences between them decrease.

5.2.2.1.2. Regional Politics of Nations
The polis in ancient Athens was made for the amateur. Its ideal was that every citizen should play a part in all of the many activities of the polis. We must have right politics as part of right livelihood. We might explore a convergence of thought of Jefferson, Gandhi and Mao, according to W. I. Thompson.

What matters is not perfection, but the basic value orientation of the polity. The developed countries may prefer Jefferson's republican simplicity to Hamilton's national power; Jefferson's vision of republican simplicity would be more manageable than Hamilton's vision of national power and commercial complexity. The latter has been tried and the need for it may be gone; it is time to try the former. "That government is best that governs least," according to Jefferson.

Although the smallness of cultural units would not guarantee freedom, with a smaller scale tyranny, at least the tyrant is visible, flight would be possible, and revolt more likely. The best disinfectant against the danger of a selfish demagogue is wise and skeptical education. Lawmakers and executives would be chosen by lot, rotation, election or a combination of procedures. Similar procedures used in Athens, Florence and other places. Thoreau's Walden is an extended sermon on the necessity of natural simplicity as the only way to avoid desperation of power and possessions.

People must be free to choose. If people are left alone to do what they please, to follow their nature, a new social order will emerge of itself. Nature is not a forced order.

Cultures cannot be planned, nor are they logical. As long as they are coherent, contradictions may abound. The form of rearrangement is immaterial. With a cultural unit approach, groups may pursue anarchistic isolationism or disinterested internationalism. It would be against any kind of morality to prescribe forms of government and administration for peoples.

Other nations may prefer Gandhi's vision or Mao's original vision of small communities. China or Greece may provide some alternatives; others may be invented. In the eutopian approach, groups may pursue anarchistic isolationism or disinterested interrepublicanism. What matters is not perfection, but the basic value orientation of the polity.

Privatism or socialism could work, depending on population size, resource distribution, traditions, or other factors. Privatism works well within a system, with intrinsic responsibility. The problem with the socialism is its contrived responsibility; who shall watch the watchers? Commonism, a systems of cultural commons, or altruism, might not work as large systems.

Anarchism is not only a stateless society but also a harmonized society that exposes humans to the stimuli provided by both agrarian and urban life, physical and mental activity, communal solidarity and individual development, spontaneity and self-discipline, elimination of toil and promotion of craftsmanship, regional uniqueness and world brotherhood. An anarchistic society would establish harmony of human and nature and human and human.

5.2.2.2. Responsibilities of Nations
The planet is experienced on a smaller frame of reference than global unity or nations; people live on the local level. Local knowledge is knowledge in place, earned in place by generations of inhabitants, through visions and trials, experience, and stories. Thus, individuals are preserved in societies that are preserved in places that are preserved by individuals and societies. Laws, politics, architecture, sports are things of place. They are shaped with local knowledge. A local area is limited by the limits of vision, a horizon. As protectors of place, Nations have explicit functions.

5.2.2.2.1. To Conserve Ecosystems: Boundaries
Nations have the responsibility of keeping their environment healthy, of conserving local ecosystems and places. Human activities cannot be isolated from societies or ecosystems. Cultures must adapt to ecosystems or biological regions to survive. All beings modify and exploit the earth to some extent. Humans do. For successful exploitation, power must be limited and density controlled at a national level, which could balance communities and places. A human ecology must provide each living human being with a satisfactory environment that must be in equilibrium with the rest of the system.

5.2.2.2.2. To Manage Resources: Distribution

Every nation has the power to use its local sources in any manner, within the limits of damage and pollution set by an international association. Every nation has the duty to conduct activities in a manner respectful of their effects. With the information available now, from a more extended resource inventory and with optimal ideas about renewal, climatic conditions, traditional land-use patterns, local cycles, and ecological requirements (limits), conservation is more effective. Its goal is to support a steady state economy within optimum ranges based on natural and human limits.

Technology can be used to increase carrying capacity to some extent, but not infinitely. Although, technologies tend to homogenize people and places, the same technologies may be used in different ways, especially adapted to local requirements, for instance, the use of tin cans as cases for radios. Heterogeneity is beneficial to all countries; it enriches the cultural resources, provides niches for individuals, and supplies many patterns that may he adapted. It also increases the speed of cultural evolution or the richness of exchange.

A nation could promote appropriate technology to manage resources for its region. Dangerous technologies would he reduced through wholesale substitution, if not of materials, than by labor-intensive solutions. Traditional housing, for instance would be preferred; its form and design are integrated into the culture, it is adapted to the local climate and is usually less expensive, due to use of local materials. Much traditional architecture is authentic and unselfconscious; its forms fit the context of place and develop in response to place. With arcologies, the urban ecologies designed by Paolo Soleri, the city can change its relationship with nature; an arcology is a good solution for an urban culture, as it solves the problems of waste, resource-use, scale, obsolescence, and segregation.

One necessary condition for the preservation of finite resources is sovereign power. To share resources without the discipline of power invites the tragedy of the commons. The limit of sharing has to coincide with the limit of sovereignty; otherwise runaway destruction could result. Every nation has the responsibility to conduct its economy without causing damage to its ecological base or to other nations. Environmental risks and damages must be identified and solutions found before economic processes can be implemented.

5.2.2.2.3. To Maintain People: Population

A nation is responsible for maintaining the health of cultures and individuals. Traditional cultures provide personal security, respect for the individual, responsibility for actions (self-discipline), social integration, concern for others, and reverence for nature. Traditional social structures, with networks of marital relations, inheritance, and rationalizing myths, are closely adapted to the local environment.

Preservation of identity appeals to qualities inherent in established ways and to people's desire to maintain their distinctive customs against change. There are also esthetic reasons for preservation: to preserve styles, merit, and achievement. Ethnic identity and consciousness of gender make finer grids of groups. Devotion to groups, clubs, corporations, teams, co-ops, can provide a better individual identity. Cultures allow different frames of accomplishment. The sum of cultures provides a greater sum of accomplishments. A global reference for a competition or cooperation is restrictive; instead of one winner at a global level, there are 2,000 winners in 2,000 cultures. Limits allow different forms of expression and knowledge.

Cultural identity is necessary to the benefit of places; for, if everyone is a citizen of the world, who will protect small places of little economic or scientific importance? In the one world system, dependence on free conscience to produce conformity is vulnerable to the smallest minority of nonconformists. And there will always be some minority.

Nations educate their members; they are responsible for the ecolacy, numeracy, and literacy necessary for individual survival and actualization within the culture. The emphasis would be local: local culture, history, geology, botany, and economics. Cultural education may not emphasize competition or excellence for economic or political purposes, as is so often done in industrial cultures.

Cultures thrive when inspired by a common vision and supported by common values. Variations of custom, languages, religion, organization, philosophy, and perception between communities are what enrich the totality of experience, as the talents and skills of individuals enrich communities. Progress is measured by the degree of differentiation within a society. People need to work on their own solutions in their own places, resulting in maximum diversity and satisfaction.

Every nation that claims sovereignty accepts responsibility for keeping its population within the ecological limits of its place—that is, the biological and cultural carrying capacity. The carrying capacity is the maximum population supported indefinitely in a given habitat. Solar energy is limited; reserves of fossil fuels are limited; ecological productivity is limited. The carrying capacity of human population includes consumption and production impacts without damage to the integrity of the ecosystem. Carrying capacity is not a rigid number, however; it can be increased or decreased by numerous factors.

A single population policy for every nation is unfair, since nations are at different stages of development. There are dilemmas posed by necessity to equate global balances and national needs. Every state needs a comprehensive population policy, closely related to environmental and technological policies, and within the constraints of their agriculture. Every nation that claims sovereignty must accept responsibility for keeping its population within carrying capacity (as a fuzzy set). Carrying capacity can be expanded to include the notion of self-reliance. This offers more flexibility for trade. Mao committed China to a policy of *tsu li kong sheng*, "regeneration through one's own efforts"; this is self-reliance.

5.2.2.2.4. To Provide Paths of Power to Individuals
For Aristotle, politics was the science of the possible. The city (*polis* in Greek) was a human artifact whose structure could be modified by reason; it was potentially a work of art, limited only the capability of the artist. Nations

present the possibilities of power for individuals.

The function of politics is to ensure that decisions are taken at the right level. A nation protects individual freedoms, guards regional culture (values and identity), and holds groups accountable for the use of power. Regional politics limits the scope of institutions by showing that the institutions can be destructive to society as a whole.

The restriction of freedom, either through tyranny, cultural uniformity, or crowding, results in a decrease of variety, which is created by spontaneous play, which is necessary to flexible and enduring social systems. It is not necessary to prescribe forms of government and administration for peoples. Many forms of government that are size-specific, such as democracy and communism, could be possible in scaled nations. Although the smallness of cultural units would not guarantee freedom, with a smaller scale tyranny the tyrant is visible and corrective action possible and more likely.

Social and personal advantage can be combined in secure social orders. In societies where non-aggression is conspicuous, an individual serves her own advantage as well as that of the group with the same act. Ruth Benedict used the term high synergy to describe such secure societies. The institution insures mutual advantage; the acts are mutually reinforcing. High synergy institutions transcend the polarities of selfishness and altruism. Virtue pays because the rewards for selfishness coincide with benefit for the society. The social structure of low synergy cultures insures opposition and counteraction; the advantage of one individual is a victory over another, as in a zero-sum game. Wealth may be distributed or concentrated, depending on factors, such as synergy, generosity, reciprocity, and cooperation.

New politics can start at the community, over community issues, like housing, transportation, or pollution. People need to save their own identities and places first from corruption and degradation. Power can be shifted to local levels through self-reliance and participation.

The size of nations would be defined by place and culture. Such a limit would increase power to individuals. There can be no separation of politics and ecology. Every political act has ecological consequences and every ecological decision is a political demand for control over use of the environment.

5.2.2.2.5. To Provide Opportunities for Needs of People
Every nation strives for self-reliance. Communities can be self-reliant by producing enough food and shelter, by limiting their population to what can be produced, by sharing tools, by recycling and repairing, by using handicrafts rather than manufactures (shoes, furniture), by using local products and raw materials (soil, minerals, plants), by using general and not specialized machines, by having multipurpose factories, by networking with other communities, and by doing without things that are not needed (bombs, food additives, plastic bottles). Food would be produced and available within local groups, so there would be no reliance on large-scale food production and distribution. Local production would eliminate transportation cost and waste and diminish dependency.

Many leaders of nonindustrial areas have attempted to reduce links with overindustrialized areas. They have attempted to balance population and resources on a local level; they have placed local values before international ones. Julius Nyerere in Tanzania promoted an African socialism. Mao Tse-Tung placed the peasant before the urban dweller in China. For India, Gandhi envisioned a familiarization of society, where property had a common ownership. Each village was a complete nation, independent of its neighbors for vital needs, characterized by self-rule and self-restraint. Later, Schumacher addressed himself to India, urging officials to try to keep poverty rural, and develop village systems to solve it, as worked out by Gandhi, instead of urban industrial complexes.

National control would mean the regionalization of transportation and communication, the administration of social services by a smaller and more responsive bureaucracy, and the resurgence of more direct forms of economic interaction, such as labor-gift and barter exchange in local neighborhoods. A free market system involving each nation could work; one major difference is that supply would be regulated by an international association. Nations could coordinate worker controlled industries and producers cooperatives, forged from kinship or cooperation. Credit unions and mutual insurances could replace big banks and insurance companies. The nature of work could change with a change in scale; it would be self determining and nonexploitative, resulting in greater harmony between worker and employer,

Traditional cultures often have wealth-leveling properties, absolute property ceilings, fixed wants, and production coupled with need; this results in a stable economy. Efficiency and productivity are less important than use and appropriateness. Advertising, the creation of desires and needs, is less important in face-to-face economies. In a small state, people can decide how to use scarce resources and how to distribute them. They can decide whether to be conservatively sustainable or to grow and gamble on innovation and substitution. Local communities have different economic attitudes. Canada, for instance, may cut and sell Canadian timber at a loss, but British Columbia may decide not do that with its timber.

A rational approach to economics is not adequate because of differences in wealth; whether saving, spending, or investing, what is rational to a pauper is not rational to an industrialist or the reverse. But, a rational response to an irrational system increases the wobble of the system. And an irrational response hurts the individual. That is where an international equalization is useful—to put a rational approach in perspective. Economics is connected to ecologies, at any level. Agriculture needs to be connected to optimum rates of production, which are far below the maximum. Society must start paying the true costs.

The populist governance model gives responsibility to communities. Food would be produced and available within own groups, so there would be no reliance on large scale food production and distribution. Local producing would eliminate transportation cost and waste and diminish dependency. A lower population fed by organic agriculture will result in greater flexibility.

How fast can a country become self-reliant? What political or social damage would change do? How would international problems be solved; for instance, when cutting trees in Nepal causes floods in Bangladesh, and deaths because crowding caused the poorest to live on flood plains? The poor in the highlands everywhere effect those in lowlands, often adversely. How should these be treated? depopulated, emigrated? Every nation can be self-reliant; almost none are self-sufficient.

Self-reliance, through decentralization, is freedom. Decentralization is a structure most appropriate to the U.S. idea of freedom; it is also the most cost-effective. The task is to make new one more visible. What is at stake is the right of nonhuman beings to exist. Freedom (in decentralization) is opportunity to define local norms for behavior; a mandate for different traditions in unique communities. Equilibriums can be reestablished through decentralization. Different kinds of constraints on a system are possible. Variety permits a wider range of responses to change in environment. Variety also produces the unexpected.

5.2.2.2.6. To Provide Paths for Resolution of Conflicts
Given differences between cultures or human groups, from images to languages, there is potential for misunderstandings and conflicts between them. A nation has to provide ways to resolve those conflicts. Conflicts can be resolved through communication. If that does not work, arbitration can be made available. Courts would be used as a another resort. Without these paths, and others, retreat or violence are more likely.

5.2.3. *Being in an International Framework*

A global coordinating body could help with communications between nations. It would help different cultures adapt to each other and learn from each other. Global interaction has been a tendency for over five hundred years. How should an individual or a culture be in an international context? What kinds of visions should we follow or goals to make?

5.2.3.1. Necessity of the Framework (UN Currently)

Founded in 1945, to replace the League of nations of 1919, the United Nations (UN) describes itself as a "global association of governments facilitating co-operation in international law, international security, economic development, and social equity." From 51 countries, the UN has expanded to 191 member states in 2006, which the UN considers to be virtually all internationally recognized independent nations, except for Taiwan and several others.

The UN, with its system of 30 affiliated organizations, attempts to solve global problems, from disease and poverty to the environment and war. The UN agencies define the standards for air travel, telecommunications and consumer products. It has developed international campaigns against drug trafficking and terrorism. Its agencies try to assist refugees, to set up programs to clear landmines, to expand food production, and to reduce disease.

The United Nations has six main organs: The General Assembly, the Security Council, the Economic and Social Council, the Trusteeship Council, the Secretariat, and the International Court of Justice. When nations become Members of the UN, they agree to accept the obligations of the UN Charter, an international treaty that sets out basic principles of international relations. The Charter expresses four purposes: To maintain international peace and security; to develop friendly relations between nations; to cooperate in solving international problems; and to harmonize the actions of nations. In September 2000, the members of the UN met to set an international agenda for the new century. The Millennium Declaration lists measurable goals in seven areas: Peace, security and disarmament; development and poverty eradication; protecting the common environment; human rights and good governance; protecting the vulnerable; meeting the special needs of Africa; and strengthening the UN itself.

The UN has been successful in encouraging dependent people to become independent and then incorporating people into its system. In 1960 the General Assembly adopted the Declaration on the Granting of Independence to Colonial Countries and Peoples, which resulted in 60 former colonial Territories attaining independence and joining the UN as sovereign Members. When the UN was formed, 750 million people lived in non-self-governing territories; by 2006, that number was reduced to about 1 million.

The UN has been successful in affirming the fundamental equality of all people and to counter racism. A long UN campaign in South Africa contributed to ending the system of racial segregation known as apartheid. In 1994, a UN observer mission observed that country's first all-race elections. A World Conference in 2001 examined ways to combat racism, racial discrimination, xenophobia and intolerance.

An important mandate of the UN is the promotion of higher standards of living, full employment, and conditions of economic and social progress and development. The UN web site notes that as much as 70 per cent of the work of the UN system is devoted to accomplishing this mandate, based on the belief that eradicating poverty and improving the well-being of people everywhere are necessary steps to create conditions for lasting peace.

5.2.3.1.1. Structure of the UN Main Organs
The structure of the UN is geared give a voice and a vote to all Member nations, to formulate policies on the goals of the system and to resolve international conflicts.

5.2.3.1.1.1. General Assembly
The General Assembly is a "parliament of nations" in which member nations consider the world's most pressing problems. The membership includes every defined nation and each member has one vote. Decisions on key issues, such as admission of new members, the UN budget, and international peace and security, are decided by two-thirds majority. Other matters are decided by a simple majority. Recently, efforts have been made to reach decisions through consensus, rather than through formal vote.

The General Assembly holds an annual regular session from September to December, although it may resume later or hold a special or emergency session, if necessary, to address subjects of particular importance. At its 2001 session, for instance, the Assembly considered over 180 topics, including globalization, AIDS, conflict in Africa, protection of the environment, and consolidation of new democracies. The Assembly does not have the authority or power to force any member to act on UN decisions, but the UN considers that its recommendations "are an important indication of world opinion and represent the moral authority of the community of nations."

5.2.3.1.1.2. Security Council
The Security Council, under the UN Charter, has primary responsibility for maintaining international peace and security. The Council may convene at any time that peace is threatened. Under the Charter, all member nations are obligated to carry out the decisions of the Council.

The Council has 15 members. Currently, five—China, France, the Russian Federation, the United Kingdom and the United States—are considered to be permanent members. The remaining 10 are elected by the General Assembly for two-year terms. Decisions of the Council require nine 'yes' votes. A decision cannot be made if there is a veto by a permanent member.

When the Council identifies a dispute that may become volatile, it explores ways to settle the dispute peacefully. It may suggest principles for settlement or encourage mediation. If fighting has begun, the Council tries to secure a ceasefire. It can send a peacekeeping mission to separate the forces until a truce can be set up.

The Council can take other measures, such as economic sanctions or an arms embargo, to enforce its decisions. It can, in extreme situations, authorize member nations to use "all necessary means," including collective military action, to see that its decisions are carried out. The Security Council has established well over 50 peacekeeping operations. The Council can also make recommendations to the General Assembly on the appointment of a new Secretary-General and on the admission of new members.

5.2.3.1.1.3. Economic & Social Council

Under the overall authority of the General Assembly, the Economic and Social Council coordinates the economic and social work of the UN system. As a central forum for considering international economic and social issues, and for formulating policy recommendations, the Council fosters international cooperation for development. It consults with non-governmental organizations (NGOs) to maintain a vital link between the UN and civil societies of member nations.

This Council has 54 members, who are elected by the General Assembly for three-year terms. The Council meets throughout the year and holds its major session in July, when a special meeting of Ministers discusses major economic, social and humanitarian issues.

The Council's subsidiary bodies meet regularly and report back to it. The other bodies focus on issues such as social development, the status of women, crime prevention, narcotic drugs, and environmental protection. There are five regional commissions to promote economic development and cooperation in their regions.

5.2.3.1.1.4. Trusteeship Council

The Trusteeship Council, considering its work complete, is composed of the five permanent members of the Security Council. The rules of procedure have been changed to allow it to meet if required. The Trusteeship Council had been established to provide international supervision for 11 Trust Territories that were administered by seven member nations, and to ensure that adequate steps were taken to prepare the Territories for independence. By 1994, the Trust Territories had attained independence as separate nations, or they had become part of neighboring independent countries. If the mandate of the Council is not changed, then it will probably be abolished.

5.2.3.1.1.5. Secretariat

The Secretariat carries out the administrative work of the UN, as directed by the General Assembly, the Security Council and the other organs. The Secretary-General, as head of the Secretariat, provides overall administrative guidance. The Secretariat consists of several departments and offices. Its staff of about 7,500 is drawn from 170 countries.

5.2.3.1.1.6. International Court of Justice

The International Court of Justice is the main judicial organ of the UN. The Court consists of 15 judges elected jointly by the General Assembly and the Security Council; its purpose is to settle disputes between countries. Although participation in a proceeding is voluntary, if a nation agrees to participate, then it is obligated to comply with the Court's decision. The Court also provides advisory opinions to the General Assembly and the Security Council.

In 1998 the General Assembly called a conference in Rome to establish an International Criminal Court (ICC). The ICC Court formed in 2002 and heard its first case in 2006. It is the first permanent international court charged with trying those who commit the most serious crimes under international law, including war crimes and genocide.

5.2.3.1.1.7. Special Agencies of the United Nations
Specialized agencies, as part of the UN system, address almost every area of economic and social endeavor. The agencies provide technical and practical assistance to countries around the world. In cooperation with the UN, they help formulate policies, set standards and guidelines, foster support, and mobilize funds. These organizations have their own governing bodies, budgets and secretariats. They report to the General Assembly or the Economic and Social Council.

Close coordination between the UN and the specialized agencies is ensured through the UN System Chief Executives Board for Coordination (CEB), which includes the Secretary-General and the heads of the specialized agencies, funds and programs, the International Atomic Energy Agency, and the World Trade Organization.

The International Monetary Fund, the World Bank, and 12 other independent organizations are linked to the UN through cooperative agreements. These agencies, among them the World Health Organization and the International Civil Aviation Organization, are autonomous bodies created by intergovernmental agreement. They have wide international responsibilities in the economic, social, cultural, educational, health, and related fields. Some, such as the International Labor Organization and the Universal Postal Union, predate the UN itself.

The Office of the UN High Commissioner for Refugees (UNHCR), the UN Development Program (UNDP), and the UN Children's Fund (UNICEF), work to improve the economic and social condition of all people.

The World Bank provides loans and technical assistance to developing countries to reduce poverty and to advance "sustainable economic growth." The World Bank, for example, provided more than $17 billion USD in development loans for the fiscal year 2001 to more than 100 developing countries. The ILO (International Labor Organization) formulates policies and programs to improve working conditions and employment opportunities, and sets labor standards for all countries. The FAO (Food and Agriculture Organization of the UN) works to improve agricultural productivity and food security, and to better the living standards of rural populations. The IMF (International Monetary Fund) facilitates international monetary cooperation and financial stability and provides a permanent forum for consultation, advice and assistance on financial issues. The ITU (International Telecommunication Union) fosters international cooperation to improve telecommunications, coordinates usage of radio and TV frequencies, promotes safety measures, and conducts research. The WMO (World Meteorological Organization) promotes scientific research on the Earth's atmosphere and on climate change, and facilitates the global exchange of meteorological data. The IMO (International Maritime Organization) tries to improve international shipping procedures, raise standards in marine safety, and reduce marine pollution by ships. The WIPO (World Intellectual Property Organization) arranges international protection of intellectual property and fosters cooperation on copyrights, trademarks, industrial designs and patents. UNIDO (UN Industrial Development Organization) promotes the industrial advancement of developing countries through technical assistance, advisory services and training. And, the IAEA (International Atomic Energy Agency) is an autonomous organization that emphasizes safe uses of atomic energy.

5.2.3.1.2. Purposes Goals & Actions of the UN
Like any human institution, one important goal of the UN is to strengthen itself. Programs that involve every nation and its people reinforce the image of the UN as an international body, despite some failures and criticisms. Funding, however, is used by many nations, as a stick to drive the UN in different directions.

5.2.3.1.2.1.To Maintain Peace & Security
The primary purpose of the UN is to preserve world peace. Under the UN Charter, member nations agree to settle disputes by peaceful means and refrain from threatening or using force against other states. UN peace efforts have produced some dramatic results. The UN helped to defuse the Cuban missile crisis in 1962 and the Middle East crisis in 1973. In 1988, the UN sponsored an offer of a peace settlement ended the Iran-Iraq war, and in 1989, UN-sponsored negotiations led to the withdrawal of Soviet troops from Afghanistan. In the 1990s, the UN was instrumental in restoring sovereignty to Kuwait, and it played a major role in ending civil wars in Cambodia, El Salvador, Guatemala, and Mozambique. UN efforts helped to restore the democratically elected government in Haiti. The UN helped to contain conflict in other countries through disarmament and peacemaking.
5.2.3.1.2.1.1. Arms Control & Disarmament
The 1945 UN Charter envisioned a system of regulations that would ensure the least diversion of the world's human and economic resources towards armaments. The use of nuclear weapons weeks after the signing of the Charter highlighted the necessity of arms limitation and disarmament. In fact, the first resolution of the first meeting of the General Assembly, on January 24, 1946, was to establish a Commission to deal with problems raised by atomic energy and to make specific proposals for the elimination of atomic weapons and other weapons of mass destruction from national armaments.

Halting the spread of arms and reducing and eventually eliminating all weapons of mass destruction are major goals of the United Nations. The UN has established forums to address multilateral disarmament, including the First Committee of the General Assembly and the UN Disarmament Commission. Items on their agenda include consideration of a nuclear test ban, outer-space arms control, a ban on chemical weapons, nuclear and conventional disarmament, nuclear-weapon-free zones, the reduction of military budgets, and measures to strengthen international security. The UN supports multilateral negotiations in the Conference on Disarmament and in other international bodies. These negotiations have produced agreements such as the Nuclear Non-Proliferation Treaty (1968), the Comprehensive Nuclear-Test-Ban Treaty (1996), and treaties establishing nuclear-free zones.

The Conference on Disarmament has 66 members representing all areas of the world, including the first five major nuclear-weapon states (the People's Republic of China, France, Russia, U.K. and U.S.). This independent Conference is linked to the UN Secretary-General through a personal representative, who serves as the secretary-general of the conference. Resolutions adopted by the General Assembly often request the conference to consider specific disarmament matters. The conference annually reports its activities to the Assembly.

Other treaties brokered by the UN prohibit the development, production and stockpiling of chemical weapons (1992) and bacteriological weapons (1972); ban nuclear weapons from the seabed, ocean floor (1971) and outer space (1967); and ban or restrict other types of weapons, such as landmines. By 2001, over 120 countries had become parties to the 1997 Ottawa Convention outlawing landmines. The UN encourages all nations to adhere to treaties banning weapons of war. The UN is also supporting efforts to prevent, combat and eradicate the illicit trade in small arms and light weapons, the weapons of choice in most, 46 of 49, major conflicts since 1990. The UN Register of Conventional Arms and the system for standardized reporting of military expenditures help promote greater transparency in military matters.

The International Atomic Energy Agency, through a system of safeguard agreements, attempts to ensure that nuclear materials and equipment intended for peaceful uses are not diverted for military purposes. And, the Organization for the Prohibition of Chemical Weapons collects information on chemical facilities worldwide and conducts routine inspections to ensure adherence to the chemical weapons convention.

5.2.3.1.2.1.2. Peacemaking
UN peacemaking attempts to bring hostile groups to agreement through diplomatic means. The Security Council may recommend ways to avoid conflict or secure peace through negotiation or through recourse to the International Court of Justice. The Secretary-General also can play an important role in peacemaking, by bringing any threat to peace and security to the attention of the Security Council; the S-G can use the offices of the UN to carry out mediation or to exercise quiet diplomacy, personally or through special envoys, to resolve disputes before they escalate.

5.2.3.1.2.1.3. Peacebuilding
The UN has started to address the underlying causes of conflict, such as health, wealth, and education. Development assistance is a key element of peace-building. In cooperation with UN agencies, donor countries, host governments and local and international NGOs, the UN works to support good governance, civil law and order, elections and human rights in countries struggling to deal with the aftermath of conflict. At the same time, it helps these countries rebuild administrative, health, educational and other services that have been disrupted by war. UN-supervised elections in East Timor in

August 2001, allowed people to cast their ballots for a democratically elected assembly.

Some of these activities, such as the UN's supervision of the 1989 elections in Namibia, mine-clearance programs in Mozambique and police training in Haiti, take place within the framework of a UN peacekeeping operation, and may continue when the operation withdraws. Others are requested by governments, as is the case in Cambodia, where the UN maintains a human rights office, or in Guatemala, where the UN helps to implement peace agreements.

In Africa, UN field missions continue peace-building activities in Guinea-Bissau and Liberia; and they remain in Angola and Burundi to support various initiatives aimed at promoting reconciliation. At the request of the Security Council, the Secretary-General has provided a comprehensive analysis of conflicts in Africa along with recommendations on how to promote durable peace.

5.2.3.1.2.1.4. Peacekeeping

All UN peacekeeping operations must be approved by the Security Council, which sets up UN peacekeeping operations and defines their scope and mandate in its efforts to maintain peace and international security. Most operations involve military duties, such as observing a ceasefire or establishing a buffer zone while negotiators seek a long-term solution. Others may require civilian police or other civilian personnel to help organize elections or to monitor human rights. Operations have also been deployed to monitor peace agreements in cooperation with the peacekeeping forces of regional organizations. These forces are provided by member states of the UN, which does not maintain an independent military.

Since the UN deployed peacekeepers in 1948, 123 countries have voluntarily provided more than 750,000 military and civilian police personnel to engage in 54 peacekeeping operations. UN peacekeeping is a vital instrument for peace. Currently, 47,650 UN military and civilian personnel, provided by 87 countries, are engaged in 15 operations around the world.

Peacekeeping operations may last for a few months or continue for many years. The UN's operation at the ceasefire line between India and Pakistan in the State of Jammu and Kashmir, for example, was established in 1949, and still continues. UN peacekeepers have been in Cyprus since 1964. By contrast, the UN was able to complete its 1994 mission in the Aouzou Strip between Libya and Chad in about a month.

Total UN peacekeeping expenses peaked by the end of 1995, when the total cost was just over $3.5 billion. Total UN peacekeeping costs for 2000, including operations funded from the UN regular budget as well as the peacekeeping budget, were $2.2 billion. UN peace operations are funded by assessments, using a formula derived from the regular scale, but including a surcharge for the five permanent Security Council members.

5.2.3.1.2.2.To Develop Friendly Relations between Nations

Through its activities, the UN tries to increase the participation of developing countries in the global economy. The UN Conference on Trade and Development (UNCTAD) promoted international trade. UNCTAD also works with the World Trade Organization (WTO), in assisting exports from developing countries through the International Trade Centre.

The UN provides the means to settle disputes peacefully. The UN has played a major role in helping defuse international crises and in resolving protracted conflicts. It has undertaken complex operations involving peacemaking and humanitarian assistance, and it has worked to prevent conflicts from breaking out. After a conflict, it has increasingly undertaken action to address the causes of war and to lay a foundation for durable peace.

5.2.3.1.2.3.To Cooperate in Solving Problems

Many nations have problems as a result of historical paths and economic inequities. Many problems are geological or meteorological. Other problems arise from conflict.

The UN offers help with resettlement, after a crisis subsides. The UN helped to repatriate refugees to Mozambique, provided humanitarian assistance in Somalia and Sudan, and undertook diplomatic efforts to restore peace in the Great Lakes region. It has helped prevent new unrest in the Central African Republic, and it is helping to prepare for a referendum on the future of Western Sahara.

The UN offers help with reconstruction. In Kosovo, the UN is rebuilding schools and providing student supplies, as part of a wide-ranging assistance effort. The Security Council established an interim international administration there in 1999, following the end of NATO air bombings and the withdrawal of Yugoslav forces. Under the umbrella of the UN, the European Union and the Organization for Security and Cooperation in Europe are working with the people of Kosovo to create a functioning, democratic society with substantial autonomy. Municipal elections in October 2000, and the casting of a Constitutional Framework for Provisional Self-Government, paved the way for Kosovo-wide elections for a legislative assembly on 17 November 2001.

5.2.3.1.2.3.1. Promote Human Rights

World War II atrocities and genocides led to a consensus that the new organization, the UN, must work to prevent such tragedies in the future. So, the pursuit of human rights was central to the creation of the UN. An early objective was to create a legal framework for considering and acting on complaints about human rights violations. The UN Charter obligates all member nations to promote universal "respect for, and observance of, human rights" and to take joint and separate actions to that end.

The Universal Declaration of Human Rights, proclaimed by the General Assembly in 1948, sets out the basic rights and freedoms to which all human beings are entitled: The rights to life, liberty and nationality; the rights to freedom of thought, conscience and religion; the rights to work and to be educated; the rights to food and housing; and the right to take part in government. The UN states that the Declaration is not legally binding to nations. Then, it states that the rights are legally binding due to two International Covenants, to which most nations are parties. One Covenant deals with economic, social and cultural rights, and the other addresses civil and political rights. With the Declaration, they constitute the International Bill of Human Rights.

The Declaration laid the groundwork for more than 80 conventions and declarations on human rights, including conventions to eliminate racial discrimination and discrimination against women; conventions on the rights of the child, against torture and degrading punishment, the status of refugees and the prevention and punishment of the crime of genocide; and declarations on the rights of persons belonging to national, ethnic, religious or linguistic minorities, the right to development, and the rights of human rights defenders. The UN Commission on Human Rights (UNCHR) is the primary UN body charged with promoting human rights, through investigations and offers of technical assistance.

The United Nations and its various agencies are central in upholding and implementing the principles enshrined in the Universal Declaration of Human Rights. A case in point is support by the UN for countries in transition to democracy. Technical assistance in providing free and fair elections, improving judicial structures, drafting constitutions, training human rights officials, and transforming armed movements into political parties have contributed significantly to democratization worldwide.

UN human rights field activities are currently being carried out in nearly 30 countries or territories. They help strengthen national capacities in human rights legislation, administration and education. They investigate reported violations and assist governments in taking corrective measures when needed.

Promoting respect for human rights is increasingly central to UN development assistance. In particular, the right to development is seen as part of a dynamic process which integrates civil, cultural, economic, political and social rights, where the well-being of all individuals in a society is improved. The eradication of poverty is a key to the the right to development.

The UN is also a forum to support the right of women to participate fully in the political, economic, and social life of their countries. The UN contributes to raising consciousness of the concept of human rights through its covenants and its attention to specific abuses through its General Assembly resolutions or Court rulings.

5.2.3.1.2.3.2. Promote Health & Human Development
The UN programs and funds for health work under the authority of the General Assembly and the Economic and Social Council to carry out their economic and social mandates. The World Health Organization (WHO) coordinates programs aimed at solving health problems and at the attainment by all people of the highest possible level of health. It works in such areas as immunization, health education and the provision of essential drugs.

The UN has special health programs for children. Every year, 3 million children are saved by immunization, but almost 3 million more die from preventable diseases. UNICEF, WHO, the World Bank Group, several private foundations, most of the pharmaceutical industry, and many governments have joined hands in a new initiative (the Global Alliance for Vaccines and

Immunization) to reduce deaths from diseases to zero. Other UN agencies work with local officials and NGOs to meet the health needs of children in conflict situations, such as this UNICEF-led immunization campaign in Afghanistan. The UN Children's Fund (UNICEF) is the lead UN organization working for the long-term survival, protection and development of children. Active in some 160 countries, areas and territories, its programs focus on primary health care, immunization, nutrition, and basic health education

UN programs try to eradicate diseases. UNICEF, UNDP, the World Bank and WHO joined forces in 1998 to launch a new campaign to fight malaria, which kills more than 1 million people a year. Joint initiatives to expand immunization and develop new vaccines have enlisted the support of business leaders, philanthropic foundations, non-governmental organizations and governments. The UN supports programs on HIV/AIDS, including grass-roots education campaigns, in 155 countries. Many other UN programs work for development, in partnership with governments and NGOs. Smallpox was eradicated from the world through a global campaign coordinated by WHO. Another WHO campaign has eliminated polio from the Americas, and aims at eradicating it globally by 2005.

The UN Human Settlements Program (UN-Habitat) assists people living in health-threatening housing conditions. UNHCR's assistance for Pakistan's Afghan refugees focuses on education and health. To pay for this assistance, the UN has raised billions of dollars from international donors. In 2001, the Office for the Coordination of Humanitarian Affairs launched 19 interagency appeals, raising more than $1.4 billion to assist 44 million people in 19 countries and regions.

5.2.3.1.2.3.3. Promote Education
UNESCO (the UN Educational, Scientific and Cultural Organization) promotes education for all, cultural development, protection of the world's natural and cultural heritage, international cooperation in science, and freedom and communication of the press.

5.2.3.1.2.3.4. Encourage Economic Development
The UN is in a unique position to promote development; it has a global presence and a comprehensive mandate to address social, economic and emergency needs. The UN tries to be neutral and not represent any particular national or commercial interest. And, it offers a voice for every country, regardless of wealth or power, on major policy decisions.

The UN has played a role in building international consensus on action for development. Beginning in 1960, the General Assembly has helped set priorities and goals through a series of 10-year International Development Strategies. While focusing on issues of particular concern, the Decade strategies have consistently stressed the need for progress on all aspects of social and economic development. The UN continues to formulate new development objectives in such key areas as sustainable development, the advancement of women, human rights, environmental protection and good governance. The UN continues to build new programs and actions to fulfill the objectives.

At the Millennium Summit in September 2000, leaders of nations adopted a set of Millennium Development Goals aimed at supporting development; at eradicating extreme poverty and hunger; at achieving universal primary education; at promoting gender equality and empowering women; at reducing child mortality; at improving maternal health; at combating HIV/AIDS, malaria and other diseases; and at ensuring environmental sustainability. These goals have specific measurable targets to be achieved by the year 2015, such as: Reducing by half the proportion of those who earn less than a dollar a day; achieving universal primary education; eliminating gender disparity at all levels of education; and dramatically reducing child mortality while increasing maternal health.

The UN and its agencies, including the World Bank and the UN Development Program (UNDP), are the premier vehicle for furthering development in poorer countries, providing assistance worth more than $30 billion a year. The UNDP is the largest multilateral source of grant technical assistance in the world. The UN also publishes annually the Human Development Index (HDI), a comparative measure ranking countries by poverty, literacy, education, life expectancy, and other factors.

5.2.3.1.2.3.5. Offer Poverty Relief
Other UN social service programs address poverty and relief, especially in vulnerable Africa. A UN System-wide Special Initiative on Africa, a 10-year, $25 billion endeavor launched in 1996, combines all UN efforts into a common program to ensure basic education, health services and food security in Africa.

Relief work for Palestine refugees has been carried out since 1949 by the UN Relief and Works Agency for Palestine Refugees in the Near East (UNRWA). As of 2006, the Agency provides essential health, education, relief and social services, as well as implements income-generation programs for more than 4 million Palestine refugees in the region. A UN Coordinator oversees all development assistance provided by the UN system to the Palestinian people in Gaza and the West Bank.

5.2.3.1.2.3.6. Provide Human Assistance
Disasters can occur anywhere, at any time, from flood, drought, earthquake or conflict. The cost to human communities is lost lives, displaced populations, communities incapable of sustaining themselves, and great suffering.

After a disaster, or famine or war, the UN system provides emergency assistance, in the form of supplies, food, shelter, medicines and logistical support to the victims, many of whom are children, women and the elderly. When disasters occur, the UNDP for instance, coordinates relief work at the local level, while promoting recovery and long-term development. In 2001, for example, following a devastating earthquake in India, the agency moved quickly to help local communities, while working to reduce long-term vulnerability to natural disasters.

In providing humanitarian assistance, the UN has to overcome major logistical and security constraints in the field. Reaching the affected areas can be a major obstacle, getting adequate supplies another. Recently, many crises have been aggravated by an erosion of respect for human rights. Humanitarian workers have been denied access to people in need. Warring factions have deliberately targeted civilians and aid workers. Since 1992, over 200 UN civilian staff members have been killed and 265 workers have been taken hostage while serving in humanitarian operations. In the effort to prevent human rights violations in the midst of crisis, the UN High Commissioner for Human Rights has taken an active role in the UN response to emergencies.

The UN coordinates its response to humanitarian crises through a committee its humanitarian bodies, chaired by the UN Emergency Relief Coordinator. Members include UNICEF, UNDP, WFP, and the UN High Commissioner for Refugees (UNHCR). Major non-governmental and intergovernmental humanitarian organizations, such as the International Committee of the Red Cross, are represented as well. The UN Emergency Relief Coordinator is responsible for developing policy for humanitarian action and for promoting humanitarian issues, such as helping to raise awareness of the consequences of the proliferation of small arms or the negative effects of sanctions.

People who have fled war, persecution or human rights abuse, that is, refugees and displaced persons, are assisted by UNHCR. At the start of 2001, there were 22 million people of concern to UNHCR in 120 countries, including 5.4 million who are internally displaced within a nation. About 3.6 million Afghans accounted for 30 per cent of refugees worldwide, followed by 568,000 refugees from Burundi and 512,800 from Iraq.

War and civil strife have separated an estimated 1 million children from their parents since 1994, made 12 million more homeless, and left 10 million severely traumatized. UNICEF seeks to meet the needs of these children by supplying food, safe water, medicine and shelter. UNICEF has also promoted the concepts of 'children as zones of peace.' It also created 'days of tranquility' and 'corridors of peace' to help protect children in war and provide them with essential services. And, in countries undergoing extended emergencies or recovering from conflict, humanitarian assistance is increasingly seen as part of an overall peace-building effort, along with developmental, political and financial assistance.

5.2.3.1.2.4.To Harmonize the Actions of Nations

There is a musical analogy with the health and operation of ecosystems, and with the health and harmony of nations; health equals harmony.[19] The four essential elements of music are rhythm, melody, harmony, and tone color. Their combined effects form a web of sound. The combination can lead to the idea of physical motion. Rhythm can lead to monotony. Melody is associated with emotion. A good melody should be of satisfying proportions.

Unlike rhythm and melody, which come naturally, harmony gradually evolved from an intellectual conception that was unknown until the ninth century A.D. The earliest form of harmony was called organum, when you harmonized in intervals of thirds or sixths above the melody. Harmony is the study of chords and their relationships (chords are sounding together of separate tones, a full chord is made of three or more tones).

What can music tell ecology? Harmony continues over time. If a forest has harmony it has to be seen over time, long periods of time. Furthermore harmony is related to wholeness. The word "whole" comes from the Indo-European root *kailo*, which is also the root for the words health and holy. The concept of the whole forest is relevant. A forest that has very complete complement of interacting beings. A whole forest can renew itself without replanting and pesticides.

David Bohm, in his theory of the implicate universe, proposes that health is a result of a harmonious interaction of all the analyzable parts that comprise the extricate order—cells, tissues, organs, the body—with the surrounding larger environment. Health is a quality that is grounded in the total order of the environment (or implicate order). Health is a dynamic quality of the entire movement of the environment (holoverse) as it flows. As organisms sometimes interfere with others or with the flow of change, the harmony breaks down—we call that disease. Health is the dance of bodies that interpenetrate (in Paul Shepard's image).

None of the bodies are completely independent or completely bounded; they are interdependent and open systems. A body is only maintained by a flow of energy and materials from its environment—much of this flow is in the form of other entities, usually much smaller, such as prey, insects, bacteria, viruses.

What can music suggest to a global political framework? The essence of harmony is allowing all elements to have a voice or sound. That is one purpose of the UN, to allow each nations to have a voice. Harmony is more likely if no one nation can dominate the others all the time at every level.

5.2.3.1.2.4.1. Governance of Nations
The UN has helped run elections in countries with little democratic history, including recently in Afghanistan and East Timor. In East Timor, UN-brokered talks between Indonesia and Portugal culminated in a May 1999 agreement that opened the way for a popular consultation on the status of the territory. Under the agreement, a UN mission supervised voter registration and an August 1999 ballot, in which 78 per cent of East Timorese voted for independence over their regional autonomy within Indonesia. In August 2001, a major step was taken in that direction, with the election of a Constituent Assembly which drafted the constitution for an independent and democratic East Timor. The people of East Timor, in August 2001, cast their ballots for a democratically elected assembly, under UN-supervised elections.

For countries in transition to more open government or democracy, the UN provides technical assistance for holding free and fair elections, improving judicial structures, drafting constitutions, training human rights officials, and transforming armed movements into political parties. In 1994, a UN mission observed South Africa's first racially-open elections. The UN has supervised elections in Namibia and elsewhere.

The United Nations works to support good governance, through civil law and order, elections and human rights, in countries struggling with the aftermath of conflict. The UN works to promote dialogue between parties, to establish a broad-based, inclusive government, with an appropriate political framework and leadership. In the Pacific, the UN helped the government of Papua New Guinea and the Bougainville parties reach a comprehensive agreement covering issues of autonomy, referendum and weapons disposal. In Haiti, following international action to restore the democratically elected government, the UN offered a comprehensive program that emphasized human rights, consensus-building and conflict-reduction, with the strong participation of civil society. The UN supports good governance with its programs.

5.2.3.1.2.4.2. Environment of Nations

Environmental conventions sponsored by the UN have helped to reduce acid rain in Europe and North America, to cut marine pollution worldwide, and to phase out production of gases destroying the ozone layer of the planet. International diplomacy, as a result of other conferences, such as UNCED, may recognize that nature is a finite source of resources, as well as a finite sink for wastes and a finite regenerator of cycles. The UN provides some oversight on overuse of resources, such as forests and fishing grounds.

5.2.3.1.3. Activities of the UN

The UN has developed many public forums, so that people from many nations can address the challenges and problems that are either world-wide or global.

5.2.3.1.3.1. Conferences

When an issue is considered particularly important, the General Assembly may convene an international conference to focus global attention on the issue and to build a consensus for consolidated action. A recent example is the UN Conference on Environment and Development, also called the Earth Summit, in June 1992, which led to the creation of the UN Commission on Sustainable Development to advance the conclusions reached in Agenda 21, the final text of agreements negotiated by governments at UNCED.

There are other examples. The International Conference on Population and Development, in September 1994, approved a program of action to address the critical challenges and interrelationships between population and sustainable development during the next 20 years. The World Summit on Trade Efficiency, held in October 1994, focused on the use of modern information technology to expand international trade. The World Summit for Social Development, held in March 1995, underscored responsibilities of nations for sustainable development and found commitment to plans that invest in basic education, health care, and economic opportunity for all, including women and girls. The Fourth World Conference on Women, in September 1995, sought to accelerate implementation of historic agreements reached at the previous World Conference on Women. And, the Second UN Conference on Human Settlements (Habitat II), in June 1996, addressed the challenges of human settlement, development and management in the twenty-first century.

5.2.3.1.3.2. International Years
The UN declares and coordinates "International Years" in order to focus world attention on important issues. Using the symbolism of the UN, a specially designed logo for the year, and the infrastructure of the UN system to coordinate events worldwide, the various years have helped advance key issues on a global scale.

5.2.3.1.3.3.Agreements Treaties & International law
The United Nations Charter specifically requires the UN to undertake the progressive codification and development of international law. Over 500 conventions, treaties and standards have resulted from this work, and they have provided a framework for promoting international peace and security and for spurring economic and social development. Nations that ratify these conventions are legally bound by them.

The International Law Commission prepares drafts on topics of international law which can then be incorporated into conventions and opened for ratification by States. Some of these conventions form the basis for law governing relations among States, such as the convention on diplomatic relations or the convention regulating the use of international watercourses.

The UN Commission on International Trade Law develops rules and guidelines designed to harmonize and facilitate laws regulating international trade. The UN has also pioneered the development of international environmental law. Agreements such as the convention to combat desertification, the convention on the ozone layer, and the convention on the transborder movement of hazardous wastes are administered by the UN Environment Programme.

The UN negotiates treaties such as the Convention on the Law of the Sea, to avoid potential international disputes. Disputes over use of the oceans also may be adjudicated by a special court. The Convention on the Law of the Sea seeks to ensure equitable access by all countries to the riches of the oceans, to protect the oceans from pollution and to facilitate freedom of navigation and research. The Convention against Illicit Traffic in Narcotic Drugs is the key international treaty against drug trafficking.

The United Nations fosters international efforts to create a legal framework against terrorism. Twelve global conventions on the issue have been negotiated under the auspices of the United Nations, including the 1979 Convention against the Taking of Hostages, the 1997 Convention for the Suppression of Terrorist Bombings, and the 1999 Convention for the Suppression of the Financing of Terrorism.

The International Court of Justice (ICJ) is the main court of the UN. Its purpose is to adjudicate disputes among states. The work of the ICJ continues from 1946. The IJC has heard cases where the Democratic Republic of Congo accused France of illegally detaining former heads of state accused of war crimes and where Nicaragua accused the United States of illegally arming the Contras—the source of the Iran-Contra affair.

5.2.3.1.3.4. Trials of the Courts
The UN also runs international criminal tribunals, including the International Criminal Tribunal for Rwanda (ICTR), as well as ones for the former Yugoslavia (ICTY), the Special Court for Sierra Leone, and the Ad-Hoc Court for East Timor.

5.2.3.1.4. Strengths of the UN
The UN has increased the involvement of nations with global issues, from disease to health and population. The UN has involved schools in its programs, through programs such as a "Model UN."

The efforts of the UN have resulted in upsurges of activism and declines in conflicts. A report produced by the Human Security Centre at the University of British Columbia, with support from several governments and foundations, documented a dramatic, but largely unknown, decline in the number of wars, genocides and human rights abuses over the past decade, after the end of the Cold War. The report, published by Oxford University Press, argued that the single most compelling explanation for these changes is found in the activities of the UN.

The report singles out several specific investments that have been particularly effective. There has been a six-fold increase in the number of UN missions mounted to prevent wars, from 1990 to 2002. There has been a four-fold increase in efforts to stop existing conflicts, from 1990 to 2002. There have also been: A seven-fold increase in the number of groups and other government-initiated mechanisms to support peacemaking and peacebuilding missions, from 1990 to 2003; an eleven-fold increase in the number of economic sanctions against regimes around the world, from 1989 to 2001; and, a four-fold increase in the number of UN peacekeeping operations, from 1987, to 1999. These efforts were both more numerous and often substantially larger and more complex than those of the Cold War era.

The UN has been able to broker independence for some nations. In East Timor, UN-sponsored talks between Indonesia and Portugal culminated in a May 1999 agreement which paved the way for a popular consultation on the status of the territory and eventually for an independent and democratic East Timor.

The UN has tried to consider nationless people. The UN has extended its efforts to groups of people within nations. For example, in 1977 the UN organized a meeting to discuss the creation of indigenous rights under international law. Indigenous peoples usually do not have armies or national currencies, perhaps not enough to define them as nations.

5.2.3.1.4. Inadequacies of the UN
The founders of the UN expected that the organization could prevent conflicts between nations and make future wars impossible, by fostering the ideal of collective security. Those expectations have not been completely realized. During the Cold War, about 1947 to 1991, the division of the world into hostile camps made peacekeeping extremely difficult. Following the end of the Cold War, the UN was expected to become the agency for achieving world peace and co-operation, as military conflicts continued to increase. The

breakup of the Soviet Union, however, left the U.S. in a unique position of global dominance as self-anointed peacekeepers. This has created a variety of challenges for the UN. Even where it has been successful, the UN has been unable to create peaceful conditions lasting enough for its peacekeepers to withdraw.

Perhaps because of its nature, or its relative powerlessness, the UN has had failures, problems, and issues. The intergovernmental nature of the UN means that it must reach consensus; it is an association of 191 member states and not an independent organization. Even when actions are mandated by the Security Council, the Secretariat is rarely given the full resources needed to carry them out.

The UN fails at times. In some cases, UN member nations have shown reluctance to enforce Security Council resolutions. Iraq may have broken 17 Security Council resolutions dating back to June 28, 1991 as well as trying to bypass the UN economic sanctions. The U.S. violated international law when it invaded Iraq. The UN did not respond; nor has it responded to other violations of international law by the U.S., especially related to the treatment of prisoners. For nearly a decade, Israel defied resolutions calling for the dismantling of settlements in the West Bank and Gaza.

The UN failed to prevent the 1994 Rwandan genocide, which resulted in the death of nearly a million people, due to the refusal of the security council members to approve any military action. The UN failed to intervene during the Second Congo War, 1998-2002, which claimed nearly five million people in the Democratic Republic of Congo, and failed to carry out and distribute humanitarian aid. The UN failed to intervene in the 1995 Srebrenica massacre, despite the fact that it had designated Srebrenica a "safe haven" for refugees and assigned 600 Dutch peacekeepers to protect it. The UN failed to successfully deliver food to starving people in Somalia; the food had been seized by local warlords, and a U.S./UN attempt to apprehend the warlords seizing these shipments resulted in the 1993 Battle of Mogadishu.

The UN has been unable to control sexual abuse by UN peacekeepers—men from several nations have been repatriated from UN operations for sexually abusing and exploiting girls as young as 12 in a number of peacekeeping missions. A 2005 internal UN investigation found that sexual exploitation and abuse has been reported in at least five of 16 countries where UN peacekeepers have been deployed, including the Democratic Republic of the Congo, Haiti, Burundi, Cote d'Ivoire, and Liberia. This abuse seems to be widespread and continuing, despite revelations and investigations by the UN Office of Internal Oversight Services.

The UN has scandals, problems and security issues. The inclusion of nations such as Libya and Sudan, whose leaders have weak records on human rights, on the United Nations Commission on Human Rights of nations, is an issue of concern. These countries argue, perhaps with some justification, that Western countries, with their history of colonial aggression and brutality, have no right to argue about membership of the Commission. One solution would be to qualify members by their current records on rights.

The Oil-for-Food Program was established by the UN in 1996 to allow Iraq to sell oil on the world market in exchange for food, medicine, and the other needs of ordinary Iraqi citizens who were affected by international economic sanctions, without allowing the Iraqi government to rebuild its military after the first Gulf War. The program was discontinued in late 2003 amidst allegations of widespread abuse and corruption; several people were implicated in bribery. Under UN auspices, over $65 billion USD worth of Iraqi oil was sold on the world market. Officially, about $46 billion was used for humanitarian needs, and additional revenue was used to pay for Gulf War reparations through a Compensation Fund, the UN administrative and operational costs for the Program (2.2%), and the weapons inspection program (0.8%).

The UN is limited by its lack of power. Although the UN has been effective at times dealing with limited kinds of conflicts, it has had problems dealing with unresolved, long-term conflicts, such as the Basques and the Spanish or Israel and Arab countries. UN concern over the Arab-Israeli conflict spans five decades and five full-fledged wars. The UN has defined principles for a just and lasting peace, including two benchmark Security Council resolutions in 1967) and 1973, which remain the basis for an overall settlement.

Sometimes the UN seems powerless with its own agencies. How should the UN deal with the World Trade Organization? Should it make it a nonprofit? How should the UN regulate goods and people? Is the free movement of goods or people across any boundary a good idea? The World Trade Organization needs to be made sustainable. Perhaps, it could be incorporated into the UN. But, the WTO must have environmental assessments, which are more important than WTO rules. New rules would give preferential treatment to trading partners with strong environmental policies and labor practices, and human rights.

The UN depends on voluntary dues from its member nations. Its funding is often too little. Expenditures of the UN system on operational activities for development, mostly for economic and social programs to help the world's poorest countries, amount to approximately $6 billion a year, excluding the World Bank, International Monetary Fund and International Fund for Agricultural Development. This amount is roughly equal to 0.75 per cent of world military expenditures of over $800 billion.

5.2.3.1.5. *Proposals for a New Framework*
In 2004, allegations of mismanagement and corruption regarding the Oil-for-Food Program for Iraq led to calls to reform the UN. There have been many calls for the reform of the UN, but there is little clarity or consensus about how to reform it. Some nations want the UN to play a greater or more effective role in world affairs, while other nations want its role reduced to symbolic humanitarian work.

An earlier, official reform was initiated by UN Secretary-General Kofi Annan shortly after starting his first term on January 1, 1997. Reforms mentioned included changing the permanent membership of the Security Council, which still reflects the power relations of the victors in the 1945 war; making the bureaucracy more transparent, accountable and efficient; making the UN more democratic; and, imposing an international tariff on arms manufacturers worldwide.

In September 2005, the UN convened a World Summit that brought together the heads of most member states, in a plenary session of the General Assembly's 60th session. The UN called the summit "a once-in-a-generation opportunity to take bold decisions in the areas of development, security, human rights and reform of the United Nations." Secretary General Annan had proposed that the summit agree upon a global "grand bargain" to reform the UN, revamping international systems for peace and security, and human rights and development, to make them capable of addressing the extraordinary challenges facing the UN in this century. World leaders agreed on a compromise text with such notable items as: The creation of a Peacebuilding Commission to provide a central mechanism to help countries emerging from conflict; the agreement that the international community has the right to step in when national governments fail to fulfill their responsibility to protect their own citizens from atrocity crimes; a Human Rights Council, since created and operational; an agreement to devote more resources to UN's internal oversight agency; several agreements to spend billions more on achieving Millennium Development Goals; a clear and unambiguous condemnation of terrorism "in all its forms and manifestations"; a Democracy Fund; and, an agreement to wind up the Trusteeship Council due to the completion of its mission.

The UN is a recognition of our human limits—also that otherness needs to exist. It is too unsatisfactory, but too important to abandon.

A global unity cannot govern itself; it requires an external controlling agent. But, small nations could govern themselves, and the UN would be not a supergovernment, but a global center for small-scale business and small-scale politics. The UN should not be a union or an association, but a weak federal government with a few more powers than the largest nation. Perhaps the UN should also have a division of power similar to nations, that is, an executive branch, a representative legislature, with equitable representation, and a judiciary.

The traditional way of governing, from the Medes and the Persians, to the Swiss and the U.S., has been to reduce the size of the governed unit, not the size of the governing unit. The Roman approach was to divide and rule. The Duke of Sully and Henry IV of France planned to limit the size and number of European states to fifteen of equal size. Hitler applied the same strategy to Prussia and Austria. Kohr alleges that all successful empires share this small-cell pattern.

One way to divide a great power is to host a war to deunify it. Another way would be to give them a gift, according to Kohr, of proportional representation in the global federal union, such as the UN. A conventional federal principle of government grants each sovereign unit an equal number of votes irrespective of size. International law does not distinguish between degrees of sovereignty. Otherwise those with more population, territory, or wealth might be considered better. In theory, regions of nations could represent their regions, regardless of what other federal union they might belong to. Centralized systems would have to be decentralized for membership. For checks and balances to work the UN has to be larger than the largest of nations.

How would the UN limit size, though? By territory, population? What would a maximum be? 20 million? How can we have equality of nations? Should that be decided by equal numbers? Equal territory or places? A global organization, such as the UN, can be a suboptimal solution with plenty of flexibility. It can be satisficing rather than optimal.

The UN would be an agent of disunity, of political anarchies. Its concern would be with global things and coordination (rather than strict order). All nations would have to be dissolved through representation to allow voting. But have a maximum size. The natural list of nations already exists, within the unions formed violently in the past 200 years. Aragon, Valencia, Catalonia, Castile, Galicia, Warsaw, Bohemia, Moravia, Slovakia, Ruthenia, Salvonia, Slovenia, Croatia, Serbia, Macedonia, Transylvania, Moldavia, Walachia, Bessarabia, Macedonia, Sicily, Basque, Catalania, Scotland, Bavaria, and Wales, among many.

A central governing body for the earth has two very important functions: To insure a diverse biosphere, on which all humanity depends, and to equalize the opportunity of humans to live in health. There is no organization that addresses either of these functions. A global organization is necessary to coordinate the system. Either individual nations or a partially-responsible global institution is inadequate. The global organization must have the regulatory powers to maintain a healthy environment and to coordinate the constituent nations. It might have a new name as well, with new powers and responsibilities. In his pamphlet Common Sense, Thomas Paine encourage people to revolution. Later, he proposed that the U.S. help form an "Association of Nations." As a working title, the Association of Nations can replace the United Nations, which are not really united and which do not really represent all nations.

5.2.3.1.6. *Strengths and Weaknesses of a New International Body*

5.2.3.1.6.1. Potential Strengths of the Frame of an International Body
A holocultural framework, such as the Association of Nations, can identify and attempt to solve global problems, such as the greenhouse effect or acid rain, that cannot be solved at the level of a culture or nation. It can address the working of opposites in human affairs, where the solution to one global problem may cause another.

By being a global framework, it can adjust international economics. Local communities are based on traditional cultures, which have long-term lasting power. Traditional cultures often have wealth-leveling properties, absolute property ceilings, fixed wants, and production coupled with need— all of which results in a stable economy. Efficiency and productivity are less important than use and appropriateness. The framework can promote limited and rational economic development and coordinate international economic exchanges, protecting those cultures that choose to remain outside networks. It can put restraints on the current international community, from large corporations to large federations.

The framework can provide a holistic education of all cultures, besides that of the local culture. It can archive knowledge of other cultures. The experiences of many lives are encoded in myths, along with natural phenomena, supernatural beliefs, moral values, and features of the culture. All interpretation and recounting of the past is mythmaking. Mythic symbols store information concisely, which makes it possible for a person to assimilate the collective experiences of a culture. That is why myths reflect the detail of a culture.

The framework may be capable of realigning social boundaries to ecological realities; the boundaries of a watershed or ecotone would be more appropriate than geometric lines. A natural region supports a great deal of life without human intervention; it produces enough life to support a reasonable number of humans. We need to know natural associations and limitations because these determine the harmony of development.

A framework can justify a wide diversity in nature and accommodation to natural laws. It can recognize the value of the total biosphere and respect all forms of life, past, present, and future. It can do so, because, unlike traditional or industrial cultures, it is conscious of itself and its purpose.

5.2.3.1.6.1.1. Being Conscious

Creating a holocultural image requires changing the gestalt of images of self, nature, and society. That effort is revitalization. Unlike classic cultural change, revitalization requires the explicit intent of the members of society; it depends on restructuring elements already in use or known. Where the culture remains responsible for the performance of ritual or the preservation of doctrine, the images are preserved. When the images are anticipatory, they lead to development and social change. Attractiveness reinforces the movement towards them. We are dependent now on our consciousness of the entire system of nature and humanity. Undertaking a conscious orderly change in our living habits, before it is forced on us by an unbalanced environment, gives us more options.

5.2.3.1.6.1.2. Recognizing Context

Cultures change as the result of human interactions in nature. Nature and cultures are in a constant state of flux; cultures have much in parallel with biological species. Our thoughts and ideas, tools and cultures, are as much a part of nature as other species or peat bogs. To preserve our cultures and natural environments, we must understand that they are examples of a dynamic order brought forth by the earth in its history. We are physically dependent on nature. We are psychologically dependent as well; without signals from nature, our minds become closed and dead. We also are physically and psychologically dependent on culture. Yet, the diversity of habitats and cultures, is allowed to erode.

A global framework for cultures depends on important principles drawn from ecology. One role of ecology could be to urge the toleration of fluctuation, irregularity, uncertainty, and diversity. As adaptive systems, cultures change as ecosystems change. And sometimes ecosystem change is a result of cultural change. They are linked together.

If humans adapted more closely to the complexities of natural ecosystems, then human cultures would be more diverse and stable. If humans adapted to the complexities of natural ecosystems, then human societies would be more complex. The proper attitude of an ecological framework is care, a positive spontaneity, but also a "letting be," a reverence toward the wild alienness of nature, a willingness to comply with the limitations of natural systems, and a willingness to reduce the dominance of natural systems.

What this means practically is that the local environment would determine the extent of a culture. The framework would recommend wilderness areas sufficient for a culture, although the shape and expression of these areas would depend on the kind of culture. Eugene Odum has calculated that for the temperate southern United States it takes two acres of wilderness to support each human being.

Cultures can determine the minimum, or optimum, amount of wilderness areas to support local ecosystems; for instance, very large areas are required in tropical ecosystems or deserts, relatively little ones in grasslands and temperate forests. They can determine the natural productivity and the percentage to be used by humans, as well as artificial productivity and costs. Cultures can key their population to natural productivity for long-term sustainable existence. And, they can multiply any increase by trade-offs, such as a reduced standard of living or exchange with another group.

The framework could recommend an optimum size for each human population. A nation must have a population large enough for economic advantages in food production, education, and entertainment, and for political tools. As Leopold Kohr has noted, the size of a culture is determined by the function it fulfills. The function of a state is to provide its members with protection and other advantages that they do not have as independents.

When a state becomes too large, it cannot offer protection—it cannot offer even clean air or water. The country of Andorra, with about ten thousand people is stable, sovereign, and healthy; the Greek, Italian, and German city-states that furnished much of Western civilization often numbered less than twenty thousand individuals. As the size of a nation increases, the negative factors of civilization, such as overcrowding and breakdowns, increase. Technology has the capacity to allow some expansion, but not an infinite amount. A comprehensive population policy must be created for larger cultures, and it must fit into the context of wilderness and other cultures.

5.2.3.1.6.1.3. Being Comprehensive
A holocultural framework includes all human cultures without judgment. The framework provides a higher resolution image of the whole, since it incorporates all human cultures. It includes all its members, recognizing that each says something worthwhile. It is not details or knowledge of the operation that is critical, but an understanding of the wholeness of order.

The framework can interact with nature much like the mythic, but understand the rational and mechanical sides of thought. It would not be a conglomerate of sciences; it would not be limited by the facts of any science, even ecology. The insights of people of every culture must be considered.

Each person tells of a way the world is; together, these ways make a holistic framework.

The framework includes ultrahuman cultures in its consideration. It can create wilderness zones that would have various limitations for conversion or use. It can reserve large areas of wilderness for ultrahuman beings and biogeochemical processes.

The framework can attempt to combine the best single elements of industrial culture with the superior components of primary cultures, in parallel with Gordon Taylor's paraprimitive solution. High technology can offer immense benefits, with restraint and appropriate limits. Primary cultures can satisfy the human needs for belonging and status.

5.2.3.1.6.1.4. Making Authentic Images

Individual cultures, in their unique cosmologies, create images of the human place in nature, in terms of mastery, community, or participants. The holocultural framework offers a holistic value of human worth, outside of any one local perspective. It promotes and protects universally accepted values: Reciprocity—the repayment of obligations; territorial integrity for cultures; legitimacy—the value of children born in wedlock; and the working of opposites—life and death, sacred and profane. It can promote basic rights human rights: The right to land, food, shelter; to equal opportunity to develop, regardless of race or sex; to participate in global affairs as desired; and to live without excessive discrimination or conflict.

5.2.3.1.6.1.5. Protecting the Diversity of Cultures.

Each culture is a response to a unique place, and so there is a diversity of cultures. Industrial culture condemns to backwardness any culture that is not part of its global electronic neural system. This definition of backwardness means only a lack of fast things or professional enslavement. Primary cultures do not lack art or play, or food, tradition, freedom, or happiness.

It might be good for cultures to be uncoupled economically; it might be a sound option for traditional societies unwilling to make the same mistakes as industrial ones. The framework would keep cultures separate and coordinate any exchanges between them. It would resolve disputes that arise from territorial expansion, the past movements of people and borders, or the unequal expansion of cultures in the same territory, such as the Sinhalese and Tamil in Sri Lanka.

5.2.3.1.6.1.6. Providing Order

The AN would have to be stronger than the largest nation, through arms control, disarmament, and its own weapons program. It would have to disarm the nations substantially. Police operations would be quite similar to the current United Nations, although there would be differences. The AN would have a permanent police force, kept in regional divisions. The funding for the police force would be as a result of the income of the AN, not dependent on voluntary membership fees.

The first force of Police would always be unarmed. If a second force is necessary it would be well-armed. In fact, AN police forces would be better armed than any single nation. A maximum residence time would be set, and an exit strategy required.

Of course, the AN would work to prevent conflicts. Although many conflicts would be reduced by the changes in the Eutopian framework, there will always be conflicts between cultures. AN forces would try to solve the problems through understanding, compromise and consensus.

5.2.3.1.6.2. Potential Weaknesses of an International Framework

History does not show a progressive unfolding of human betterment; loss and defeat are much of the texture of daily life. A framework will not be able to solve all problems, especially ubiquitous ones like hunger. No human construct is perfect and completely comprehensive. No human framework can expect to solve every problem to everyone's satisfaction. The framework can be expected to exhibit a number of weaknesses.

5.2.3.1.6.2.1. Being Abstract

A holocultural framework is a general human construct, which may not be implemented. There is no working model of global unity. Our experience with international cooperation on an immense scale is minimal. Our ability to plan our cultures and foresee our impacts is minimal. Other abstract ideals, including democracy and communism, have been disappointing and severely modified in practice.

Kinship is more rigidly localized than other dimensions of culture, which can be more rapidly disseminated and assimilated. The transition from kinship to a simultaneous abstract global citizenship may slow. Kinship loyalty sometimes clashes with global perspectives. A framework trying to lessen the conflict and resolve contradictions may be faced with more conflict.

5.2.3.1.6.2.2. Being Uncritical

Such a framework, by definition, accepts any human culture, even bad ones. It cannot make judgments about use. In avoiding ethnocentrism, it must accept failure. It may not be able to deal fairly with cultures that are dying out, because they are unfit or because they are victims of a large coercive culture. Yet, it cannot artificially support bad images. It must preserve the process of making and sustaining a way of living, not every individual culture.

This framework does not reject or judge cultures, but incorporates all the practicality and paradox. It makes no distinctions between right and wrong or good and bad; these polarities are more like positive stimuli useful to development. Hence, there is no evil, as considered in many cultures, only suffering that results from lack of wisdom. Many customs, like sacred cows in India, at first glance, seem to be dysfunctional. But, even sacred cows provide dung for cooking fires.

5.2.3.1.6.2.3. Being Contradictory

It used to be, as Karl Marx said, that village life enslaved the human mind with traditional rules and subjugated it. No more—too much communication is a greater threat. Our excess communication tends to wear out our ability to feel empathy and react to suffering. Some cultures may overcommunicate and others may undercommunicate. Undercommunication may result in ignorance and suffering; overcommunication may result in passiveness and insignificance. The framework will have to abide more than one contradiction.

5.2.3.1.6.2.4. Being Weak
The framework may not have the power or authority to make agreeable boundaries. It may be unable to set aside large enough areas for natural processes. It may not be able to dictate population restrictions for some cultures without seeming to be genocidal or prejudiced. It may not be able to achieve an agreeable redistribution of some kinds of wealth. Any action may result in some dislocation and suffering. It may be impossible to limit the interdependence of nations.

The framework may not be able to deal with incompatible cultures or the divisive forces of large industrial cultures. Some cultures may refuse to participate. It may not be able to handle large differences or to limit the influence of powerful corporations, which have no local accountability. Some traditional cultures may have trouble incorporating new ideas, such as the equality of women.

5.2.3.1.6.2.5. Being Fallible
A holocultural frame may try to address global problems that may be insoluble within its range. Some of its actions may have negative consequences for some cultures. For instance, in mediating boundaries that have changed over centuries, it may be difficult to rectify imbalance, theft, or suppression. Cultures have dominated, displaced, merged, or destroyed other cultures for millennia. No one knows how far back to trace a wrong. The dividing line might always seem arbitrary. It may be appropriate to return lands to the Pawnee, but not to the people that the Pawnee displaced.
5.2.3.1.6.2.6. Being Naïve
What does it mean to be naïve? Artless? Ingenuous, which we already consider a weakness of utopias? What is naïve? That people will accept inequity as it worsens? That people will always accept cheating and discrimination? Is it naïve to think that corporate greed will benefit starving children? Is it naïve to think that people will give up heroic luxuries to help people somewhere else on the planet? That nations will find it in their interest to break apart along ethnic or economic lines? A eutopian framework may always seem naïve by some definition or example, but by contrast with hard "realities" it will always seem less naïve.

5.2.3.2. *Responsibilities of a Global Framework*
There is already a world system. But it is not, and should not be, a stagnant, monolithic industrial system—to say that there is a human body is not to say that all organs have decided to become kidneys. A global order is necessary to govern this system. The Associated Nations (AN), an elected body, should have the regulatory powers necessary to maintain an healthy global environment It should have regulatory and advisory powers to maintain the independence and integrity of its constituent nations. It should

have regulatory and punitive powers to rectify resource and human rights infringements; only this body would have police powers and impersonal weapons. Various advisory bodies would recommend policies and actions to nations. The Associated Nations has six basic functions: To ensure a diverse biosphere; to manage resources; to protect unique cultures; to coordinate representation; to provide services to nations; and, to create peaceful conditions.

5.2.3.2.1. To Ensure a Diverse Biosphere.
To ensure a diverse biosphere, on which all humanity depends. The Associated Nations works to conserve genetic resources and ecosystems. Preservation of entire systems is addressed on a global scale. The Associated Nations is responsible for planetary monitoring of all major biomes and their ecosystems. The destruction of basic landscapes sets the frame for proper conservation and development policies. Many natural and artificial values are conserved this way.

In ecological ignorance, our ancestors cut down the cedars of Lebanon, ruined the Mediterranean, created dust bowls and deserts. History supports the notion that no civilization has ever recovered after ruining its environment. Some, like Egypt or Rome were replaced from the outside. Others, such as Ur or Rapa Nui, were rebuilt by wealthier invading peoples. A few, like the Mayans, settled for a lower level of complexity.

Ray Dasmann distinguishes between ecosystem people and biosphere people. Indigenous traditional societies are examples of the former, and technological societies are in the latter. The former live within a single ecosystem usually and are dependent on it for survival. If ecological rules, such as "do not overkill," are violated, they perish. Island people do not tolerate overpopulation. But biosphere people can draw support from any ecosystem on earth; if one place is ruined by exploitative pressure, then another place can be drawn from. But with absolute increase in human numbers, they cannot be completely insulated from ecosystem failures. Knowledge of local collapse in distant states, which are part of the resource commons could precipitate an ultimate collapse.

A natural way of extermination is by stimulating overgrowth. The natural way of preserving things and increasing the base of life is to contain growth; instead of expanding form, it duplicates it. Julian Huxley calls this adaptive radiation. Speciation uses a wider range of noncompetitive food sources than the expansion of a single species. This type of adaptation occurs in humans also. The relationship between groups can be characterized as symbiosis, living together. Biologically symbiosis increases the chances of its organisms for survival. Humans should choose goals that are symbiotic from the alternate paths.

But problems arise when societies become larger and inflexible, when the variety that insures tribal and small communities yields to nation states. Nation states have no value in a global order. The designation of cultural units does not involve a major revolution. Revolution is a false dilemma, it does not reflect the possibility of thousands of microrevolutions on farms, factories, and families, all at local levels.

5.2.3.2.1.1. Basic Landscapes

The basic landscapes and their divisions are described. By keeping these divisions separate, and limiting the kinds of activities in them, the landscapes themselves will be healthier. Not all activities are compatible; furthermore, living systems have developed in relative isolation, and function best with a limited amount of interference from other species or other systems.

5.2.3.2.1.1.1. Foundation Landscapes

Foundation landscapes protect natural processes. There is no scientific answer as to how much of the earth's surface should be reserved. Areas of the planet that have effectively remained unused are placed in this category, which is approximately 30 percent of the planet. Representative areas of all types, including many polar regions, deserts, and tropical forests may add up to 50 percent of the total land area. Large undeveloped and uninhabited areas, such as Antarctica, are designated foundations. A very large percentage of oceans, lakes, estuaries, and wetlands are included in this category. The category is further subdivided by the impact of human presence.

Foundation landscapes enclose the most sensitive and fragile areas. This would include the majority of wild areas. No human presence would be permitted in the most sensitive parts; data would be obtained from satellite mapping. In less sensitive areas, visitation would be permitted for scientific studies or other acquisition of knowledge; most machinery would be excluded.

5.2.3.2.1.1.2. Preservation Landscapes

These lands are those that have cultural values and are maintained by limited human intervention in that state, such as ruins or many kinds of grasslands. Many of these areas would permit only limited access for cultural or recreational purposes.

Large areas under continuous habitation by archaic cultures, primarily foraging or Swidden agriculture, would fall in this category; exploitation, which shaped some of these landscapes, would continue at traditional levels and with traditional ways. Herding and nomadism by archaic cultures would be normal, but only with traditional tools. Other landscapes maintained by human or domestic animal presence would be included, for example, parts of the Mediterranean, some of the English landscape, Japanese shrines, or various central continental grasslands.

5.2.3.2.1.1.3. Conservation Landscapes

These areas assume the regular exploitation of ecosystems by humanity, but well below natural, nonhuman-subsidized regeneration rates. Natural wildlife would be controlled and exploited by humans, including the commercial exploitation of uncultivated forest. Commercially exploited areas, natural forests, shorelines, wetlands would be included in this category; exploitation of wild plants and animals would be part of normal activity. Transport machinery, such as rail, air or road, would be permitted as impacts would be limited to right-of-ways. The greater pressure on these conservation areas would require greater care. The kinds of communities permitted in these areas would include communities that depend on natural ecosystems and permanent camps. Recreation would be allowed, but with limited machinery.

5.2.3.2.1.1.4. Domestic Landscapes

These areas are those that have simplified for human needs and must be maintained with human labor. Forests, grasslands, seas, and wetland areas would be manipulated for human benefit. Typical activities would include traditional agriculture (nonirrigated) and animal husbandry, with appropriate tools, which may be mechanized, herding, and animal shelters. Managed forests, using appropriate methods of cultivation, would be present, as would modern large-scale agriculture, using modern methods of cultivation, and livestock, including some factory farming, automation, industrial methods, and a larger scale of energy, which implies the dramatic conversion of the natural landscape. Special and general recreation would occur, with a provision for large-scale human recreational needs, such as hiking, skiing, and boating, using limited mechanical aids, excluding built-up settlements. Rural communities would be evident, with minimal services.

5.2.3.2.1.1.5. Artificial Landscapes

These areas have been completely modified and have few remaining natural features. Human dominance would vary from light residential areas, with permanent paved roads, following existing ones where possible or if not new roads planned to make minimum impact, restricted lanes and volumes of air and water transport, to residential areas with full services, including light commerce at low density, with provision of facilities and services, including some cottage employment, increased commerce at medium density, and recreation of any kind, with any machinery, to cityscapes dominated by central area functions, such as communications and services, at high density, interspersed with manufacturing transitional areas for light industry and services. Although a high biomass of animals and plants may exist, there would be low diversity and few wild species. There would be an isolated area for heavy industry and the disposal of noxious waste.

5.2.3.2.1.2. Global Ratios

Each land or ocean system would be classified and put into an appropriate category, ranging from pristine to heavily industrialized land. Each category would occupy a different percentage of the planetary surface, depending on calculations of minima and maxima and depending on cultural values and decisions. At a minimum, approximately fifty percent of the land area would occupy the first division (eighty percent of ocean and water surfaces); sixteen percent in each of the other three (four for water); leaving two percent for completely artificial landscapes—industrial or city (two for water). These figures are consistent with several earlier proposals. Eugene Odum suggests thirty percent forest cover world-wide, with sixty percent in tropical areas. Paul Shepard offers seventy-five percent of the total land area left wild in a techno-cynegetic society. Constantin Doxiadis suggests fifty percent of the surface area in wilderness. We cannot preserve less until we learn more about the requirements for large cycles.

5.2.3.2.2. To Manage Common Resources

The Associated Nations would have the power to designate areas for conservation, including the oceans and atmosphere. It would regulate all industrial and residential use of common resources. Furthermore, it would form new institutions, both regulatory and advisory, such as a Associated Nations Environmental Agency, to deal with resource availability and alternate technologies, create global scientific bodies to study global ecological balance, collect data on global systems, explore remote areas, and maintain a central library of all information on sciences, technologies and cultures. It would maintain reserves of food and minerals for emergencies and catastrophes. The Associated Nations could perform a resource function for all nations, maintaining large crop margins, for instance for seven years, to secure survival. Future survival should depend on systems sufficiently flexible and elastic to sustain moderate failures in parts of the world without causing catastrophes to a connected food system. This attitude applies to the entire technology and survival controversies: Irrigation, tankers, nuclear power, pesticides, population, deforestation, and genetic engineering.

Finally, the AN would recommend optimum populations for nations, although it would not enforce those figures. Optimal sizes would be calculated, based on social and ecological limits, as well as on traditional values. Every nation needs a comprehensive population policy, closely related to environmental and technological policies, and within the constraints of their agriculture. A single population policy for the world is unfair, since cultures are at different stages of development with different values. There are dilemmas posed by necessity to equate global balances and republican needs. Since the allocation of resources to a nation and the representation of a nation would be determined by area and not population, there would be no reason for a nation to exceed the optimum figure. If a nation wanted to expand its population, it could do so through a number of means: Trading off with other nations or through the development of new food technologies, such as attached greenhouses for every building. If growth exceeded a safety margin established by the Associated Nations, demographic policies would be strongly recommended by the Associated Nations, without prejudice or malice.

Humans have modified their surroundings as much as possible within their power to improve their lives. Recently, they have done so to improve nature. Believing that nature was incomplete, they added plants and animals, then added fields, structures, canals and dams to feed the plants and animals. In *The Origin of the Species*, Darwin observed that insular biotas were glaringly depauperate in general, until supplemented by human culture:[20] "man has stocked...far more fully and perfectly than has nature." Unfortunately, filling up nature and perfecting the earth did not proceed with ease; there were setbacks. Exotic animals and plants ran wild and became pests. Fire control caused raging fires. Dams became the sources of diseases. Canals introduced pests. Plantations ruined soils. Irrigation projects salted up the soil. Peter Matthiessen noted that where great, wild creatures ranged, vermin prosper. If the influx of new organisms of all kinds continues unabated, all life on earth will eventually become homogenous or drastically changed; then it will also be strained through the filter of adaptability to humanity and their managed crops. This flora and fauna will undergo change as our living habits change. On the other hand, if we plan our future, we can include squirrels instead of rats, butterflies instead of cockroaches.

The induced instability of ecosystems is an important cause of economic, political, and social disturbances throughout the world. The disturbances are passed on to humanity. And where our intervention has unbalanced nature, we need to repair. Each biota has developed only once in the history of the world. And once lost can never be regained. Some environmental degradation can be reversed, but not biome or species extinction. We do not know how many whole systems that we have destroyed. Nor do we know which element of a system is a more crucial one. Very little is known of degradative synergies from noise, heat and pollution.

5.2.3.2.2.1. Renewal of Resources
Ecosystems damaged by social activities may reacquire lost ecological qualities by natural processes. Ecosystems dependent upon periodic natural disturbances, for instance floods or fires, may be markedly changed if these disturbances are controlled. Damaged ecosystems may also be rehabilitated to a condition that includes some of their original characteristics and some beneficial to humanity. Much of our manipulation of nature is highly desirable for us, perhaps even for some natural systems. Some possibly may be enhanced by management techniques to an improved condition different from the original. Some may remain degraded.

Ecosystems have enormous powers of recovery from traumatic damage. They can overcome the effects of outside disturbances by progressively reestablishing ecological equilibrium, even if not exactly to the original state. Frequently, other potentials are activated by the outside disturbance. Unfortunately, the key word is outside. No disturbances are outside, anymore. If all ecosystems are disturbed, no improvement can come from outside either.

The rate of healing of injured systems is often more rapid than expected. Good management and human commitment can aid the process. The recycling of degraded environments is one of the urgent tasks of our age. Marsh envisioned man as a coworker[21] with nature in the reconstruction of "the damaged fabric which the negligence and wantonness of former lodgers has rendered untenable."

Under loving care, even very degraded ecosystems can be made productive and satisfactory for humanity, although not the same as the original. "Even the most successful programs of reclamation and the best artificial environments cannot of course duplicate the subtleties and complexities of natural environments; but most of them will improve in time," states Rene Dubos. Of course, they might, as they become less under control and less invaded. Perhaps humans have a secret desire for simple environments. Dubos seems entranced by the bleached islands of Greece, as well as by deserts. Do we want all earth to be those abstractions? Dubos has spoken eloquently of the humanized landscapes, but there is no one to praise what has been lost. There are inherent values in wilderness as much as in the humanized landscapes. The impoverishment of Southern Europe may be aesthetic, but it leads to human impoverishment.

Should ecosystems be restored to a close approximation of the predisturbance condition? It is always feasible to establish more than one type of ecosystem on a disturbed site. Due to climactic change, faithful restoration may be impossible. Certain ecosystems are perturbation dependent. Untouched reference areas could be preserved as models.

5.2.3.2.2.2. Conservation of Resources

The Emperor Asoka, in Third century BC India, took a positive stand on wildlife conservation. The same Asoka earlier had caused roads to be built with periodic rest stops, for the care of animals. In most literatures there is little mention of the long history of rural conservation. The rural economy is the result of centuries of careful cultivation. Wise people have always treated resources with care. Many countries in Europe and Middle east had strict regulations for management of water, wood and farmlands. Vergil's *Georgics* were written in support of government policy to remedy the decay of rural lands.

Carrying on from the UN, the AN would work to conserve genetic resources and necessary wetlands and watershed forests. The Biosphere Programme of UNESCO is a worldwide monitoring of all major biomes and their ecosystems based on international agreements. Conservation efforts are concerned with: The dynamics of a system; the interactions within the system and effects of climactic and system changes, including human involvement; the varying time scales of concern ; and, the preservation of natural communities with a high degree of integrity, subject to intrinsic processes.

Conservation is basically a problem in ecology and must be addressed on a regional and global scale. Conservation is practiced as an affluent token; even poorer societies are conserving with the expectation of tourist income. Volunteer financing is inadequate. Long-term AN financing is necessary to extend the effort beyond the lifetimes of politics. The cost of saving the wild for a common heritage must be borne equally. If Brazilians cannot extract minerals from the Amazon basin, if an Indian peasant loses a bullock to a Bengal tiger, there must be some balance.

Richard Allen contends that the way to save the world is to invent and apply patterns of development that conserve living resources essential for human well-being and survival. Although resource conservation is thought of as specialized and limited, it cuts across all human activities, and should be incorporated.

5.2.3.2.2.3. Management of Resources

History records the debris of some civilizations that tried to manage their resources and failed; they existed in the Americas, the middle East, Africa, Asia, the Pacific, and Europe. Natural resources were originally defined as objects provided by nature for human use. This concept has been expanded over thousands of years to include minerals, wildlife and people. Eric Jantsch claims that humanity now acts as a systems manager at all levels, where management is an activity that aids evolution, acting with it, recognizing and applying an ethics that transcend an individual level.

Even most of the noncultivated land surface of the earth is being managed; elephants, giraffes, crocodiles, wolves, caribou, snail darters, redwoods, prairies flowers are managed or else destroyed. Many are done in by human recreation, with its attendant necessary vehicles. Even a modern, balanced exploitation may destroy forests and fisheries. Currently, many resource managers espouse the ideas of equilibrium maintenance and maximum sustainable yield. These ideas are poor guides to management. By trying to maintain habitats in equilibrium, we often set them up for catastrophic decline, for instance, in fire-climax pine forests, or destroy resident species, such as the condor.

The use of maximum sustainable yield in wildlife management has resulted in the degradation of the populations involved, whales and salmon, for instance. A carrying capacity is not constant; species that live near the limit of capacity cannot be killed at a maximum. Even small numbers, for the Sandhill crane, less that six percent, hunted could result in extinction. This may be true of wolves, bears, mountain lions, and other species.

Some managers, like whalers, are far worse. They do not try to manage for a continued maximum yield; they try to maximize the economic value of a resource, in spite of an awareness of extinction—the rape of one "resource" provides the capital for the rape of the next.

The idea that everything should be managed is based on an extreme belief that nature is a resource to be processed. Furthermore, management is self-perpetuating and self-justifying. The objective of resource management is to increase the measure of quality of life for affluent people in overdeveloped countries.

Management, even conservation management, has been based on economic objectives. And, as Aldo Leopold pointed out, the weakness of relying on economic motives is that most members of the earth's community, such as wildflowers and song-birds, have no economic value. Yet all the members of the community contribute to the integrity of the whole, which is vital to maintaining what we do consider important. Those beings with no economic value are ignored, or worse, labeled as weeds or vermin and destroyed so that crops and animals with short-term advantages for human ends can be substituted. The goal of this institute is that kind of temporary control.

The impulse to manage nature is an expression of the judgment that we know how the world should be run. But we are finding that we do not know at all. We did not know about the effects of DDT or radiation or chemical dumps or special drugs. The whole approach of the conservative position ignores the physical and ecological dimensions of resources. The vandal position is even more basically ignorant. Laws of ecology must be obeyed for these laws determine our existence and that of "resources." There can be no "balance" between obeying some laws and disobeying others.

We are unbalanced. Our whole industrial world view is unbalanced. Balanced resource management will still unbalance nature, though perhaps at a slower rate. The balance of nature has to come before the balance of resources. We will continue to be unbalanced until we enlarge our understanding of nature and let ecological limits suggest new technologies and techniques. A balanced relationship between humanity and environment is necessary.

Such a balance must be based on conservation, if it is to avoid harmful 'side-effects' and provide benefits. We must invent patterns of development that also conserve living resources essential for survival and well-being. This kind of conservation is not a special and limited activity; it is a process that affects all human activities. Conservation must be integrated with development to ensure that vital parts of the biosphere are protected or modified only in ways it can sustain.

A conservation strategy has to identify the most significant objectives, according to criteria of biological importance and urgency of need. Damage to life support systems that are becoming irreversible—extinctions, habitat destruction—these need the highest priority. Every independent group should prepare proposals for cooperative programs concentrating on biomes that cross boundaries, that is, tropical forests, rivers, and global common areas, such as oceans and atmospheres.

Common resources can be managed, if the system is managed so as to minimize fluctuation and interference, so as not to impact the stability of the process, so as to harvest an appropriate production, but so as to be aware that even a stable sustained yield of a renewable resource might change deterministic conditions so that resilience is lost and a chance event could trigger sudden change and the loss of integrity of the system. Some resources can be restored or renewed, although intervention may be inappropriate if natural cycles, including catastrophic events, are not understood. Natural processes of recovery work slowly, but good management can accelerate them.

5.2.3.2.3. To Protect Unique Human Cultures
Cultural patterns relate human communities to the ecological areas in which they are embedded. Any culture is only one of many possibilities. There is no single or correct way. By 1900, humanity had spread through 1,000 different cultures and 3,000 languages—-roughly equivalent to the number of natural biogeographical provinces and subprovinces on earth. Whenever groups were geographically separate, there was differentiation, which enforced separate cultural identities.

The real feelings of innumerable groups of people center on much smaller regions of the world than nations. For example, Britain is composed of Scotland, North and South Wales, Northern Ireland, Anglia, and Saxony. It may mean more to be Welsh or Irish than British, or Quebecois than Canadian, Kurd than Iraqi, Mongolian than Chinese. Forced cultural integration breeds tensions; in the USSR by 1988, the tensions exceeded the force and advantages of integration. Rwanda, and Tanzania are additional cases.

Many cultures in established countries, like Scotland in Britain or the Nyiha in Tanzania are organized cultural communities, but are not permitted to join the UN because they do not possess armies. A new world order would permit autonomous groups to join the Associated Nations according to cultural or linguistic affinities and not merely force of arms. Nations could break up into preferred "natural" units. Every cultural group, or nation, is considered equal, regardless of size or sophistication. These things would contribute to their protection from forces that fragment and destroy cultures.

5.2.3.2.4. To Coordinate Representation of Cultures

The Associated Nations, would function as a global coordinating body with powers and limits. In order to coordinate representation, the AN would create a representative body. Each nation would provide a set number of representatives to the governing body of the Associated Nations, which would provide a forum for designing the governance of the earth, one in which everyone can participate.

5.2.3.2.5. To Provide Services to Nations Groups & Individuals

Garret Hardin noted that the Marshall Plan, which channeled $12 billion for rebuilding Europe after 1945, was not entirely altruistic; it was meant to keep the USSR out of Europe. After the Marshall plan succeeded in Europe, Mr. B. Hardy convinced Truman to extend the plan to the world; the result was the beginning of foreign aid in 1949. But, the plan did not work as well. Over $80 billion and 25 years later, most aided countries are still poor. What was the difference? The plan in Europe recreated an industrial civilization. Foreign aid expected illiterate, fatalistic, poor populations to try something new to their experience. Although it was funded at about the same level ($3 billion per year), it was expected to help 20 times as many people—2 billion instead of 100 million. Furthermore, the expectations were wrong. A. van Dam suggested that the Marshall Plan extended to the world in the same spirit and at the same level would prove more rewarding and stimulating. That amount of investment is only equivalent to the production of two day's goods and services in North America, Europe and Japan. Linear thinking, combined with economic altruism, can lead to great short-term successes, but to long-term problems.

Strictly, human altruism occurs only on a tribal level. Biological heredity makes kin altruism possible. Money makes a flexible and reciprocal altruism possible between unrelated members of the species. Money also makes people less materialistic; it is a symbol. It frees people from the calculation of gift-barter. Telescopic philanthropy—the term is from Charles Dickens—is not coupled with responsibility. Our gain is unrelated to any effect on the recipients. That irresponsibility may be part of appeal. Hardin wrote that human actions should be guided by charity, but he applied the older understanding of the virtue, which he noted confers benefits and refrains from injuring, but does not shrink from inflicting suffering to achieve real good. Amiability, or good nature, is a weakness not to be confused with charity. It is the source of foreign aid, which ruins the longer prospects of a self-reliant life.

Any kind of aid is a distribution from a commons, as Hardin notes. Dealing with a global commons is more effective through laws that end destructive behavior. Furthermore, laws are a second-order altruism; an individual does not risk acting as a lone altruist, in violation of Hardin's Cardinal Rule of Policy, which is to never ask a person to act against his own self-interest. If it can be demonstrated that the long term effects of egoistic actions are harmful, people may be persuaded to forgo short-term gains. To prevent a tragic end to commons, the system must be changed. People will be reluctant to change because of the uncertainty of technological forecasting and political stability. Political change may be similar to lifting one's self by the bootstraps.

The tragedy of the commons could happen in mass economy, not necessarily in an information economy. Hardin believes that coercion, centrally controlled by majority rule, is required for survival. Self-interest and knowledge of capacity could also avoid tragedy. J. Martino claims that private property can eliminate the tragedy also; self-interest of the owner dictates. In this case, a global socialism would work because it would be responsible to national cultural units, whose interests would be represented. Economic cooperation in world of scarcity will not solve environmental problems.

The Associated Nations, by comparison, would furnish only temporary aid in the form of help and education. The kinds of aid would be threefold. (1) Rescue and assistance. Responses by the UN to earthquakes in Peru (1970) and Nicaragua (1972), droughts in Africa, floods in Bangladesh, and other disasters, are indicative of the promise of cooperation, although many efforts have been minimal or diverted into administrative mazes.

(2) Civic action would be concerned with representation and voting. Mass media would be available to every culture for referenda. Civic action would include technical projects, such as farming or reforestation. Civic action might also address inequity and population or immigration concerns. Civic action groups, similar to the U.S. Civilian Conservation Corps (1930s) or the U.S. Peace Corps (1960s-), could apply appropriate technology on request. Richard St. Barbe Baker suggested armies for reforesting the Sahara; the technical feasibility has been demonstrated in places, but any whole effort is crippled by politics.

Special education would be a priority. Education would be especially important at this common level, since cultures would dispense local specific information. All scientific and technological knowledge shall be available to all states, as regulated by the Associated Nations. Scientific research and development, especially on environmental problems, will be promoted in all states. The Associated Nations will support a free flow of scientific information and experience. The Associated Nations will also ensure that appropriate technologies are available to all countries. The Associated Nations will award basic educational and research grants to all humans, for whatever use desired. An earth university might be established. For public health, the AN would create indicators of social and biological health, as well as monitor health, trade, and social quality. It would establish centers on epidemic and disease control, recognizing that health in general depends on healthy global cycles and ecosystems. For financial health, the AN would standardize exchange rates and provide banking facilities. It would work to stabilize the prices of commodities and materials and set common business standards in terms of work and pay units and wade values—the unit of wage shall be a human work unit, which shall have equal value for all. The Associated Nations would provide laws and courts to address problems of justice.

(3) National armed forces could be replaced by an unarmed Associated Nations (AN) police force; Associated Nations enforcement would consist of a persuasive presence for the observation of law and order. The UN force in Cyprus (1960s) performed this function admirably. An Associated Nations charter would ensure the inviolability of personnel and their right to intervene in any conflict when asked by any group. With world consciousness, the weak and disadvantaged can get food and shelter by appeal or right, without plundering, without war. War would be allowed to evaporate with the protection of all people by a central governing body. Fighting would occur, between individuals and small groups as interests conflict and communications falter. Nonviolence is possible only between rational individual human beings. Sometimes force is necessary. Therefore, some armed security would be necessary, and part of the police force would be armed. A shift from military to police forces could provide that security. This police force could provide humanitarian intervention.

5.2.3.2.5.1. To Manage Populations

Human populations tend to expand, especially after agriculture, to fill up the human niche, to use every possible resource and to reduce every kind of flexibility. People then become excited by the intensity of people and addicted to the luxuries of trade. For humans not to destroy the planet, we have to plan an a satisfactory or optimum population rationally or irrationally.

At low population densities, management only needs to apply to interpersonal behavior. Management in this sense is at the limits. A global framework could proscribe behavior at the limits, and prescribe on a cultural level. It could balance the equation of access, rights, and distribution.

5.2.3.2.5.2. To Adjust Human Equity & Species Equity

The AN would be responsible for distributing a portion of the wealth of the earth among humanity. In this sense it would be socialistic. It would regulate resources for a common good, that included all living beings. A redistribution of the imbalance of wealth would require an attitude like altruism.

5.2.3.2.6. To Create Concord (Peace) & Accommodate Discord

Like the UN before it, a global framework would try to create the conditions for peace and eliminate war. What is war, again? War means fighting or hostility, campaign or invasion. But, more than just being a kind of conflict, it has the connotation of physical harm or complete destruction. Long ago, war changed the level and scale of violence, by involving more people and by making the fighting more detached. Now, war is guaranteeing its own continuity. The dangers of the military-industrial complex, that Eisenhower warned of, have increased exponentially. The original axis of military and industry now includes, in the U.S., the enthusiastic complicity of the entire legislative branch of the government, which is supported by the military and industries, and the inbred ideas of the new forms of think-tanks, which are supported by the military and industries. All four are staffed by escalating revolving-door policies. The profit-driven American way of war, where the U.S. presents itself as the arsenal of democracy and the reluctant guardian of freedom, works to ensure the coca-colonialization, that is, the economic colonialism, of weaker countries and the physical subjugation of disagreeable countries.

Wars are advertised and sold to the citizens of a nation using the same dishonest and fallacious, but effective, techniques. Supposedly, one can consider war as the imposition of order through the death and destruction of people causing disorder. Is war simply contention or conflict? Contention means verbal strife or dispute. Dissension means difference of opinion or opposing groups. Conflict means strife, struggle, collision, hostility, fight or battle. These words may have been adequate at one time, but war, as institutional destruction, has to be eliminated; the word has to be refer to behaviors that are no longer exhibited. So, what will remain? All those smaller pieces, such as fighting, conflict, dispute, and strife. These will not go away. But, they can be kept small and handled by different kinds of treatment, and maybe rarely, force. Discord is a good word to collect the human behaviors. Discord means a disagreement, from the words meaning 'hearts apart.'

What then is peace? Is it dull and uninspired? Why is it desirable, if it is dull and impossible? The word 'peace' is from the Latin 'pax,' which is from IE 'to fasten.' Peace can also mean concord, harmony, amity, friendship, or just 'quiet.' Popular definitions of peace start with 'freedom from war' and go on to 'freedom from public disorder,' 'freedom from disturbance' and 'freedom from disagreement.' This is a negative way to define freedoms or peace. Peace must therefore be order or agreement.

Agreement is a going together without conflict, which is what morals are, a going together. Accord is the fitness of things considered together. Concord means of the same heart and mind. It also means agreement or harmony. Concord can mean the friendly relationship between nations or a treaty. Concord is a better word; it avoids the negative connotations of peace.

The problems of war, aggression, nationalism, disarmament, degradation, goodness and peace are problems of human nature, that is, of symbols, cultures, politics, and ecology. They are not simple problems and not easily solved. They are interrelated as human groups and natural ecosystems are interdependent ecologically, politically, economically, and technologically.

Human interactions are dominated by symbols. The most powerful set of symbols, embodied as nationalism, has a direct relationship to war. The intellectual rationalization for the continuous preparation for war is the old Roman adage: "If you want peace, prepare for war." This adage has been so completely taken into the modern heart that most of the larger nations have spent half of every century in war, according to Pitirim Sorokin. Preparation for war has always lead easily into war. There seems to be no reason that the present preparation will lead anywhere else.

Starting peace means ending preparations for war. Modern communications, radio and television, could reveal the concern for peace virtually everywhere. But, they also aggravate the images of inequality. It is unrealistic to expect cooperation without some fair redistribution of resources and manufactures. Equalization would allow trust. Trust would allow many customs and prejudice barriers to fade away.

Communication through art could have a fundamental role in

promoting peace. Frederich Schiller believed that there was historical proof that art can achieve what violence and law cannot—art could educate and liberate the individuals of society in a gradual and peaceful process. In spite of the cultural forces dominant at any moment, an individual has the potential to determine a different and peaceful course.

5.3.5. *The Dance of Art Money and Ethics: Advertising Good Places*
Advertising creates the mythic images of our industrial cosmology—Marshall McLuhan called advertising the "cave art of the twentieth century." The myths are powerful, but trivial, and memorable, but inadequate to convey the meaning people need to live. Perhaps the myths are restricted by their content. If so, then ecologists and artists, and urban planners, historians, and politicians need to use the strengths of advertising to convey ecological sense and traditional wisdom, the feelings of balance and the dreams of nature.

Our dream of nature, and it is still a dream, in modern Western culture, is the dream of order and beauty. But, as Aldous Huxley noted, the dream of order begets growth and tyranny, the dream of beauty, monsters and violence. Our dreams are nightmares because they are not complete. The nightmares are symptoms that reflect unbalanced and immature cosmologies, that is, images of the earth. A traditional cosmology evolves with people's needs, fears, and knowledge. But, if it is incomplete, or if it does not fit environmental conditions, it may fail. Many early cosmologies, primitive or advanced, failed to fit the earth.

The modern industrial image of nature as a resource has resulted in pollution, material shortages, and environmental degradation. A culture that degrades its ecosystem risks its own extinction.

Industrial cultures, however, are not the only cultures in existence. There are hundreds others, although at one time, around 1900, our species had over 1,000 different cultures and 3,000 languages, roughly equivalent to the number of natural biogeographical provinces and subprovinces on earth. Each culture exists in a particular location with a unique history. Later developments are not more adaptive than earlier; nor do they replace them. Ethnic groups are not evolutionary stages culminating in The U.S., but are equally valid ways of life. Each culture is only one of many possibilities, a way. There is no single or correct way.

Each culture has a root metaphor. In the West, it is the machine. The advent of the machine made processes of order more amenable to description. Although only a closed system itself, the machine was a fruitful metaphor for living systems. The theory of the living organism as a mechanical contrivance explained biological phenomena from the physiology of an organism to the processes of cells. The cybernetic machine metaphor was successful at explaining detailed processes without answering fundamental questions of meaning.

Science makes extended use of the metaphorical process to construct its models. For example: "Man is a system" according to Erwin Laszlo or "Man is a computer" according to Michael Arbib. Kenneth Boulding offered the perfect machine metaphor for the operation of the earth: as a spaceship. As a metaphor, a spaceship suggests the limits of earth and the value of a limited life-support system—unfortunately, it also implies something of human creation that can be controlled and fixed by human intention.

The use of the word "ecology" by Ernst Haeckel implied that the natural world was a place to live, a house, rather than a machine to control. Making the earth into a house is fundamentally a poetic activity, according to Gaston Bachelard. Poetry also is a way of understanding the universe through metaphor, a literary device that transfers the characteristics of one term to another. As Picasso said of art, poetry also is a `lie that tells the truth.' For example, William Shakespeare said "The body is a garden; and William Harvey said "the body is a machine." The body is not a garden or a machine, but the metaphors extend our understanding of the body.

Poetry is communicative of the quality of things. Like science, it discriminates the unsuspected in the commonplace. It is not different from science, but more diffuse; not better than science, but more comprehensive. It accepts ontological parity, the equality of beings; aspects of the world are not negated or reduced by one another. As metaphorical knowledge, which may be prerational or metarational, poetry can avail itself still of scientific references. Poetry can measure a whole qualitatively and mimetically, a germ or the cosmos with its imagery. Poetry is a tool for comprehending partially what cannot be known totally. A poetic language could include a view of the interrelatedness of all existence in a sublime ecology.

People need to be made aware of the power of self-determination. People need to feel things, like the immensity and uniqueness of nature or the strangeness of a biting tick, before they can act. Poetry can help people feel themselves as part of the web of life or on an oasis in space. That feeling, more than laws or injunctions, can justify preserving the ecological systems of the earth on which we live. Humanity is a poetic species, as Richard Rorty noted, "one which can change its behavior by the words it uses." We need desperately to change our behavior.

Mythology can join science with feeling to help us change. Mythology is not limited by method. Mythic symbols store information concisely, which makes it possible for a person to assimilate the collective experiences of a culture. Myth combines us with other beings. Mythologies are in fact great poems that function to awaken the experience of awe and humility before mystery, create a cosmology, validate and maintain an established order, and bring the individual into harmony with the whole.

5.3.5.1. Monetary Lies & Pecuniary Pseudotruth
Unfortunately, the myths of the predominate industrial cosmology are inadequate. The myths are powerful, but trivial and misdirected. Poetry and art are undervalued as forms of communication, not to mention as ways of shaping and making. Business has transformed much of art and poetry into advertising, to match the style and attention span of the people in industrial cultures. Advertising, quite literally from the *Wall Street Journal* to college textbooks, refers to its activities as "shaping the American dream." Like art, advertising creates an image of a way of experiencing. Unlike art, it limits its focus for a specific goal—profit. Like art, it mirrors us. Unlike art, it intensifies and glorifies only the positive aspects of culture, ignoring the dark, negative

aspects that are equally valid.

Its simplicity is irresistible. Our environment deteriorates according to ecologists, but gets better according to economists. And their pictures are prettier. People want to hear that it is getting better. Advertising tells them it is. People want to act stupid, greedy, and selfish, and spend the inheritance of their children on themselves. Advertising tells them their actions are rewarded. The real issues of life and death, destruction and hope, make people feel helpless and anxious, so advertising draws their consciousness to comfortable trivia.

Despite the ugliness of the dreams of progress and growth, of waste and stylistic frenzy, advertising, using sophisticated techniques and narrowing the focus out of context, makes the dreams desirable and irresistible. People in agricultural and hunting cultures interiorize the abstract industrial vision. African farmers are convinced to buy inorganic fertilizers, even though it degrades the soil; women to buy powdered milk for their children, even if it kills them. Tractors replace draft animals in the paddies in the Philippines, even though they are costly and less energy-efficient; French winter fashions are found desirable in tropical Brazil, even if they can only be worn in air-conditioned villas. People in industrial societies are convinced that their children will be ruined without personal computers. Disposability is offered as a fix to a wanting in the temperament. Advertising fuels the acceleration of conspicuous and compulsive consumption.

5.3.5.2. Ecological Persuasion
Yet, advertising may be the most effective means to reshape desires and reform buying habits. Advertising presents the symbols of modern experience, even if they are just the trivial ones. It could present healthy symbols equally well. Advertising does incorporate traditional values, like family, friendship, and love, although to sell beer and cereal and, sometimes, churches and hospitals. And, like art, advertising lies, although Jules Henry thought it was instead a new kind of truth—``pecuniary pseudo-truth''—not intended to be believed, or certainly, proved.

Advertising is beginning to support more informational functions, such as the dangers of drug abuse and smoking. Advertising creates values—fur coats, fast cars, dark beer, slim cigarettes are certainly recent and artificial values—but it could be used to create positive ecological values and new identities that show that our needs for prestige, esteem, and belonging can be met without stylistic waste at mindless speeds. Advertising could promote new attitudes about appropriate technology, the rights of other cultures, and the place of people in nature. Good advertising could be as subversive and conservative as ecology. It could avoid confrontation with people's values; emphasize positive aspects without negative ones. A good ad could capture and carry the most self-indulgent viewer; for the most part, ads don't require effort, literacy, or consciousness, just attention.

Advertising has been serving the dream of progress, but progress is leading to catastrophe, a long, slow, global catastrophe. When people experience local, sudden catastrophe, they usually respond immediately, with heroism and sacrifice, aiding the victims of earthquakes or floods, sometimes famine. Advertising could bring to consciousness the slow catastrophes of erosion and population overshoot, and, perhaps, invoke the same altruistic and effective responses to them.

To work towards this service, conservation groups could define and promote an integrative mythology as the basis for the framework of diverse efforts to protect life and the environment. Conservation groups could provide a meaningful philosophical foundation, as well as coordination for other humane, social, and conservation programs. But, the approach must be egalitarian: Respect for life cannot neglect human life and suffering. The approach must be eutopian: A new cosmology cannot ignore adaptive cultural traditions that arose in place over centuries. Furthermore, in addition to formal education, they could provide re-education through the most effective means, such as advertising. Conservation groups could spend money advertising ``humane consciousness,'' moderation, and the joy of living, instead of just consuming or winning. Ecological ads would be unique and compelling, simple and effective. They would advertise not a product, but a way; not for a profit, but for a dream.

The other day, tired of scribbling, I went to visit friends, who were watching a car race. It occurred to me that only with entertainment industries is there so much technical fizz and coordinated enthusiastic teamwork. Imagine all that energy and enthusiasm directed to appropriate technology for reforestation or the proper use of forests. Imagine television coverage of forest work with the same amount of attention and detail. Why not a competition for the most beautiful or productive forest or teams working to restore devastated areas—broadcast by a major network as an important event. It also occurred to me that this remorseless entertainment is an anesthetic against the fear or emptiness or self-searching or death. Continuous entertainment is a kind of guarantee of health, riches, and long-life. Everything that is pleasurable, thought George Orwell, seems to be an attempt to destroy consciousness. Ecoforestry cannot ever compete with entertainment if it raises troubling questions or difficult expectations. As long as the industry can guarantee many forests through the arithmetic of fantasy, we will always seem to be complainers and false prophets—until it's too late, then we will be blamed for not avoiding the catastrophes.

Maybe the situation is not that bad. Maybe we can present images that rival the industry images. Maybe we too can speak the languages of euphemism that large corporations use to conduct their businesses of larceny and fraud. Positive images and pleasing language skills are everything these days; no one really looks for substance. The devotion to money, beauty and youth is our focus. I think one way to compete might be to present conservation biology or ecoforestry as a medical discipline, aimed at restoring forests to health—and advertise it that way. As with any medicine, the patient actually does most of the work to become healthy, although the doctor gets the credit and the payment. This would also lead to more respect for the practitioners, but also to more responsibility and more rules. The first rule, which we might take to be basic, is identical to the first vow of the Hippocratic oath, "Do no harm."

5.4. Creating & Maintaining Eutopias Now

To avoid fanaticism and violence, Karl Popper has suggested that utopians should try to build an open, progressive, partially-planned society, instead of a finished, closed, completely-planned society. Indeed, this is how general systems theory would describe a working, successful society. Such a utopia would have to accept the imperfect nature of man and the changing ambiguity of nature. Utopias is the dream of reason. Eutopias is the dream of small traditions and cultures, reasonable or not. Where an imagined utopia offers revelations promising a desired future, Eutopias offers references from selves and cultures for producing good places on earth now. There is no mechanical prescription for making good places; there is no blueprint or timetable. The current institutions cannot create good places; the market has not been able to create health and equity; even radical ecologists have not been able to create a way—Eutopias is a fourth way. It is not an institution that benefits only the rich; nor is it a schedule of temporary handouts. It is a plan for a framework for local self-reliance and global exchange, that is respectful of traditional cultures and ecological networks. So far, there is only the idea or poetic image. Human will to power might be found in the will to imagine, and then to speak and become. What is our moral responsibility for this power? We can choose to alter our world with new images moderated by new ideals, such as good places, eutopias. Eutopias should offer knowledge and power with charity.

The criteria for eutopias include: Its benefit for humanity; the inadequacies of the present system; a drastic system change as a result of catastrophic awareness; and a low, but not too low, political feasibility. The benefits must be worthwhile to justify the costs. Benefits cannot be vague and unsatisfying when the costs are immediate and painful. Poetry and education must prove the benefits, so that the eutopian alternative can be begun. This code emphasizes its flexibility.

The best thing to do is stop—stop growing, stop producing, stop running. Suspend the race and contemplate a direction. We know that whole countries have built again from ruins. So there is nothing to fear from stopping—if we know there would be no problem going again. What are the dangers of fast social transformation? Lack of justice? Lack of order? That is what the Eutopian framework is for.

The steady state would provide a period of rest, and time to explore human values and quality considerations. This strategy would avoid eventual hardening of the choices. But it must be instituted at once. The crisis caused by exponential growth and destruction cannot be solved just after some final limit is passed and the ultimate catastrophe begun. The crisis of ignorance cannot be solved by hurrying ahead and creating more problems.

Eutopias exists in the extended present, incorporating past traditions and future values. It would concentrate earthward (down) and inward. Heaven may be a perfect home, but eutopias is here and now. Eutopias is a new comprehensive philosophy to make sense of the world. Eutopias is comprehensive and global. A broader frame of reference is assumed. It is concerned with evolution unfolding, evolving, producing new emergent forms, not just a static description. Eutopias is grounded in environmental concerns. Its values must be highest cultural and natural values. It must develop from existing social and political forces. Eutopias is vitally concerned with the well being of society. It regards society as a *sui generis* entity, not just an aggregate for analysis. Conservation is a means to an end, which is human fulfillment in harmony with nature. Human happiness depends on a balance between needs and commodities. In a throughput process it is not possible to economize all inputs simultaneously. There are many criteria for inputs to be preserved. Options must be site and culture specific. Eutopias recognizes and preserves slow cultural knowledge. A social base may be partly developed through ecological education. Social diversity may have cross-cultural appeal. Eutopias would retain the capacity to change and innovate, with changes in environments and human values.

Eutopias would detoxify national rivalries. Racism, sexism and ageism would lose their importance in a cooperative society of advanced communication, automation, equality, humane scale, and meaningful preservation. Eutopias is politically aware. We make political statements by the way we live. Every tradition is only one tradition among many. The higher sanity requires of philosophies and therapies is open, planetary dialogue between modern experience and sacred tradition. Eutopias requires a planning process that bridges all cultures and sciences. It must be a participatory political movement. It must appeal to a large segment of the total human society. Since not all interests will be satisfied, there must be opportunities for transformations or alternate paths. Eutopias would be a framework for microeutopias, where different human experiments are tried. Its variability would insure that we could reject local visions that fail.

The eutopian frame can be justified. It is not just one kind of global society in one place. If we try to make one society, it will change over time, because people are in different places. Solutions come from living in place.

How can we form society within an ecological perspective? By following the principles of ecology and applying them to the characteristics of good places. According to David Orr, certain design principles work with ecosystems and nations. Small units dispersed in space, redundancy, short linkages between modules, simplicity, diversity of components, self-reliance, decentralized control, large margins, quick feedback. A megaframe like Eutopias would allow this.

Eutopias requires a change of attitude. We have to change the framework so that we can change to new minds. We no longer have an external point of view. We are inseparable from the environment and each other, but we differentiate. Eutopias is a nostrum, really, a description of good places for all beings. Its connotation is as a panacea or questionable remedy. This is appropriate since a panacea is a cure-all, a remedy for disease, and a solution to catastrophe.

5.4.1. *What Eutopias Can Do*
Eutopias is a self-conscious panacea. It requires an understanding of the anatomy, physiology, and diseases of the body in question, now the entire human and wild planet.

5.4.1.1. *Eutopias Can Eliminate Bad Approaches & Actions*

Human approaches to the challenges of nature have resulted in many losses. The lure of size and simplicity has resulted in many failures that become traps difficult to avoid or leave. The stresses from these things have resulted thefts, as attempts to balance or correct the situations. The very size and impact of humanity has made theft the only easy option, much easier in the short run than planning or self-restraint.

5.4.1.1.1. Eutopias Can Reduce Losses

Eutopias can reduce the losses of nature and culture by creating a framework to protect them. Eutopias can reduce the losses of health, fitness and accord, by emphasizing them and creating circumstances for their continuity. Eutopias can reduce the losses of equity, renewal and design by offering new designs that allow for a normalization of equity and for the normal processes of renewal.

Losses from accidents and diseases can be reduced by preparedness. Losses from earth and climate changes can be reduced, also, with preparedness for 'normal' events, such as hurricanes, earthquakes, and droughts. Design can also be used to reduce impacts from these events; for instance, by denying building permits on floodplains. The losses from some events, such as droughts resulting from El Nino, can be ameliorated, by having surplus food and supplies stockpiled.

5.4.1.1.2. Eutopias Can Reduce Thefts

Stopping a theft can be as simple as stopping a thief. But, theft has become such a complicated thing, many steps removed from the people who make the decisions and from those who carry them out. Eutopias would address the processes and trails of theft.

5.4.1.1.2.1. Reduce Theft of Life from Ecocides and Democides

Animal and plant lives are stolen for the profits of a few; ecological and human systems collapse as a result of biocide and ecocide. Hundreds of millions of human lives are stolen every century at the behest of a few. Millions die from starvation when regional crops fail; millions more die when the distribution system fails or is perverted for a few. This democide is unacceptable. The plague of power is responsible for the dialogues of death, and the absoluteness of some power is responsible for the massive scale of deaths in Russia, China, and some other nations.

Three reasons for these deaths seem more contributory than others: Inequity, runaway cultural antagonisms, and the use of absolute power. Inequity is simple to understand; some people have more valuables than others. Often, equalization does not happen until during or after a collapse, as it may have happened with the Mayans in 795 AD (or 1211 YBP). Cultural antagonisms seem to worsen when the different cultures are forcibly combined in nations as the result of colonial wars. Totalitarian regimes, especially with great power and in secrecy, behind walls or threats, kill almost as many people as famines—more, when one realizes that many famine deaths come from denial of distribution. Famine itself is the regional failure of food production or distribution. However, the denial of distribution, as when food is saved for trade or the elite, such as the English did to the people of Ireland and India in the 1800s, can contribute to the severity and extent of a famine.

Eutopian responses to these three reasons is: To equalize wealth as much as possible, to separate cultures into separate nations, and to make laws to control ecocides and democides. Laws without supervision and enforcement would not be effective. The UN outlawed war, but when the U.S., U.K., Iraq, Korea, or others decide to violate it, no one enforces it. The AN needs to have the power of enforcement, backed by all member nations. The AN needs to have the moral force to keep national governments open and responsible. The workings of government should be transparent to the people, whether the government is democratic, royal or charismatic. The AN must be sure that people can bear witness to every regime in the world, from Korea and Cambodia to the U.S. and Russia. Bearing witness should reduce the number of secret pogroms. Restricting and checking the power of leaders, in a eutopian framework, overseen by the AN, should greatly reduce democides, including genocides and mass murders. There are no permanent solutions. Eutopias can reduce the theft of life by making it more valuable and more visible.

5.4.1.1.2.2. Reduce Theft of Common Sense
Eutopias can reduce the theft of common sense by fostering and respecting common sense in communities and nations, as well as increasing its value and appreciation.

5.4..1.1.2.3. Reduce Theft of Choice
Eutopias can reduce the theft of choice by creating a framework that offers more choices for people in different communities and nations. It can also address the economic and political processes that reduce choice.

5.4.1.1.3. Eutopias Can Reduce Failures
Eutopias can reduce failures through education and opportunity. Perception, intelligence, and imagination can be taught. Integrity, will and charity can be shown by example. And, if there are enough teachings and examples, these human capabilities will be developed and applied to domiture, that is, civilization and nature. With will and imagination, people can design and build good places.

5.4.1.2. *Eutopias Can Integrate Tools & Designs*
Tools and designs are important extensions of the human mind. Their purpose is to foster and assist survival, not to make it more difficult. Tools and designs can be made appropriate to environmental limits and cultural preferences, both of which are often ignored by industrial approaches.

5.4.1.2.1. Eutopias Use Tools Effectively
Eutopias can illustrate how people can use tools with awareness of their effects and impacts. The principle of caution is followed.

5.4.1.2.2. Eutopias Can Thread Characteristics with Plans
Eutopias can thread the characteristics of nature, that is fields, ecosystems, and places, with the characteristics of cultures and good societies to make good places ecologically and culturally.

5.4.1.2.3. Eutopias Can Avoid the Traps of No-places
Eutopias can avoid the lure of or the accidental assembly of no-places. By exposing the lures of no-places, and showing the connections that make no-places into traps, eutopias can neutralize the plague of placelessness.

5.4.1.2.4. Eutopias Can Suspend the Designing of Nowheres
By promoting the understanding of the inadequacies of bad characteristics and bad designs, eutopias can stop the plague of uniformity and paucity. Through an understanding of the consequences of human ambitions and actions, eutopias can avoid many of the evils that result from a civilization on technical autopilot.

5.4.1.3. *Eutopias Can Increase Understanding*
Understanding is a powerful thing. Understanding why an animal bites can dissipate the desire for revenge or punishment. Understanding why things break down can result in an examination of the context and effects of tools, and maybe a simplification.

5.4.1.3.1. Eutopias Can Help Understand Ways of Knowing
The ways that human beings know things is part of the human adventure. There are many ways of knowing, from traditional ecological knowledge to the most abstract science. None of these ways is the only way. None should supplant the others entirely. This is the importance of education, that it be applicable to local place, yet broad enough to put that place in a larger context, of the environment or planet or universe. These ways of knowing allow people to learn the operation of nature and fit human activities in it. This understanding points to the need for basic sciences and crisis sciences.

5.4.1.3.2. Eutopias Can Help Understand How Things Go Together
Ecology is a science of relationships and patterns. Understanding the components of an ecosystem, and the characteristics of an ecosystem, can be applied to the growth, change and development of human systems.

5.4.1.3.3. Eutopias Can Help Understand How Things Happened
History can allow understanding of the regular patterns of human life, as well as the dramatic changes, such as agriculture or urbanization, and how these changes have affected the patterns. History is a record of the cumulative human impacts on living systems, as well as of a few famous people or battles.

5.4.1.3.4. Eutopias Can Help Understand How Things Renew
Systems automatically renew themselves, especially living systems. Systems that do not renew themselves very well, such as agriculture and cities, can

be put on track for renewal by linking them with the surrounding natural systems. Eutopias can foster the renewal of human systems by integrating them into natural self-renewing systems.

5.4.1.3.5. Eutopias Can Help Understand How Nature & Culture Work

Nature and Culture are systems. Domiture is the combination of those two systems. Culture was once called a "Second Nature," but human culture has expanded so dramatically that the two systems are better identified as one developed system, now. The fitness of human systems are intimately related to the fitness of species and natural ecosystems. The human attachment to place is critical to understanding why people live where they do.

5.4.1.3.6. Eutopias Can Help Understand How to Live in Place

Eutopias can offer understanding of how people live in places, not only how they adjust themselves to a place, but how they adjust the places to their needs and desires. This mutual adjustment can be ruinous or beneficial. Emotional investment in a place, even love for that place, is crucial to the preservation of the genius of place.

5.4.1.4. *Eutopias Can Start Making Good Places*

Eutopias can start making good places by addressing the economics and politics of human cultures. Economics and politics are large-scale human programs to relate human needs to resources and distributions of resources and goods.

5.4.1.4.1. Eutopias Can Show How to Preserve & Restore, Design & Plan

Eutopias can provide an ecological planning process that offers a structure of limits and divisions for the planetary system that would permit the preservation and restoration of natural cycles and places. An ecological design process would be applied to ecosystems as well as to cities and fields.

5.4.1.4.2. Eutopias Can Illustrate Ways of Making a Living

Eutopias, through a holistic examination of how people make their livings in place, can show how changes can make better places. Economies can be as diverse as tropical or desert places; there is no evolution to one economic style, such as capitalism. Eutopias can show how to integrate individuals, communities and corporations into place.

The current, dominant economic and financial order is unfair. It needs to be radically reshaped. It is better to do this as part of a directed plan than after some kind of collapse. Power and wealth must be more equitably distributed. A Eutopian plan would try to ensure that the underrepresented would be allocated more resources. Which would increase the demand for basic services. But, would that let them disconnect from any dependence on a world market? Wouldn't that be the goal for every nation? To be self-reliant in terms of food and basic production? Then, nations could reject technologies and products that did not fit their cultures or that would affect their own resources.

These are all transitional processes, backed by the educative process and political pressure. A specific political process could be worked out later. There will be a painful readjustment to the realities of our new intricate involvement in the whole order of nature and her ecological balance. Social strains at this time will be unavoidable. A great amount of capital of energy and metals will be wasted. Sophisticated technology may allow a rebirth. A new world will have to be based on a gradually decreasing population. Production will have to be redirected to communal needs in transportation, housing, food, and recreation. It will be a much more humane world, moving from a materialist society based on industrial production and consumption to a contemplative culture based on ecological consciousness and symbiosis. But, people and cultures have to learn how to harmonize human culture with a deeper understanding of the ecology of earth, to become partners, rather than stewards or bosses.

This is the time to define goals in terms of population, quality of life, and preservation of biomes. Goals are not some final state reached once and for all time, but a horizon to be strived for, never reaching. Order is the highest ideal of mind; but chaos is necessary to shape and change it. Natural order is dynamic, creative, logical, and temporal. We live in natural order. To preserve what we are, we must admire the matrix out of which we arose. What is desirable is a relationship with a certain amount of conflict. Global peace may be dull indeed, but global war would be deadly. We need competition as well as cooperation. We could make a golden age in the present, not in the past (where Plato put it) or in the future (where O'Neill puts it). Life in the past was sometimes good regardless of environment. There are enclaves of well-being in all parts of the world, in Asia and Africa, in Australia and South America. Why not such good places for all? There is no technological reason why gracious living can not be available for all.

Economies can emphasize different things, from producing family needs (reciprocity), to distribution and redistribution of luxuries, to trade (mercantilism), to unbounded capital and to bureaucratic efficiency. It may be time to emphasize a form of aesthetic efficiency, that is the shared production of what is wanted without as much regard for cheapness and mass production.

5.4.1.4.3. Eutopias Can Explore Ways of Governing
Eutopias can examine how people govern themselves. Political styles can be equally diverse; there is no evolutionary path to one political style, not democracy, socialism or community anarchy. Eutopias can suggest ways to fit governing to culture and place.

Politics can use different types of leadership or rules. The rule of law is fine. Perhaps a rule of religious tolerance would allow people to live together, something on the order of the golden rule. Does it always come down to one person, president, pope, king, or dictator? Representing all? In small groups or communities, anarchy could work fine. Rather than rule, perhaps understanding. Would a rule of knowledge work? Or would people have to know too much? When it comes to politics, as with mythology and religion, different people have different levels of understanding. So, government should be simple enough for everyone to participate knowledgeably in.

5.4.1.4.4. Eutopias Can Try Ways of Integrating Religion & Art
Religion is a part of culture that binds people to their ancestors as well as the invisible powers of place. It focuses on the changeless aspects of natural and human processes. Religion concerns itself with an image of the world, that explains what the world is like. It also explains how we can influence it and why we would want to influence it. Art is a part of culture that expresses the invisible parts of society and the environment.

Religion can lead to understanding of the world; it can lead to ecological balance. Art can lead to peaceful ways of interacting with nature and other human beings. Art ruthlessly examines society. Religion reinforces the integrity of society. Art is a survival technique for humans on a wild planet. Religion relates the human to the wild.

5.4.1.5. *Eutopias Can Start Making a Framework for Revolution*
One premise of eutopias is that many things have to be changed simultaneously; some things have to be eliminated, and other things have to be invented. This revolution in thinking and acting, especially on a global and national level, will have to be governed by the consent of people in those nations. The structure of human life, in unique cultures in specific places, the basic everyday experience of human life, will basically remain the same, but the superstructure, that is concerned with global trading and distribution and taxes—that will change.

5.4.1.5.1. Creating an Associated Nations Framework
The police force would be used for positive nonviolent interventions to help people with problems or disagreements. Such interventions would be cooperative efforts by neighboring nations, coordinated through a revitalized Association. All states now have armed forces, whose primary duty is killing their enemies, internal or external, in unending conflicts. The unarmed police force would have different goals: Rescue from catastrophes such as earthquakes; civic assistance, such as vote getting or monitoring; and simple police action, being a persuasive presence in areas of conflict. The AN would insure the inviolability of the police to go anywhere on assignment and to intervene in any conflict when asked by any party. If the AN had most large-scale weapons, it might short-circuit the vicious cycle of armament races, and it is conceivable that the AN would need to use weapons in some circumstances. The UN has successfully used police for the observation of peace and for enforcement, in Cyprus for instance. The UN has used police in response to natural catastrophes, such as earthquakes, in Peru and Italy for instance.

A global association would also coordinate the distribution and use of common resources, which would also be owned by the association as representative of all nations, rather than of individual nations; resources across the planet are uneven and have precipitated numerous disputes for thousands of years. The agency would address real global problems, such as global warming, which has resulted in grain harvest shortfalls in recent years. Climate itself would be a concern.

For any nation, the association could advise on topics ranging from justice to wilderness. Wilderness has an important role in human freedom, as well as in providing ecosystem services. The association could insist on self-reliance, by connecting human population to ecosystem productivity. It could also make sure that local air, soil, and water resources are stabilized.

For all nations, the association could provide education on health and appropriate technology. It could work to provide basic needs for food and health. It could insist on the truth of the ecological situation, on the real costs of economic decisions and growth, especially those that destroy ecological capital, in the form of wilderness ecosystems. It could recommend changing the system to allow taxes on destructive activities, such as excessive carbon emissions, and to normalize the values of resources and wilderness.

5.4.1.5.2. Encouraging & Fitting New Nations

The AN will offer any culture the opportunity to have a vote in the global management of human cultures and natural processes. Those cultures may choose to remain in their current national framework and share one vote, or become independent and exercise a whole vote.

Three levels of responsibility—individual, national, and global—are identified and discussed; each has responsibilities for specific attributes, such as population or health. This does not mean that only nations will exist within a global framework; alliances and networks will form and reform.

The eutopian code divides the earth into zones for preservation, conservation, domestication, and human communities. Human activities are limited to specific zones and, within those, the global authority controls all air, water and land use under complete sovereignty. Political units are formed from existing cultural units; an optimum human population is of each nation is based on a calculation of net community productivity on arable land through traditional agriculture. Common planetary resources are assigned according to the optimum population figure. The development of the nations is regulated by the Associated Nations through charters. Self-reliant nations would decide their own appropriate technology, crops and institutions based on traditional values and are responsible for the ecological education of their constituents. Residents of nations have equal rights and work opportunities, and have the responsibility to participate in government and to live as wisely as possible, to make good places.

5.4.1.5.2.1. Connection & Size

When small societies start to grow, they become successful in different ways. But, that success leads to increases in size, which can lead to a tragedy of scale. Each major technological breakthrough permitted a step increase in size. The size of a local population increased the likelihood of its success. For cultures, size was important. More successful cultures (as measured by size and continuity) were larger and more aggressive. Humans naturally increase the size of societies, but do not know how to stop or limit it. Ambition contends with common sense? Is the problem growth or growth without development for the scale? Henry Simons designated the great powers as "monsters of nationalism and mercantilism" and suggested that they are the obstacles to world peace, and must be dismantled for us to survive.

Leopold Kohr relates cancer to size. But, is it largeness or sameness without function? Cancer allows the mass of one unit to become too big. The cells outgrow their limits. Political cancer is a matter of proportion between large and small units. Cancer is a small-cell phenomenon, but it converts all cells to itself. Would a theory of social gravitation work? At one scale we have fusion and energy, but if the scale is too large that becomes crushing and instability.

The processes of social development can create traps that then determine the direction of development. Changes in scale, such as population size or sedentary living, can decrease the number of options possible, while providing different attractive options, such as the accumulation of luxuries. In this sense a trap is a sudden reduction in options or flexibility due to changes in scale or repetitive pattern.

The sheer size of a united China meant that tributes were enormous and that any commercial income could not compete well with the mass of tribute. The commercialization of states seemed to benefit from proximity to rich routes, small state size and rivalries.

The size of a cultures might not be optimal, since they grow unplanned and wild. Kohr quotes Arnold Toynbee as linking the rise of universal states to the downfall of civilization. Toynbee suggests that one solution might be the return to the Greek ideal of a self-regulating balance of small city-states, *Homonoia*, rather than further macropolitical solutions. Leopold Kohr sees gigantomania as the economic problem of systems. Kohr notes that our choice is not between crime and virtue but between big crime and small crime, not between war and peace, but between great wars and small wars.

Local equalities are easier to acquire first, more than global equalities. We live local lives in home places, with local limits and local pressures. We can calculate an optimum size population of a culture or community, by relating it to the carrying capacity of the land and society. We can establish optimum scale of populations through limits of carrying capacity. We may also calculate an optimum size for the planet, based on the sum of local cultures. An optimum global population might be of the order: Between 0.5 billion and 1.5 billion people, the sum of local optima.

For the Chipewyan people in Canada, for example, the commitment to caribou hunting is ecologically inefficient, since people could spend more energy on secondary sources of food. For the Chipewyan, a deliberate "underutilization" of moose, rabbit, grouse, birds, and fish, is the result of cultural values: The willingness to live below the carrying capacity of the local environment—a characteristic of most hunting/gathering societies—the complex practice of drying caribou meat, and the reciprocity of the kinship system, that is, the act of giving as the basis for future relationships. The cultural decision to hunt caribou as the primary item of subsistence has produced a unique pattern in the utilization of land and in the formation and distribution of social groups. Many foraging groups, such as the Chipewyan, have been successful by staying below the maximum carrying capacity. Culturally, an optimum population has to be large enough to allow variety.

We may not know what is the minimum, optimum or maximum use of an ecosystem. Science might try to identify minima or maxima but management can aim at optima or satisficia. Francisco Varela analyzes the evolutionary process as satisficing rather than optimizing; a suboptimal solution is adequate. A free market has to be limited by conservative calculations of ecological balance. It is almost impossible to estimate the economic value of natural balance.

Kohr's reasons for the greatness of small states: There is a cultural diversion of aggressive energies, or artists are cheaper than soldiers; there is a relief from social servitude, as a result of time and leisure; there is the variety of human experience; and there is the testimony of history. Kohr concludes that it was always[22] "the small state, not the empire that survived. That is why small states do not have to be created artificially. They need only be freed."

5.4.1.5.2.2. Connection & Speed

The speed of our economies might not be optimal, either. Alvin Toffler has described the fast economies that are forming and concludes that slow economies will have to speed up their responses or risk becoming uncoupled from the fast lane. Yet, it might be good for countries to be uncoupled. Uncoupling economically might be a sound option for traditional societies unwilling to make the same mistakes as industrial ones. Local communities are based on traditional cultures, which have long-term lasting power. Traditional cultures often have wealth-leveling properties, absolute property ceilings, fixed wants, and production coupled with need—all of which results in a stable economy. Then, efficiency and productivity are less important than use and appropriateness.

Furthermore, Toffler says that the nonindustrial countries are faced with a shortage of economically-relevant knowledge. Are they? What kind? The knowledge of how to find or grow edible and medicinal plants? The knowledge of how to make appropriate houses and cooking utensils? Toffler touts knowledge-based agriculture as a cutting edge of economic advance; how knowledgeable can it be, if it ignores the erosion of soil and the destruction of beneficial insects? Traditional communities have lost more knowledge than we will have in the near future. What happened to our rich biological knowledge of animals and plants, to our rich mythical knowledge of animals and plants?

The path to economic power is through the application of the human mind, according to Toffler, and he urges that "revolutionary" forms of education are necessary. What is more revolutionary than traditional education? Learning about plants, animals, families, and cultures is more relevant than theoretical knowledge; computers and economics can be learned after adolescence. We have more than enough information and secondary knowledge.

Economic success is secondary, as is money, the accumulation of goods, and prestige. We are accomplished in the secondary meanings of life. The satisfactions from being in a culture in place, from planting trees, growing apples, watching birds, playing with children, and making love are primary. And, they are not speed-dependent. Some things have proper speeds. Music is not made more efficient or better by increasing the revolutions of a disk. Food or relaxation require a human speed. We lack the wisdom to act as if we believed this. Is fast technology a necessary part of happiness? Those who are uncomfortable with primary meanings tend to become addicted to power, speed, and possession, as a frantic way to avoid awareness, silence, or responsibility, as a replacement for being grounded in nature.

Nature provides the source, of wonder, of the sacred, of otherness, and of the wild. By submitting ourselves to positive accelerating feedback loops in economics, we distance ourselves from such primary meanings. Nature possesses power that is not speed dependent. Human consciousness has already had a "revolution"—from the wild to the tame—and many of us regret it; a further revolution to remoteness sounds more depressing. Animals used to be directly experienced; now, they are humanized and domesticated. Humanizing the world has made it tedious, uniform, and dull. Economics is dull! Toffler's assumptions are dull! The needs he describes are transitive wants, and their only measurement is quantitative. For fertile nature, we have substituted a sterile model of production and economy. The model is reductive: trees become resources, people become labor. More is more, faster is better. Although speed is our normal response to dullness, the celebration of speed for itself is ultimately unsatisfying.

What is the result of our fascination with speed in everything? Dismissing nature in disgust, we attempt transcendence through speed. We speed away from nature, from our own bodies, and base our civilization on that momentum, praying, requiring, that it never stops. People's souls die, but secure in their power, they manage the things of civilization and inhabit the treeless flatscapes of the malls of commerce, comforted by the banishment of wilderness and the capture of animals in zoos and of free people in reservations, satisfied that their young are mercilessly tied to televisions and computers, acquiring information without touch and speed without grace.

Nations and communities do not all have to follow the same path and the same rules at the same time and at the same rate. Cultural success is not the "survival of the fastest" any more than it is of the biggest or shallowest or newest. Perhaps if we remain unconscious, there will be a power shift to the fastest that will homogenize and level all human cultures. But, we can consciously imagine alternatives and work to preserve cultural and natural diversity and the richness of existence.

We have the knowledge to save cultures, to restore places, to participate in the cycles of the earth, but extra speed and power are not required. The pace of nature is generally balanced and well-established; we violate it at our risk. If we adjust to the pace of the growth of trees and to the movements of animals, we would not be risking catastrophic extinctions and famines, shortages of water and fuel wood, and the death of humaneness.

We do not need to give our power to faster economies. We need to shift power to local communities through self-reliance and participation. A community protects individual freedoms, guards regional culture (values and identity), and holds groups accountable for their use of power. In communities, people can decide to be conservatively sustainable or to grow and gamble on innovation. Communities can have different economic attitudes, paces, and goals. A community that is balanced and flexible, in tune with natural cycles, based on traditional values—in which industrial production is limited to appropriate goods—can absorb the shocks of change far better than an immensely big, powerful, accelerating, postindustrial, national vehicle.

5.4.1.5.2.3. Change & Exchange
In an article on good forestry, Hugh Williams links the maximization of the moral good of creativity to the maximization of public good, then to forests specifically. Williams also proposes maximal creativity as an ethical imperative. Maximizing creativity, however, would lead to chaos, both in one's self and in ecosystems. There has to be a balance between creativity and stability, between innovation and habit. We should not being trying to maximize creativity in human beings or forests, but rather seeking stability and relative harmony. Maximizing creativity may be a meaningless exercise.

In a system of ethics, we might consider maximizing a value, but then we have to decide if it is being maximized for one species or the system, or if it is being maximized for the present or the future, or whether it can be maximized at all. John B. Cobb Jr. suggests that we should act to maximize value in general, at least for every entity with intrinsic value, rather than maximize value for one human or all humans, that is, the greatest good for the greatest number, in the present or the future. Perhaps though, we should aim for an optimum or satisficium here also.

An economic maximum is a monotone value, which only increases or decreases. There are no monotone values in ecology. Desired substances have an optimum value—more calcium is not always better.

Before anything cam be maximized or optimized, we have to be able to measure accurately. We can measure wealth with modified Index of Sustainable Welfare to avoid distortion by size or by the combination of repair and maintenance with production.

5.4.1.5.3. Providing Paths for Individuals & Communities
A maximum isolation is bad. A minimum is bad. An optimum is good. Isolation is dangerous, especially isolated theoretical knowledge. We strive for optimal solutions and control, but should settle for suboptimal and partial control, a satisficing solution.

Eutopias suggests small solutions to big problems. Protecting and restoring ecosystems is a local effort. Reducing gases, that contribute to the instability of the climate, reducing consumption in general, reducing the human population, and reducing conflicts, which contribute to the escalation of wars, are local efforts. Integrating food into ecosystems, to regenerate soils and repair ecosystems, integrating technology into a culture, integrating economies into ecosystems, and equalizing wealth, are local efforts.

Although not every global problem has a local solution, people will have to address them in small ways, too. Climate would be very difficult to change, much less control on a global level.

5.4.1.5.4. Promoting Health at All Levels
Eutopias is healthful. Positive health results from being on good terms with cosmos. The idea of right to health should be replaced by moral obligation to

preserve ones health. We need to become attuned to the earth, to commit our fate to nature, and not just say that we have faith in modern technology to save us with an artificial environment. We must be flexible, not detached or noncommittal. We must commit ourselves and be able to adjust to necessary changes—to be in a state of risk. The harmonious interplay between humans and environment results in adaptive fitness, which requires a constant expenditure of effort to maintain. We must maintain an environment for plants, animals and humans that is healthy for all. Conservation and creation must be tempered with preservation. We are too ignorant to tamper with everything. More searching and researching are necessary.

Ecological health requires a single system of environment combined with high human culture, with a matching flexibility, to create an on-going, open, complex system, characterized by a slow change in its basic characteristics. High culture is not a return to the innocence of the Inuit, or the sparseness of the cave. It includes necessary institutions for the arts and sciences limed in transactions with the environment. Flexibility is needed; within limits, a variable can move to achieve adaptation.

The ecologist must create flexibility and then prevent civilization from immediately expanding into it. Flexibility is uncommitted potentiality for change. Flexibility must be distributed among many variables of a system. Freedom and flexibility in regard to most variables is necessary during the process of learning and creating a new system by social change. There are still many possible futures for the earth and humanity, but they become fewer as we burn or destroy the earth's flexibility and our options. Recommendations to reserve flexibility must be tyrannical.

The ecological health of a civilization depends on a single system of environment combined with high culture in which the flexibility of the civilization must match that of the environment to create an ongoing complex system, open ended for the slow change of even basic characteristics. Health is the capacity of the land and water for self-renewal. Conservation is the effort to preserve this capacity

Although the nature of the biosphere is largely determined by evolution, by organisms adapted to specific parameters and to each other, the anthroposphere tends to be artificial and managed, with only human needs considered. We need to keep as much of the natural world as possible in the anthroposphere; there is a human need for variety, individuality, and the challenge to understand the nonhuman. Emersion in trees and bees is necessary to nourish human attributes that are in short supply: Awe, compassion, reflectiveness, and brotherhood. As humans move from concrete to trees, there may be a profound transformation in a scientific return to animism. The metaindustrial culture is one in which the trees are counted in a census of members of a community. In the shamanistic tradition, people are not viewed as individuals, their history and experience is seen as result of being part of the group.

One significant book in the Hippocratic corpus was *Airs, Waters and Places*, which showed how well-being is influenced by the quality of air, food, land and general habits. It is as important to know from whence your body atoms and molecules came as it is to know the history of a used car.

Atoms that came from stars and rocks make up molecules of seeds, flowers, defecation, and rotting leaves, which are cycled through our bodies. Bodies are open systems exchanging materials with the whole environment. It is therefore important to choose carefully what is put into the body. Good food comes from healthy plants and animals, unprocessed and unpoisoned. Cells and enzymes react poorly to poisons and preservatives. Physical, mental and spiritual well-being are dependent on a healthy diet. As much as possible, one should know the origins of one's food— the soil, the plants—and be able to determine what becomes you.

Illness can only be understood in context, in relation to network of interactions in which person is imbedded; the health matrix. Ill health may be a natural stage of growth and interaction. Temporary illness as part of dynamic balance (especially childhood diseases?). The observation and study of balanced relationships in complex systems should allow us to recapture an experience of harmony and intimation of divine from scientific knowledge of processes. "A truly ecological view of world has religious overtones," according to Rene Dubos.

5.4.1.5.5. Integrating Acts with Poetic Wisdom
A planet that is mindless is not entitled to moral or ethical consideration. The earth has a mind but ecocrises are driving it to madness. The alternative to ecological insanity is wisdom. Wisdom is the functioning of a mind that is respectful of its own boundary and processes, according to Gregory Bateson. Evolution is trial and error process of learning; all learning contributes to evolution of global mind. So the cure for ecocrises is the education of minds.

We need reeducation in the demands and recompenses of a sane, realistic world. Peace of mind, security and self-respect must arise out of being someone in a real community, and these will be valued more than conspicuous possessions and idleness. The process would be labor-intensive rather than capital intensive, and intimate rather than pretentious.

A high culture must respect the wisdom of its experience, using necessary technological devices (computers, televisions); be diverse enough to accommodate the genetic and experiential diversity of people; shall limit transactions with the environment, consuming natural resources (capital) only to make necessary changes. High cultures must depend on renewable resources from photosynthesis to wind, tide, and sun to continue "making," which is the source word for poetry, good places.

Poetry expresses the image of human potential, of what better circumstances may have formed. Poetry tells of a goal, even if it is the moral superiority of suffering in the 'third world.' By presenting a goal, poets can become the "unacknowledged legislators of mankind," as Shelley defined them. Poetry creates a fourth world, of unique groups sharing part of the wealth of the earth in a global community. This fourth world is where the past is reconciled with the present and the terrible beauty of the future is born. The terror of beauty, as Rilke recognized, results from its power to shake humans from the refuge of a small identity into an immense strange world.

The lives of humans and all beings has become a collective responsibility. Humanity has to learn to live again on a finite and varied earth. Learning is a transforming experience. Poetry objectifies conscious experience and makes it easier to communicate. Nationalism (1930s) used poetry in service to the state. Used for each nation in this way, poetry shows the diversity of human experience. The essential unity of the earth can be discovered through its infinite diversity. Poetry gives groups and individuals their identity; it articulates societies and authenticates forms of exchange. By transcending the limits of single cultures, it draws all cultures together. The tradition of poetry does not belong to just three worlds; it encompasses them and links them together in a fourth. Poetry is wise language.

5.4.2. *Moving Forward Backward Inward & Outward*
Human ills cannot be cured by a return to idyllic hunting and gathering groups or to a quasi-agricultural, ecologically-caring society. There is no possibility of complete return. Most industrial nations are urban, and are becoming more so, as agricultural countries pack their surplus peoples in cities. Nor can there be a return to 4th century B.C. Greece, or to 17th century China, or to 1910 France, or to any time. Many traditional cultures no longer exist; others are disintegrating under pressure from industrial cultures. Nor can there be a jump to a complete technological future, where technology transforms hydrogen into wealth for everyone. Eutopias works with traditional cultures and realistic planning.

5.4.2.1. *Uncertainty & Incomplete Knowledge*
The detailed planning of complex open systems is not necessary. Planners are not in a position to attempt detailed models of future situations because many relevant parameters remain unidentified, and many of those known cannot be quantified. Plans can be made within the limits of variables, although it is not safe to be limited by lethal variables, as Gregory Bateson recognized. Closeness to limits reduces flexibility, that is, the uncommitted potential for change. To minimize untested conclusions, Eutopias is based on the values and forms of traditional cultures. This could allow time for rational planning to catch up.

We have to invest and cultivate our inheritance. We must enlarge our human identity, to include other beings and the earth, to include our own posterity and its image of the future, without which we lose the will and capacity to solve problems. Creating the future is necessary to maintain the present. It is meaningful to construct a world that we will never live to see, to plant trees that take two hundred years to mature, to save some of the forests and soils—not for the oil and timber elite or even for the backpacking elite, not for social abstractions or for personal profit, but for our heirs, for them to see and decide to save or to use.

Eutopias addresses the inadequacies of the present system; it offers a drastic system change from the institutional gridlock of elitism, but the change is not so drastic that the feasibility of acceptance is too low. The benefits must be worthwhile to justify the costs. The benefits cannot be vague and unsatisfying when the costs are immediate and painful. Communication and education must prove that the benefits exist, so that the eutopian alternative can be exercised. It must be a participatory movement, and it must appeal to a large segment of the total human society. Since not all interests will be satisfied, there must be opportunities for transformations or for alternate paths.

The eutopian framework is an open, flexible, and partially-planned global relation, instead of a finished, closed, completely-planned society, as imagined in utopias. Eutopias accepts the imperfect nature of humans and the changing ambiguity of nature. Eutopias detoxifies cultural rivalries. Racism, sexism, ageism, and speciesism lose their importance in a cooperative society of advanced communication, automation, equality, humane scale, and meaningful preservation.

5.4.2.2. *Action Responsibility & Wisdom*
Now is the time to define goals in terms of population, quality of life, and preservation of biomes. Resolving conflict through social debate would free unprecedented resources to satisfy social needs. That which has been hitherto left unsaid—the goals of humanity-could become explicit. Goals are not some final state reached once and for all time, but a horizon. Eutopias offers continuity towards a horizon.

Solutions to uncertain futures can be found in the characteristics of good places and in the principles applied to them. The proper action come out of common sense. We need to be sure that we allow ecosystems to regenerate healthy conditions while we take our needs from some of them. We need to plan for at least seven generations ahead, being flexible and keeping some options open, and being as self-reliant as possible. We need to be frugal with most resources and keep seven years of food and supplies in reserve. We need to identify an optimum population, over a minimum and maybe fifty percent below a maximum. We need to be as playful and joyful as any previous generation.

Science presents us with too many facts, yet we crave to have more. Philosophy presents us with too many values, but we attend to too few. Technology presents us with too many things, but we do not know what we need. We do not need more information or rules, but we do need meaningful ideas. Our attitudes and feelings toward nature need to be revitalized with evocative metaphors that let us accept responsibility for that part of the earth that we build, namely human culture and human landscapes. In order to know what is important and what is valuable, we need wisdom that we may not have.

The words 'view,' 'vision,' 'witness,' 'wise,' and 'idea' are all derived from the Indo-European *weid* or *wid*, meaning to see, understand, or know. Wisdom is knowledge of the larger interactive system, which if disturbed, can generate exponential curves of change. Greed is unwise. Wisdom is recognition of and guidance by a knowledge of the total system. The system punishes any species unwise enough to quarrel with its ecology. Greed, size and pride are unwise. Any course of action, like that just discussed, that ignores ecological stability and intentionality, i.e., the logic of nature, is unwise.

Hans Vaihinger (1911) in *The Philosophy of As If* suggested imitation as a solution to our lack of wisdom. Humans have no choice but to live by fictions; as if this world is the ultimate reality, as if there were free will. Humanity must plan for its future as if its days were not counted (or at least for several billion years). Jonas Salk urges us to behave "as if" we were wise, by using good sense. Wisdom is a new kind of fitness. To survive, we must accommodate ourselves to the new conditions of a radically different life. Survival in this sense is not a win or lose proposition, but a double win.

Wisdom is knowledge of the larger interactive system, which if disturbed, can generate exponential curves of change. Wisdom is the recognition of and guidance by a knowledge of the total system. Lacking knowledge, lacking wisdom, we must behave "as if" we were wise, as if we had good sense. Humans have no choice but to live by fictions, as if this world is the ultimate reality, as if we are responsible for our actions. Humanity must plan for its future as if its days were not counted (or at least for several thousand years). Wisdom is a new kind of fitness. To survive, we must accommodate ourselves to the conditions of the earth.

Wisdom is the disciplined use of the imagination with respect to alternatives, exercised at the right time and in the right measure. But we need practical wisdom, prudence, and intellectual control in virtue, in place of the theoretical wisdom taught by schools. The truths of our unique cultures and the wild earth are apprehended through myths. The poetic language of mythology can fit all the facts and values, things and images, into our hearts so that we can feel them and act upon them—so that we can make good places.

Related to wisdom, there are many corrective factors of human action: Contact, art, love, and religion. Love is the formation of Martin Buber's I-Thou relationships between human and society and environment. Socrates stated that Eros is midway between wisdom and ignorance. He who has no sense of his own deficiency will have no love of wisdom. Love is the desire that good be one's own for as long as it can. Arts and the activities of the mind can correct the excesses of pride. Contact between man and nature and animals can correct the problems of abstraction. And, ecodeontics (or religion), the binding of humans to the invisible powers of place, can correct the effects of detachment.

5.4.2.3. Could it work?
Will eutopias work? Yes, if—and that word makes a difference. We can try to be wise, and act "as if" it might work. Will we survive? Has some limit been exceeded? If not, do we have time to correct our actions? Time has become a real problem, especially since calendars were invented to keep track of big events. If the climate or our lives were more regular, we might not be so concerned with time. The idea of a regular or eternal return might be satisfying enough. If a fundamental limit has been exceeded, what should we do? If it is too late, and it is very difficult to know this definitely or absolutely, then we could accept our fate, and party. Or we could act "as if" we were wise.

Hello, can we start now?

6.0. Ecodex (Coda)

Eutopias is a total reconsideration of the current *pattern* of technologies, cultures, value systems, and behaviors, evolving into a low-profile technological ethic suitable for an ecorenaissance. It is a code for preserving those parts of the earth that are needed for renewing the holecosystem and for habitats for the billions of animals, plants and living beings that are part of the earth. It is a code for allowing fair use of that part of the earth that is human. It is a code for human equality in opportunity and worth. It is the demand for a margin from catastrophe, so that if humanity is unable to live peaceably, the rest of the earth will not become extinct as well.

Death and life are seen together. Everything gives in its death; stars die, trees die; humans need to return to the earth what they took from it. To paraphrase a line from Keats, the poetry of the earth is never dead, but is could become unreadable to us, as remote as the stars.

The new theme for people's minds may begin in prose, but it should culminate in poetry. The human mind, under pressure from the dialectic process, grows into more subtle noetic experiences, until ecstatic insight blossoms. We must learn to be an individual in a human society in an ambihuman ecology with amphibian grace.

What mysteries of the universe we cannot understand, we must accept in faith. One secret is that all things are secret. The working out of the cosmic process is effected by the actions of human beings, by hate or love. Love is reverence for the experience of all beings. Through love, as well as effort and intelligence, humans can make good places on earth.

6.1. Principles
Principles,[18] remember, are fundamental rules, or laws, that match characteristics to standards to maintain the characteristics—standards are examples of values established by mutual consent. The Eutopias framework recognizes and incorporates into its application a number of basic principles.

The Eutopias framework possesses three levels of authority, each with its own area of responsibility. There is a global authority to protect both the planet and human cultures. This authority, the Associated Nations (AN), is responsible for all land, air, and water utilization, for global cycles, and for interactions between nations. The AN gives equal opportunity to nonwestern, nonindustrial cultures to flourish.

Nations or republics (from the Latin words meaning 'thing of the people') are based on traditional cultures, which have long-term, lasting power. Nations are responsible for protecting local environments and for providing a context for individuals. Both globalism and the simple community are necessary, if the community is not to be diseased and the globe impersonal.

The locus of political sovereignty is the individual, who is limited in giving away proxy rights. Politics has to be a participatory process, where an individual has some power over decisions affecting him or her. Participation is necessary, not only politically, but to establish the existence of common values throughout the population as a whole. Individuals have responsibilities for themselves and to their cultural governments.

6.1.1. *General Principles*
- The principle of lawfulness. Every fact can be analyzed into lawful components. The discovery of new patterns can confirm, but not prove, the principle.
- Preserve the earth, the heritage of all living beings. It has been modified and maintained by living processes over billions of years, and is required for the continuity of life.
- Keep humanity participating in the entire ecology of the planet. As with all beings, both the whole ecology and the species-specific are necessary for survival.
- The natural resources of the earth—the air, water, soil, plants, and animals—are to be preserved, and where possible, restored or improved.
- Allow all beings the equal opportunity for existence; this does not mean that they cannot be exploited or separated, just that they are not eliminated from the system.
- Humanity must build its civilizations within the framework of a planetary ecology. The human-created environment is necessary for human well-being.
- Economic development and social progress are necessary for the welfare of humanity. But must be conducted within environmental policies.
- The goal of economic and social development is to provide favorable and meaningful human habitations and activities.
- Human settlements must be planned and constructed within environmental constraints and according to ecological priorities.
- Technological processes must be brought into balance with the cycles of the earth. They must not damage or degrade natural cycles. Processes that cannot be controlled or rendered harmless, such as nuclear waste or inorganic pesticides, must be banned.
- Nonrenewable resources must be used sparingly, to avoid exhaustion before a steady-state economy has been achieved. The benefits from their exploitation are to be shared by all.
- All communities and citizens are responsible for the environments. They cooperate through a united body to preserve and promote the whole environment for the well being of all species and posterity.
- All humans have equal right to their share of the resources of the earth and to the amenities of civilization.

6.1.2. *Global Principles*
- No one group has sovereignty over the earth. The Association of Nations (AN) has regulatory powers necessary to maintain a healthy environment.
- The AN will establish a body for managing the earth's resources. And encourage states to establish local institutions.
- The AN will manage the earth through a fund from all states.
- The AN has regulatory and punitive power over all waste and pollution.
- The AN has regulatory power over all mineral resources in the earth, and

distributes them equally, according to the principles herein.

6.1.2.1. *Regulation*
- The AN will be the intergovernmental body for the world to guide common policy.
- World-wide and interstate matters will be handled by all states working through the AN. Cooperation is essential to preserve, control and improve environmental and human conditions.

- The AN must ensure that rational planning considers the irrational, that human development considers the nonhuman. Therefore it has the power to refuse state plans.
- Only the AN shall have large-scale police capabilities. Only the AN shall have appropriate weapons. All mass destruction weapons, such as nuclear bombs, killer satellites and biological bombs, shall be reduced and recycled.
- Where population growth exceeds the safety margin established by the AN, on the basis of organic carrying capacity, demographic policies may be imposed by the AN, without prejudice or malice.
- The AN shall create a world bank for the exchange of all nations.
- The unit of wage shall be a human work unit, which shall have equal value for all.
- The AN shall stabilize prices of commodities and materials, and earnings from employment of labor.

6.1.2.2. *Resources*
- Limits use of other species within the limits of the dynamics of those species.
- Respects the use of materials through limited quantities and recycling.
- Respect the cycles of a system that renew or circulate elements.
- All scientific and technological knowledge shall be available to all states, as regulated by the AN.
- Scientific research and development, especially on environmental problems, will be promoted in all states. The AN will support a free flow of scientific information and experience. The AN will also ensure that appropriate technologies are available to all countries.
- The AN will award basic educational and research grants to all humans, for whatever use desired.
- The AN shall maintain quantities of food and currency to provide for disasters of natural and human cause. And shall be responsible for transfer of financial and technical assistance as required.
- The AN shall provide social security to those unable to work because of age or inability.

6.1.3. *Local Community or National Principles*
- The community is the unit of survival and must be kept healthy.
- A community is composed of many interacting species and must be kept diverse.

- A communities embodies the rhythmic changes in the activities of individuals and groups, from which emerges periodicity, including genetic or system changes.
- A mature community is self-perpetuating and homeorhetic, with a dynamic balanced energy-matter budget.
- A community can change state and replace another community, as a result of orderly processes, such as succession or intentional development.

6.1.3.1. *Management*

- Preserve all components, structures, and functions of system, that is, the health of a system providing services to the community or nation.
- Protect and maintain diversity; preserve the overall natural patterns of the system.
- Utilize natural processes for regeneration and protection.
- Current knowledge of the supporting ecosystems of a place is necessary.
- Acceptance of ecosystem limits of a place is necessary.
- Reduction of human demands on a place is necessary.
- Use of a place cannot be independent of human equity.
- The scale of human infrastructure and building should reflect the scale of the landscape.
- Human designs should follow the sensory force of a place and enhance the spirit of place.
- An optimum diversity in a landscape should be valued above a maximum or minimum.

6.1.3.2. *Political*

- All states shall be equal , regardless of size or sophistication. Every state has the right to its own integrity.
- States shall have sovereignty over their cultures, people, and organic and inorganic goods, within the limits of human and environmental rights and health.
- In accord with the AN charter, states have the right to use their assigned resources in any manner, within the limits of damage and pollution previously set.
- Nations have duties to ensure that activities are in conformity with principles set forth in the Association of Nations.
- Nations have duties to conduct their activities in a manner respectful of their complete effects.
- Nations must adopt an integrated and coordinated approach to planning and design, for the benefit of the environment and populations.
- Every nation has the responsibility to conduct its economy without causing damage to any other state or to the whole environment; each state must compensate for damage.
- Environmental risks and damages must be identified and solutions proposed.
- Through the AN, states shall develop laws on human and environmental rights, and activities.
- Education of the people on local culture, ecology and science is the

responsibility of the state. The AN will provide aid for promoting enlightened opinion and responsible conduct. Mass media will disseminate educational information to protect and improve the whole ecology.
- Mass media will also be available in state centers for referendum needs.
- If population growth does not adjust to social and economic changes, it must be controlled by state policies.

6.1.4. *Individual*
- The individual is the unit of experience and reproduction and must be kept healthy.
- An individual identifies with her home (habitat) and must keep it healthy.
- An individual depends on his niche (work or way of producing food).
- An individual acts for her self-preservation and self-interest first.
- An individual engages in ethical behavior, as part of a cultural group.
- Humans have the right to ecological freedom and equality. Equality is best facilitator of excellence. They have the right to the dignity and well-being provided by civilization.
- The AN or any state will not have the right to determine values for any other state, within the basic limits of human and environmental rights and equality.
- Individuals are responsible for protecting the environment and improving damaged areas.

7.0. End Matter

This section contains specific notes from the text, as well as definitions of terms, a bibliography, and an index of subjects and names.

7.1. End Notes

[1] Some of these numbers are from Rudolph J. Rummel and are estimates

[2] From J. Hoyt, HSUS, 1984.

[3] From J. Cousteau et al., 1984.

[4] From N. Myers et al., 1984.

[5] Called by P. Shepard 'philopatry'

[6] See also C.H. Waddington 1968.

[7] Soleri 1966.

[8] Wackernagel and Rees, 1996.

[9] Aristotle, in the *Politics*.

[10] A. Huxley, in *Ape and Essence*

[11] In an editorial in *The Ecologist*, "Aid—the Arch Enemy."

[12] Kaplan 1973.

[13] Especially in the works Norberg-Schulz 1980.

[14] Kaplan 1973.

[15] Jane Jacobs, Systems of Survival: Moral Foundations of Commerce and Politics.

[16] In *Franju*.

[17] In *Farm Animal Welfare and The Human Diet*.

[18] John B. Cobb Jr. in *Is it too late? A theology of ecology*.

[19] From Copland's book on Music, "What to Listen for in Music."

[20] Charles Darwin, Origin of the Species, p. 390.

[21] G. P. Marsh, Man in Nature, p35.

[22] Kohr p. 196.

7.2. Definitions

Adaptability. The ability of an organism to change itself to the limits of the system. The ability to adjust to different circumstances, which can increase potential for survival in the environment.

Ambihuman. Everything that is not human; nonhuman; ultrahuman; 'surrounding the human'

Carrying capacity. The number of people who can be supported indefinitely in a territory, with a given culture, with a given style, and using a given technology (may refer to any organism, as well as to population or use).

Catastrophe. A down-turning or disruptive event. A slow down-turning is a bradycatastrophe.

Characteristics. Qualities that distinguish unique individuals, systems, or patterns. Gregory Bateson calls them differences that make a difference.

Conversation. The communication between two or more beings; 'turning with'.

Conviviality. Social, jovial (from the Latin convivium, living together).

Corridor. A narrow strip of land that differs from the matrix on either side.

Biological movement corridors can stem inbreeding depression, lessen demographic stochasticity, and fulfill the need for movement

Design. From the Latin meaning to "mark out." The verb form means to make a pattern or plan. To intend for a purpose.

Difference. The condition of being unlike or dissimilar; 'carrying apart'.

Disturbance. Regular but unpredictable events that destroy a percentage of organisms and their relations.

Diversity (as in biological diversity). Species richness. Different age and size classes in a population. Genetic differences in a species. Kinds of habitats present in an ecosystem. The kinds of communities occupying the habitats. Kinds of ecological processes that maintain habitats. The variety and richness of the planet's genetic heritage.
Alpha diversity—number of species in a habitat (local diversity)
Beta diversity—change in diversity along habitat gradients
Gamma diversity—the composite diversity across a whole region

Domiture. The system of culture embedded in nature (has to be a larger term to enclose the previous nature/culture dualism. It has to include human reason and human emotion, rather than simply putting them on opposite columns., as with order and chaos, higher and lower, linear and cyclic), as well as agriculture and wilderness.

Ecology. The science that deals with the relations of organisms to their environment (which includes other organisms). From the Greek meaning "study of the house."

Economics. Literally, "the management of the house" or law of the house. The formal study of how people use and share resources to make a living.

Ecopoetics. A neologism meaning 'making the house,; or expressing the house. This is how the invisible or power is represented in art, which is a subcategory.

Ecosystem. An adaptively organized system of living beings and elements that recycle important elements within the system (after Lynn Margulis); the smallest unit that recycles biologically important elements.

Eutopia. Good place (as used by Thomas More).

Eutopias. Good places that can be made culturally and ecologically.

Exploitation: The normal use of a resource by a species. It may also create diversity in ecological systems.

Flexibility. The potential for changer within a system. It is not being over connected. Not being too rigid or efficient. Able to slough off species or living forms and incorporate new. A measure of unused potential (once the potential is used, the system becomes less flexible) or the capacity to adapt to larger systems.

Form. The contour or structure of something; mode; essence; 'shape'

Frame. Something that encloses or encircles; equal to vehicle or ground.

Gaia. The hypothesis of the living earth; Homer's term; James Lovelock's theory.

Gigatrend. A long-lasting pattern in a human culture, such as accumulation of goods, or the height of early agriculturalists.

Harmony. The simultaneous occurrence of tones; agreement in feeling.

History. A sequence of states. In complex systems, the earlier state, also called the 'past,' contributes to or constrains a subsequent state, such as the magnetic hysteresis of ferromagnets or the behavior of organisms having a form of memory.

Holarchy. A whole order

Holocosmology. The whole framework of human cosmologies

Holon. A Janus-faced entity, simultaneously a part and a whole; Koestler's term

Holopoetic. Referring to making wholes.

Home. A place for one or more persons, invested with emotion and time.

Identity. Identity is that persistent quality that serves nothing; it is. A system's identity can be described apart from its performance in interactions, but not isolated.

Image. The reproduction of an appearance of something; 'imitation'.

Interaction. Reciprocal effects by two living beings (on nonliving things) on each other.

Interference. Exploitation and disturbance on a scale that destroys the ability of a organisms or their ecosystem to continue. The complete disruption of an ecosystem, as a result of a large event such as a meteor strike, volcanic eruption or human conversion. It is an activity that can degrade, destabilize, or destroy entire ecosystems. Interference is not a form of disturbance, exploitation, or competition; it is destruction without gain to any species; sometimes it is caused by planetary events, but in the case of human interference, it is the destruction of the structures and processes of evolution for large-scale, one-species, short-term gain

Industrialism. A form of social and economic organization characterized by large industry, mechanization, fossil-fuel use, and concentrations of workers.

Landscape. A heterogeneous land area composed of a cluster of interacting ecosystems that are repeated in similar form throughout. Landscapes vary in size, from bioregions to a few kilometers in diameter.

Law. A law is a stable pattern inherent in things; it has to be perceived or discovered (like gravity).

Limit. The word limit comes from the Latin word for boundary, border or frontier. It means boundary, restriction, or utmost extent, either largest or smallest. A limit is the point or line where something must end.

Matrix. The most extensive and connected landscape element type, which plays a significant role in landscape functioning. Or, that element surrounding a patch.

Maturity. Ability to move to a greater efficiency over time (in an ecological system).

Metaphor. Based on the Greek words meaning "carrying beyond." A metaphor is a figure of speech that combines two frames of reference.

Model. A stylized or hypothetical representation of an object. A generalized description based on analogy or metaphor.

Morals. Customs or manners. The "way of going together" (from the Latin root).

Nation. A people or tribe. A people living in a territory united by a single government. A stable, historically-developed community of people with a distinct culture occupying a common territory.

Nature. The wild environment of humanity, the self-making process of living. Nature is a feeling system, with mutual experience and history.

Net. An openwork fabric of woven threads forming a mesh in various sizes.

Optimum. What is an optimum? Must it have a less than maximum in every case? An optimum for rats includes challenges and dangers or bad behavior. Simon uses the term satisficed, also used by Varella.

Order. A condition of comprehensible arrangement among elements of a group; a number of successive differentiations.

Organicism. For L. Bertalanffy organicism was necessary to accomplish three specific jobs in biology: appreciation of wholeness (regulation), organization (hierarchy and level laws), and dynamics (process, behavior of open systems).

Overshoot is that growth beyond the carrying capacity of an ecosystem leading to collapse or die-off.

Panecology. The study of all forms of ecosystems, including human ideational.

Panethic. The human recognition of the importance of interrelations of all beings.

Participation. The state of being part of a system. Joining or sharing with others. The system is embedded in larger systems and global cycles, cyclicity. Relationality to the other systems.

Pattern. Regularity in a system, from physical systems to cultural ones.

Place. Emotionally-invested space, living space.

Principles. Fundamental rules that we can use to create images or models.

Process. A sequence of states, or a trajectory of states, describing as path. If it involves the emergence of new things it is described as an evolutionary process.. Also, ongoing movement.

Productivity. The conversion of energy into flesh.

Properties. Qualities common to all members of a class. A property is an attribute proper to a thing or characteristic quality.

Proposition. That which is expressed in a statement, having logical constants, asserting or denying something. Propositions can be tested for truth.

Quality. Refers to a basic nature or characteristic element. A characteristic of something; a feature; 'of what kind'

Quantity. An amount of something; the character of a proposition

Quantum. A quantity of something; indivisible unit; 'how great'

Radical. Referring to root.

Range: The territory occupied by small-scale societies.

Reciprocity (general): The distribution of goods by direct sharing, without comparison or accounts, but with the understanding of an eventual balance.

Resilience. A measure of how fast variables return to equilibrium after a perturbation in a system.

Resistance. The degree to which a variable is changed after a perturbation.

Reverence. Schweitzer's 'honor-fear' a feeling of respect, awe or love.

Ritual. A religious ceremony; the technique of constituting an order.

Rule. A social convention set up by the people in a culture.

Satisficium. An amount that leads to satisfaction, that may be more then the minimum, less than a maximum and different from an optimum.

Science. Knowledge. A form of systematic knowledge derived from observation and experiment.

Socialism. A system of ownership by the people or community.

Society. An interacting group of people sharing a common culture.

Stability. Ability to provide constant internal environment. Ability to maintain identity under the flow of external forces and disturbances. Forms: Reliability, Resistance, Accommodation, Resilience. Related to compartmentalization, communications, richness of interactions, connections.

Standard. A model of quality that can be repeated.

State. A condition in time. The state of an organism, for instance, depends on its history and its environment.

STEM. The universal field of space-time/energy-matter.

Subsistence: The production of basic resources necessary for survival, including shelter and food.

Sustainable. The ability of a system to maintain its structure and function indefinitely.

Symbol: Anything with a culturally-defined meaning.

System. A complex unit (in space-time) whose components keep structure and function stable despite changes and disturbances. A system is a complex object, every part of which is connected with other parts of the object in such a way that the whole possesses emergent properties that the parts lack.

Tragedy. A dramatic work of struggle ending in ruin; 'goat song'.

Topolatry. Worship of place.

Topopoetic. Place-making.

Trap. The use of resources by a people, where the replenishment rate is constant ands the rate of use exceeds it, resulting in ecosystem degradation that is less reversible.

Trend. A temporary pattern in a human culture, such as human infertility or globalization of capital, which can be reversed.

Umwelt. A perceived world; von Uexkull's term for animal world.

Unity. A condition of accord; the state of being one.

Variables. Qualities with no fixed value, changeable.

Vitality. Activity, health.

War. The condition of open armed conflict between factions or countries. A formal nonmonotonic condition of destruction (that is, all living beings are affected).

Wealth. Having rare things. Having more than the minimal requirements to live. Having great quantities of things that are valuable as measured by price. Having extra needs met, from physical to self-actual.

Wild. Pre-reflective, undomesticated.

World. Our planet and its inhabitants; or the perspective of the inhabitants (from the German word for "man-image").

7.3. **Bibliography**

Alexander, Christopher. 1977. *A Pattern Language*. New York: Oxford University Press.

Aristotle. 1952. *The Works of Aristotle*. Tr. by I. Bywater. W. Ross, ed. Oxford: Clarendon Press.

Arbib, Michael. 1972. *The Metaphorical Brain*. New York: John Wiley and Sons.

Bachelard, Gaston. 1969. *Poetics of Space*. trans. M. Jolas. Beacon Press, Boston, pp. 4-6.

Bacon, Edmund. 1967. *Design of Cities*. New York: Penguin Books.

Bacon, Francis. 1901. *Novum Organum*. J. Devey, ed. New York: P.F. Collier.

Ball, Philip. 1999. *The Self-made Tapestry: Pattern Formation in Nature*. Oxford: Oxford University Press.

Bateson, Gregory. 1979. *Mind and Nature*: A Necessary Unity. New York: E.P. Dutton.

Bateson, Gregory. 1987. *Steps to an Ecology of Mind*. Northvale, NJ: Jason Aronson Inc.

Becker, Ernest. 1973. *The Denial of Death*. New York: The Free Press.

Bellah, Robert N. et al. 1991. *The Good Society*. New York: Alfred A. Knopf.

Bergonzi, B. 1969. *Great Short Works of Aldous Huxley*. New York: Harper and Row.

Bergstraesser, Arnold. 1962. *Goethe's Image of Man and Society*. Freiburg: Herder.

Birch, Charles, and Cobb, Jr., John B. 1981. *The Liberation of Life*. Cambridge: Cambridge University Press.

Bly, Robert, ed. 1980. *News of the Universe*: Poems of the Twofold Consciousness. Sierra Club, San Francisco.

Boguslaw, Robert. 1965. *The New Utopians*. Englewood Cliffs: Prentice-Hall.

Bookchin, Murray. 1989. *Remaking Society*. New York: Black Rose Books.

Bookchin, Murray. 1989. *Toward an Ecoological Society*. New York: Black Rose Books

Boulding, Kenneth E. 1956. *The Image: Knowledge in Life and Society*. Ann Arbor: University of Michigan Press.

Boulding, Kenneth E. 1966. *Beyond Economics*. New York: Harper & Row.

Boulding, Kenneth E. 1969. "The economics of the coming spaceship earth," In *Population Evolution and Birth Control*. San Francisco: Freeman.

Campbell, Joseph. 1969. *The Flight of the Wild Gander*. New York: Viking Press.

Campbell, Joseph. 1972. *The Masks of God: Primitive Mythology*. New York: Penguin Books.

Campbell, Joseph. 1972. *The Masks of God: Creative Mythology*. New York: Penguin Books.

Cicero, M.T. 1933. *De Natura Deorum*. Tr. by H. Rackham. London: Wm. Heinemann. Pps. ii, 154.

Cobb, John B. Jr. 1971. *Is It Too Late?* New York: Glencoe.

Conrad, Peter. 1999. *Modern Times, Modern Places*. New York: Knopf.

Daly, Herman E. and John B. Cobb, Jr. 1989. *For the Common Good*. Boston: Beacon Press.

Daly, Herman E. 1993. The steady-state economy, In Herman Daly and Kenneth Townsend, eds., *Valuing the Earth: Economics, Ecology, Ethics*.

Cambridge: MIT Press.

Doxiades, C.A. 1975. *Building Entopia*. New York: Norton.

Doxiades, C.A.. 1977. *Ecology and Ekistics*. Boulder: Westview Press.

Drengson, Alan. 1989. *Beyond Environmental Crisis: From Technocrat to Planetary Person*. New York: Peter Lang.

Dubos, Rene. 1972. *A God Within*. New York: Charles Scribner's Sons.

Dubos, Rene. 1980. *The Wooing of Earth*. New York: Charles Scribner's Son.

Ehrlich, Paul. 1981. An ecologist standing up among seated social scientists. *Coevolution Quarterly* 31:24-35.

Einstein, Albert and Leopold Infeld, 1960. *Evolution of Physics*. New York: Simon & Schuster.

Eisenberg, Evan. 1998. *The Ecology of Eden*. New York: Vintage.

Evernden, Neil. 1981. *Out of Place* (unpublished manuscript).

Evernden, Neil. 1992. *The Social Creation of Nature*. Baltimore: Johns Hopkins.

Eyre, Samuel. 1978. *The Real Wealth of Nations*. London: E. Arnold.

Fowles, John. 1970. *The Aristos*. New York: The New American Library, Inc.

Fowles, John. 1979. Seeing Nature Whole. *Harper's*. 259:49-56

Fowles, John. 1980. Is nature necessary? *Harper's*.

Fox, M.W. 1980. *One Earth, One Mind*. New York: Coward, McCann and Geoghehan Inc.

Fox, M.W. 1980. *Returning to Eden: Animal Rights and Human Responsibility*. New York: Viking Press.

Fraser, J.T. 1975. *Of Time, Passion and Knowledge*. New York: George Braziller.

Fromm, Erich. 1956. *The Art of Loving*. New York: Harper.

Fromm. Erich. 1976. *To Have or To Be*. New York: Bantam Books.

Fuller, R. B. 1969. *Utopia or oblivion*: The prospects for humanity. New York: Bantam Books.

Fuller. R. B. 1970. *Operating Manual for Spaceship Earth*. New York Pocket Books.

Goldsmith, Edward. 1988. "The Way: An ecological worldview," Pp. 160-185 in *The Ecologist*, Vol. 18, No. 4/5.

Goodman, Paul and Percival Goodman. 1947. *Communitas: Means of Livelihood and Ways of Life*. New York: Abrams.

Goodman, Paul. 1962. *Utopian Essays and Practical Proposals*. New York: Random House.

Gray, Russell D. 1988. Metaphors and methods. In Mae-Wan Ho and S. W. Fox, eds., *Evolutionary Processes and Metaphors*. New York: Wiley.

Gregg, Alan. 1955. A medical aspect of the population problem. *Science* 121 (3,50):681-2.

Haldane, J.B.S. 1927. *Possible Worlds and Other Papers*. London: Chatto and Windus.

Hall, Edward T. 1969. *The Hidden Dimension*. Garden City, New York: Doubleday.

Hall, Edward T. 1976. *Beyond Culture*. Garden City, New York: Anchor Press.

Hardin, Garrett. 1977. *The Limits of Altruism: An Ecologist's View of Survival*. Bloomington: Indiana University Press.

Hardin, Garrett. 1985. *Filters Against Folly*. New York: Penguin Books. (Discounting the future or who can afford a forest? pp. 71-76. The effect of scale on values, pp. 128-140.)

Heroditus. *The History Book* 1:22-23.

Huxley, Aldous. 1945. *The Perennial Philosophy*. New York: Harper.

Huxley, Aldous. 1977. *The Human Situation*. P. Ferrucci, ed. New York: Harper & Row.

Illich, Ivan. 1978. *Towards a history of needs*. New York: Pantheon.

Illich, Ivan. 1973. *Tools for Conviviality*. New York: Harper & Row.

Kepes, Gyorgy. 1965. *Structure in Art and Science*. New York: G. Braziller.

Klein, David R. 1970. *IUCN Publ. New Series* No. 16:209-242.

Klein, David. 1972. Toward an ecophilosophy. Tomte Symposium on Ecology and Land Use, Steinsgard, Norway.

Klein, David R. and R. G. White, eds. 1978. *Parameters of Caribou Population Ecology in Alaska*. Fairbanks: Biol. Papers Univ. AK, Special Report No. 2.

Klein, David. 1976. "Wilderness Part 1. Evolution of the Concept." *Landscape* 20: 36-41.

Klein, David. 1983-4. Personal communications.

Koestler, A. 1978. *Janus*: A Summing Up. New York: Random House.

Kohr, Leopold. 1957. *The Breakdown of Nations*. New York: E.P. Dutton.

Kohr, Leopold, 1973. *Development Without Aid*. New York: Schlocken.

Kohr, Leopold. 1977. *The Overdeveloped Nations*: Diseconomics of Scale. New York: Schocken Books.

Kozlovsky, Daniel G. 1974. *An Ecological and Evolutionary Ethic*. New York: Prentice-Hall.

Kropotkin, P.A. 1972. *Mutual Aid: A Factor in Evolution*. New York: New York University Press.

Krutch, Joseph W. 1970. *The Best Nature Writing of Joseph Wood Krutch*. New York: Pocket Books

Lackner, S. 1984. *Peaceable Nature*. New York: Harper and Row

Laszlo, Ervin. 1987. *Evolution: The Grand Synthesis*. Boston: New Science Library

Lorenz, Konrad. 1974. *Civilized Man's Eight Deadly Sins*. trans. M. K. Wilson. New York: Harcourt, Brace, Javonovich.

Lovelock, James E. 1991. *Healing Gaia: Practical Medicine for the Planet*. New York: Harmony Books.

Margulis, L. 1974. *Five kingdoms*—classification and the origin and evolution of cells. Evol Biol 7:45-48.

Marsh, G.P. 1964. *Man and Nature*, The Earth as Modified by Human Action. St Clair, MI: Scholarly Press.

Maslow, A. H. 1971. *The Farther Reaches of Human Nature*. New York: Viking Press.

Maturana, H.R. and Varela, F: 1987. *Tree of Knowledge*. Boston: Shambala.

McHarg, Ian. 1969. *Design with Nature*. Garden City: Natural History Press.

McLuhan, Marshall and Quentin Fiore. 1967. *The Medium is the Massage*. New York: Bantam.

Meadows, Donna et al. 1972. *The Limits to Growth*. A report for the Club of Rome's project on the Predicament of Mankind. New York: Universe books.

Meeker, Joseph. 1974. *The Comedy of Survival*. New York: Charles Scribner's

Sons.

Montaigne, Michel de. 1958. *Complete Essays*. Stanford: Stanford University Press.

Montesquieu. 1949. *De l'Esprit des Lois* (The Spirit of the Laws).

More, Thomas. 1982. *Utopia*. London: Penguin Books.

Morris, Richard and Michael W. Fox. 1978. *Animal Rights and Human Ethics*. Washington: Acropolis Books.

Mumford, Lewis. 1922. *The Story of Utopias*. New York: Boni and Liveright.

Mumford, Lewis. 1961. *The City in History: Its Origins, Its Transformations, and Its Prospects*. New York: Harcourt Brace and World.

Mumford, Lewis. 1966. *The Myth of the Machine*. Technics and human development. New York: Harcourt, Brace & World, 1966.

Myers, Norman. 1984. *Gaia: An Atlas of Planet Management*. Doubleday and Company, Garden City, New York.

Naess, Arne. 1972. The shallow and the deep, long-range ecology movement. A summary. *Inquiry*, 16: 95-100

Naess. Arne. 1974. *Gandhi and Group Conflict* Oslo: Universitets forlaget.

Naess, Arne. 1987. Okologi, Samfunn og Livsstil (Norwegian version later published as *Ecology Community and Lifestyle*. New York: Cambridge University Press).

Needleman, Jacob. 2003. *Sense of the Cosmos*. New York: Monkfish.

Norberg-Schulz, C. 1971. *Existence Space and Architecture*. New York: Praeger.

Odum, Eugene P. 1970. ``Optimum population and environment: A Georgian microcosm." *Current History* 58:355-366.

Odum, Eugene P. 1971. *Fundamentals of Ecology*. 3rd Edition. Philadelphia: Wm. B. Saunders.

Orr, David W. 2004. *The Nature of Design*. New York: Oxford University Press.

Passmore, J. 1974. *Man's Responsibility for Nature*: Ecological Problems and Western Tradition. NC: Duckworth.

Pepper, S. 1961. *World Hypotheses*. Berkeley: University of California Press.

Pimm. Stuart L. 1991. *The Balance of Nature*. Chicago: University of Chicago Press.

Polunin, Nicholas, ed. 1980. *Growth without Ecodisasters?* New York: Wiley.

Reichel-Dolmatoff, G. 1977. Cosmology as Ecological Analysis: A view from the Rain Forest. *The Ecologist*, Vol 7, Pp. 4-11.

Relph, Edward. 1976. *Place and Placelessness*. London: Pion.

Roszak, Theodore. 1972. *Where the Wasteland Ends*. New York: Harper and Row.

Roszak, Theodore. 1975. *Unfinished Animal*. New York: Harper and Row.

Roszak, Theodore. 1979. *Person/Planet*. New York: Harper and Row.

Salk, Jonas. ND. *Survival of the Wisest*. New York: Harper and Row.

Schumacher, E.F. 1973. *Small Is Beautiful*. New York: Harper and Row.

Schweitzer, Albert. 1957. *The Philosophy of Civilization*. Translated by C. T. Campion. New York: Macmillan Co.

Searles, H. 1962. The role of the nonhuman environment. *Landscape* (Winter 1961-1962):31-34.

Sharp, Henry. Comparative ethnology of the wolf and the Chipewyan. In *Man and Wolf*. H. Frank, Ed. Dordrecht: Dr. W. Junk.

Shepard, Paul and D. McKinley, eds. 1969. *The Subversive Science*. Boston: Houghton Mifflin.

Shepard, Paul. 1978. *Thinking Animals*. New York: Viking Press.

Shepard, Paul. 1982. *Nature and Madness*. San Francisco: Sierra Club Books.

Skolimowski, Henryk. 1981. *Ecophilosophy*. Boston: Marion Boyars

Slater, Phillip. 1974. *Earthwalk*. New York: Bantam Books.

Snyder, Gary. 1990. *The Practice of the Wild*. San Francisco: North Point Press.

Snyder, Gary. 1995. *A Place in Space*. Washington: Counterpoint.

Soleri, Paolo. 1969. *Arcology: The City in the Image of Man*. Cambridge: The MIT Press.

Speck, W. A. 1975. Mandeville and the Eutopia seated in the brain. In Primer, Irwin, ed. *Mandeville Studies* (1670-1733). The Hague: Martinus Nijhoff.

Stevens, P. S. 1974. *Patterns in Nature*. Boston: Little Brown Co.

Stone, Christopher D. 1974. *Should Trees Have Standing?* New York: Avon Books.

Stulman, Julius and Ervin Laszlo. 1973. *Emergent Man*. New York: Gordon and Breach.

Susser, Bernard. 1981. *Existence and Utopia*: The Social and Political Thought of Martin Buber. Rutherford: Fairleigh Dickinson University Press.

Tinbergen, Jan, Coordinator. 1976. *Reshaping the International Order*, Report of the Club of Rome. New York: Dutton.

Thomas, Lewis. 1975. *Lives of a Cell*. New York: Bantam.

Thompson, W. I. 1971. *At the Edge of History*. Harper & Row.

Thompson, W. I. 1974. *Passages About Earth*. New York: Harper and Row.

Todd, John. 1977. Towards a sacred ecology. In *Earth's Answer*. pp. 170-183. M. Katz et al., eds. New York: Harper & Row

Todd, N. J. and J. 1994. *From Eco-Cities to Living Machines*: Principles of Ecological Design. Berkeley: North Atlantic Books.

Toffler, Alvin. 1970. *Future shock*. New York: Random House.

Tuan, Yi-Fu. 1974. *Topophilia*: A Study of Environmental Perception, Attitudes, and Values. Englewood Cliffs: Prentice-Hall.

Uexkull, J. von. 1957. A Stroll Through the World of Animals and Men. Schiller, Claire, ed. 1957. IN: *Instinctive Behavior*. New York: International Universities Press Inc.

Vaihinger, Hans. 1961. *The Philosophy of As If*. C. K. Ogden, trans,. Bloomington: Indiana University Press.

Varela, Francisco et al. 1974. Autopoiesis: The organization of living systems. *Biosystems* 5:187-196.

Waddington, C.H., ed. 1969. *Towards a Theoretical Biology*. Chicago: Aldine Publishing Co.

Weltfish, Gene. 1965. *The Lost Universe*. New York: Basic Books.

Wheelwright, P. 1962. *Metaphor and Reality*. Bloomington: Indiana University Press.

Whitehead, Alfred N. 1933. *Adventures of Ideas*. New York: Macmillan.

Wilson, E.O. 1984. *Biophilia*. Cambridge: Harvard University Press.

Wittbecker, A. E. 1970. *Eutopias: A Commonwealth of Earth*. Newark: Shamrock Press (bound printed manuscript).

7.5. Biography

During a brief career in astrophysics and astronomy at the University of Arizona, where he worked on mathematical models of stars and on spectrometric analysis, Alan Wittbecker spent his daylight hours climbing trees and trying to track mountain lions; his companions were a mouse and squirrel, who shared his trailer near the observatory on Mount Lemon.

Encouraged by research budget cuts to pursue a different direction, Wittbecker went to graduate school in psychology, anthropology, veterinary medicine, philosophy, and ecology. As a graduate student in 1970, he was a cofounder of the G. P. Marsh Institute for Research in Ecology, where he worked for 22 years, including three separate years as Director, as the position rotated annually. He worked on a wide variety of projects, from forest monitoring and ecosystem restoration to country-wide wolf monitoring, in many countries, including Bulgaria, Canada, Mexico, Norway, and Russia. When funding was in short supply, he worked in other occupations, including librarian, systems engineer, editor, graphic artist, typesetter, housepainter, television repairman, cook, swimming coach, carpenter, clinical psychologist for a drug abuse clinic, Austin Healy auto mechanic, tree-planter, and college instructor.

In 1976, with three partners, Wittbecker cofounded Nieman Ryan Community Designs, specializing in private and urban local landscapedesign—but, also designing books, posters, journals, packages, landscapes,and buildings. In 1983, he finished his doctorate in Human Ecology at International College. He continued his postgraduate education in landscape ecology, forestry, conservation biology, zoology, and genetics.

In 1991, Wittbecker founded SynGeo ArchiGraph, a firm specializing in global and regional ecological designs; he created designs for several bioregions and a global framework. A year later he set up the educational program for the new Ecoforestry Institute, becoming an Instructor in 1994, journal Editor in 1995, Director from 1997 to 2000 and Consultant, 2003-06. He has worked on public and private forests from British Columbia to California.

He is the author of eight books, including *REviewing REthinking REturning*, which won an Eppie award for best nonfiction on the web, *Fragments*, a finalist with the National Poetry Series, and *Good Theories Good Practices*, which won an award for best essay, for "The Health of Forests," and over 100 articles. He has also written series in ecology and forestry for newspapers and journals.

A veteran of the U.S. Air Force, Wittbecker is also a returned Peace Corps Volunteer from Bulgaria, where he monitored wolves in the Central Balkan Mountains. He has used his education and interests to explore a spectrum of ecological applications, from research on forest pests—larch casebearers, cedar powderworms, and bears—to the political implications of the protection of species and habitats. When not engaged in preservation activities, he enjoys walking, swimming, reading, and drawing, at the Altazor forest in western Idaho. You can reach him at: home@eutopias.net.

Author's Notes
This book was taken from a much larger, unfinished work-in-progress, which is available as a notebook on our website, www.eutopias.net. The sections in that work are numbered sequentially, and the numbers are kept for this book, even though over eighty percent of them do not appear. There are, alas, a few misspellings, some bad grammar and many unfinished thoughts. Some of the ideas in this work were radical thirty-seven years ago, although some have become acceptable or commonplace. Others are still considered awkward or unpalatable. I trust you will be able to participate in this conversation despite these flaws and shortcomings. Thank you for your consideration. To make up for the loss of trees and their services, as a result of my use of paper in these books, I have planted over nine thousand trees, during a period of twenty years, at the Altazor Forest in Idaho. More plantings are planned in 2006 in Oregon and Virginia farms.

Colophon

Type: Palatino (designed by Hermann Zapf in 1948
    at Stempel AG)
Display Type: Palatino
Book Design: Rian Garcia Calusa Designs
Cover Design: Rian Garcia Calusa (based on the 1934
    cover page of Thomas More's *Utopia* by the
    Limited Editions Club)
Graphics: Alan Wittbecker
Author Drawing: Merissa DePasse, 1996
Editing: J. Garcia B. of Rian Garcia Calusa
Hardware: Macintosh G5
Software: Adobe InDesign & Acrobat
Furious Charge & Entertainment: Pippi Frog
Spiritual & Material Support: Precious Woulfe

www.ingramcontent.com/pod-product-compliance
Lightning Source LLC
Chambersburg PA
CBHW031312170626
46807CB00001B/394